Make Me A City

Jonathan Carr

Make Me A City

a novel of Chicago

SCRIBE
Melbourne • London

Scribe Publications
2 John St, Clerkenwell, London, WC1N 2ES, United Kingdom
18–20 Edward St, Brunswick, Victoria 3056, Australia

Published by Scribe 2019

Endpaper image: Chicago Fire Map, 1871 © Bridgeman Images

Every effort has been made to trace owners of material in copyright where permission to
reproduce is obligatory, but Scribe has been unable to reach all such owners. Please do
write to us at the address above to clarify any usage prior to future reprints.

Typeset in Garamond

Printed and bound in the UK by CPI Group (UK) Ltd, Croydon CR0 4YY

Scribe Publications is committed to the sustainable use of natural resources and
the use of paper products made responsibly from those resources.

9781911617150 (UK edition)
9781925322989 (Australian edition)
9781925693515 (e-book)

CiP records for this title are available from the British Library and the
National Library of Australia.

scribepublications.co.uk
scribepublications.com.au

In memory of Nickie, who typed my first manuscript.

Contents

'Almost every person I met regarded Chicago
as the germ of an immense city ...'

PATRICK SHIRREFF,
A Tour Through North America (1835)

'The habitual weakness of the American people is to assume
that they have made themselves great, whereas their greatness has
been in large measure thrust upon them by a bountiful providence
which has given them forests, mines, fertile soil, and a variety
of climate to enable them to sustain themselves in plenty.'

ISAAC STEPHENSON,
Recollections of a Long Life, 1829–1915 (1915)

'We struck the home trail now, and in a few hours were in that
astonishing Chicago — a city where they are always rubbing the
lamp, and fetching up the genii, and contriving and achieving new
impossibilities. It is hopeless for the occasional visitor to try to keep
up with Chicago — she outgrows his prophecies faster than he
can make them. She is always a novelty; for she is never the
Chicago you saw when you passed through the last time.'

MARK TWAIN,
Life on the Mississippi (1883)

1800–1812

The First Settler

(Extract from *Chicago: An Alternative History 1800–1900* by Professor Milton Winship, University of Chicago, A.C. McClurg & Co., 1902)

In the beginning was a game of chess, and on the outcome of that game would hinge the destiny of Chicago. That is my proposition, and that is what my *Alternative History* shall seek to demonstrate. Doubtless, there will be readers who find the notion preposterous. From them, I ask for patience. Just as playing chess takes time, so too does my explanation, and just as chess can be complicated, so too is this history.

Let us cast our minds back to May 6, 1800. Jean Baptiste Pointe de Sable was seated in a slat-backed rocker on the front porch of his mansion in the late afternoon. A gentle breeze was up, the air wafted sweet with the flowerful scents of early summer, the mosquitoes were not yet on the wing. There was a magnificent view, had he chosen to admire it: to his left, the setting sun shone a coppery light upon the waters of the great Lake, while directly before him stretched the greenery of the vegetable garden. Beyond, his horse grazed in a paddock that led down to the riverbank where a line of Lombardy poplars he had planted many years before cast lengthy shadows.

Pointe de Sable, had he risen to his feet, would have been able to see a chance of sandhills on the far side of the river, marked here and there by stunted cedars, dwarf willows and pine trees. This was the same formation of sandhills that, twelve years later, would provide cover for the Potawatomies who attacked the American garrison in retreat from Fort Dearborn. But on that balmy evening in 1800, no fort had yet been built. There were no soldiers. The only people who lived at Echicagou (as it was called), apart from Pointe de Sable and his family, were a few Frenchmen in his employ.

Normally, at this time in the evening, he would relax with a horn of whiskey and a pipe of tobacco. He might take the opportunity to reflect on his good fortune, on the trade he had developed, on the prosperity he had secured for his family. The extent of that prosperity would have been evident enough to an observer from the cluster of outbuildings that lay on the other side of the mansion. There was a dairy, a bakehouse, a stable, a smoking-house, a poultry coop, a workshop and a warehouse. His livestock comprised thirty cattle full-grown, two spring calves, thirty-eight hogs, forty-four hens and two mules, in addition to the horse already mentioned. And that is not yet taking into account his wheat field, nor the income he earned as a trader. He dealt in everything from furs to guns, calico to corn, tobacco to whiskey.

Perhaps though, rather than indulging in self-congratulation, Pointe de Sable might have ventured instead into nostalgia, remembering the day he first crossed the Echicagou portage as a young man in his twenties, bound for a farming life in Peoria, with not a notion in his head that one day this desolate, marshy place would become his home. Nobody lived here then. Echicagou was nothing but a place of passage, a portage between the Lake and the Illinois River, frozen in winter, swampish in spring, and cussed hot in summer.

Those are the kinds of thoughts that might have passed through his mind, had this been any ordinary day. But it was not. Pointe de Sable was tuckered out with anxiety as he sat in his rocker that evening. He drank no whiskey and smoked no pipe. And he admired no view because his eyes were tight shut. All his thoughts were concentrated on one matter only. And it would hardly puzzle a dozen Philadelphia lawyers to unriddle what that matter was. The most important contest of his life was about to take place. If he won, his unwelcome visitor had promised to leave and never come back. But if things went the other way, if the unimaginable happened and he lost, the person to leave Echicagou and never return would be himself.

Presently, all the particulars pertaining to that extraordinary contest shall be revealed. First, let us establish some facts.

Mr Pointe de Sable was born in about 1745, though exactly where remains a mystery. His father came from the Dandonneau family of La Rochelle in western France, while his mother was a freeborn slave. Pointe de Sable, in other words, was a mulatto. And that fact, I believe, is why my fellow historians have attempted to gloss over the identity of the true founder of Chicago, instead conferring the title on a white man called John Kinzie, whose own parentage was of dubious worth, to say nothing of his character.

In the historical records, we first come across Pointe de Sable in 1779, by which time he is about thirty-four years old and a successful trader in furs and sundry other items in what is now Michigan City. It was a time of fighting and confusion. The British, claiming he had sided with the French, imprisoned Pointe de Sable in their fort at Michilimackinac. The remarkable story of how he came to be released from jail and employed by his former captors at The Pinery, we shall leave for our protagonist himself to describe. The Pinery, incidentally, stood on the site now known as St Clair, and in one of those twists of fate that can only be seen with the benefit of hindsight, much of that district's fine timber would later be used to build Chicago.

When Pointe de Sable moved to Echicagou in 1785, it was an inhospitable, mosquito-infested wilderness. Over the next few years, he cleared a swath of land (between today's North Water Street and Michigan Avenue) and built the mansion and outbuildings already mentioned. In these endeavors, he was helped by Catherine (her Indian name was Kitihawa), a squaw from the local Potawatomie tribe who became his wife. And so it came to pass that by 1800, with his land, livestock and trading post, he had become as established and successful at Echicagou, in his own small way, as a Potter Palmer or a Marshall Field.

One afternoon in early May, his six-year-old grandson Wabaunsee alerted Pointe de Sable to the imminent arrival of visitors. Two figures were visible near the landing stage on the far side of the Lake. The boy, having reported this news, ran off to play his 'cyotie cat' trick on them. Deep in the woods, overlooking the main path, he kept a wild tabby cat he had trained to hide in the branches of a cottonwood tree, from where it would hiss and spit as strangers drew near. When they passed below, the cat would hurl itself down into the undergrowth, howling like a coyote. It was an act that never failed to startle first-time visitors, and a prank his grandfather had forbidden him to play.

We will now let Pointe de Sable himself describe what happened that afternoon. Please bear in mind that our founder never saw the inside of a schoolroom, and make allowances, therefore, for the quirks of diction and spelling that I transcribe here as they were originally set down.

EXTRACT FROM THE JOURNAL OF JEAN BAPTISTE POINTE DE SABLE

Mai 2 the yere 1800

This day comes truble to Pointe Sable. Happns like this. I ridin to the lake from Kaskaskia on mine hoss Ladie Strafford when

I sees litle Wobonsee runnin my way. I pulls the hoss up sharp
and she hisses like a fire puttin out, afore I dissend carefull to
ground. My legs ake after ridin and gone done stiff and I spose
thats the ole Reaper comin after me. Look at me, too bent to
swing a full ax and hair all curlish gray like a cloud tho there
aint none today, its a still evenin and nuthin moves nowhere,
othrwise the boy skimmin full chisel thro the grass.

Visitrs, tells Wobonsee, yellin in his pipeskweek voice. Visitrs
½ league from the landin, and he comes runnin on and dont
ware no shirt nor shoes and his hair all streamin blak like a tale,
and I deceivd visitrs be good news for that we needs more powdr
and shot and whiskey. I tether the ole Lady Strafford and she
looks ten times grummer than the one in the painting, for that
shes wantin the stable door and fresh hay and a daintie pillow
for her proudliness. Next moment Wobonsee comes skiddin to
a stop afore me and stands the copy of a brave, tho he onely done
six sumers, and togethr we spy the men far off. The boy soon runs
away westwind and the world turns peacefull till a flok of wild
geese they go aclamorin and beatin them wings in a frenziness
and twist high in the air and beak at the pinky sky afore divin to
the water, and the waves come risin and frothin and that noise it
sounds like a war cry and I feel afeard, lookin at my reflexshun in
the water that was clear afore, but is now gone crakked.

When I go home the first thing I sees is a wite man lookin
like a gost. Tells me to brung whiskey. I ask him polite his
busyness and he tells me stop askin dang stupid questions dont
I be seein hes lukky to escape with his life for he been attakt
by wild beests in the woods. And I think to tell him no need
for worryin hisself for the onely beest in them woods be litle
Wobonsees cyotie, that aint nuthin more than a noisome tabby
cat, but I dont say nuthin. I brung him whiskey and leeve him
alone till my ole frend Lalime arrives, puffin his breth for that he

aint no peg pony, and Lalime he tells me this visitr he brung be considrable of a chief from St Josefs, and he called Kinzie man.

After Cathrin feeds us chiken meat and jonniecakes, Kinzie man wipes his mustash and belchs like a bufalo. He dont say much, exept onely that the paintings on my walls be mighty girlish. Then he takes mine rockin chair from off the veranda, unbuttns his cote, stuffs tobcco in his cheek and tells Lalime to brung more whiskey. Lalime, he wants to make us frends. Probly thats why he say Kinzie man is the beatingst chess player in St Josefs. He knows I play chess, but he dont have no idea how deep it lays in mine bones. No, Lalime dont know the way mine father lernt me to play when I was a boy, that I nevr forgotn. I replie we can game, if the visitr wants. But Kinzie man dont want to play nuthin. Lalime has anuther idea, that I tell a story to pass the time, for he knows I have some up mine sleeve. In the end I agree, evn I dont like to raconterise to a man I dont trust.

Chess was still in mine mind. I guess thats why the storie I tellin them goes like this. When I was a prisonr in fort Maklimakinak I oftntimes challinged gainst the gards at chess and beat them. One day the guvner calls for me. Hes herd this Negro he play chess good, and he dont beleeve it. I am brung to sit in the guvners parlor. The chessbord on the table in front of me is prettyer than I evr seen afore with peeces made from walrus ivory and carvd jus fine, and I gottn a hankerin that if I ever escape I find a bord like that misself one day.

The guvner marchs in. He wares a long red cote and brassie butons and a porcpine fether in his hat and he talks in a slantendikular way, like a rope gone done tied up his tonge. I dont like his proudliness, and I knows I must lose gainst him but I thinkin to misself how to take the shine off of his viktry. Thats why I tells him I can beat him even with mine eyes shut, for that I figger his viktry dont be so gloryous if he win a blind man.

The guvner be insultd and his temper go ablazin, and he says if I wantin to play blinded then by Jove and by Darn I shall. When hes cooled down its too late to think again, for I seen this in the English, how they be afeard to look weak and foolsh in front of themselfs and for a guvner to be changin his mind, this a skeery thing to do.

They make me blinded with a blak stokkin. Then the guvnor gets anuther idea, how to shame me propper. If I winnin the game, I can have mine libertie, he tells, wich is just and reasnble, aint it? Yessir, thank you sir, I must say, most reasnble. But if I losin, he go send me in chains on the first ship to the Indies. I sits there, cussin my fat lips that gets me in this predikment, while the guvner makes an Englsh open, wite pawn E4. I take a long breth, and try to remembr all I know. And wen I can see good the pikter of the chessbord in the darkness of mine mind, I tell the guvners adjitant to move for me the blak pawn E6, wich is the French defense.

I always make a pause now in the tellin of this tale. I reckon I do this for to allow the listners to vision the moment and ask what happns next and how kwik I lose and how come I get all the way bak from the Indies. But Kinzie man dont say a word, onely sits there in mine rockin chair, drinkin whiskey and chewin tobcco and spittin on the floor. He looks at me like he dont beleeve a word of it. So I niver tell what happns next and dont say nuthin more, exept onely to misself, that this Kinzie man be the kind that always wants to play the biggst toad in the puddle.

How boorish of Mr Kinzie not to want to know what happened next. Although we learn later in the journal that Pointe de Sable won the game, and thereby gained his freedom, we never hear how on earth he managed it. We must assume, though, that it was executed with aplomb, given that a further entry reveals the regard in which he would come to be held by the very same English governor who spoke in that 'slantendikular' way. Pointe de Sable's journal discloses that it was the governor — his name was Sinclair — who taught him how to write. It was also the governor who introduced him to the world of fine art. That was doubtless why, at the time of Mr Kinzie's visit to Echicagou, there were no less than twenty-eight paintings in Pointe de Sable's possession, displayed on the walls of his mansion.

His granddaughter Eulalie recalled that, for her, two of those paintings were of particular importance. The first pictured the English Lady Strafford (after whom Pointe de Sable named his horse) at her country seat, surrounded by some of her most prized possessions. One reason Eulalie remembered this painting so well, she would admit to me in conversation late on in her life, was because she knew it was 'a favorite of Gray Curls''. 'Gray Curls' was the secret nickname she used for her grandfather. Many years later, this painting would come into the ownership of Chicago's first mayor Mr William Ogden, and hang in the entrance hall of his imposing North Side house. The second painting was a slight piece called 'The First Mansion at Echicagou' by an unknown artist. Eulalie had a sentimental attachment to this work because it depicted her childhood home, complete with her beloved 'Gray Curls' seated in his rocker on the porch.

I would like to dwell for a little longer on Eulalie as the four-year-old girl she was in 1800. By all accounts, she was strikingly beautiful. Her full lips, limpid eyes and high cheekbones, set off by a light brown skin, lent a particularity to her features that was extremely unusual in a child of such tender age. Most remarkable of all was the bounteous head of fair hair she had inherited from her father, the handsome, dissolute Jean Baptiste Pelletier. Those magnificent tresses settled in natural waves and an earlock curl dangled in front of her left ear, a style she copied from the painting already mentioned — 'Lady Strafford's Vision'. On Sundays, when their neighbors gathered in the Pointe de Sable home for prayer, she would be slicked up like a lady. And all this finery, readers will be surprised to hear, was achieved in complete silence.

For Eulalie, poor child, had never been heard to utter a single, solitary, intelligible word. Communication was achieved through the eyes and hands, through smiles and sighs. Although there was no doubting her intelligence or emotions or powers of observation, she would not speak. Many remedies had been tried, including a mix of herbs, bear dung and crushed elk bone administered by a notable Potawatomie witchdoctor. Nothing had worked. It was a mystery to her family and, needless to say, a powerful worry.

On the first morning of Mr Kinzie's visit, Eulalie positioned herself in one corner of the spaceful keeping room. It was a splendid day. The front door stood wide open and sunlight streamed inside. There was a dazzle to the polished puncheon floor. At the far end, around a low table draped by an embroidered cloth of French lace, stood the armchairs in which Pointe de Sable and Jean Lalime had sat the night before, together with the rocker appropriated by Mr Kinzie. In front of the table was a fireplace. The walls were brightened by Pointe de Sable's paintings, arranged in close proximity to each other. The exception was 'Lady Strafford's Vision', which hung alone above the finest piece of furniture in the house, a cabinet of French walnut. Through its glass doors, the family's best utensils were on display — pewter pots, clay jugs, china plates and a tall pair of fluted silver candlesticks. Beside the cabinet stood one other rarity that must be mentioned for the significant role it shall be called upon to play in this story. Enthroned on its own stool stood the largest copper kettle in the household, said to hold a measure of ten gallons. It was maintained in gleaming, pristine condition.

Mr Kinzie had risen late. Eulalie watched him cross the room, a high, winding man with pointy whiskers and glittering eyes like boiled candy drops. His skin was the color of tobacco and he had long bent fingers, only the tips of which he used to pick things up. He paused to eye the contents of the cabinet, ran a finger over the surface of the copper kettle, and then approached the dining table that fronted the window. She became aware of a mighty rich and, to her young senses, unpleasant smell. The house had plenty of odors, safe scents that drifted through from the bakehouse and the timber store at the back to mix with the cedar-scented soap her grandmother believed could be used to clean everything. Those familiar smells were now overwhelmed by the perfume worn by Mr Kinzie, a kind of cologne that made Eulalie think of bitter oranges and the bite of salt and the flash of lightning in the sky. It made her eyes water.

Mr Kinzie sat down at the dining table and Susannah, Eulalie's mother, put a plate of porridge in front of him, with maple sap to the side.

The porridge was too cold. Where was the coffee? Where was the bread? Were there no ham fixings for a visitor? Not even no eggs? What kind of inn was this? And what is your name, maid, he wanted to know, and where is your husband?

Susannah, who was heating up coffee from the grains, told him there would be no bread until they baked later in the day, that she had seen no sign hanging at the door to advertise an inn, and that it was no business of his to know where her husband might be. (Jean Jacques Pelletier had, in fact, traveled to Peoria with Susannah's brother — also, confusingly, called Jean Jacques — where the two of them would, no doubt, be on a drunken spree.) She was no maid, she added, but the daughter of Mr Pointe de Sable, by whom he had been made welcome.

That brisk speech caused Mr Kinzie to change his attitude. He now behaved with lick-spittle civility. He was charmed to make her acquaintance, he said, touching his hat and smoothing his mustache. And he asked her to forgive him for being in a pucker, but he never slept well in a strange bed — especially, he added, when he had to sleep alone. No, no, she should not suspicion him because of that remark, for it was made with an honest heart. He explained that he had lost his wife but recently in distressing circumstances, and it was 'exceedingly irksome to discover the blessed realm of sleep'. It was a habit of his, apparently, to use highfalutin phrases in an attempt to impress.

And it is to her credit that Susannah did not fall, hook line and sinker, for such bunkum. She was right to be skeptical of his sentimental yarn about a deceased wife. History records the marital affairs of Mr Kinzie with accuracy, and somewhat differently. At the time of this visit to Echicagou, he was thirty-seven years of age, and recently married for the second time. His first wife, Margaret, together with their three children, had deserted him. He had married his second wife over two years previous, on January 23, 1798. She was expecting their first child.

Mr Kinzie's tongue continued to wag. He told Susannah tall tales about his adventures, described the glamorous life to be lived in far-off Quebec and Detroit, and even managed to make St Joseph sound like a rip-snorting place. Why was a beautiful woman wasting her youth in this backwater? 'Trust me. I've seen more of life than you. The world is bigger than you think. Even if you does choose to stay here,' he told her, 'I can make life better for you, if you cop my meaning.'

Eulalie did not know what he meant by that, but she did know what she thought of him. She stepped out of her corner, marched forward and stared direct at Mr Kinzie. She pointed one finger at him and, for the first time in her four years on earth, there emerged from her mouth a word.

'Snag,' yelled Eulalie. 'Snag.'

Mr Kinzie jumped back in his chair, knocking his porridge plate off the table. It shattered on the floor.

'Snag, snag, snag,' Eulalie shouted three more times, before stepping outside. She did not run (or so her mother claimed later), as most children would have done. She walked, tresses in place, smoothing her skirt, a proper little Lady. Stopping at the open window to look back inside, she felt herself enveloped in a maternal embrace.

Together, they watched Mr Kinzie finish his coffee. That seemed to calm him down. He stuck his forefinger into the pot of maple sap and twirled it around, before licking off the juice. Doubtless, he found it awful sweet. But he did not notice how the sap had gotten trapped in his mustache. As it dried, the hairs began to curl up at the ends, stuck together, ridiculously erect. He pushed back his chair, stood up and released a long, loud fart.

Nobody could find an explanation for why Eulalie had broken into speech for the first time. Pointe de Sable, though, guessed where the word must have come from. My Euladie (as he fondly called Eulalie) would have heard it used when she accompanied him on a recent river journey. In those days, 'snag' was often shouted by the look-out on a boat to alert the pilot to the menace of driftwood hidden in the channels and shallows ahead. With hindsight, we can appreciate that this little girl had foreseen the threat represented by this unwelcome guest, this dangerous piece of human driftwood, if you will. Twelve years on, that diminutive word would be used again by sixteen-year-old Eulalie as another warning of danger. But on that occasion, as we shall hear in due course, the circumstances would be infinitely more terrifying than those that prevailed at breakfast on the first morning of Mr Kinzie's visit.

That same afternoon, Eulalie was in the kitchen standing on a stool, helping her mother mix flour for griddlecakes, when Mr Kinzie returned to the house. She heard a curious *thump* on the porch followed by a rooting of hogs. His nailed boots mounted the steps. He was in good spirits, whistling a tune that was popular at the time: 'Hail Columbia, happy land! Hail ye heroes, heav'n borne band ...' Eulalie slid off her stool and took up a position by the door to the keeping room. Gray Curls and Lalime — or 'Uncle Jean', as she knew him — were seated in the easy chairs surrounding the fireplace.

Unknown to Eulalie, Gray Curls and Uncle Jean were engaged in a heated conversation because Mr Lalime had finally revealed the true purpose behind their visit. He had brought Mr Kinzie to Echicagou, he said, at the request of a powerful trader in St Joseph, called Mr Burnet. Mr Burnet had instructed Mr Kinzie to purchase Pointe de Sable's estate, to include his mansion and its contents, his land, his outbuildings, his livestock and his trading store. Pointe de Sable, taken aback by the news, had given an immediate, unambiguous response. He would sell nothing to nobody. It had long been his desire, as his friend Lalime knew very well, that everything he owned should one day be inherited by his grandson Wabaunsee.

Lalime told Pointe de Sable he might have no choice. 'If you refuse,' he said, 'they'll use the law.'

'And what be those laws in particular you talkin'? That a man don't have the right to live on the land he cleared?'

'Not when an American wants that land. When an American uses the law against someone like you …' Lalime shrugged, '… the law goes down on its knee and curtseys. That's the fact, no matter the way it's done. You'll suddenly find the law says it's not allowed for *gens de couleurs libres* to own property in Echicagou, even though it did not say that yesterday. Or they'll prove it was never your land in the first place.'

Lalime reminded Pointe de Sable of the infamous agreement reached at Greenville in 1795 when the Potawatomies were hoodwinked into ceding six square miles of land at the Echicagou Portage to the United States.

'But Greenville don't mean nothin' to the Potawat'mies,' exclaimed Pointe de Sable. 'They never gone done buyin' or sellin' land 'cause they believe all the land everywhere, it belong to the Great Spirit.'

Lalime agreed, but said it made no difference. Powerful people in St Joseph wanted his land and buildings, and they would stop at nothing to get it. 'I think you should accept what is inevitable,' said Lalime, 'and negotiate the best price you can. I know these people. If you don't agree, they'll use force.'

Despite this warning, Pointe de Sable refused to have any dealings with them. Instead, he made a plan. As he puts it in his journal:

> I tell Lalime I shall rip misself to St Josefs on Ladie Strafford
> for to find an attrney while he be keepin Kinzie man busie, so
> he dont suspectin nuthin. Let him start makin an account of
> everthing, noting it all down, from evry plate in the kitchn to
> the last bushel of grain in the storehouse.

Mr Kinzie made his entrance just as this conversation came to a close. He sailed past them to retrieve the rocker off the porch, returned with it, sat down in front of the fireplace, and, as though he were quite alone in the privacy of his own chamber, he removed his boots and socks, and began to wiggle his toes.

Pointe de Sable made a point of treating his guest with civility. He brought Mr Kinzie a glass of whiskey and asked about his walk around the estate. The inquiry elicited no more than a nod of the head. Rocking back and forth, Mr Kinzie took out his tobacco pouch, dipped a wad in his cheek and chewed, seemingly lost in his own world. From time to time he smiled, as if at some private joke.

For a few moments more, not a word was spoken. The windows were open. There was a warm, treacly scent to the air, tinged by the aroma of baking bread. From the kitchen came the sound of more dough being beaten. The only strangeness was the snuffling of the hogs who, unknown to Pointe de Sable, Lalime or little Eulalie, were fighting over the remains of the dead 'cyotie cat' Mr Kinzie had deposited on the steps outside.

At last, their visitor broke his silence. Gesturing towards the copper necklace Pointe de Sable was in the habit of wearing, he turned to Mr Lalime. 'What does it mean, Jean,' he said, 'that your friend wears Indjun jewelry?'

Lalime looked embarrassed. Pointe de Sable, though, maintained his equanimity and even managed a smile. 'The same like it always means,' he said. 'I been wearin' this necklace since I first come to Echicagou, Mr Kinzie.' He explained that it was a gift he had been given by a Potawatomie chief, when he arrived to establish a homestead. He said no more than that, doubtless because he knew Mr Kinzie would have mocked him were he to claim the necklace had special powers that derived from a Potawatomie legend about a monster called Nambi-Za, who ruled the nether regions of Lake Michigan.

'That one's wearin' jewelry as well,' observed Mr Kinzie, pointing towards the painting of 'Lady Strafford's Vision', that hung above the French cabinet.

Pointe de Sable agreed that indeed she was. Perhaps in an attempt to allay any suspicions on the part of Mr Kinzie regarding his newly hatched plan to seek urgent legal advice in St Joseph, he went on to speak about the picture's meaning and provenance. Truly, this was one of the most exquisite paintings it had ever been his privilege to behold. As Mr Kinzie would observe, both Lady Strafford and her horse were depicted with such skill they might almost be alive. Note the horse's posture, and the beads of sweat on its flank. See how strands of hair escaped from Lady Strafford's earlock curl, how the flush on her cheeks changed with the light. And if Mr Kinzie would care to take a walk around the room, he would find her eyes seemed to follow him everywhere, never once averting their gaze.

'What a hussy!' growled Kinzie, not shifting from the rocker.

Pointe de Sable was not put off his stride. As always when talking about 'Lady Strafford's Vision', he got carried away. 'Look closely, Mr Kinzie,' he continued. 'Is not everything authentic? Do you not feel the delicate mist in the air? Does it not seem possible to stroke with your own hands the velvet of Lady Strafford's crimson gown and the flimsy white lace at the cuffs?'

'I'd settle for stroking what lies underneath,' said Mr Kinzie, spitting on the puncheon floor. 'You too, eh Jean?'

Mr Lalime pretended to be examining his hands.

Pointe de Sable described the other features of the painting that delighted him, the mansion in the background with its Corinthian colonnades, the sweeping lawns and flowerbeds in bloom, the ornamental lake, and the small oval building in the foreground. Pointe de Sable believed this to be an oracle.

'And what does she ask the oracle?' Kinzie inquired.

Pointe de Sable told Mr Kinzie he did not know.

His journal, though, explains otherwise. There, we learn that he considered it no accident that Lady Strafford had posed for the painting in the midst of her estate, surrounded by her possessions. She was a worried Lady. These were troubled times, and she wanted to find out from the oracle what would happen to her property, to her family and to herself.

'This the first picture I purchas'd,' said Pointe de Sable, 'from Governor Sinclair at Michilmackinac. That gentlem'n brung it cross the seas from England. The painter that gone done it, he wern't no greenhorn.'

Had Mr Kinzie taken note of the signature at the bottom of that canvas, and mentioned it to the more refined folk in St Joseph, he might have figured the painting was worth a great deal more than a few shiners. But he did not, so he remained ignorant of the fact that 'Lady Strafford's Vision' was executed by George Stubbs, one of the eighteenth century's most celebrated English painters.

'You oughtta be selling more of this firewater,' said Mr Kinzie. He leaned forward, clearing his throat with a mix of a *hem* and a cough, and spat out a wad of masticated tobacco (which 'gone done slidin like a brown slug cross the polshed timbrs'). 'That's your problem.

You don't understan' the mind of the Indjun. You ain't serious about bringing them grog.'

Pointe de Sable was about to speak out, about to tell Mr Kinzie he did not run a low-down drinking den. He was about to speechify along the lines that if you make the Potawatomies drunken on whiskey today, how they gonna pick up a hoe tomorrow? And if they don't pick up them hoes, how they gonna pay for the whiskey? He was about to punch Mr Kinzie with those points. But he never got to do it because there was a sudden rumpus, a high-pitched whooping, a burst of color, a flash of steel, a degree of youthful rowdiness the Pointe de Sable homestead had likely never seen before. All eyes turned to the open doorway. There stood six-year-old Wabaunsee, ululating, his eyes in a trance, painted for war like a Potawatomie brave. His slight back was arched as he thrust forward first one stamping foot, and then the other. From the corner of the room, Eulalie had a clear view of her cousin. Lines of red paint crossed his cheeks and chest. He had tied his hair into a scalp-lock and planted it with feathers. In his hands he was clutching what looked like a real tomahawk. She had no idea where that had come from, but she did not trust him with it. Her cousin could be plenty wild and dangerous, even without a weapon.

Mr Kinzie leaped out of his chair, coughing out the tobacco in his cheek. Uncle Jean began to sweat profusely. Only Gray Curls stayed calm. He stood up and raised a hand. Wabaunsee was advancing, waving his tomahawk this way and that. 'I'll hang your scalp,' he screamed at Mr Kinzie, 'from my belt.'

Eulalie was scared. She feared he might do it, and though not certain it would be wrong, given the identity of Wabaunsee's proposed victim, she thought it likely would be. Her cousin had never attacked her with a blade, but she had often been on the receiving end of his temper and she knew what that felt like. So it did not seem inconceivable to her four-year-old self that he might take on a bad grown-up and win.

At this point, though, Gray Curls intervened. He seized hold of the tomahawk in Wabaunsee's hand and told him to wait outside.

'That savagerous little animal,' hissed Mr Kinzie. 'I will make him pay.'

'You have children?' asked Gray Curls. His voice sounded deep and soft as the big feather bed in his room, where Eulalie would go to hide beneath the covers when she wanted to be alone. 'Because if you do, you know how deep they feelin' sometimes, even they not able to put the feelins' into words.'

Eulalie could feel her grandfather's eyes on her.

'And what kinda man is it, Mr Kinzie,' continued Gray Curls, 'that gits hisself huffed over a tabby cat?'

Mr Kinzie swapped a new wad of tobacco from one cheek to the other. He talked about a man in St Joseph, about buying land and buying buildings, about Gray Curls being allowed as a 'favor that ain't deserved' to take his paintings with him when he left Echicagou, like the one of 'that hussy' on the wall.

'And you and your friends,' asked Gray Curls, 'where you expectin' us to go?'

Mr Kinzie twitched his shoulders. 'It's a big country, ain't it?'

Eulalie did not know what all the talk meant, but it frightened her. She did not want to go anywhere. She certainly did not want to leave her home. And whereas before she merely disliked her cousin, now she hated him. Because it was obvious to her that none of this would be happening if it wasn't for Wabaunsee and his 'cyotie cat'.

In view of what will happen in the future, perhaps the fractious relationship between Eulalie and Wabaunsee as children should be placed in a broader context. Wabaunsee was a bully, though perhaps no more so than any other boy of that age. He would play tricks on Eulalie, pull her hair, trip her up and encourage his 'cyotie cat' to hiss at her. No wonder, then, that she kept her distance from him. But perhaps, too, she resented what she had doubtless already intuited, though she was too young to understand why: Wabaunsee was her grandfather's favorite.

Pointe de Sable doted on the boy not, as some might assume, because he was his only male grandchild. He doted on him out of shame. To explain: Wabaunsee was the illegitimate child of Pointe de Sable's son Jean Jacques and a Potawatomie woman to whom Pointe de Sable had never been introduced. Maybe that would not have mattered overmuch, had Jean Jacques been a responsible father. But he was unreliable, lazy and frequently drunken. Pointe de Sable tried to shoulder as much as he could of his son's neglected parental responsibility. That was why he wanted his estate to bypass Jean Jacques in favor of Wabaunsee, and that was why the boy would always be his blind spot.

Maybe it happened that evening. Maybe the next. She could not be certain. In later life, when she had frequent nightmares, Eulalie would look back with disbelief at how deeply she had been able to sleep as a child, before, that is, the arrival of Mr Kinzie. It was as though she were someone else in those days, a fairytale girl with fancy clothes who lived in the magic world of her grandparents with its comforting smells of baking, of newly split timber and cedar-scented soap.

She could tell, before opening her eyes, that it was still dark outside. Even so, she woke up instantly. She reckoned it must have been the perfume that jolted her into consciousness — the sharp mix of bitter oranges and the bite of salt and the flash of lightning. The door was closing, softly, to the room she shared with her mother at the far end of the house's long corridor. Only a moonlit gleam came in through the shutter, enough to illuminate Mr Kinzie's shape curving away into the darkness, like one of those trees on the riverbank bent over by a big wind. Her mother was sitting upright, holding the blanket to her chin. She was whispering questions: why are you here, what do you want? 'Please go away, Mr Kinzie. You'll wake Eulalie.' He was kneeling in front of her mother's low bed.

She could not hear or understand everything Mr Kinzie said but, despite her tender age, she knew he was trying to persuade her mother to do something she did not want to do. There was nothing normal about the way he spoke. Sometimes he sounded too kind, sometimes he seemed to be threatening her. Over the last few days, Mr Kinzie had paid a lot of attention to her mother. Eulalie hated Mr Kinzie for that.

The tone of his voice changed again. He was lonely. He had feelings for her. If she let him come underneath that blanket, he promised all Pointe de Sable's problems would disappear and nobody would take his property away from him. Mr Kinzie would return to St Joseph and never come back. St Joseph was a fine town, and he wanted her mother to go there with him. 'I like you very much, Susannah. Fate has brought us together. I will change your life.' Her mother interrupted, pushing his hand away, telling him to stop this silly talk. He would wake the child. Eulalie shut her eyes tight and held her breath. There was a rustle of cloth and she smelled his grunty breath. A finger touched her lips, and stayed there. It was terribly cold, like a piece of ice.

'Out like a log,' Mr Kinzie informed her mother.

As if they were communicating in the same unspoken language, she understood that the freezing finger was an order to stay silent. After what seemed like ages, the finger withdrew.

Her mother asked him to leave.

'Send me away, Susannah, and your lives here are finished. Your father will lose everything. It's an easy decision, ain't it?'

There was another burst of the bitter perfume as Mr Kinzie rose from his knees. He was trying to get into the bed. Her mother was holding the blanket tight, pushing him away. Where Eulalie's strength came from, she had no idea. Her fear seemed to evaporate. She threw herself at Mr Kinzie's back. She bit through his shirt and scratched at him and maybe she would have screamed except that his hand was pressed down on her mouth and he was throttling her with the other, and his face was against hers, full of stinky breath. Her mother was begging him to let her go. 'She's only a child.'

Mr Kinzie hissed instructions at Eulalie. She was to wait in the corridor, 'in silence, not a squeak out of you. Understand?' If she did that for him, he promised she would be safe and her mother would be safe. 'But if not ...' He squeezed her throat until she was choking again and there were tears in her eyes. Her mother was begging Mr Kinzie to leave her be. At last, he released her.

'Do what he says,' whispered her mother in a halting voice. 'Everything here is fine.'

'That's better,' said Mr Kinzie. 'Much better.'

He opened the door, pushed Eulalie outside and pressed his finger once more against her lips. As soon as the door closed behind him, she ran.

The timbers pounded beneath her feet, and in no time at all she was past the bedroom doors of that long dark corridor and inside the keeping room where the night air was still heavy with smoke and whiskey, damp and warm against her cheeks, with no thoughts inside her head except that she must stop Mr Kinzie and save her mother and save Gray Curls and if she did that she would save everything and nothing would have to change, and they could stay there for ever and ever.

She must have picked up a wooden bowl because that was what she used, with both hands, to pound the nearest, shiniest object she could see, which was her grandmother's favorite copper kettle, the biggest of all her kettles, the one displayed on its own small stool, the one Eulalie had never seen her use. It sounded like a gong, then a bell, then a drum, and then — as it toppled to the floor — like all three of them together.

The house awoke. It exploded with shouts and people and lamps, and there was running and guns and fear, and someone must have taken away the wooden bowl because the next thing Eulalie remembered was finding herself hidden in the folds of her grandmother's nightdress.

That old copper kettle would survive both the Great Chicago Fire of 1871, and a subsequent fire in 1874 at the home of lawyer J. Young Scammon, where it was being held in temporary storage, along with other items of interest to the Chicago Historical Society. You can still see the dents made on its surface, all those years ago, by the four-year-old granddaughter of Mr Pointe de Sable.

Everyone assumed that Eulalie's outburst was caused by a nightmare. And she, poor girl, whose utterances had gone no further yet than 'snag', was able neither to explain nor understand what she had witnessed. When she grew older, though, she would be under no illusions about what had almost happened that night.

The copper kettle was placed back on its stand and calm restored. Everyone returned to bed. Everyone, that is, except Wabaunsee. He waited until all were fast asleep again before stealing into the room where the guests, Uncle Jean and Mr Kinzie (now back in his allotted bed), were lodged. As Pointe de Sable put it in his journal, Wabaunsee:

> ... fans the bag of Kinzie man, finds a perfum in a silvry pot engravd with flowres and lettrs, and empties it over the visitrs face. Kinzie man wakns, cryin out that his eyes be on fire, and that probly not far from the truth neither because next day they be glowin red and streamin like a tragdy.

Pointe de Sable was a man whose behavior was guided by an innate sense of right and wrong. In his journals, he refers more than once to his belief that 'there is indeed justice in the world', as if he imagines the existence of heavenly scales in which all our deeds on earth will one day be weighed. Those scales, he thinks, will ultimately favor right over wrong, truth over falsehood, honesty over deceit, and the triumph of reason over force. It is an inspiring, optimistic doctrine that history has all too often proven to be misplaced. But it was presumably this conviction that persuaded Pointe de Sable to concede that the visitor be permitted to punish Wabaunsee. For however rude Mr Kinzie might be, however sinister his intentions, however wrongful his killing of the 'cyotie cat', he was still a guest of the household. Wabaunsee had acted towards their visitor in a way that could not be condoned.

Pointe de Sable left the house with Mr Lalime early the next morning to work on a new storehouse he was building. This was a terrible miscalculation. A distraught Eulalie appeared some time later and tugged frantically at his sleeve, while pointing towards the house. Though he dropped everything and ran as fast as he could, he arrived too late to stop the worst of the beating. Mr Kinzie, instead of waiting for Pointe de Sable to bear witness to the punishment, had chosen to exact his revenge at once in an empty household. He was still crouching over Wabaunsee, who lay prone on the puncheon floor, limp and defenseless. Blood wept out of purple welts ('big like wagon weels') across his back. As yet another blow rained down, the boy neither flinched nor uttered a sound. Pointe de Sable hurled himself at Mr Kinzie, who was now in the process of taking a knife to Wabaunsee's cheek. 'The wild beest wants to be an Indjun savidge, says Kinzie man, then by damnashun he can look like one.' Before it could be stopped, the boy's cheek had been slashed. He would be scarred for life.

Pointe de Sable ordered Mr Kinzie to leave his house at once, or he would personally take the whip on him. 'You try to whup me, ole mulatto man, says Kinzie man, and I brake your legs. He swallws anuther horn of mine whiskey, and then he leeves.'

Wabaunsee, despite his fragile state, remained impassive as his wounds were tended by the ladies of the house. Pointe de Sable sat by his side for the rest of the afternoon. At some point, he removed the copper necklace he wore and placed it around the boy's neck, telling him to wear it always for protection. It would keep him safe in the future, he said, in times of danger and misfortune. He does not mention in his journal whether, as he handed it over, he also told Wabaunsee the Potawatomie story about Nambi-Za, to explain the necklace's significance; probably, though, he would have recounted that tale often enough before. Nor does he record his own feelings at surrendering the necklace to his grandson. There is little doubt, given his belief in the power of the talisman, that he would have been only too aware of how vulnerable its loss rendered him. As to whether Wabaunsee was a worthy recipient of that precious gift, only time would tell.

One can assume that his brutal treatment at the hands of Mr Kinzie did much to harden the boy's immature heart against white men. A few days later, when a group of Potawatomies passed through Echicagou, Wabaunsee asked his grandfather whether he could travel with them to visit his mother. This was not an unusual occurrence, so Pointe de Sable saw no reason to object. Although he had never met the boy's mother, he suspected she was a kindly influence on Wabaunsee, and that after such an ordeal it was a good idea for the boy to seek her support.

The decision to allow him to leave was one he would revisit time and time again. Wabaunsee departed with that group of Potawatomies, never to return. The loss of his grandson would break Pointe de Sable's heart, and trouble his conscience for the rest of his life.

Mr Kinzie did not leave the house that afternoon, as had been demanded of him. When at last he rose from Wabaunsee's bedside in the early evening, Pointe de Sable found the visitor making a list of his household possessions. 'I sees the list. 1 coper kettle 10 gal (damagd), 1 coper kettle 7 gal, 1 coper kettle 3 1/2 gal.' And so on. He called Jean Lalime aside and insisted that Mr Kinzie leave at once and never come back, only to be reminded that the visitor was backed by powerful men in St Joseph. Despite his abhorrent cruelty towards Wabaunsee, said Lalime, nothing would be achieved by sending Mr Kinzie away. He would only return with reinforcements. These men wanted Pointe de Sable's house, his land and outbuildings and trading post and, one way or another, they would have it. One must wonder, given this response, whether Lalime was merely being realistic, whether he was utterly spineless, or — worst of all — whether he was in league with those 'powerful men' himself. Pointe de Sable never seems to doubt his friend, despite the fact that Lalime had acted as the conduit for Mr Kinzie in the first place.

Despite this warning from Lalime, Pointe de Sable refused to capitulate. 'Then we must be findin' a way,' he said, 'to stop them wantin' it.' Mr Kinzie, he told Lalime, had to be persuaded to return to St Joseph and tell those 'powerful men' they were wasting their time, that the Pointe de Sable house had no value, that the land was a swamp, and that the trading post did no business worth the name. But why on earth, asked Lalime, would Mr Kinzie do that?

Pointe de Sable drew him close and revealed an ingenious, madcap plan. Mr Kinzie was one of the best chess players in St Joseph? Very well. Lalime should tell Mr Kinzie that Pointe de Sable was willing to wager his entire estate on the outcome of a game of chess. Not only that, but Pointe de Sable would offer to play the game blindfolded. Lalime was alarmed by the idea. And, anyway, what would happen if there was no winner? 'Then we goe play till there be one. Dont be worryin', Jean, I seen this kinda man afore. He can't say no to a challinge from an "ole mulatto man". He nevr dream he could be losin'. Beleeve me, he will.'

Lalime tried to persuade him it was a foolish idea, that Pointe de Sable could never win, not even with his eyes wide open, because Kinzie was a brilliant player. Pointe de Sable, though, simply repeated his proposal and set conditions. First, Lalime would referee the game; second, Kinzie would sign an agreement strong enough to put before an attorney in Washington that, if he lost the game, he would report back to those 'powerful men' in St Joseph that Pointe de Sable's land, property, possessions, and trading post were worthless. And if Mr Kinzie won the game? 'Then I sell ever'thing to you, Jean.' But why would he sell it to him? ''cause if I have to sell to someone, I bettr sell to a frend than a nogood. But dont be worryin. This nevr gonna happn, Jean. Nevr.'

The entry in Pointe de Sable's journal that describes the chess contest is touching, and it is worth repeating here, but I must warn my readers that the account breaks off shortly after the game itself begins. Only many years after the event took place, did Eulalie reveal to me how that evening ended.

EXTRACT FROM THE JOURNAL OF JEAN BAPTISTE POINTE DE SABLE

Its a prettie sumer evenin. I sit with mine eyes tite shut for that I figgerin if I done rite or wrong. I dont touch mine pipe nor whiskey but start thinkin on the bord, on evry peece waitin in its place to play, for to make the pikter strongr in mine mind. Lalime comes out. He tells me Kinzie man he made the consent and signalized the agreement, and it can be brung afore all the attrneys in St Josef and Detroit and Washingtn and nobodie nevr find no leak. And he garanty it all writ down lawful with warranty deeds. I thank my frend from mine hart. You, I say, you be a trustin kind of man. But tell me this, Jean, why you sweatin so bad? He tells me mebbe he comin down with the agues or fevers, it that time of year. Then he looks away. I know it aint no fever. Hes skeered bout wot happns. Thats cause hes afeard for me and I thinkin mebbe I should tell the truth how that my father lernt me chess with the blindfold, the bettr to see the storie on the bord in the darknss of mine mind. Mebbe I should tell him it was no surprse I win guvner Sinclare with mine eyes blinded cause thats how I play the best. Mebbe I should tell that the guvner be so impressd he set me free and give me the walrus ivry chessbord for a gift. Mebbe I should tell that for a Englsh, the guvner was a trusting kind of man, the same as you, Jean Lalime. Mebbe I should tell mine frend these things, but I nevr do for that we go inside straitways to play the game.

Cathrin and Susanna are lookin afeard as deer by the door, and My littel Euladie tugs at mine cote, pointin at Kinzie man. I run mine fingers thro her goldish curls, and wisper that I hope them curls never go gray like mine. She repeatin to me the word she lernt, the first word she ever talkd, wich word be SNAG. I unnerstan. She tellin me go carefull of Kinzie man, that he like to a snag hiddn up ahead in the great rivr of life.

Lalime brung out the set of walrus ivry and counts evry peece and puts them in the propper place. And afore Kinzie put the blak stockin on me so tite my eyes cant take breth I lookin at that bord close for the last time and I see it in mine mind like a gloryous pikter, evry peece in its place and ready to move. And I smile for that in front of all the roylty and nobilty, the pawns awready skrapin there hoofs on the bord, ready to surprse that paleface Kinzie man like the pawns in the world, they always do brung surprse. For its the pawns of the 3rd rank that do the winnin, not the bishps or nites or castls, and they be the soul of chess, like we pawns be the soul of the world too, also.

Mine eyes go into the blakness. Lalime says that Kinzie's made an Englsh open, wite pawn E4, so I tell him to move the

blak pawn E6 wich is the French defense I use gainst guvner
Sinclare and thats how we start, and this is a good sign because
I know if there be any justce in the world, I wont nevr lose to
Kinzie man.

Promises

August 14, 1812

It is hot and humid with only the faintest breeze, so slight Eulalie cannot see a single ripple break the surface of the wide, slow river. The water reflects the harshness of the midday sun in a shiny pewter glow. Mosquitoes flit above the surface. She digs in one heel to gain a better purchase in the mud as they scrub and beat the last sheet against the flatness of the scalding rock, working from one end each. Cicely begins to sing in her lilting, tuneful voice. 'Walkin' all the way to Heav'n' is one of Eulalie's favourites. She hums along to the chorus.

After the sheet is washed and wrung, they lay it alongside the others, flattening the spiky grass as they do so, weighing down each corner with a stone. They shake out the sodden bottoms of their skirts and retreat to the shade of a cluster of scrub oaks. While Cicely checks on Juba, her sleeping baby, Eulalie sits with her back to a tree trunk and dabs her neck with a pocket handkerchief, warning herself not to scratch the bites. She will treat them later with the lotion Isaac has given her, made from wild garlic, witch hazel and cedar oil. She is hot and tired from the morning's work. But she is also excited and cannot stop herself from glancing again towards the path that leads to the Fort.

She inspects her chafed, puffy hands. The soap they used was poor, more gritty ash than grease. Removing her hat, she adjusts the earlock curl. That's the problem with doing the laundry. You end up looking dishevelled, and she hates that feeling, just as she hates wearing the same patched, threadbare skirt, day after day. Isaac has promised to buy her new cloth as soon as they reach St Joseph. And if there's none to be had there, they will buy it in St Charles. For a few moments, Eulalie thinks wistfully of St Charles and its fine streets and shops, and how thrilling it will be to present Isaac to her grandfather.

She looks across at Cicely. 'Still sleepin' the sleep of the just?' *The sleep of the just* is a new expression she has borrowed from Isaac. It is the kind of saying Gray Curls would like too.

Cicely smiles. She swats away a fly from Juba's forehead before planting a kiss on his chubby black cheek. The baby stirs but does not wake. One of Eulalie's hands has dropped to her belly. She takes a deep breath, enough for both of them. There is a scent in the air, coming off the baked earth, that starts her hunger pangs. How she longs for real food, and more of it. Anything but the turnips and potatoes they've been eating, day in day out. Tomorrow, she thinks with sudden gaiety, from tomorrow everything will be different.

She sneaks another look at the path leading back to the Fort and tells herself that looking again will do no good, and may even put a curse on his coming. If he does not arrive soon, they will run out of time. Mrs Heald wants them back at the Fort as soon as possible. Much still needs to be done in preparation for the journey. Eulalie knows what Mrs Heald is like. Stay out too long, and she will send someone to look for them.

Even if Isaac doesn't come, she tells herself, she should make the most of this time away from the Fort. Tempers in the barracks room, where they are confined, have become more frayed than ever since Captain Heald announced that Fort Dearborn was to be 'temporarily vacated'. Tomorrow, the whole garrison, together with those few white settlers who live at Echicagou, are to travel in convoy to Fort Wayne. Everyone is on edge. There have been scareful stories circulating about surprise Potawatomie attacks, about the horrific ways in which they scalp their victims, about what they do ... and this is communicated only by the boldest women, and only in frightened whispers ... about what they do to those they take captive. Eulalie, as usual, has kept her own counsel. She tries not to show her fear. She tells herself that she, unlike everyone else, has Isaac to protect her.

She kneels beside Cicely. 'He's having your smile,' she tells her. 'I never seen it before. But today it's clear as a bell.'

'Thank you, miss.'

She admires Cicely. Despite her circumstances, she already seems wise and grown up. Even Mrs Heald talks to her differently, with more courtesy than she usually employs to address a slave. Eulalie wishes she felt wiser and more grown up herself. Sometimes, she fears Isaac might change his mind. One day, perhaps he will see through her, judge her to be like all the others, nothing more than a frivolous, untried young woman.

'Don't worry, miss,' says Cicely. 'I'm sure that doctor he gonna come.'

She feels herself blush. 'You think so, Cicely?'

'As sure as sugar is sweet.'

That assurance is a comfort. She joins Cicely in gazing at baby Juba as he sleeps and is filled with a feeling of inexpressible wonder at the miracle of a child. It seems incredible and yet it is true, that this same miracle is happening inside her now, that every moment of every day her own babe is taking shape, with new eyes and hands and feet. Such an extraordinary thing, and now the process has begun, nothing can stop it. Even if Isaac cannot come today, what is one lost hour when they have years together stretching ahead of them? She feels a surge of excitement at the prospect of tomorrow's journey. All will go well, and within the week they will be in Fort Wayne, officially married in the church. As soon as Isaac's duties allow, they will make the trip to St Charles. He says there is even a chance he might be posted there. She cannot wait for them to meet, the two most important people in her life, Isaac and Gray Curls.

'What're you thinking, miss?'

'Whether it be a boy or a girl,' she says.

Cicely reaches across and places her hand beside Eulalie's, on her belly. Closing her eyes, she begins to chant something in her own tongue. Eulalie feels drowsy. She hears the roll of the river, insects circling, the occasional crack of a twig. The chant rises to a crescendo.

Cicely opens her eyes. 'That one a boy, I reckon. Will you go tell 'im today, miss?'

'Yes.' She can feel her lip trembling. She touches the necklace at her breast, for luck. The truth is that she cannot wait to tell Isaac about the baby, now that she's certain. And why not tell him, too, that Cicely is sure he will become the father of a son? She imagines how he might react, with one of his slow, gradual smiles — the best ones always seem to come like that, as though they have travelled from somewhere deep inside him. By the time the smile surfaces, his whole face has been filled by it. His mouth widens, the lines of his teeth show, his eyes narrow and sparkle, dimples appear in the middle of his whiskered cheeks and often, too, he will begin to chuckle, though he confines that chuckle to the depths of his throat, as if he knows he shouldn't really be doing that as well, because this is only meant to be a smile, but he simply cannot stop himself. Yes, that is how she hopes he will react to the news, with one of his slow, gradual smiles.

She looks up and something catches her eye across the river. Their old home is partly visible through the screen of Lombardy poplars. The sight of a man crossing the front porch pains her.

———

When Eulalie heard that 'Uncle' Jean Lalime and his wife wanted her to keep house for them in Echicagou, she had been reluctant to go. Who else would be able to care for her grandfather, in his condition? In the end, though, it was Gray Curls himself who persuaded her she should take the opportunity. She had to start living her own life, he said, and not be held back by his. The more he insisted and the more she reflected, the better she came to understand that, despite what had happened in the end, Echicagou still held fond memories for her.

It was where she grew up, where she had been happy. She could remember everything about that great house: the smoothness of the long corridor beneath her bare, skidding feet; Gray Curls dozing in his rocker on the porch; and the golden shine of the biggest copper kettle she had ever seen. There was the smell of freshly baked bread, the clucking of hens, the cedar-scented soap that got into everything and her grandfather's kinnikinnick tobacco, sprinkled with 'grains of paradise' brought all the way from Africa. With the Lake to the side, and the river in front, the house seemed to float like a magic island at the centre of the world. When she reminisced like that, even her cousin Waubansee, she decided, had not been *too* cruel. And it was only when they left, when they got to St Charles, that everything went wrong. Pneumonia took her mother; some kind of ague her grandmother. And her father? She hardly saw him. He would disappear for weeks, and come back drunken and irritable.

The position with Uncle Jean would only be temporary, Gray Curls assured her.

On her arrival in Echicagou, she discovered that Uncle Jean had moved house, having sold their old residence to Mr Kinzie, a fact he made Eulalie promise on a Bible never to reveal to her grandfather. After only a few months had passed, Uncle Jean was dead, stabbed eight times in the back by that villain who was now crossing Gray Curls' front porch. Reports of Indian incursions led to orders that all settlers should move into the Fort, and that was where Eulalie had stayed since the winter, waiting for her father to take her back to St Charles. But he had never arrived.

'Miss? You's all right?' Cicely follows her gaze and shakes her head. 'Oh, you mustn't go thinking of that man no more.' She speaks softly but firmly. 'When you the wife of Dr Isaac he don't matter never again, ain't that right?'

She agrees that it is right.

'And don't let nothing never bring you back to this place. Promise that?'

She promises Cicely she will never return to Echicagou. That is easy to do. But although she knows there is good sense in what Cicely is saying about Mr Kinzie, the truth is that she does not think she will ever be able to forget him completely. There are very few things she has not told Cicely, but the full story about Mr Kinzie is one of them.

Juba splutters awake and Cicely gathers him in her arms, rocking him back and forth. She begins to sing that song again, 'Walkin' all the way to Heav'n'. Eulalie closes her eyes and hums along. The melody lulls her and, as a rare breeze fans her cheeks, she forgets about Mr Kinzie and her childhood in the old house. Instead, she dreams of the future. She and Isaac are seated in the second-floor parlour of the house on Jefferson Street in St Charles, above Gray Curls' trading store, carriages passing by in the street below, the walls bright with paintings and the air thick with his pipe smoke. He is telling them one of his stories, about where he's lived and who he's known and what he's done. Like Cicely, she rocks their newborn son in her arms.

Something makes her open her eyes. A few feet away, dressed in his bright blue silk coatee, stands Isaac. A gun hangs at his shoulder. In one hand he holds a fresh cutting of elk root plant. With the other he reaches forward, to help her to her feet.

He leads the way from the riverbank towards the sandhills. She follows in a happy trance, holding up her damp skirts as she walks. Sometimes, instead of taking a step, she skips. Patches of yellow and blue wildflowers shine as bright as his coatee in the brilliance of the sun. She squints, the light is so strong. Prairie grass, tall and wavy, tickles the backs of her hands.

She has warned Isaac of how little time they have. Perhaps that explains his haste. Even so, she is disconcerted by how often he checks behind to see they are not being followed. She does her best to reassure herself. Has she met anyone stronger or more capable than Isaac? At Fort Dearborn, even Captain Heald regularly defers to him. *But first we must ask Dr Van Voorhis. Send for Dr Van Voorhis. Dr Van Voorhis will know. Dr Van Voorhis will decide.*

As she watches his tall, lanky figure striding through the grass, clearing a path for her, as the trample of their footsteps and the chatter of cicadas and the midday heat establish a rhythm, she begins to feel better. But then there comes another troubling, dizzy turn. She wonders if this might be another daydream, that one day she will awaken and find that Isaac is not real, that she has made him up like a childish story, that nothing has ever happened, that no seed has been sown, that no baby boy is growing in her belly. After a while her head clears again, leaving only a sense of amazement that a man like this could have chosen her. How painful it has been, these last few months, to listen to the women chatter about him in the barracks room and jest about which of the unmarried girls would one day be the lucky one. She cannot wait to see the looks on their faces when they find out.

In the lee at the top of the first sandhill, she finds him waiting for her. There is such vitality to him. He is crouching. Hair springs out of his round black hat, gathered in a bundle about the neck. His shoulders press against the coatee that enfolds them. She cannot imagine he will ever grow old. He is like one of those beings you hear about in stories who have been granted everlasting youth. His skin is fresh, his expression is playful and behind those dark eyes resides such courage and intelligence she is assailed by a renewed sense of disbelief that he should be hers.

'Let's try another way,' he says, grinning as he takes her hand, and the next moment she is on her backside and they are sliding down a sandy slope. Her poor skirt. At the bottom is a patch of hard earth. They lie on their backs and giggle until he takes her in his arms and she clings to him as his lips press against hers, and there is sand everywhere but she does not care because she feels giddy to the point of madness that so much life and love and luck could be hers.

He is telling her something, a quotation from an English writer, that the taste of her lips is like lunacy and like poetry and like love, like all three of them together, and that it is the best taste in the world. And she replies that of course it must be all three, because everyone knows he's a poet, and he must be a lunatic to love her. 'And, of course, you're a doctor, too.'

'And your husband,' he says.

She is pleased to hear him say that again. She will never forget how he put it, the day they were wed beneath the giant cottonwood tree. He knew all the words. Because there is no church in Echicagou, he had said, and no priest, because we are apart from civilisation, let us take our vows in the open, with God as our witness. In the name of God, I, Isaac Van Voorhis take you, Eulalie Pelletier, to be my wife, to have and to hold from this day forward, for better, for worse, for richer, for poorer, in sickness and in health, to love and to cherish, until we are parted by death. Will you take me for your husband?

Tenderly, he squeezes her hand. The next moment she is lifted to her feet, and they begin to run through the grass.

She arrives behind him and out of breath. He has already removed the branches that conceal the bed of dried cotton seeds and shrivelled brown leaves they have gathered in the natural hollow at the centre of the tree's misshapen trunk. Giant silvery-grey ridges form three-quarters of a circle, each protruding root as solid looking as a piece of masonry. She stumbles, and has to reach out to stop herself from falling. A piece of bark peels off in her hand and she makes a show of giving it to Isaac. 'Mix this with basil and a dash of wild onions,' she says, 'and you can make a tea that, though bitter in taste, will heal aching bones.'

'You will soon know more than I do,' he says, smiling. 'The bark also makes good horse fodder.'

He has not told her that before. She will remember it. She sits down and removes her hat, letting her hair fall loose. He takes off his boots and stretches out beside her. Normally, they begin to make love at once, but today he props himself up on one elbow. He touches her necklace. 'Copper,' he says. 'The leaves are finely wrought.'

'It's Potawatomie,' she tells him. 'Belonged to my cousin. Wabaunsee.'

'The one that went back to the tribe?'

'Yes.'

With his forefinger, he flips through the copper leaves — she has counted twenty-four of them — and they tickle as she feels them part at her neck like the pages of a book.

'They are the scales on a dragon's tail,' she says. 'It's an old Potawatomie story.'

'About Nambi-Za?'

'Yes, that's probably the one.' The truth is that she cannot remember. It is another of those stories she must ask Gray Curls to repeat. She had forgotten about the existence of the necklace until she came upon it this morning, wrapped up at the bottom of her trunk. 'He gave it to me the day he came to St Charles to tell Gray Curls he was a brave, and was his grandson no more.'

Wabaunsee did not really 'give' her the necklace. He left it behind. Doing that, she decided, was another way — and a cruel way

— of saying he had cut himself off forever from Gray Curls, who had given it to him in the first place. She did not want her grandfather to know, so she hid the necklace and kept it for herself.

'I cannot wait to be gettin' into Fort Wayne,' she says, running her fingers through his hair. 'Mrs Heald says Cecily and me, we're to travel in the wagon with the youngsters. We're to be keepin' them in order.'

'That will be a good place to be.'

His tone disturbs her. 'The journey troubles you?'

He shakes his head. 'Everything is settled,' he replies. 'We set off after breakfast.' He lies down on his back, hands behind his head.

She wonders if he does have worries, but is not telling. Mrs Heald has told them that the details of the route have been agreed with the Potawatomie chiefs, and that any rumours circulating about their departure being dangerous must have been planted by cowards or spies. Only yesterday a group of Miami braves arrived, with a famous American captain, and they would be coming with them too. 'As if,' said Mrs Heald, 'we do not already have quite enough of our own soldiers to protect us.'

'Take a blanket with you to sit on,' advises Isaac.

She stretches out beside him. 'Or I shall need that elk root, mixed with alcohol?'

He grins. 'It's a long ride. We'll all be sore by the end of it. That's why I was looking out for some today.'

She peers up through the leaves of the cottonwood tree, a vast tangle of green triangles with their tips as sharp as needle points, and spends a few moments looking into the pale blue sky beyond. How serene it looks, how perfect, and how very distant.

He plays with her earlock curl. 'You never said where the idea for this came from.'

'A picture,' she says, 'hanging in our old house 'cross the river. They say I looked at it for hours. You'll be seein' it in St Charles. Then you can tell me which you like the more, her curl or mine.'

'I can already tell you that.' He rolls over and kisses the nape of her neck.

She stretches the skin tight, and he kisses her there again. The necklace tingles, making her shiver. She wants to weep for happiness.

'Will you wear this in the church?'

'I will.'

'Promise?'

She places her hand on her heart. 'I promise you everything,' she murmurs.

This is the second promise she has made this morning. She's sure of that. But she is struggling to remember what the first one was.

'We don't have much time,' he says, as he begins to undo the top button of his coatee.

'I know. But wait on,' she says. 'Wait on ... please ...' She sits up. She knows it is unfair to leave Cicely on her own, and what if Mrs Heald has already sent someone looking for them? She knows it is madness to linger, today of all days. But that is what she wants to do and so, dang the consequences, that is what she will do.

'I have news,' she whispers, her lip trembling.

He pulls away and looks at her.

She is about to tell him about the babe, when another idea stays her tongue. How cruel, but how wonderful too, to hold him just a little longer in this state of suspense.

'What is it?' he is forced to ask.

'Wait on,' she says giggling, as she releases more buttons on his coatee.

She insists he allows her to undress him and, as if they have all the time in the world, she removes the coatee first, easing it off his shoulders before she shakes it free of sand. She lays it beside them, folded and flat, and while she is doing this she notices that he is beginning to smile, one of his slow, gradual smiles, and she hears a chuckle begin deep in his throat as her fingers fumble with the top button of his shirt and then she can control herself no longer, and nor can he, and they fall upon each other mostly clothed and moments later he is inside her. She moans, again and again.

Until, above her panting breath, she hears the thin, distant cry of Cicely.

'Eulalie? Eulalie?'

She rises to her knees, adjusting her skirts and manages a strained response.

'Mrs Heald,' Cicely calls out, 'she sent that man lookin' for us.'

'I'm comin'.'

They straighten their clothes, and after exchanging a hurried kiss, Isaac takes from his pocket a sheaf of letters. He asks her to keep them safe with her. 'It will be easier for you to carry them tomorrow,' he says, 'than me.'

She slides them beneath the bodice at her breast, the paper cool against her skin, joyful that he has entrusted his precious writings to her. She shall keep them there, even when she sleeps. It will be as though Isaac is speaking directly to her heart.

He embraces her so hard she can feel *his* heart, beating like an Indian drum.

'Isaac?' she whispers. But before she can continue and say she is with child and it is a boy and does he agree they must call him Isaac, he has pulled away.

Cicely calls out again, 'Eulalie? Eulalie?'

'I'm comin'.'

The last thing she sees is Isaac doing up the top button of his blue silk coatee, and there is only time for one brief look into each other's eyes before she turns and hastens back through the long grass towards the river to help Cicely collect the clean linen. They must return as quickly as possible to Fort Dearborn.

A Doctor in St Charles

October 13

Awakened this morning by a hullabaloo at my own front door.
The peace was being disturbed by Sable, the old mulatto with
the store on Jefferson Street. I remarked that the hour was
still early and that even the good doctor needs a wee repose. I
would be down in due course. I manage only a short nap before
rising. My wife and I pray that I shall be permitted to save
another life today.

    The patient is Sable's granddaughter. She is confined to bed
in a garret room above his store. The fire in the hearth needs
tending and the window closing, I warn him, to avoid the
influx of poisonous miasma from the street. The girl has been
in an accident, though I have not yet been able to ascertain
the circumstances. Severe cranial bruising is evident, with
some associated lacerations. Her mind is in disarray. She is
aged sixteen years, a specimen of slight build with a peaked
complexion, of developed hips and mammaries. Her hair is thick
and fair. Her character tends to violence. Although slumberous,
she attempted to resist an examination of her heartbeat. I
administered laudanum for pain relief and to ease her sleep, in

addition to castor oil and molasses. When my wife asks, I tell her that I am treating a member of Sable's household.

October 14

Sable tells me the girl was in Chicago during the Fort Dearborn affair. Although the massacre occurred two months past, he had heard nothing, either from or about her, until the previous morning. He found her on his doorstep, 'hugging herself and scratching her neck and she don't know what she's seen or who she's been with or maybe she knows but she don't say ...' The man's a blatherskite. I raise my hand. Your point, I tell him, is made. I carry out a further examination. This time the girl is more slumberous than before and offers no resistance. I advise Sable to keep her well happed, tucking the blanket beneath her to show him how. I would return again on the morrow. 'Is the girl with child?' he asks. No, I say, she is not. I have noticed this before with these people. They are obsessed by matters copulative. I tell him it is the girl's *mens*, not her *corpus*, that should be his concern. When my wife asks, I tell her the patient's life is in the balance.

October 17

Sable tried to lecture me on the Fort Dearborn affair today! At least the girl wasn't scalped or worse by those savages, I reminded him, as so many of the Americans were — ladies in particular. The corpuscular indignities that were inflicted upon the fairer sex by those brutes have no place, said I, in the imagination of a Christian. He went quiet. My wife would doubtless chide me for speaking with such candor, but I believe the truth must out. A doctor cannot be squeamish. I enquire about the girl's appetite. He says she is eating more bread and broth. That is the effect of the castor oil and molasses, I tell him. The scars will take time to heal, but in a day or two, she will be back on her feet. When my wife asks, I tell her that the patient is showing no signs of recovery.

October 21

The girl continues to be without her senses. Sable says she calls out names. What names, I ask? He lists them: Cicely, Kinzie and one of Indian origin — 'my grandson' he says without shame. It was the grandson who brought the girl to St Charles. Is her recital of names a sign, asks Sable, that her wits are returning? I tell him that such a conclusion would be premature. A woman's mind, in the grip of such powerful and dangerous delusions, does not recover without due treatment. Prescribed calomel. ½ teaspoon of grains daily. When my wife asks, I tell her the patient's mind is diseased.

October 26

Today, I uncover subterfuge. Sable has been giving the girl patent medicines. Alas, these people imagine a doctor is like a magician. Explain to them the truth, that cures don't happen overnight, and they run off (or hobble off, in Sable's case) to a huckster calling himself Professor This or That and thereby contaminate my treatment with quack potions and unguents. I make my displeasure clear. Tell him to throw them away, or I would be compelled to cease my visits forthwith. When my wife asks, I tell her there have been complications.

October 28

Double dose of laudanum. Sable helped me hold the patient down while I bled her. Shortage of leeches in town so I lanced the flesh, piercing a vein in the forearm, which set off a caterwauling. She howled the name 'Isaac' repeatedly. I asked

Sable if she knew her Bible. In her madness she must have seen me as Abraham, herself as my sacrifice. Removed a pint of dark, malodorous blood. When my wife asks, I tell her the patient continues to teeter on the edge of life and death.

November 6

Informed Sable that the girl is with child. He says she had already told him, and was it not obvious? Her belly is swollen, she vomits. I note his presumptuous tone and remind him that a doctor works only on the evidence of medicine and science. 'How far into her term is she?' he wants to know. I estimate between four and five months. He says that is what the girl told him, too. His attitude is most disagreeable. If he did not always plank the cash, I would have second thoughts about treating the girl. I tell him I will return in three days' time. He does not respond. When my wife asks, I tell her the patient is still in limbo and may pass through either portal.

November 9

Sable is reluctant to admit me. He alleges that my treatment is not taking effect and that the girl grows weaker by the day. I remind him that I trained with the esteemed Benjamin Rush in Philadelphia. Sable has a duty to obtain the best possible medical attention for his own flesh and blood. We proceed to the parlor, a room full of paintings. D___d if I know how or where a colored person got them, or why. The girl is there, dressed to the nines, despite her perilous condition. She has even braided her hair and painted her face. I do believe she tries to catch me with her eye, the hussy, as if I were a libidinous young billy rather than a doctor of medicine, not to mention a husband of mature years. Sable is fussing about, asking if she's comfortable, if he can get her anything etc. The girl always did like to 'slick herself pretty', he tells me. I am sure she did, think I, because I am by now well aware of her kind, and the sin they bring into the world. When my wife asks, I tell her the patient needs our prayers.

November 12

I enter without knocking, to prevent any recurrence of what happened last time. Sable is telling the girl a story about a monster living beneath a Lake with the face of a cat and the back of a dragon, and a shiny copper tail. I am politeness personified. Please continue, say I, it sounds delightful. You must wear copper to make yourself safe, Sable tells her, because that fools the monster into thinking you are one of them. The girl herself was adorned with a hideous copper necklace. A story with a sting in the tail, I quipped pleasantly. 'Surely the opposite,' she said, tossing her hair and giving me another of her pussy looks. It is the first time she has said anything moderately intelligible in my presence. The treatment, I tell Sable, is working. But she now needs purging. 'What for?' he asks. To clear her wind tunnels, I explain. He frowns. Mr Rush, I point out, would advocate the same. I prescribe jalap. When my wife asks why I did not tell her the member of the Sable household was female, I remind her that a doctor must keep details about his patients confidential. How demeaning that my helpmate should be consorting again with the town's gossips.

November 14

For once, Sable does not seem displeased to see me. He takes me into the parlor and closes the door. He whispers, very hugger-mugger. He says the girl gave him four letters to send to a judge in Fishkill, New York. But when he has 'tortoised' to the stage, he finds there are five letters, not four. The four that are sealed, he duly dispatches to Fishkill. The fifth is open and grubby. It appears old Sable can read a wee bit. Says he's never seen 'scribing so straight and pearty' nor a letter filled with such 'love and learning'. The letter was written to the girl by an Isaac Van Voorhis, son of the judge in Fishkill. 'Though Isaac don't say he's the father of the babe, there ain't no doubting it.' I beg to differ, but hold my tongue. 'I don't never meet him but I know he's a good man. How she must be missing him. You see the tragedy, doctor? Isaac Van Voorhis, he don't come a-living from Fort Dearborn.'

He begins to weep. In my presence! I take the opportunity to tiptoe upstairs, to examine the girl. I am relieved to note that the shameful behavior I observed on recent visits does not reoccur. Depraved female patients who attempt to beflum their doctor by flaunting the flesh are a pest, and we must always be on our guard. She is awake. I advise her that if she continues to follow my treatment there is hope that both she and the babe will be saved, as long as she doth truly and honestly repent. 'Repent for what?' says the ingrate. I point out that although she may be able to deceive her doting grandfather, she will have no such success with a doctor and gentleman of science. She is unwed, I remind her. 'You don't know that,' she retorts. The babe in her womb, I insist, was conceived in sin and will therefore be brought into the world only if God so chooses. Again, I advise her to repent. She does nothing of the kind. What an effluence of words pours forth, so vile they cannot be repeated, not only against my own person but against the stronger sex in general. If Isaac were here, she dares to say, he would put me in my place. The girl needs a sound wallop. Told Sable that the diseases of the mind, as Mr Rush has shown, have their genesis in the flesh. When my wife asks why I did not say the patient was a young woman with child, I give her the same response as before.

November 18

Sable says she does not wish to see me. Hostility towards our
profession is to be expected, I explain, given her ailments. It
would be folly to let her dictate to him on the matter. We find
the girl in her room, mixing yellowed Indian tobacco in Sable's
pipe. She pretends to ignore me. She adds grains from another
pot and tells the old man she likes the smell. 'They're grains of
paradise, ain't they?' she says. Sable says indeed they are, and
that they come from Africa. He then attempts philosophy. 'The
smoke is like hope, because it never dies,' he tells her. 'Jus' because
you can't be seeing it no more, don't mean it ain't there.' I point
out that he is hardly comparing like with like, before reminding
them that I do have other patients to visit. Sable launches an
extraordinary, unwarranted attack. Have I no heart? Do I not
understand how the girl has suffered, and how she needs to have
some hope in the future? 'Medicine,' he pontificates, 'din't never
save no soul.' The impertinence. I tell him I am not a priest or
midwife, but a doctor. My interest is in ailments of the flesh and
diseases of the mind. The girl then makes a comment I shall not
repeat. I tell Sable I will return only when she remembers her
manners. When my wife asks why I did not tell her I was in the
habit of conducting aural examinations of the girl's heartbeat, I
give the same answer as before.

November 23

The patient is deteriorating. It is always the same. In an
emergency, they come begging for our help. She is already half
asleep. I administer a triple dose of laudanum before examining
her eyes, pulse, tongue and ears. When I test her heartbeat, her
eyes flicker and I detect a modicum of resistance. I administer
a further dose of laudanum and leave Sable alone with her. I
tell him to build up the fire and smoke his pipe. He can tell her

one of his stories, if he wants. That should aid slumber. When I
return, the room is well heated and she is in a profound sleep. I
send a reluctant Sable downstairs into the shop. I must do tests,
I inform him, regarding the progress of her term. I raise the girl's
shift and carry out an aural examination of her heartbeat. The
mammaries have begun to swell in accordance with lactatory
activity. I then raise the blanket and part her legs to locate the
infant's exit route. The odor is intense, and unpleasant. The lips
are concealed by much maiden hair and, despite the plentiful use
to which they have doubtless been put, are in need of dilation.
I manipulate them, as is necessary, with my fingers. When my
wife asks why I did not tell her I was prescribing laudanum, I
give the same reply as before.

November 24

I have to force my way into the house. Sable is in a temper
again. He will not pay 'another cent' for my services. The girl
is no better today than she was yesterday. I remind him that,
in accordance with the Hippocratic oath, I cannot abandon
a patient, especially when not one, but two lives, are at risk.
I therefore offer my services today at no cost. I administer
sufficient laudanum and suggest we both retire to his shop. It is a
dark, disorderly place with not a spare foot of space. He seems to
sell everything from corn to whiskey to cloth. I inquire whether
his crippled state is the result of falling beneath the wheels of
a carriage. I have seen such an effect before. He says he did not
fall, he was beaten. I express no desire to hear the details.

    In due course, I proceed upstairs. Although the room is
already warm, I build up the fire and remove my coat. The
patient is asleep. I raise her shift and proceed with an aural test
of her heartbeat, before carrying out a full examination of both
mammary glands. It was an oversight not to cover them again

once the examination was done. I had raised the patient's hips
for ease of movement and was making excellent progress with
dilating the lips through which the babe must pass, when the
door burst open. My concentration, when at work, is absolute.
Otherwise, I would surely have heard Sable climbing the stairs.
I tried to usher him out, requesting that he keep silence for
fear of waking the patient. But rather than follow instructions,
he struck me a vicious blow across the jaw with one of his
sticks. I landed on the girl who, though still drowsy, awoke
before I could stand up or cover her nakedness. She went into
a conniption fit, uttering a string of profanities, and sunk her
teeth into my arm. Blood was drawn. Sable continued to wield
his stick against me. It was unwarranted and unseemly. When
my wife asks why my breeches were undone I give the same reply
as before. And I remind her that colored people always lie.

1834–1835

1834

Next Year Will Be
Even Better

John was troubled by the fact that he could remember neither the precise day nor the particular circumstances under which he first set eyes upon her wispish, bustling figure. It did not matter how busy he had been. That encounter should have struck him with the force of a blinding light. He ought to have been able to remember every word they exchanged as accurately as he could recite passages from Homer or list the Elements of Euclid. But he was unable to do so. He knew only that they must have met for the first time in the old store, sometime in May or June. Probably, she had been looking for ink and paper. That was what she usually bought. She wrote a lot of letters, she told him. And how often did Miss Eliza Chappell come back over the next few weeks? Eight, ten, twelve times?

That second summer in Chicago was the finest of his life, to which the arrival of Miss Chappell added the most thrilling element. John had never been happier. There was something magically unstoppable about the way things were changing, as though nature itself might have been behind the frantic mix of hastily constructed houses, the stores and warehouses that he watched rise higgledy-piggledy out of the virgin swamp to the grind of saws and the thump of hammers in clouds of sawdust, the air reeking with the scent of fresh-cut timber and filled with oaths in half-a-dozen different tongues from morn to dusk. And maybe nature was in collusion too with the plumes of blue-grey smoke, with the glow of lamps and candles reflected off the waters of the Lake by night, just as it was responsible for the earth's invigorating perfume after a summer squall, for the release of the rich odour trapped in the clayey depths of its old soil.

John, whenever he wasn't working, would briskly walk the growing grid of dirt tracks, dotted here and there with shacks and frame houses, that stretched and criss-crossed the flat, empty land in the four directions of the compass. He would count the new houses going up and answer questions from newcomers like the old-timer — at just eighteen years of age — he had already become. Always, he was on the lookout for lots worth bidding for. He imagined a future in which Chicago was five, ten, even fifteen times bigger.

Every day, supplies were coming in. Every day, more wagons were pitched on empty lots. Everywhere you looked, there were horses grazing. At least once a week, a ship would anchor offshore in the Lake, unloading people and goods. Prairie schooners kicked up funnels of dust as they skirted the line of sandhills and clipped into town, bearing another complement of young Yankee settlers or immigrants from the Old World or sometimes a whole family, the final stage from Detroit now completed after travelling for weeks over rutted tracks from far-off New Hampshire or New England in search of a new life. Like him, they believed that this was no false dawn for the West. Chicago was as young and ambitious as John Stephen Wright. Together, they would forge a glorious future for themselves.

He and his father built a new store that summer, providing a fine opportunity to discourse with Miss Chappell on one of his favourite topics — frame houses. They had been invented by Mr Snow only two years before, he told her, when he built a warehouse with nothing but a bag of nails and a pile of two-by-fours. And now they were everywhere. What would Chicago be without them? He wasn't claiming they were pretty — the Kinzie family's old log mansion was the finest building in town — but they were practical. Think of the lumber that was saved. There was no need for a skilled carpenter. Anyone could put up a frame house as long as they had the proper lengths of scantling and sidings, ordered in the right proportion.

'And a plentiful supply of nails, Mr Wright?' he remembered her suggesting. 'Perhaps ...' (and at this point she read from the sign on the counter) '... perhaps *cut nails from 3p. to 20 p. of superior quality by the keg?*'

John laughed. 'Scantling, sidings and nails will hold this town together. You'll see, Miss Chappell. Believe me.'

'Chicago is a town already?'

He pointed to the sign propped up on the counter: *Next year will be even better.* 'It shall be soon, Miss Chappell. And a big one.'

'Then perhaps I should address you as Mr Prophet, not Mr Wright?'

He liked that. 'Now, if you are ready to start building at once, I can offer you an excellent price on nails, if only you would buy three kegs at once?'

She smiled, in a tight-lipped way. 'Perhaps I should alter the spelling? P-r-o-f-i-t?'

On another occasion she said, to his delight: 'Conversation with you is like gazing up at the *aurora borealis*, alive with shooting stars. You never know where the next bright idea will come from.' He would never forget her saying that.

But the truth was that the more they talked, the less certain of himself he began to feel. Ideas were one thing, points of view another. Miss Chappell already seemed to know what she believed in. One day, he had been telling her about a corner lot he had bought for $12,000 on Water Street for a down payment of just $300. The location was excellent. He had no doubt it would be worth three times that amount within a year.

'Tell me Mr Wright,' asked Miss Chappell, 'how does this property speculation profit humankind? Does it educate our children? Does it grow food? Does it improve our health? Does it strengthen our faith? Does it develop civilisation? Does it assist us in ridding this country of the abomination of slavery? Does your property speculation heighten our love for Almighty God?'

For all his learning and quick wit, John floundered in his response to this battery of questions. He stood behind the counter and fiddled with a box of nails. His mind was racing. The problem was that the questions she posed were the same ones that, in moments of quiet reflection, troubled his own soul. What good was he doing in the world, with all this activity, with all this buying and selling, with his frantic purchasing of new lots? What did he really think, in his heart, about the rights and wrongs of slavery? Was it enough to argue that anti-slavery agitation was a matter of high-up political maneuvering that did not concern him? Was it enough to say, each to his own? Was it enough to pledge never to employ a slave himself, while at the same time refusing to cast judgment on those that did?

'It is a question of morality, Mr Wright. I suggest we all need to take a moral stand.'

He admired her for saying that. He understood she meant more than simply following the teachings of our Lord. All he could do was nod his head and agree. She raised a small, gloved hand and smiled. 'I'm sure not all speculation is bad,' she said. 'In fact, I wondered if I might ask you to speculate on my behalf?'

John looked at her in surprise.

'I am, as you know, a teacher without a school. Might you be able to speculate as to where a Normal school might be established in Chicago, so that the child of the humblest cottage and the finest palace can meet on equal terms? And might you also, perhaps, speculate as to how that school might be equipped with furniture by the beginning of September?'

And with another smile, tight-lipped but so infectious that John found himself smiling back, the slight Miss Chappell swung around on her heels as neatly as a dancer on the turn, opened the door and stepped lightly across the boards at the entrance in the direction of Dearborn Street, where he heard she had taken lodgings.

He watched her until she was out of sight.

Shortly afterwards, he closed the shop and went to visit his friend Mark Beaubien. This fall, when they moved into the new store, the room they were currently renting from Mark would become vacant. It would be big enough for a schoolroom. If Mark agreed, he would be happy to pay the rent for it out of his own savings. And then who knows? Maybe next year he would build Miss Chappell a school of her own. How grateful and indebted to him she would feel, though he would make nothing of it. His mother would also be delighted to hear he was building a Normal school. The matter of education for all was dear to her heart and it would give him enormous pleasure to break the news to her. How proud of him dear *Mater* would be.

John's upbringing had been strict, one in which innermost feelings were not discussed. His communications with women, in particular young women, had been limited. In the presence of Miss Chappell, he often had the uncomfortable sensation that he was not sure what he was doing or what he was meant to do. He knew only that the day felt empty when it passed without sight or sound of Miss Chappell.

Perhaps his inability to recall anything about their initial encounter was because he did not, in the beginning, find her mightily attractive. His first impressions had been of a slight, feathery creature. Everything about her looked fragile and petite. And yet he came to realise that this appearance of physical frailty was deceptive. She showed stamina. She was energetic. He had never met anyone who was as full of ideas, nor anyone who was as confident, intelligent and forceful. She was also, he discovered, remarkably brave. On one occasion, he expressed his surprise that she had lost some teeth so early in life. He had become accustomed to the quirks of her diction — the breathy sounds that substituted for the harder sounds a full set of teeth would have given her. In fact, he found her voice charming, and that made it even more difficult to argue against her.

'I have lost *all* my teeth, Mr Wright,' she corrected him. 'It is as well that I am partial to porridge, batter cakes and apple dumplings.'

The rot began with prolonged salivation by calomel, she explained, which had been prescribed for other maladies. The surgeons that came afterwards could find nothing good in any of her teeth, so they had been extracted, one by one, over a number of years. A majority had been removed shortly before she came to Chicago, which had affected her speech. And her diet was much changed, too. She mentioned this terrible misfortune as if it were the most natural thing in the world.

He looked at her directly, where she stood upright and diminutive, across the counter. Her eyes were green and turned his way. They were flooded, it seemed, with sunlight.

'I think of it this way, Mr Wright,' she said. 'I shall never again suffer from toothache. Is that not a most particular blessing?' She grinned, in her tight-lipped way.

He grinned back. And as he did so, something stirred in his heart. For the first time, perhaps, he was seeing her properly. He had never gazed at a young woman like that before. It was not done. And yet it was being done, and done without embarrassment. How could he have failed to recognise her beauty? It struck him now, with the force of an epiphany, how happy he felt in her presence, and how much he desired more of it. Their eyes were engaged in a conversation that went beyond any words they had exchanged. He did not intend to be the first to look away.

But they were interrupted. A customer came in and asked for

rope. Or maybe for timber or nails, or a hammer or a hoe. Whatever it was he asked for had long since vanished from his mind. The look they shared, though, had not. That, he decided, would be his first memory of her, even though it could not have been.

'I am twenty-eight years old.'

'Impossible,' he said. 'The registrar's pen must have slipped.'

'You flatter me, Mr Wright, and I shall not object. And you are, I am guessing, at least nineteen?'

'I will be next year,' he said. He busied himself with re-arranging those boxes of nails again, which did not need re-arranging.

'I thought you should know that about me,' she said. 'So there is no misunderstanding.'

Misunderstanding, exactly, about what? He wanted to tell her that age should not matter where feelings were concerned. 'I believe my mother must have been about that same age,' he said, 'before she wed.'

She raised one fine eyebrow.

'What I mean is ...' But he did not know what he really meant. He reminded himself that he was John S. Wright, already a notable merchant and storekeeper in Chicago, and the owner of over three hundred and fifty acres of real estate. He reminded himself that there was nothing in the world he could not do if he applied himself, and that included conducting a conversation on his own with Miss Chappell.

'I'm sure you must miss your mother, Mr Wright?'

He agreed he did. 'She will be moving to Chicago,' he said, 'in the spring.'

She was pleased to hear that. 'Sometimes we don't realise how much we miss those we love,' she said, 'until we are driven apart from them.'

This was another of those things he would remember her saying.

One fine afternoon in mid-October, John closed the new store and set off across town. There had been a lot of ribaldry about the distant, isolated lot on which it had been erected. Nobody would cross that open prairie to buy a bag of nails, especially after rain. John had played along with the joke. 'We shall call it,' he told his father, 'The Prairie Store.' They had confounded their critics. They were already doing double the business they did in the old store. John was certain it wouldn't be long before the centre of town shifted in their direction.

The day was so warm it might have been left behind by summer, were it not for the turning of the leaves and the groundfall of nuts beneath the cluster of water hickory that grew on the northern edge of his land, nearest to the river. He was taking a short cut across his friend Philo Carpenter's lot. Then he would walk along Madison Street and cross to Water. He wanted to inspect a lot that was up for sale at the corner of South Water and Dearborn. John pushed back his hat and whistled a tune. He wished he had been born more musical than he was. Maybe, when he had more time, he would have another go with the fiddle.

He paused to watch three or four men working on a new house near the intersection with Halsted Street. It was a frame, of course. He could see the stack of two-by-four scantlings, ready to be nailed up. He walked across to bid them welcome. This was a habit he had picked up from Mark Beaubien, whose warm, generous greeting for his father and himself, when they first arrived off the boat, had made a deep impression on him. He asked where they were from, said they had made the best decision of their lives in coming to Chicago, and told them where to find his store.

On he strode.

The lot he was on his way to inspect had last been sold in March. John was considering how much he was prepared to pay. There were no other vacant lots on South Water Street and the values had been rising even faster than he had anticipated. He'd done another census — one hundred and fifty new buildings with a population increase from eight hundred to eighteen hundred. He was as optimistic as ever. Next year would indeed be even better.

That optimism may have partly explained what he did next. Before proceeding to the corner lot he would agree to purchase later that afternoon for $1500 (a staggering threefold increase on the $500 for which it had been sold in March), John stepped into a new store on Water Street. The sign hanging outside said that it belonged to a Mr J. H. Mulford from Albany, New York, purveyor of: *Fine setts of jewellery; Diamond pins, ear rings and finger rings; Necklaces, Medalions and other Trinkets; American watches in Gold and Silver Cases.*

1834

Letters from Chicago

Chicago

October 14, 1834

My dear F_____,

You must be weary of my endless descriptions of the difficulties
we face here and my carping on about the fact that no civic
organization exists to address some of the most glaring problems.
Greed, dear F_____, seems to consume those in society on
whose shoulders such a responsibility might be expected to fall.
And yet I believe there are grounds for hope. The congregation at
Reverend Porter's church continues to grow, talented people have
chosen to make Chicago their home, and there is a determination
to better themselves in many I meet that could, if properly
harnessed, be a force for good. But enough of generalizations.
Let me tell you about someone I have met.

Mr W. is the young man who provided me with a
schoolroom, for which he has done all and more than I could
expect. He even paid a carpenter to make desks and chairs for
my charges. (I have thirty-two unkempt little angels at the latest

count, their souls lined up like rows of rough-cut diamonds in need of a good polish.) Mr W. behaves like a man who fears time will end and find him wanting. He seems to work on a dozen different projects at once. There is something of the distracted scholar in his appearance, with his curly uncombed hair and fraying sleeves, that I confess I find charming.

Though there is nothing dishonorable either in Mr W. nor in the attention he shows me, the sibyls in Chicago warn me it is unwise to keep his company. Eliza, they whisper, Mr W. is considerably younger than you (I suspect they mean, by that, 'indecently younger') and he is not yet established in the world. But I have never been swayed by this kind of talk. You know how I am, and how opposition spurs my resolve. I regret to say that Revd Porter, for all the goodness he shows towards me, is one such voice. There is another reason, left unsaid, for their reservations. Mr W. behaves with a haste and foresight that frequently troubles the more staid among those that are, as they say here, 'in society'. Prolific and persuasive with the pen, he is also skilled in oratory. Do you wonder then, my dear, at my interest in him?

Let me make a wild conjecture, in a manner I would not dare with anyone else in the world but you. If a gentleman such as Mr W. were ever to honor me with an offer of marriage, what should I do? When I try to imagine what kind of life it might be, I see only through a glass darkly. I worry that if I yoked myself to a man such as Mr W., even though he is most diligent in his attendance at church, I would be unable to serve God as wholeheartedly as I desire. I shall give you two reasons why.

October 15, 1834

My candle gave out last night, and I had none in reserve. And perhaps it is a blessing, given the matter at hand, that I am writing this at first light, my mind and soul refreshed by prayers and sleep.

The first reason is this. Mr W., despite my arguments against land speculation, sees nothing unjust about the practice. There is a mad race for the acquisition of property in Chicago and he considers it no sin that land 'bought' off the Indians for three cents an acre is now being sold at $100 a squire. He seeks to justify his gain as a reward for the risks he has taken. 'Risks?' I retort. Our newspaper, the *Chicago Democrat*, says there has never been such a boom in real estate prices in America. The value of empty lots (i.e. open prairie depicted by lines on a chart) goes up each week like magic. For which reason, I contend, the only 'risk' he faces is that of being beaten to a purchase. These exorbitant profits are arithmetical anomalies that militate against every lesson taught in our Scriptures.

The second reason is even more worrisome to me. He declines to view slavery as an abomination before the Lord that must be abolished. His first line of defense is to argue he will practice no slavery himself, but nor will he presume to pass judgment on those that do. Why will he practice no slavery himself, I ask? Because, he says, he does not care for it. As though, I goad him, slavery were a dish not to your liking? We debate in this fashion. He pretends neutrality where there can be none, while I too often become prey to my feelings. He will admit to me, when pressed, that the question of slavery is not yet entirely clear to him. But beyond this point, I cannot take him.

You see my dilemma. And it becomes more complicated by the day. I believe Mr W. might have feelings for me. No, that is disingenuous. I cannot and would not deceive you dear F_____. The truth is that he has proposed marriage to me twice already, and each time I have refused him. But I have not refused as directly as I might have done, and I suspect my ambivalence has not escaped his notice. For this reason he is discouraged, but by no means vanquished.

He continues to court me. Only last week, he brought me a silver-plated watch he had ordered some weeks previous from a jeweler called J.H. Mulford. It had to be sent direct from New York it was of such rarity (and, doubtless, expense). I am looking at it now. Inside the cover, my initials have been engraved above an inscription in Latin: '*Sed fugit interea, fugit irreparabile tempus*'. Whenever I want to check the hour, it is as though I hear his voice, hectoring me: 'But meanwhile it is flying, Miss Chappell, irretrievable time is flying.'

I confess that if Mr W. were to request my hand again, I shall not know what to do. More importantly, I do not yet know what the good Lord wants me to do.

I must finish here. The other lodgers are stirring, and it is time to prepare myself for the new school day. You know how much I would value, as always, your thoughts on my little quandary.

Your sister-in-Christ,
Eliza Chappell

Chicago
October 24, 1834

My dear F_____,

Thank you for your sound advice. I have been avoiding routes close to The Prairie Store. I even bought this notepaper elsewhere, though I confess that purchase felt akin to a betrayal. You will be glad to hear that, as you advised, the twin forces of time and absence do seem to be exercising a calming influence over me.

As regards the Lane Theological Seminary's Debate, I appreciate your keeping me informed on the issue. Like you, I have no time for the perverted notion promoted by the colonizers, viz. that the issue of slavery can be solved at a stroke by shipping off America's Negroes, most of whom were born and bred here, to Liberia. The next time I bump into Mr W., I shall demand to know whether he is one of those that favors the 'Liberian option'.

To divert both myself and you — O most patient and understanding of correspondents — I want to speak of someone else I have met ...

One crisp, cold Saturday morning, Eliza set out for Wolf Point. There was a strong breeze, the path was muddy and the surf on the Lake was splashing onshore in foamy hoops. The Sauganash Hotel's bright blue shutters and smoking chimney were welcoming enough, but they could not entirely quell the sense of remoteness afforded by its isolation. This was where the traders and fur trappers were said to have congregated in the early days, when there was no village to speak of. The hotel had never attracted neighbours and the location still lived up to its name. At night, the wolves howled. Reverend Porter had been attempting, without success, to bring the word of the Lord to one of the Sauganash's residents. When Eliza suggested she try her luck in his place, the offer was swiftly accepted.

Mark Beaubien, the landlord, ran a house in which gambling and drunkenness were condoned, but Eliza did not share the reverend's disapproval of him. Despite his rough habits and liking for revelry, Mr Beaubien seemed to be a man with a big heart. As Mr Wright had put it, anyone able to play the fiddle like a maestro was surely allowed a few flaws. Today, as she went inside, he greeted her with a cheerful mock bow and asked after the school.

'I am hoping some of the young Beaubiens will appear one day soon,' she said.

He assured her they would and insisted she drink a freshly brewed coffee with him to ward off the cold. 'With a drop of whiskey, p'raps, for sweetener?'

'Mr Beaubien, you are incorrigible. Thank you, but no.'

Eliza took the seat he offered, and looked around. A couple of men stood near the hearth, cracking walnuts and tossing the shells into the fire. A huddle of children, lost in their own world, were playing a game in the far corner. The air might be smoky and soured by old ale, the timber walls might be covered in too many animal skins for her taste, but she decided that the hotel, in the absence of a rowdy clientele, was a comfortable enough place.

While they sipped coffee, she told him why she was there. She saw no point in skirting the issue. 'I understand Mrs Eulalie, as she likes to be called, has rejected the Lord. I hope to change her mind.' She did not add that she also hoped Mrs Eulalie would find her an easier confidante than the reverend. 'Reverend Porter suspects she might be a little touched.'

'Aren't we all?' Mr Beaubien's laugh seemed to bounce back off the ceiling. 'That lady,' he said, serious again, ' 'as seen a lot more trouble than you or me, Miss Chappell. We must remember this.' When she asked him to explain, he shook his head. He always, he said, kept his confidences. 'And, I tell you another thing. Mrs Eulalie make the best Indian cures I ever seen. 'Ow she know, this is a mystery.' To demonstrate the point, he exercised a shoulder. 'Come 'ere one week ago, and you don't see this moving.'

Eliza knocked, entered and was invited to take a seat. The room was small, but had been decorated to feel light and cheerful. The bed cover was bright; there was a vase of cut flowers on the sill.

Arranged on a small table against the wall were jars containing the Indian remedies.

Eliza's first impression was of a handsome lady, well-attired, about forty years of age with a sallow complexion, presumably the residue of mixed blood. Her hair was fair and plentiful, worn 'a la giraffe' with an old-fashioned earlock curl. An antique Indian-style necklace hung at her neck. At first, she seemed to mistake Eliza for a customer. Indeed, Mrs Eulalie's grey eyes observed her with an intensity that she found unsettling. It was not unlike a doctor's examination, without the instruments. Removing the Bible from her bag, she explained that she had come in place of Reverend Porter.

'I won't be needing no Bible talk, Miss Chappell. Not today, not never.'

Rebuffed, Eliza contrived to move the conversation elsewhere. By the time she left, an hour or so later, it had been agreed that she could call again. Eliza felt that Mrs Eulalie had taken a liking to her. For her part, she was intrigued.

On the next visit, Eliza made more enquiries about her family. After Mrs Eulalie had spoken fondly about her grandfather, she asked about her father.

'If he's still alive, he'll probably be liquoring himself someplace. And my mother, because you'll be asking about her next, she passed on when I was still a young pup, after the Banishment.' Banishment, she said, was when her family left Chicago. 'I was birthed here, Miss Chappell.'

Surely, Eliza pointed out, there would have been nobody in Chicago in those days but the Potawatomies?

Mrs Eulalie shrugged, as if it were of no matter whether she believed her or not. 'The house is still there. It ain't moved nowhere.'

'I would love to see it. Perhaps we could go together?'

She shook her head. 'I never going back. But you can probably get invited for one of the parties. I was birthed, Miss Chappell, in the house 'cross the river from the Fort.'

'But the only house there is Mr Kinzie's.'
'That's right. My grandfather built it.'

... I am baffled as to why she would make such an assertion. Until
then, our conversation had been stilted — she is not the most
willing of communicators — but there was nothing unusual in
what she actually said. On the surface, dear F_____, little had
struck me as untoward, though it might be considered odd for
a widow to travel to Chicago in middle age from St Charles,
Missouri to practice Indian medicine. But did I, too, not come
here on my own? In Chicago, are we not all from somewhere else?

An appropriate word for her predominant mood is
'dolefulness'. The source is difficult to divine, but perhaps
derives from too much introspection. Perhaps. Might the
brightness of her surroundings be an attempt to counter her
despondency? Have you come across such examples before?
You are the most astute observer of human behavior I know.
How interested I would be to hear your impressions about Mrs
Eulalie, from what I have told you thus far.

Your sister-in-Christ,
Eliza Chappell

Chicago
November 5, 1834

My dear F_____,

I do not know where to start. Let me try to relate what
happened today in as straightforward a way as possible, and we
shall see where that takes us.

It began with a note being delivered at school, requesting my attendance at an address on Clark Street. As soon as I had released my little angels from their books — I am pleased to say their company now includes a Beaubien and two Potawatomie boys — I set off across town. Today, we saw the first signs of winter. I had to fight a cold, stiff wind off the Lake, keeping my head down and my back bent. You have never seen so many new buildings going up at such a rapid pace. People today were crawling over these half-finished structures like ants, sawing and hammering away in a fog of sawdust, trying to get roofs up before the snow begins to fall. Many of the latest arrivals, I hear, have come from very far away, Germany and Sweden in particular. In fact, I heard my first Swedish spoken today. In its intonation and rhythm, it reminded me of a plodding carthorse. Probably, Swedes are common as muck in Boston but all foreigners — as opposed to Easterners — are still something of a novelty for us.

On a gray day like this, Chicago looks its most makeshift and miserable, more like a white man's version of an Indian camp than a real town. The balloon-frame house style used here, that Mr W. espouses so fervently, is not well suited to winter, as I am learning to my cost in my own lodgings. Some houses have been knocked together in such a hurry, they are already splitting and leaning sideways. Only a few of the better streets are provided with boardwalks, most stores don't have proper signs or lamps, the stench from the open drains can be overwhelming, there is the constant hazard of fresh horse manure and now that the winter is imminent wild dogs, hunting for scraps, have begun to roam the streets in packs. One has to watch for mud and potholes, and always remain alert to the reckless approach of a wagon that seems to consider every creature on two legs either invisible or expendable. You can imagine, then, the effect on the spirits when one has to walk on streets of this rudimentary nature. Nothing has been built to last.

I thought of you, dear F_____, as I made my way downtown this afternoon, envious of how you could choose, whenever you felt like it, to step outside and stroll along Boston's Main Street full of solid brick houses, with their glass windows and roofs of slate, pausing perhaps to look into the cheerfully decorated shop windows that will soon be full of Christmas fare. Indeed, writing that sentence down reminds me how terribly far we have to go in Chicago.

I knew the address to which I had been directed on Clark Street was close to Revd Porter's church but imagine my alarm when I discovered it was the shack immediately next door, its front yard notorious as a den for drinking and gaming. Revd Porter has often condemned this hovel from his pulpit, calling it a repository for 'drunken brawls and a gaming hell'.

Could this be the correct address? Nobody seemed to be about, except the driver of a cart that was stuck. He swore and kicked at the offending wheel.

Forgive me, my dear F_____, I fear I do not have the energy tonight to tell you what was about to transpire. Indeed, I still do not know whether I should be pleased or appalled by what happened. I shall write again tomorrow. Perhaps, by then, my thoughts will have resolved themselves.

Your sister-in-Christ,
Eliza Chappell

Drunken on Love

John stepped past the overturned bench in the yard and arrived at the front door of the two-room frame house that occupied the lot next to the First Presbyterian Church on Clark Street. It was a cold, windy November afternoon. The rutted street was full of caked mud. He worked free the wedge that held the door shut, and tried to push it open. The hinges were so stiff that in the end he had to use his shoulder. The former occupant, as well as serving liquor, had been a hog butcher. The place reeked of dead meat. Once inside, he pushed back the shutters, took a deep breath and looked out. Someone would build soon enough on the vacant lot in front, on Dearborn Street, and that would provide a buffer against the wind off the Lake. At the horizon, a low sky merged with the churned grey of the water. Removing his gloves, he rubbed his hands together to bring feeling back to his fingers.

A cart drawn by a pair of oxen was creaking past. A few yards on, a wheel caught, the cart came to a halt, tipped to one side, and the mishap was soon being reported to the world by its driver in a stream of ripe curses. At least the wind was blowing them away from the church.

John turned and went into the dark back room, a handkerchief over his nose. The place was filthy. Rotten floorboards creaked underfoot. Bits and pieces of equipment were scattered across the floor, evidence that someone had left in a hurry. Three or four meat hooks dangled from a beam. The chimney had leaked. A single upright chair stood lopsided, on three legs.

He should have waited for a day of milder weather. The rooms should have been given a good airing. The floors should have been swept and scrubbed. There ought to have been a vase of flowers. Yes, he should have waited and prepared properly for the occasion. But patience, virtue though it might be, had never been his. Any moment now, and she would be here.

He hastened towards the back shutters to let some fresh air in. Tripping over an abandoned meat hook, he was flung forwards. He lay for a moment on the floor, recovering his breath. *If you don't slow down, John,* he could imagine his mother saying, *you'll do yourself an injury.* Luckily, not much damage was done. He was still in one piece. While inspecting the unsightly tear in his breeches, he became aware of another presence in the room.

Miss Chappell stood in the doorway, wrapped up, her scarf over her nose and mouth.

He scrambled to his feet. 'Welcome, Miss Chappell.'

She greeted him. 'So this *is* the place you meant,' she said, removing the scarf for a moment to wrinkle her nose very prettily. 'But why? And please tell me, Mr Wright, what is the abominable smell?'

John tried to push some shape back into his hat. 'I believe,' he said, 'that the odour can be traced back to the activities of the previous occupant.'

'He was a butcher?'

'Mr Hezekiah Weed was indeed a butcher, and not a very honest one.'

He followed Miss Chappell as she retreated towards the relative fresh air of the front room, where she stood to one side of the open shutter. The cart was still stuck in the street, its owner still swearing. John leaned out the window and demanded that the man mind his language, that he was outside a church, that there were ladies present.

'I shall be out in a moment,' he said, 'to see if I can help you.'

'Then we'll stay quiet as a church mouse, sir,' said the man. He slapped the flank of one of the oxen. ''Ear that, you big critter? The nice gent'man's goin' to get you outta trouble.'

Miss Chappell frowned. John hastened to explain what had happened. Mr Weed was discovered to have bought some diseased carcasses at a bargain price and dressed up the rotten meat in herbs to hide the smell. He put the meat on sale. Three people were dangerously ill, and others were suffering from bouts of violent sweating and stomach cramps and the flux.

'Mr Weed vanished overnight. He apparently got word that a lynch mob was about to pay him a visit.' John smoothed down his coat. 'On his departure, I purchased the property.'

Miss Chappell studied him with suspicion. 'And you asked me to come here this afternoon so I could congratulate you on your latest speculation?'

'Not exactly, Miss Chappell.'

At which point, there was another interruption from the carter. He had his elbows on the sill and was peering inside. His face was unshaven, his teeth few. He pinched his nose. 'Gawd, wot a stink! And g'day to you, miss, tho' it ain't one,' he said, tipping his hat. 'You comin' or not, then, Mr Gent'man Samar'tan? Or you one of them that's all talk, and no action?'

John told him, politely but firmly, to wait by the cart and he would be out in a moment. He had not planned to break the news in such circumstances, but there was no point in waiting. 'I wanted,' he told Miss Chappell, 'to show you your new schoolhouse.'

It was two long weeks before John saw her again. He asked Mr Joseph Meeker, his carpenter, to accompany him. Together, they waited for her to emerge from her classroom. She greeted them graciously and, for once, John let Mr Meeker do most of the talking. Mr Meeker described how he planned to repair and extend the shack, with an office at the back for Miss Chappell and the schoolroom to the side. John asked her whether she had any recommendations of her own because it would, after all, be her school. Miss Chappell flushed, when he put it like that. He suspected she remained skeptical that such a wreck could be transformed in the way Mr Meeker had described. She did, though, ask that the front room be equipped with shelves around the walls, so that it could become the library. John took that little intervention as a good sign.

Over the next few days, when the weather was reasonable, he would hurry across to Clark Street, after closing The Prairie Store for the afternoon, and work at cleaning the premises. He wanted every inch to be scrubbed clean, with all traces of the former activity eradicated, before Mr Meeker began his work. One day, Miss Chappell not only visited to see what progress had been made but also, to his delight, offered to help him. They opened all the shutters and let the little frame house breathe. Armed with mops and buckets, they began to remove the noxious smells and unsightly stains.

Miss Chappell came, too, on the days that followed. The work gave them an opportunity to talk about all kinds of things — Miss Chappell never shied away from difficult topics — and John found time would pass in a flash. On the final afternoon before Mr Meeker was due to start work, John lit a candle and placed it on a table that was intended to become Miss Chappell's desk. He asked her to pray with him and they kneeled together a little awkwardly, side by side, as John asked for God's blessing on their enterprise.

The candle guttered, flickering shadows against the plank walls. When they had said 'amen', and before either of them had risen from their knees, John said something else.

'I wanted you to know, Miss Chappell, that I have today signed papers before an attorney, donating this property in its entirety to our neighbour, the First Presbyterian Church.'

He heard a little intake of breath. She touched, lightly and briefly, the sleeve of his coat, a gesture she had never made before.

'That was a very good deed,' she said.

'All children deserve to be educated, whatever their circumstances.'

'Regardless of race or colour?'

'Yes.'

'Did you see that article in the *Chicago Democrat* attacking abolitionists as enemies of the state?'

He had seen it, he said, and considered it wrong and irresponsible. Following their other discussions, he explained to Miss Chappell that he had also given the issue of slavery a great deal of thought. He thanked her for encouraging him to do so. He had studied the passages in the Bible she recommended, and considered the arguments. 'I even wrote an essay to myself, listing the pros and cons. I find that putting ideas down on paper helps me to clarify my thoughts.' Although he did not tell her this, he had also corresponded with his mother on the topic and found she was strongly in favour of abolition herself, a fact that bolstered his confidence a great deal. His father, of course, was still a committed doughface.

While he was explaining his thought processes to Miss Chappell, both of them still on their knees, another idea came to him. There was one further step he could take.

It was something she had been urging him to do for long enough, but he had always demurred. It was not a question of numbers. There were probably no more than three dozen slaves in the whole of Chicago. It was more the fact that there was considerable support for slavery, both tacit and overt, among those 'in society'. Although he himself found Illinois' Black Laws unnecessary, even offensive, he knew how many of his acquaintances were in favour of them.

The Laws kept Negroes under control, and enabled the provision of cheap labour. Why should Illinois businesses be at a disadvantage, compared to slave states like Virginia?

Perhaps he was being impetuous, but in that intimate atmosphere, his misgivings vanished. 'At the next meeting of the Committee for the First Presbyterian Church,' he said, 'I shall propose the founding of a Chicago Anti-Slavery Society.'

Miss Chappell said, quietly: 'Nothing you said could have pleased me more.'

John felt gratified, almost triumphant, but also apprehensive. Maybe he had spoken too soon. His father would be impossible to convert, and he regretted the rift this would create between them. Trade in The Prairie Store would suffer as some customers went elsewhere. And there might be an effect on his real estate dealings. But on the other hand, should we not take a 'moral stand', as Miss Chappell put it?

'All men were created equal,' he went on, 'and are therefore equal before God.'

'And women?'

'And women too? Well, yes.' His father would not agree with that either, though he thought that he probably did.

'And you also believe that Negroes,' said Miss Chappell, 'should be able to buy and sell property?'

He had not gone this far in his thinking. In theory, though, he had to agree she was right. Equality surely had to extend to the purchase and sale of real estate. 'I see no reason,' he said, 'why not.'

'And what of the colonisers' idea that all Negroes should be shipped to Liberia?'

'It is impractical,' he replied, too quickly. Miss Chappell frowned. 'And,' he hastened to add, 'unjust.'

He turned to her. There were many things he wanted to say, of his hopes and dreams, of the difference they could make to the world if they approached it together, of the feelings he had for her. He said none of them. But her hand was somehow inside his, when he asked her, for the third time: 'Will you agree, my dear Miss Eliza Chappell, to become my wife?'

Those words seemed to echo around the confines of that former hog-butcher's shack. There was no creak of timber. The wind died down. The candle steadied. A stillness took hold.

Will you agree, my dear Miss Eliza Chappell, to become my wife?

At first, he detected no response at all. Then her hand, cradled inside his own, seemed to flutter. *Yes*, he thought, with a surge of hope. *That flutter must surely be the prelude to a 'yes'.*

But before she could speak, three raps, brisk and imperious, struck the front door.

Spirits, he thought. *Spirits have come to signify God's blessing on our union.*

The front door was flung open. A tall, shivering fluster of black cloth emerged against the grey light of dusk. But no heavenly spirit inhabited those dark robes. John stiffened, trying to mask his disappointment. After all, was not Reverend Jeremiah Porter the next best thing?

It was a frosty evening with no moon. John held the lantern high as he and his father crossed over the new bridge. He kept glancing towards the Sauganash Hotel, but could not see anybody on their way. At least Reverend Porter would not be attending. No doubt he knew that the previous year Mr Kinzie's Christmas party had turned into a drunken, raucous affair. Following their encounter in the future schoolhouse, the reverend had acted coldly towards John, no matter how many times he swore on the Book that nothing unseemly had taken place. These last few days, John had thought of little else but his interrupted marriage proposal.

The Kinzie house loomed up before them, even larger than it had looked from afar. The windows twinkled with lanterns, a chain of lights stretching the length of the house. A cottonwood tree stood at each side of the front gate. From some outbuildings, came the lowing of cattle. And beyond, somewhere in the darkness, he could hear the murmur of the river.

'It's much bigger than I imagined,' he remarked.

'Mind you behave yourself,' said his father. 'Everybody will be there.'

Deacon Wright did not like parties. He was only here because he yearned to be seen as 'someone' in society. John found that embarrassing.

When they stepped inside the house, he had a good look around. The main room, in which twenty or so guests were already gathered, was in a poor state of repair. He could imagine it must have once been magnificent. The puncheon floor was worn and splintered, and could have done with some polish; the furniture looked old and scratched. One glass door of an elegant French cabinet was cracked down its length and sections of the stone hearth, in which a fire was blazing, had worked themselves loose.

There was a fine crowd. John soon lost his father and had an ale in his hand. He knew almost everybody and, before long, had become engaged in a debate with his friend Philo Carpenter about which land they should prospect next. John was planning to draw a new chart of Chicago and he wanted it to be bigger and more accurate than anybody else's. While they talked, he kept checking the door, and when at last Mark Beaubien's party arrived, he found it hard to concentrate on what Philo was saying. As promised, Mark had brought Miss Chappell.

He was careful not to stare or catch her eye. Her cheeks were flushed from the cold and she looked to be engaged in an animated discussion with Mark's wife. A lock of hair had slipped from beneath her bonnet. Her head sometimes turned this way and that, like a bird taking stock of its territory.

'John, is all well?' asked Philo.

'Yes, yes, but please excuse me,' he said. 'I have an urgent matter to discuss with Mark, before he starts playing his fiddle.'

Some time would pass before he managed to engage Miss Chappell on her own. He planned an apology. Reverend Porter would have been harsh towards Miss Chappell too, after what happened. But to his surprise, she did not seem much concerned. 'I have known the reverend a long time,' she said. 'We first met in Mackinaw. He is a fine man, but perhaps a little severe. I explained we had merely been praying for the success of the school. I think he considers the matter closed.'

A pity the reverend had not closed the matter with him too, thought John. Maybe she would, even now, respond to his proposal if he were to ask again? But Miss Chappell's attention had strayed. She was staring at a picture, hanging from a nail on the timbered wall. It seemed to depict the Kinzie house, presumably as seen from the river. It even showed a porch at the front with a man in a rocking chair. At the bottom was an indecipherable signature and a title: *The First Mansion at Echicagou.*

'Mr Wright,' she said. 'You remember me telling you about Mrs Eulalie, the nurse with Indian ointments who lodges at the Sauganash? Do you think it possible she could have been born here? I mean, has this always been the Kinzie house?'

'Indeed it has,' said a voice behind them.

John turned to find Mr Kinzie standing closer to Miss Chappell than he thought proper. His eyes were red, there was liquor foam in his moustache and he was evidently, to some degree or other, drunken.

'But did your father not buy it off a Frenchman, Mr Kinzie?' he said.

Mr Kinzie gave John a black look. He demanded to know what the d___ he meant by that, 'excuse my language, miss'.

'I examined the records, when I was thinking to buy an adjoining property. I forget the Frenchman's name but ...'

'Do I know you?' interrupted Mr Kinzie.

'We met last month, at a meeting about the canal lots. I am John Wright.'

Mr Kinzie had demanded that old settlers be given priority and a concessionary price on lots. John had argued that a new canal had nothing to do with the old settlers, and that the lots should be sold at auction. He'd won the argument.

'You haven't been in Chicago long, Mr Wright. Or you would know more of its history.'

Mr Kinzie shifted around, until he was facing John square on. A heavy man, probably in his mid-thirties, with ginger hair and freckled hands, he leaned in a bit closer. 'My father built this house.' He tipped his hat to Miss Chappell. 'You are welcome in Chicago, ma'am.'

'What an unpleasant individual,' said Miss Chappell, after Mr Kinzie had gone.

John tried to make light of it. 'Perhaps I should have held my tongue, but the records do show that Mr Kinzie's father bought the property from a Frenchman. And that Frenchman, if I remember correctly, had previously bought it off another Frenchman. So to answer your question, Mrs Eulalie could have been born here, if she's of French origin.'

Miss Chappell said she didn't know about any French origins, but that Mrs Eulalie had married a Dutchman, and that she was of mixed blood. 'Everything else she told me about this house seems to be accurate,' she said. 'She knew about this picture. In fact, she said she'd love to have it back.' Either Mrs Eulalie had been here recently and was making a fool of her, she said, or ... She stopped in the middle of a sentence. Her eyes widened. She touched John's sleeve. 'Would you mind coming with me?'

They wound their way through the crowd until Miss Chappell stopped in front of a large copper kettle he had noticed earlier. She examined it in detail. But whatever she was looking for, she did not seem to find. She asked John if he could see anything on the other side, where the kettle was wedged into the corner.

John stood on tiptoe. There was nothing strange, he told her. 'There's just a dent,' he added, 'quite a big one, which explains why it's been turned that way around.'

This, apparently, was the answer Miss Chappell was hoping for, though he could not see why it was important. Old kettles always had dents in them. She had gone quite still. If anything, she looked puzzled, and a bit astonished, as she pushed the stray lock of hair behind her ear.

'Mrs Eulalie told me about that dent,' she explained. 'She was only four or five years old at the time. One night, she woke up and ran barefoot along this very corridor, picked up a wooden bowl and hammered the kettle as hard as she could.'

'What for?' he asked.

'To wake everyone up. She'd had a nightmare. It was the very first nightmare she'd ever had.' She looked at John. 'And do you see what this means? She was telling the truth. The first settler wasn't a white man at all, he was a mulatto.' She made a ball of her two small hands, shaking them lightly up and down, as if she were about to roll dice. 'Mr Wright, would you write to the *Chicago Democrat* and report this?'

John would have done anything for Miss Chappell, but he was not sure what would be achieved by harking back to the past. It was a small community. He had already crossed Mr Kinzie once — or twice if this evening were included. But her request, he thought, might at least provide an opportunity to propose another meeting. 'Perhaps, before I write a letter, it would be wise for me to meet Mrs Eulalie?'

Miss Chappell considered this. 'Yes,' she said. 'I think that could be arranged.'

At which moment, as if out of nowhere, Deacon Wright appeared, seizing John by the arm and demanding to know what he had done or said that had caused such offence to Mr Kinzie. 'Did I not tell you to mind your behaviour? He is furious. He's telling people not to go to The Prairie Store.'

Only at this point did Deacon Wright notice Miss Chappell. He apologised, in his stilted way, and introduced himself. He asked whether she would mind if he had a private word with his son?

'Of course not. But I can assure you he did nothing wrong, Mr Wright,' said Miss Chappell. 'He told the truth. And Mr Kinzie did not like it.'

When John arrived at the Sauganash the main room was empty, apart from a lone figure asleep on a bench in front of the fireplace. Everything had been tidied up from the night before. The floor was swept, the tables and benches wiped, and the furniture straightened. He could hear people moving around upstairs. Taking a corner seat, with a view of the Lake, he propped up his package — wrapped in cloth — on the chair beside him. After checking that his boots looked clean enough, he removed his hat to try to smooth down his hair. Yesterday, he had bought a pot of macassar oil. Either there was something wrong with the oil or he had applied it incorrectly because his hair had congealed into matted clumps. He replaced his hat, adjusting the angle, and looked out of the window. Beyond the bridge, a steamer was approaching the new pier.

How well he remembered his own arrival here, and the excitement he had felt when the schooner moored offshore and he and his father were transferred to land by rowboat. They had pulled up in front of the same handsome, two-storey log building with a shingled roof in which he was sitting now. The timber was whitewashed and the shutters painted blue. A sign hung above the porch — *Sauganash*

Hotel. As they walked towards it, the door opened and a man strode out, massy as a bear, hugging a small child to his chest. On his head the innkeeper wore a broad blue hat with feathers at the rim, arranged in the Indian style. He greeted them with a cheerful smile and a French accent. In a deep, booming voice he said how happy he was to see new faces arrive on this bright fall day.

'You are welcome, *messieurs.*' He threw the giggling child up into the air. 'This one is number eight,' he explained, 'and number nine is on the way. My wife she make the best griddlecakes from 'ere to Peoria. You know Peoria? It is the end of the world.'

His father said they were on their way to Galena.

'Galena, *monsieur?*' he said, shaking his head as the child tugged on his beard. 'Why Galena? Please stay 'ere. If everyone stay, we 'ave a 'appy place.' He looked at John. 'You, *monsieur*, is un *homme d'affaires?*' The compliment pleased John, for that was exactly what he intended to become. 'Then this is a good place for you. Plenty of business 'ere for everyone.'

He threw the child into the air again and called to his wife that there were visitors and opened wide the door. Coffee and griddlecakes, he said, would be on the table before they could unpack their bags. Indeed they were, and they tasted exquisite.

That was how he had met Mark Beaubien.

John smiled at the memory. Mark was the most generous and unusual man he had ever encountered. That same evening, while his father was trying to arrange storage for their merchandise, he had been fast asleep in the upstairs dormitory when he was woken by the sound of a fiddle. He had climbed down the ladder ...

'John, *mon ami.*' His reminiscences were interrupted by Mark in the flesh, the same blue hat with feathers on his head, arms loaded with logs. He piled them beside the fire and, brushing the sawdust off his coat, he came to join him. 'I know what you are day dreaming.'

John felt himself blush. He had told Mark about his feelings for Miss Chappell. But he insisted that, actually, he had been remembering the very first night he arrived there and heard him play the fiddle. 'I'd always thought of fiddlers as lean little men with small hands and slender fingers, until I saw you. And what a mix of people it was.' There had been Easterners, soldiers, French voyageurs, fur trappers, Creoles, Indians. 'It was like seeing the whole human race at once. I stood in that corner and gawped like an idiot.'

'Only two years past, isn't it?'

John agreed it was. 'I'd never imagined a white man could dance with Indian squaws.'

'They won't no more,' said Mark, standing up with a sigh. He clapped John on the shoulders. He had work to do. 'We must look forward, not back. *Le temps passe vite.*' He saw the package wrapped in cloth. 'You give it 'er now?'

John nodded. 'Thank you for doing that.'

'*Rien!* I think this make a sad lady very 'appy.'

John was left to himself. If there could be so much change in two years, just imagine how different things would be, say, five years from now. At this rate, he thought, Chicago would soon be bigger than Detroit. That was where his mind was, fixed on the future, when Miss Chappell arrived and introduced him to Mrs Eulalie Van Voorhis.

He was not sure what he had been expecting. Mrs Eulalie was as elegantly dressed and handsome as Miss Chappell had described her. Her fair hair was pinned at the back; her eyes were serious and searching. There was something about her bearing, about the way she spoke and carried herself, that he found deeply impressive. Sandwiched between these two women, John felt young and unworldly. They were more mature and experienced in life than he was. Mrs Eulalie was a nurse, Miss Chappell was a teacher, but he was simply a young *homme d'affaires* with no special talent or expertise in anything, running his father's store and speculating in real estate. His confidence was knocked by this unfavourable comparison.

Miss Chappell — and he could hardly bear to tear his eyes away from her — explained that her friend John Wright was often writing letters to the *Chicago Democrat* and he wanted to inform readers about Mrs Eulalie's grandfather and correct the claim that Mr Kinzie's father had been the first settler.

Uneasy about the direction of the conversation, John spoke up at the first opportunity. 'Miss Chappell told me,' he said, 'that you would like to have this back.'

He watched their faces as Mrs Eulalie unwrapped the picture.

'But how did you persuade Mr Kinzie to sell?' asked Miss Chappell.

John smiled. 'He thought Mr Beaubien was the buyer.'

Mrs Eulalie wanted to pay for it, but he would not accept anything. 'From what Miss Chappell has told me, it should not have remained in the house in the first place.'

'My grandfather,' replied Mrs Eulalie, still gazing at the picture, 'was a great collector. We took twenty-seven paintings with us to St Charles. This was the only one Mr Kinzie refused us. Probably, he liked to tell visitors he was the man sitting on the porch.' She examined the writing at the bottom. 'And it was the first.'

John frowned. 'I don't follow you, ma'am.'

'What it says. *The First Mansion at Echicagou.*'

'Ah, yes. A pity the signature isn't clear.'

'I think it was done by a French visitor,' said Mrs Eulalie. 'I remember my grandfather complaining how long he had to sit in the chair smoking his pipe while the man painted.' She turned to him. 'Thank you.'

John, his confidence restored, resisted glancing again at Miss Chappell. He started asking Mrs Eulalie questions about life in the old days, and why they had to leave. He included a few stories of his own. Perhaps he said more than he should have done, and asked too many questions. Mrs Eulalie soon seemed to tire of them. She stood up, saying she needed fresh air.

Miss Chappell was on her feet next, offering to accompany her.

John was left with little option but to offer to re-wrap the painting, and leave it for Mrs Eulalie in the safekeeping of Mark Beaubien.

A few moments later, he was on his own again in the virtually empty tavern. The lone figure on the bench in front of the fire was still asleep. There was no sign of Mark.

He looked out the window. The steamer had docked at the pier; a crowd was gathered around as Negro porters scurried up and down planks, boxes and crates strapped to their backs. Miss Chappell and Mrs Eulalie were walking in the other direction, towards the bridge. Miss Chappell was the smaller figure. Even from here he could detect the briskness in the short steps she took. He watched them, regretting that he was not included in their party. He thought of some of the things he had wanted to say to Miss Chappell. And he wondered when he might get another chance.

It only takes one stone to start an avalanche. That was the thought that crossed Eliza's mind as they walked beside the Lake. Discussion with Mr Wright seemed to have dislodged something in Mrs Eulalie. Her customary reticence was gone. She wanted to talk about her childhood at the house, about all sorts of things — the bread they used to bake, the hens in the backyard, the journeys she took with her grandfather.

She had spoken of many things by the time Eliza asked the question that would change her mood, if not her willingness to talk. 'So this is the first time you have returned to Chicago since then?'

Mrs Eulalie shook her head and paused. She pursed her lips. With studied determination, she now began to speak about something very different. She had witnessed, she said, the fall of Fort Dearborn in 1812. She began to talk about her husband Isaac, how brave, handsome, kind and learned he was. 'He was the doctor,' she said, 'and a poet. And a lunatic, of course, to love me.' Eliza reached across and took hold of her sleeve, as Mrs Eulalie's voice choked.

'Good men can be so hard to find,' she remarked.

After a moment's reflection, Mrs Eulalie turned to face her. 'Tell me. Have you had many dealings with doctors, Miss Chappell?'

'More than I care to remember.' She grimaced. 'Bloodlettings, blistering, purges. Calomel. The scars on my back still trouble me.'

'You remember I told you once my son was born in New York? You asked me why, and I didn't tell you. After Fort Dearborn, you see, I went to my grandfather's house in St Charles.'

Eliza wondered how she had managed to escape from Fort Dearborn, but dared not ask. At least, not yet.

'My grandfather was a good man, and he thought everyone else must be good too. That was the weakness in him. He saw the evil in other people too late. It happened like that with Mr Kinzie. It happened like that with ...' her eyes watered 'a cousin of mine. Anyway, my grandfather, he paid for the best doctor in St Charles. That's what he thought.' She paused, biting her lip.

Eliza waited. When it became clear Mrs Eulalie would say no more, she finished off for her. 'And it happened like that with him, too?'

'Yes, that's a way of putting it.' She wiped her eyes with the back of her hand. 'Isaac had taught me the Indian cures, so I decided if I was ever getting the chance, I'd try to be a doctor myself one day, even if I don't have the book learning for it.' Something, at that moment, caught her eye. She halted. 'That's elk root,' she said, pointing to a sturdy green plant with purple petals and a rosy-coloured floret. 'When elks are injured, that's what they chew.' She bent down, withdrawing a knife from her bag, and cut the root deep down in the earth. Holding it up triumphantly, she shook off the soil. 'Mixed with alcohol, this will be helping your back.'

'Thank you, doctor.'

Mrs Eulalie gave a weak smile. With the Lake behind them, she led the way along a beaten path that wound its way over some sandhills towards a copse of trees.

'So you left St Charles to have your baby in New York?' asked Eliza.

'Isaac had given me a letter to send to his father. If anything happened to him, he asked that the family should look after me.'

'He knew about the baby?'

She shook her head. 'I was going to tell him. But then ...' Her eyes seemed to glaze over, lost in recollection. 'Mrs Heald was calling for Cicely and me. We had to run.' She sighed. 'No, I never told him. I didn't want to go to Fishkill. But there was nothing my grandfather could be doing to stop him. He was old by then, walking on two sticks. And Mr Van Voorhis was a big man, and white, and a judge.'

'He was good to you, Isaac's father?'

She shook her head. 'He thought I was touched. Once baby Isaac was birthed, they sent me back to St Charles.' She swallowed. 'I never did know what they told him about me. I went to Fishkill once, soon after, but the family had moved to New York. I never saw him again.'

Eliza, who did not know what to say to that, opened her arms wide and drew Mrs Eulalie into an embrace. The poor lady tried, at first, to resist. Eliza had never seen her in such a state before. She was trembling, her breath was agitated. She would write to F_____ as soon as they got back. Sentences began to run through her head. *Though neither you nor I have yet been blessed by motherhood, can we not feel in the very core of our beings how agonizing such a loss must be, how it would feed like a canker on our hearts, how it would imperil our sanity?*

Mrs Eulalie pulled away. 'Maybe I should learn to speak more like that, Miss Chappell,' she said, 'for the good it does me.' She brushed down her skirt. 'I always was a quiet one, even as a young sprout.'

For some minutes, they walked on in silence. Eliza glanced across at her from time to time, but could not read her expression. Those raw emotions, briefly displayed, seemed to be back under control.

They stopped in front of an enormous cottonwood tree. Devoid of leaves, there was a sombre grandeur in its sheer size. Beyond a natural hollow at its roots, stood a patch of wooden crosses. Mrs Eulalie stepped forward, plucked the flower from the elk root she had gathered and placed it at the base of one such cross, before standing upright, with her head bowed. Eliza kneeled on the cold, hard ground. She prayed in silence for Mrs Eulalie's lost husband, and for all those souls that met their Maker on that fateful day.

Then she began to pray aloud. She asked that God, in his infinite mercy, might pardon all those who had transgressed against Him, however heinous their crimes.

Mrs Eulalie interrupted. 'You can't be saying that, Miss Chappell.'

'Mercy is hard,' she reminded her, 'but without it we are lost. Utterly lost.'

'You don't know. You wasn't there.'

On the way back to town, Eliza asked Mrs Eulalie for her impressions of Mr Wright. She told herself she was simply trying to create some distraction. Deep down, though, she could not deceive herself. She was keen to talk about Mr Wright, and eager to hear what Mrs Eulalie would say about him. The older woman, for all her reserve and contradictions, seemed to be possessed of a hard-earned wisdom. And although Mrs Eulalie continued to reject Eliza's attempts to bring her to the Lord, she carried herself with an undeniable grace. The confidences she had shared today filled Eliza with hope that she would yet be able to succeed where Reverend Porter had not.

Mrs Eulalie was very grateful, she said, to have the picture. How thoughtful of him. What a sympathetic young man he was. 'Make sure you don't go hiding from your own heart, Miss Chappell,' she said, ''cause love never comes twice. Take it from one that knows. It's clear as day, you have destiny with Mr Wright.'

It had been raining, on and off, for days. But today the heavens opened even wider and great torrents cascaded from the sky. It rained and rained and rained as never before, in all the time John had been in Chicago. There was no wind, and only occasional bouts of distant thunder. Not once had the downfall eased. Big drops bounced like balls. It was impossible to raise your head as you walked, or to see further than a few feet ahead, or to find the boardwalks even in those few streets where they were laid. A stranger would have had no idea where he was, nor any chance of finding out. State Road was a mud bath, full of hidden ditches and floating debris, and by the time John waded around the corner into Clark Street, he counted himself lucky to have arrived there with his shins intact and without having fallen headlong in the filth. He climbed the three steps onto the new deck. The lock turned easily. He went inside.

The schoolhouse was almost complete, and he had come to deal with the leakages that such tremendous rainfall would have caused. He inspected each of the three rooms and was delighted to find everything quite dry. The roof was watertight, the seals on the windows and shutters were sound and at neither door had anything seeped inside. Joseph Meeker had done an excellent job. Even in The Prairie Store, built with such care and attention to detail, they had not escaped a few leaks. He paced around, prodded here and there, and ran his fingers over the joints and seams. Removing his greatcoat, he hung it from a hook beside the front door, and positioned a bucket beneath to catch the drops. Unbuttoning his gaiters, he balanced them on top of the bucket before easing his feet free from their boots.

With a dust cloth, he wiped them dry. The rain continued to hammer down on the roof and he was shivering. Going into the back room, he knelt in front of the fireplace and laid kindling. That would be the final test of Mr Meeker's work.

It did not take long for the fire to take hold. As he worked some warmth into his fingers and held his sleeves forward to dry them out, he recalled once more the circumstances of his last marriage proposal. And he speculated as to when and how he might try again. First, he would need to do something about the anti-slavery society he had promised to establish. He wondered whether he could find a way out, or a reason for further delay. At least he had done what he could with the letter about Chicago's first settler. It was a relief that the *Chicago Democrat* declined to publish it.

When he was feeling warmer, he went into Miss Chappell's new study in the back extension and picked up a few of the journals arranged on her desk. He returned to the back room and unrolled an Indian mat in front of the roaring fire. After raising each foot to warm it through, he sat down. And with the rain pounding on the roof, the flames and heat felt like a little miracle. There was no rush to get home. He flicked through the journals and, after browsing a few articles, he settled on one about a new type of fence in a journal called *The Horticulturalist*.

As he read, he was reminded of a conversation he had once held with Miss Chappell about the need to encourage farming on the prairies. 'What about herds of marauding buffaloes?' she had asked. 'To keep them out would need a very strong fence, much stronger than any of the fences used out East.' She advised him, tongue in cheek, to hold off from becoming a farmer himself until such a fence had been discovered. He continued to read, with mounting excitement. The writer was describing a kind of mulberry tree, commonly known as the Osage Orange in Arkansas, with branches that were formed of a notably strong and springy kind of wood and the trees (this was the sentence that caught his eye) '... when set at a distance of fifteen inches asunder, make the most beautiful as well as the strongest hedge fence in the world, through which neither man nor animals can pass'.

He was so enthralled, and the fire was bathing him in waves of such luxuriant heat, that he barely noticed the door opening. He became aware of a draft only because it sent the flames in the hearth even higher.

He turned to find, standing in the doorway, dripping wet, Miss Chappell.

'I apologise. I was not expecting ...'

'Nor I,' he said, rising from the mat. 'Please ...' He beckoned, inviting her to come near the hearth. 'You must be wet through and frozen.'

Indeed, she was shivering so much she could not undo the ties to her bonnet. 'I am very h ... happy to see a fire.' He had never heard her stammer before.

He watched her fingers grapple with the ties for as long as he could stand. 'May I?' he said, stepping forward.

'It's new,' she said, 'and too tight.'

It was certainly tight beneath her chin, and his fingers had never been particularly nimble. He tried not to touch her, for the sake of propriety, but he could not help it. Their proximity was an embarrassment. He caught a waft of her warm breath. She avoided looking up at him. He made a joke about his clumsy fingers. She said he should cut the ties, if he could not undo them. He said he wouldn't hear of it. He wasn't *that* clumsy. He shifted a little closer. He wanted to lean still further forward, feel the rise and fall of her bosom against his chest. They were only a few inches apart. It could appear unintentional, a mistake, and if she objected she could always pull back and they could pretend it had never happened.

The knot came undone.

He stepped back. She shook out her hair. He took the sodden

bonnet, of a rather fine dark velvet material, and hung it on a hook to the side of the fireplace. 'Terrible weather. The rain,' he said.

'Yes,' she agreed, looking around. 'I was expecting a disaster.'

'It's all right. I've checked. Mr Meeker has done a fine job. There are no leaks. Please,' he said, 'try to warm yourself and dry out.'

Her skirts were soaked, and had quite lost their shape. There was a dazed expression on her face. For once, she did not seem to know what to say.

Nor did John. 'You could say Mr Meeker has fenced us off,' were the words that came out of his mouth.

'Fenced us off? From what?'

'It was intended as a joke,' he blundered on, 'meaning he has fenced us off from the rain.'

'Ah.'

He hastened to explain himself. 'I have just been reading ... er ...' He indicated *The Horticulturalist*. 'Do you remember what you once said, about herds of marauding buffaloes?'

He talked fast and felt he wasn't making much sense but he did his best to explain why the Osage Orange plant would make a perfect fence, while helping to remove her overcoat, and he noted the pale blue colour of her skirt which he didn't remember having seen her wear before and he brought through the other three chairs from the office and before long they had arranged everything so that their two coats were spread over the chairs to catch the heat, and their hats were hanging from nails beside the fireplace and he was regretting the fact that there was no means of making coffee. She was looking more relaxed now. How fine it would have been, to sit there with Miss Eliza Chappell, drinking coffee together, dry and warm in a world of their own, as the rain thundered down.

He put on another log, and stoked the embers.

'I love fires,' he said.

'You have built a very good one,' she said, as she held up the hem of her skirt to the heat.

'Mind the sparks,' he warned. He swallowed. 'I must apologise,' he said, 'for the way in which I questioned Mrs Eulalie at the Sauganash that day.'

She told him not to worry. 'Your questions, actually, were helpful. They seemed to put Mrs Eulalie in a talkative mood.'

He should have stepped back; he should have given her more space. It would have been the courteous thing to do. There were damp patches on her pale jacket, which matched the skirt, and he noted how that dampness clung to her bosom.

His eyes were looking straight into hers. He asked more questions about Mrs Eulalie, but he was only doing it to make conversation.

'She is very grateful to you,' she said. 'That picture is now on the wall of her room at the Sauganash.' She made as if to move away.

He should give her space. 'Miss Eliza ...?' His voice sounded gruff, broken and strange. And he was feeling off-balance. He was leaning towards her, his hands were on her upper arms and he squeezed soft flesh beneath. Her hair was glossy, and her cheeks flushed in the firelight.

'Are you well?'

'Yes,' he murmured. 'Quite well.'

A voice inside him yelled 'madness, madness' but he did not care. Let Reverend Porter denounce him from his pulpit for as long and as loudly as he wanted. Nothing Reverend Porter said could touch him here. It was like being drunken, this sensation that overwhelmed him. His movements were not his own. Another voice warned he was making a catastrophic mistake, that this would bring his friendship with Miss Chappell to an end, a lost friendship as irretrievable as time, and that from this moment on she would know him for what he was and shun him. She would know that lurking beneath a veneer of principles and good intentions was a man not fuelled by nobility and love for our Lord, but a common, lustful beast.

The flames filled him with hope, the rain pummelled down, they were safe in a world of their own, filled with sighs of damp cloth and a clammy warmth, and his mouth was pressing down towards hers. He couldn't stop himself. She would slap him, push him away, and never speak to him again. Reverend Porter would be able to crow that he was right about him, after all. And there was only one thing he would cry out in his defence. That he was drunken, not on whiskey, but on love itself.

Farewell, Chicago

Chicago

February 15, 1835

My dear F_____,

Apologies for such a long silence. I am glad to say my news
is better. The sickness to which you referred in your last letter
is over. You may have heard reports from others that exaggerate
the extent of my suffering. I have never been as frail a plant as I
look. And though I had bilious complaints, and was laid low by
fevers and agues, I told anyone who would listen that they should
not grieve for me because it was not I who suffered, only my body.
The truth is that I knew something the doctors did not. The
sudden chill I contracted was no ordinary winter malady.

I have sinned, and that sin is too grave to be put down
in writing, even to you.

February 16

I have lain awake all night, wondering how to continue. You and
I have pledged absolute honesty between ourselves for as long

as we shall live, and have sworn never to hold secrets from each other. And yet, I hesitate. I am seeking the courage to fulfill my side of that bargain. And I fear that if I find it, you may choose never again to call me your cousin or friend.

But I must try.

The truth is that in those few moments beside the fire with Mr W. I lost my senses. I suspect he did too. I allowed him to go too far. Only by the grace of our Lord, before all was lost, did an angel hasten to my side. I covered myself, and he drew back.

No wonder, then, that I fell sick. The doctors expected me to die. They thought the chill that had waylaid me was as natural as it was deadly. But I knew this to be punishment. I have prayed and begged for His Forgiveness and Mercy, as I have never begged before in my life.

My hope is that you, dear F_____, may take pity on me and forgive me my sin too, and advise me on how best to make amends.

Your sister-in-Christ,
Eliza Chappell

Chicago
March 10, 1835

My dear F_____,

Your letter dated February 27 has brightened my day. I do not know what I have done to deserve such a loyal friend and confidante. Your forgiveness, so generously given, means everything to me. But it would be duplicitous to pretend that the views you express about Mr W. have not caused me considerable unease.

First, though, let me reassure you that I have held nothing back about what transpired between us that afternoon. To put the matter with as much delicacy as I can manage, we went further than we should have done in our displays of affection for each other, but I promise you we did not go too far. I should also make clear, if I did not do this with sufficient emphasis in my last letter, that — for my sins — I consider myself as responsible as Mr W. for what happened.

Regarding your advice that I should carry on as normal, I am pleased to say that — apart from the break occasioned by my illness — I have not missed a single day at school. I am thrilled by the new schoolhouse. Never have I taught in a place its equal. Mr W.'s mother, recently arrived in Chicago, is helping me. She is a fine lady of strong and liberal views who has a special way with the children. They adore her. As you know, this is the worst time of year, the Lake is frozen, the skies are gray and everyone is suffering from the cold weather and poor diets and short days. The children are often sickly but how effectively does the schoolroom's cozy fire, together with ample sustenance for their inquiring minds, distract them from their privations and ailments.

My concern, then, is over the advice you give regarding Mr W. and his most recent proposal for my hand in marriage. I confess it was a surprise to hear that you are in favor of his suit, given the way in which I have represented him to you, warts and all. Although you are correct to say he has many fine qualities to commend him and that, were we to be joined in partnership through life, I might be able to smoothe some of his rougher edges and 'bolster his moral resolve', I remain troubled by the same doubts I have expressed to you previously.

The truth, dear F_____, is that whatever the stirrings in my heart, I have not yet felt an assent to a union with Mr W. in my soul, from on High, from Our Lord. If I do indeed 'have destiny with Mr W.', as Mrs Eulalie put it (a view with which I now understand you would concur), and if my heart is indeed his, why will my soul not give its unconditional assent?

Your sister-in-Christ,
Eliza Chappell

Chicago
March 23, 1835

My dear F_____,

In brief and in haste and in wonder, I have the most extraordinary and joyful news to impart. This morning, after the church service, my old friend and the noblest, most determined man I have ever met, Reverend Jeremiah Porter, called me into the vestry. Bending down on one knee, he offered me his hand in marriage.

I am delighted to report that I accepted.

The proposal did not, I hasten to add, come without prior advertisements, even though I failed to recognize them properly for what they were. I apologize, dear F_____. I should have prepared you better for this news but after sharing my enthusiasms and fears with you about Mr W. at such length, I felt it would be speculation inviting hubris to speak in a similar vein of Rev Porter. I noticed his attentions these past few weeks, but I never imagined where they might lead. I did not dream such a union might be in the Lord's plan for such a wretched sinner as I.

And yet it has come to pass.

I will write again at the earliest opportunity, and tell you everything. Until then, let us heartily rejoice.

Your sister-in-Christ,
Eliza Chappell

Rochester, NY.
June 22, 1835

My dear F_____,

It is done. I am happy to report that one week previous, on June 15, I was wed to Reverend Jeremiah Porter. I know you may still harbor misgivings about the news, but I hope you will be able to put those aside and share in my joy. I am happier, today, than I have ever felt in my life. Although I do not deserve it, the Lord has granted me the greatest of blessings. The reverend is caring, incorruptible and devout, and I shall quickly learn to love him to the full. We are to travel soon to New England to visit my husband's family before we return to Chicago, where there remains much work for us to do.

Your sister-in-Christ,
Mistress Eliza Porter

Chicago
August 1, 1835

My dear F_____,

I do not know what I would do if I could not confide in you. Something has happened. Perhaps it is only a small thing of no account that will pass soon enough, and yet it troubles me.

Let me work my way gently towards what I must tell you. When we returned from the East three weeks ago, we found Chicago in a state of giddy chaos. Land fever was worse than ever, the town was full of speculators and sharpers, and as if that weren't enough, it was also inundated by Potawatomie Indians, allegedly five thousand strong. They are preparing for their official departure, bound for a new reservation in Missouri. You see them gathered in groups about town clad in bright blankets and breechcloths, or raising a rumpus in their camps, which run in a swath beyond the town across the prairies, a vast sprawl of crude huts and wigwams peopled by braves and their squaws, by young and old, by dogs and horses. Each day, they feast at the expense of the government. I regret that whiskey is always made available to them, as I hear was also the case when they were pressed to sign the Treaty two years previous.

I have visited these temporary encampments. The Indians are often tipsy, there are frequent arguments and I expect a good number find oblivion long before night falls. They amuse themselves with gaming and horse races and dancing around great fires that are probably visible as far away as Detroit. I have suggested the reverend establish a mission among them, but he judges (correctly, I do not doubt) that this is neither the time nor the place to embark on such a challenge. His preference is to support an outpost in China.

I have not, I think, mentioned Mr Gutzlaff before? He is an intrepid explorer who has, according to my dear husband, 'crumbled down the Wall of China' and thereby opened up a new world for our church. I believe that we are all — white, Indian, Negro, Chinese — equal before the Lord. So although I

do not doubt the need to raise funds for Mr Gutzlaff's mission
in China, I also wonder whether we should not raise monies for
our benighted neighbors whose land was taken from them, after
being encouraged — while intoxicated — to sign bills of sale
for millions of acres, in the name of progress and civilization.
Believe me, this is the truth of what happened, dear F_____,
whatever the 'official' version of that transaction may be. I
believe there is a profound contradiction between the theory
and practice of our government. On the one hand we argue that
might does not justify right, while on the other we use that same
might (and other deceitful devices) to attain our ends when the
public good is supposed to require it.

To return to Mr Gutzlaff. My husband arranged a gathering
in church for The Sewing Society to raise funds for Mr
Gutzlaff's Chinese mission. We were selling items mostly of
cotton and calico, such as scarves and napkins and tablecloths,
embroidered by Society members. Also included for sale were
sundry other items that people were happy to donate for the
cause. I chose to contribute the silver-plated watch that Mr W.
gave me when we first became acquainted. For some time I had
been looking for a suitable opportunity to dispose of it, given my
altered circumstances.

It must have been mid-afternoon and I was weary after
spending hours on my feet, when I realized that none other than
Mr W. himself was standing across from me. I had not seen him
arrive and believe me, dear F_____, I was not expecting him to
come there. Since our return to Chicago, I had not set eyes on
him. And if I had thought there was the slightest possibility he
would attend, I would never have put that watch on sale.

My dear husband was standing beside me. I could neither
remove the watch, nor say it was no longer available. Though he
is the most kind-hearted of men, I feared Reverend Porter would

be perplexed and disappointed if I were to take it back. He had already commended my willingness to part with such a valuable article so that souls in far-off China might be saved.

Mr W. greeted us with a little bow. I avoided his eye and listened to a civil but awkward exchange between the two of them. Mr W. had, of course, seen the watch at once. Picking it up, he examined it as though for the first time. He read aloud the Latin inscription.

'Ovid,' said my husband.

'Virgil,' Mr W. corrected him. 'An interesting passage in the Georgics,' he added, while withdrawing a purse from his pocket. A large number of bills, and coins too, tumbled onto the table. 'Time may be irretrievable,' he said, smiling awkwardly, 'but the same cannot be said for this watch.'

He proceeded to scoop up the timepiece and drop it into his pocket. At last, our eyes met. How do I describe the distressed, regretful look that I saw in Mr W.'s gaze? His feelings, I had no doubt, came straight from the heart. I realized that, despite my marriage and months of absence, Mr W.'s affection for me remained undimmed.

When he left, Mr W. probably tipped his hat and bade us farewell, but of this I have no recollection.

Were I able to stop this account now, perhaps no harm would have been done. The truth, though, was that I became aware of a reciprocal stirring in my own heart. Old feelings and memories resurfaced. Dark thoughts assailed me. Might I have made a terrible mistake? My disquiet lasted only a moment and was swiftly quashed. But why should it have occurred at all?

'That man is an enigma,' I heard my husband remark, as he counted the great sum of money Mr W. had left on the table. The Sewing Society raised almost $150 at the event, of which

Mr W. contributed more than $90. He has never been the kind of man to flaunt his wealth in such a vulgar fashion. Why, then, did he leave such an extravagant donation?

Your sister-in-Christ,
Mistress Eliza Porter

Chicago
August 13, 1835

My dear F_____,

Such an explanation would never have occurred to me, and yet it seems plausible. You are right. Mr W. did look nervous; his manner was indeed strange. The only reason I did not notice this at the time was because he caught me by surprise. Even so, I confess another part of me doubts it can be true that Mr W. is still so enamored of me that he should suffer from what you call 'a dizzy spell of the infatuated', rendering him unconscious of his behavior to the extent that he can empty out his purse without thinking.

Your sister-in-Christ,
Mistress Eliza Porter

Chicago
August 23, 1835

My dear F_____,

We are leaving tomorrow for Hadley, Illinois, where cousins of my husband reside. I have decided to remain there until a new position has been found for Revd Porter. You — and you alone — will understand why we are moving, if I tell you that, buried deep within my heart, an old wound still festers. Absence, I believe, is its best cure and for this reason I have suggested to my husband that we leave Chicago. I suspect he is under the impression that I remain worried about the possibility of trouble and — unfairly, I know — I have chosen not to deny this. I am not proud of myself, dear F_____. I will write to you again on this matter, when I am more composed.

This letter concerns our friend Mrs Eulalie …

It was a warm, sultry morning, with very little breeze, for the Potawatomies' 'Dance of Departure'. Eliza joined Mrs Eulalie in her room at the Sauganash Hotel, from where there would be a good view of the route. Since Eliza's return, they had rekindled their friendship. Mrs Eulalie, too, was about to leave Chicago. She was returning to St Charles.

'I've decided not to keep the painting of the old house. I don't want the memories.'

'Shall I return it to Mr Wright for you?'

'In person?'

Eliza feared she might blush. She knew Mrs Eulalie, like dear F_____, did not wholeheartedly approve of her marriage. 'I shall ask Mr Beaubien to give it to him.'

Mrs Eulalie opened the window, and they stood side by side, looking out. The sky was almost colourless, the sunlight was so intense. The river looked brown and sluggish and close, while the Lake beyond seemed to have distanced itself, rimmed by a halo of summer heat that blurred the surface with a silver haze.

'I don't know what I was expecting to find here,' said Mrs Eulalie, 'except old memories that should be left where they lie. I should've spoken about what happened a long time ago, not trapped it inside. That only makes the heart turn small and cold.'

'Though I'm not convinced you have yet told me everything?' Eliza tried, gently.

'Maybe I did, maybe I didn't.'

From beyond the river came the sound of drumbeats.

'Drums make me nervous,' said Eliza. 'They seem to summon up the dark side of the human soul. Which reminds me,' she reached into her bag, 'this is for you. I hope that you might choose to read it one day.' She placed the leather-bound Bible on the table, beside the jars of coloured ointments.

'It's a pretty binding. I thank you but it ain't for me, Miss Chappell, and you know it.'

Eliza would not be discouraged. 'I don't know what it is you cannot tell me, my dear Mrs Eulalie. But I promise you there are things that hurt me too. And when that hurt becomes too much, and if I cannot bring myself to talk about it, I read the Book. There is a magnificent passage in Ecclesiastes. It always helps. *For the Lord is full of compassion and mercy, long-suffering, and very pitiful, and forgiveth sins.*'

'You are a good woman, Mistress Porter,' said Mrs Eulalie, 'and I shall miss you.' She handed over a gift of her own, tied with string. 'For your back,' she said. 'Elk root essence and alcohol.'

They leaned out the window for a better vantage point. On the far side of the river came their first sighting of painted braves. Even from a distance, there was something menacing in their movements. They took slow and fitful steps, they writhed and coiled like snakes, they paused every few yards to bend their knees and leap into the air. The drums grew louder, like a roll of thunder, and this percussion was accompanied by blood-curdling shrieks, each wave of noise made yet more terrifying by the way in which the braves clapped their mouths repeatedly with the palm of one hand. Silence had come over the Sauganash. This spectacle is godless and terrifying, thought Eliza, and coming ever closer. *We are warriors, we shall cut you down, we shall grant you no mercy.* It felt as though the drums were sounding their death knell, that this 'departure' from Chicago might be nothing of the kind. She took hold of Mrs Eulalie's hand, which seemed remarkably cool and fresh compared to her own.

The braves began to cross the bridge, hundreds of them. The timbers shook beneath their stamping feet as they wound their way over the water. The road coughed up clouds of red dust. Even the greatness of the Lake seemed diminished by their presence. This is like a tight-loaded spring, thought Eliza. Release the tension, and hell will break loose in our midst. In a single fusillade of blows, the braves will strike us down. She glanced at Mrs Eulalie. Is this how it had felt, all those years ago, as they departed from Fort Dearborn? Did this resemble the prologue to that slaughter? If so, she was not showing it. On the surface, at least, she looked eerily tranquil.

The warriors were naked but for a loincloth, their faces and bodies decorated by lines of paint — red, black and vermilion. Their heads were shaven, except for a scalp-lock adorned by bird feathers, and their dark eyes were fixed in hallucinated stares. Sweat foamed on their shoulders. They prowled forwards, their bodies twisted low until they were almost squatting to the ground, one foot flung forward and eased slowly back as the other foot advanced, a pattern of staggered steps interrupted by frenzied jumps into the sky that seemed to reach higher and higher. And, worst of all, each Indian bore a club or tomahawk with which he mimed act after gruesome act of slaughter.

Eliza brought her hands together in prayer. She reminded herself that although we human beings may be very different in our behaviour, yet we are all equal before Heaven. We are all the children of God. She thought about her husband, who had gone to pray in the church. She thought about Mr Wright.

The procession stopped below the window. Only a few timbers

separated them, a few feet and the nothingness of air. The heat was unbearable. Eliza was damp with perspiration. She felt she could hardly breathe. And she cursed her imagination, how it behaved when beset by fear. The Indian chief would now make a signal, the Sauganash would become a bedlam of Indian braves, the air would be filled by the screams of the dying. Her time had come. She prayed anew for His Mercy and Forgiveness. Even as she yearned to pull herself back from the window, her feet remained rooted to the spot. Like one entranced, she watched.

At some point, she realised Mrs Eulalie was no longer standing beside her. She swung around. The room was empty. And before she could go to look for her, a frightening disturbance broke out below. Something had thrown the braves into confusion. The outer ranks were being driven backwards by the ones in the middle. They were still 'dancing' as before, still brandishing their clubs and tomahawks, still gyrating and jumping and whooping war cries. But in their centre was a foreign element, a force of such strength that it had the effect of a whirlpool. Relentlessly, as though by the exercise of sheer will, this force was pushing the Potawatomie host back onto itself. The origin of that whirlpool, pirouetting with demented grace at its core, armed with nothing more than her voice and clenched fists, was Mrs Eulalie.

She had lost her hat, her thick blonde hair hung loose, and she swirled around in the middle of that throng, boldly, recklessly, eyeing the braves. She was shouting. If she uttered any real word at all, it was the same one, repeated over and over. Arms akimbo, she hurled herself at the front line of retreating braves. It looked as though she had a target.

Just as it seemed that the very gates of Hell were swinging open, Mr Beaubien appeared like a delivering angel in the midst of those braves and managed, somehow, to extricate Mrs Eulalie from the throng. He almost had to drag her off the brave she had attacked. Ushering her inside, he urged the Indians to continue. Mrs Eulalie went with him meekly enough, shuddering a little, but with her head held high.

Eliza rushed downstairs.

... For the last week, dear F_____, I have been attending her. I have no explanation for her conduct. She has not yet spoken, neither of that day nor of anything else, though her eyes are open and alert. She once told me it was suspected, when she was growing up, that she might be dumb. I fear some reversion to childhood behavior may have been prompted by this incident. Perhaps you have some thoughts to impart on this?

I am praying for her. And I have been reading to her from the Book, to which she has raised no objection, though it seems unlikely she is listening.

I am now certain it must be God's will that we are leaving Chicago. Nothing good has happened since we returned. This town is not for the Indians, dear F_____, it is not for Revd Porter and myself, nor is it for Mrs Eulalie. We must leave it, then, to the likes of Mr W.

Your sister-in-Christ,
Mistress Eliza Porter

1846–1852

1846

The Long Tests

The stagecoach from Chicago arrived in Cairo at night, the final twenty miles taking over five hours due to treacherous dugways and an afternoon thunderstorm. Ellis Chesbrough managed to find the last bed at the town's only lodging house. Though exhausted, he hardly slept. Rising as soon as it was light, he threw water at his face, pulled up the same creased breeches in which he had travelled for the last five days, slipped on his coat and hat, and hurried downstairs. He did not dare waste time having breakfast. On his feet, he swallowed down a cup of lukewarm liquid billed as coffee, and chewed a piece of crackling bread (cornbread mixed, he was told, with hog fat). He apologised to the landlady but he understood the *Gopher* was moored at Cairo, and he needed to get to the boat before it set out for the day.

Shrugging off the oppressive humidity, he stepped briskly across the boardwalks that lined Cairo's main street, its parade of bedraggled frame houses fronted by a muddy road and pools of stagnant water. A pale blur of pink sun was visible behind a barrage of grey clouds. The town was waking up — carters and vendors setting up stalls in a forlorn-looking market square, a drunk tipped over on a doorstep, a washerwoman with a basin on her head, probably on her way to the river too. Already, mosquitoes were on the wing. A turgid brown effluence from a flooded drainage ditch oozed underfoot. The stench was pernicious. What a miserable settlement this is, thought Ellis, every line, angle and surface warped by damp and mould. The inhabitants trudged past with stooped shoulders and lowered eyes, as if resigned to whatever wretched fate might come their way. He observed a cripple, hobbling towards him, and wondered what had caused the man's injuries. Ellis had seen too many accidents, and they always left him feeling uneasy. Could this one have been avoided? He handed the man a dime.

It was a relief when the town ended and the road took a meandering course through acres of tall, healthy canebrake. He half-walked, half-ran. The soles of his boots had soon picked up a wedge of red mud. The grasses swayed, vividly green, and over the whisper of their movement came the sound of birdsong. Ellis allowed himself a smile, recognising the dominant cries and mating calls of a warbler. There had been warblers on the farm where he grew up. That was a long time ago, before he had ever heard of surveys or railroads.

The canebrake ended abruptly, affording him his first sight of the river. Screened in part by a thicket of beech trees, the dark surface lay silvered by a gleam of sun. He could smell it already — much more pleasant than the odour in town — a pungent mix of warm mud and rotting vegetation. A few moments later, rounding a bend, he stopped stonestill and stared.

Moored alongside the riverbank was what could only be the *Gopher,* the most outlandish-looking paddle steamer he had ever seen. It was as though two oversized canoes had been strapped to the opposite sides of a giant deck. Over their twin prows towered a scaffold. Attached to the scaffold was a boom. From the end of the boom, like the swollen claw of some mythical underwater creature, a huge grapple swung to and fro. Though Ellis had never seen a snagboat before, he grasped at once the point of its design. The deck would be solid iron, a battering ram against underwater thickets; the grapple would be for seizing individual trunks. Some might have found the craft an incongruous presence in such a remote place, but such a thought did not cross Ellis's mind. He was curious about how it worked.

Figures were moving about on the deck. Ropes were being hauled in. There were three ominous blows on a whistle. As Ellis set off at a sprint, a man in uniform stepped out of the cabin at the rear. Lieutenant Colonel Stephen Long's erect bearing was unmistakable. 'Wait,' shouted Ellis. 'Please wait for me, sir.'

He had been fifteen years old when he first met Mr Long. It was 1828, his father's latest business venture had failed and, to support his mother, Ellis wanted to find work that paid more than he earned as a clerk at a mercantile house. That was not easy for a boy with no education or training. He had left school at the age of nine, when his father stopped farming, to start his first trading enterprise, and since then he had worked his way up from warehouse labourer to clerk. It was dull work with no future. So he could not believe his good fortune when he was hired as a chainman by the Corps of Topographical Engineers for a survey of what would become the first railroad in America — the Baltimore & Ohio. It was Mr Long himself who offered him the post.

Ellis applied himself to the job with enthusiasm and diligence. He had always liked figures — he had a natural ability with them — and he was obsessed with keeping accurate records of everything he did. Each evening, no matter how late they worked, he would crouch in the firelight and record the day's activities with drawings and figures, accompanied by a diary entry of lessons learned. Perhaps his behaviour was driven, he would reflect in later life, by a determination not to be like his slapdash father. 'Don't make the same mistakes,' his mother would tell him, in her lilting sing-song voice that owed its music, she said proudly, to the hills of her native Wales. One of her favourite sayings was the one his father never heeded: 'A man without prudence, Ellis, is a ship without an anchor.' She repeated it so often, and with such melancholy, that it haunted his nighttime dreams.

Very early on, Ellis concluded that his boss was the cleverest and most capable man he had ever met. Mr Long had studied at Dartmouth College, taught at West Point and enjoyed countless other adventures. He was an explorer, an inventor, a man of diverse talents. He was also strict, stern and humourless. Ellis did not mind. Deciding to learn everything he could, he accompanied Mr Long on his preliminary sorties across the ground to be surveyed, observing him closely as he took compass readings, made calculations and noted things down.

Ellis's task was to lay his chain between the two ranging rods that determined the direction of the railroad line. To keep the chain straight was no easy task in uneven terrain, and every single one of the hundred links had to be fully extended for an accurate sixty-six-foot reading. The number of completed and partially completed chain lengths then had to be counted off and reported to Mr Long.

After the first week of work, Ellis came up with an innovation. Cutting ten strips of the brightest cloth he could find, he tied one to every tenth link in the chain. When counting incomplete lengths, it meant he could count the links more quickly and reduce the likelihood of error. Mr Long was impressed. He taught Ellis how to use his prized Rittenhouse compass.

When the Baltimore & Ohio contract ended, Mr Long took Ellis with him to Pennsylvania to work on the Allegheny Portage Railroad. Ellis had a new title: 'Assistant Engineer'. He was seventeen years old.

———

Ellis was panting as he mounted the gangway. Lieutenant Colonel Long greeted him with an awkward formality, as was his way, before introducing him to the captain of the ship. 'Mr Chesbrough has come all the way from Boston,' he explained. 'He and I have some business to attend to. But in the meantime I think he will be glad to remove his coat, and set to with the men. Am I right, Mr Chesbrough?'

'You are indeed, sir.'

Ellis asked the captain whether he might be assigned to the team working with the grapple. Over the next few hours, he threw himself into the task as they hauled snags out of the water with the windlass to cries of 'heave-to'. The labour was hard, the heat intense, the mosquitoes persistent, and the crew worked for the most part in a sullen silence, punctuated by oaths. At first, they regarded Ellis with suspicion. But as the morning progressed and they saw him pulling his weight, they became more communicative. He asked many questions about the grapple and how best to manipulate it, and by the time they stopped for the lunch break he was being quizzed about growing up in Baltimore and work on the railroads.

With the sun almost overhead, the *Gopher* was moored partly in the shade of some overhanging branches. Mr Long had remained on deck all morning, barking orders about when and how to dispose of the debris collected. On a couple of occasions, Ellis heard him lose his temper. Now, he was examining the captain's logbook. Mr Long disagreed with the claim that they had removed sixty-three obstacles to navigation, and that each one was correctly noted down under a heading chosen from: *'Snags, Logs, Stumps, Roots, Impending Trees, Thickets, Planters'.*

Shortly afterwards, Ellis joined Mr Long in the captain's vacated cabin. The space was small and functional: it housed the wheel, overhead cupboards and two benches. They removed their hats and sat down opposite each other. 'Ten snagboats are under my command,' Mr Long explained. 'The others are on the Mississippi, the Missouri and the Arkansas. I have created the same recording system for them all, but its success depends on accurate records.'

'I understand, sir,' said Ellis.

Mr Long eyed him. 'I know you do not make mistakes, Mr Chesbrough. And you have initiative, unlike these snagboat captains.' Wiping the sweat off his brow, face and neck with a handkerchief, Mr Long took out his lunch.

Ellis removed from his bag the package the landlady had pressed on him as he was leaving that morning. He found biscuits, three slices of ham and some crackling bread. They ate for a while in silence.

Ellis was relieved he had caught up with Mr Long. To have come all that way and missed him would have been disastrous. But, now that he was here, he was increasingly doubtful what good it would do. The two of them had always kept up a regular correspondence, but it was over ten years since their last encounter. Mr Long must now be in his sixties. His hair had receded and turned grey, the skin about his face had slackened, removing something else in the process — it seemed — of a more qualitative nature. It was difficult to define the precise nature of the change. But it was in his eyes, in the way he barked commands, in the way he snapped at the captain. Mr Long looked distracted, irritable and worn down. He was in decline; a very different man to the inspiring genius who had been mentor to a youthful Ellis Chesbrough.

Coffee was brought to them in battered tin mugs. 'In a moment, you shall tell me your business here, Mr Chesbrough. But first I want you to understand why you find me in circumstances such as these ...' He gestured disparagingly, in a way that seemed to take in everything: the ship, the river, the sky. 'Six years ago, I agreed to investigate how we could clear the Red River Raft. I assume you have heard of it?' When Ellis confessed he had not, Mr Long explained that the Red River Raft was an ancient, treacherous, natural logjam, comprised of trees with entangled roots and branches that stretched all the way from Georgia to Louisiana. 'The Raft is the greatest obstruction to the waterways of America. It goes on for hundreds of miles. Hence my interest in the project.' This was a new kind of challenge, he explained, and surely a grand one. It might not equate to surveying for a canal or railroad where none believed one could ever be built; it might not equate to the invention of patented locomotive wheels; it might not equate to a revolutionary treatise on grades, curvatures and gravity. Mr Long's voice had changed and his eyes began to brighten. 'But imagine,' he said, 'if we could eradicate this Raft. Eradicate it forever.' He stopped, and for a moment his eyes continued to shine as though he were imagining that happy day when the Red River flowed smooth and uninterrupted, free of obstacles, its waters plied day and night by great steamers.

Ellis was relieved to hear him speaking like this. This was more like the old Mr Long, the one who had taught him how to look at the world anew, to think about angles and gauges, about 'rack and pinion' engines, about how to move canal boats up inclined planes.

Mr Long's exuberance, though, did not last. He dropped his hands. 'It never happened like that,' he said. 'And now, six years later, instead of putting all our resources into clearing the Red River Raft, as I urged Congress, my ten snagboats are dispersed across the country, picking away at minor obstacles. Fiddling, in my view, while Rome burns. It makes me furious.' Last year, though they had travelled over 2250 miles of river and removed 56,062 obstructions, that was as nothing compared to how much more dangerous the Red River Raft had become in the meantime. 'And we lost six crewmen,' he added, his eyes coming back to Ellis, 'with a further four crippled for life.'

Ellis recalled the cripple he had seen earlier that morning, and wondered if his injury had been sustained in circumstances such as these.

'It's dangerous work,' continued Mr Long. 'That is why a good engineer must go beyond his calculations and set the rules by which the work is done. I have established new Shipping Articles to be adhered to by every captain and crew under my command,' he said. 'But as we have seen this morning, the best rules cannot prevent incompetence.' He paused, tapped the tips of his fingers together. 'Never forget, Ellis, that the death of the few will always be justified by the improvements we make for the many.'

Ellis nodded, though he was not sure he wholeheartedly agreed. What if you knew one of the men who lost a limb, one of the men who died? Would that always be a sacrifice worth making? Was it always justified?

'Of the many things you taught me, sir,' said Ellis, 'the notion that we should attempt nothing unless it be for the public good has always inspired me. I think of it as the "Long test".'

Mr Long almost smiled. 'Are you not forgetting another Long test?'

Ellis hesitated. He had learned many lessons from Mr Long, but none of them struck him in the same way, as a test to which each job he undertook should adhere.

'Why have you come to see me, Mr Chesbrough, rather than write?'

'I have been offered a new position, sir, in a field of engineering in which I have no experience. I think it might be one of the most important decisions I ever make. I wanted your advice as to whether I should accept the post or not. I thought it better to speak in person.'

The position, he explained, was that of chief engineer for the western division of the Boston Water Works. As Mr Long was aware, he had no experience of hydraulic engineering. Since their days on the Allegheny Portage Railroad, whenever he had been able to find some work, it had always been on railroads. He had never surveyed for a canal, never built an aqueduct, never designed a sewage system. He probably knew less about water than most of the men on this boat.

'I take it you are afraid of failure?'

'Not only failure. I fear that leaving the railroads to start as a beginner again with water might be a backward step. In your view, sir, will we rely more on our canals or on our railroads in the future?'

'It depends where you are,' said Mr Long. 'I hear a group of local speculators have bought up ten thousand acres because Cairo is to become the southern terminal for an Illinois Central Railroad. But railroads cannot do everything and cannot go everywhere. Where would we be without water? Building a canal is a marvellous enterprise. One of the great regrets of my life is that I was never given the contract to construct the first canal I ever surveyed. I did that survey in 1816, in Chicago, but it's taken them till now, thirty years on, to start digging. It will be one of the most important canals in America.'

'Sir?'

'For the first time, ships will be able to pass from the Great Lakes to the Gulf of Mexico. Just imagine what that will mean.'

Ellis did not know much about Chicago, other than what he had seen on passing through. It was a small, nondescript town but he could see how such a canal might help to boost its fortunes.

'What did I always tell you about becoming an engineer?' said Mr Long. 'That it's not about the schools you go to, but about the depth and variety of experience you accumulate.'

'Though you would not believe that, the way some people talk.'

Mr Long sighed. 'I learned more in a month's work on the Baltimore & Ohio than at Dartmouth College and West Point put together.'

'I am encouraged to hear you say that, sir.'

'I have shared my frustrations with you, Mr Chesbrough. There is no new challenge or experience to be derived from the work you find me doing here. I have been thwarted by the government in Washington in my ambition to destroy the Red River Raft and condemned, instead, to managing ten minor projects in ten different places.' His gaze was level. 'You have been offered a fine opportunity, Ellis. Now, do you understand the second Long test?'

The captain's whistle blew. The break was over and it was time to swing the grapple and remove more obstructions. Ellis looked forward to the afternoon's work. He drained his coffee and smiled. 'Thank you, sir. Yes, I understand.'

1847

The Clochan

(This chapbook was believed to have been in private circulation in Chicago during the 1890s. Who transcribed the monologue, and when, remains unknown. The trustees of the Chicago Historical Society have declared it to be an artifact of cultural importance. It should be noted, by way of introduction, that more Irish immigrated to the United States during the 1840s, when the potato famine was at its height, than any other nationality.)

Yerra, it's no surprise you want to hear about Mochta. Everyone always does. I shall do my best, though God knows it opens fresh wounds in my heart each time I tell the tale. That great ruffian was different from the rest of us, and not only because he stood tall and strong as the rock of Teeraught. I swear God's grace surrounded him like a smothering of Blasket mist. There was nobody that didn't feel it, even when the big dolt was dizzy with drink and his speech was wandering. I saw more souls flee the living hell of that canal for the Blessed Isles than I could count, but Mochta should never have been one of them. That brother of mine was a force of nature. He should have lasted to be old, and the shame is that I could have saved him, the day fate came looking for him.

Mochta was born in '22, my elder sibling by three years, and he was the strongest man on Great Blasket. I worshipped him. He could charm a crab with his crack-toothed grin, and if I hooked a big pollack and he fetched me a friendly clout on the ear, I was in Heaven, so to speak. We were the eldest two of nine, though only five of us survived. My parents named me Dubhaltach Bruaideadh, and you can write that down as you will, for I'm not the one to tell you how. There was a school in the Lower Village, but it did not often see a teacher. In any case, the younger ones in the litter were sent to learn the chalk marks, not Mochta or me. Our work was with my father. We went fishing and hunted seals, we grew potatoes and cut the turf.

I've lived without knowing letters all my life, and I am the happier for it. I've seen what happens. Once a thing is marked down on paper, it can't be changed. It's writing that landowners and bailiffs use to cheat their tenants. It's writing that turns everything to stone. Much better, that words be left to blow in the breeze. Much better that no story is ever the same. Because that's how life is, isn't it? Everything is on the wheel, and always will be. O by Mary, writing is a curse, for what it fixes. But do as you will. Write down all the words you want. Nothing I tell you will be invented, for I've no need for anything but the truth when I speak about Mochta. I knew that rascal better than he knew himself.

One day ... it was in either '41 or '42 ... he left the Island to find his fortune in America. The years passed, and after my wife was taken one stormy night on the rocks off Inishtooshkert — the blessings of God be on her soul — Mochta sent me the passage-money for the crossing. No, I didn't think bread grew on hedges and there were mountains made of gold, whatever dreams that brother of mine planted in my head. I only wanted me and the whelp to have the chance of a second start.

We arrived at Deer Island in Boston, and the Yankees laughed when I told them my name was Dubhaltach Bruaideadh. They said I must be drunk. All Irishmen were bog-trotters on the bottle, to their way of thinking. My first lesson in English would be to learn my new name, which they told me was Dudley Brody. I didn't complain, though some from the Old Country disagreed. For me, a name is only a sound that will pass soon enough, once we're gone. So if they wanted to call me Dudley Brody, though it seemed short and ugly, I made no objection. My boy never complained either. He was three years when we made the passage, and Osgar was easy enough for the Yankee tongue, though he soon started to call himself Oscar. It made him sound stronger, he said.

Only Mochta refused to have his name changed. None of them could say it properly. They said 'Mockter', though there should be a pocket of air and a pause in the throat, *M-uch-ta*. Mr Krumpacker called him 'Mucker', and thought himself a wit for doing so. I'll tell you more about Mr Krumpacker in a minute, for he's the other half in this story.

Mochta was settled in Chicago, and there was a fine job waiting for me there. That was the yarn he'd spun. So me and the boy, we crossed the bigness of America, and one misty summer morning as the *General St. Clair* steamed across the surface of Lake Michigan, smoother than any sea could be, I sneaked out of steerage and went up on deck towards the prow, holding the boy tight, and dreamed of throwing out a net to see what manner of fish swum beneath all that quietness. As I was looking towards the horizon, a creamy-white beach rose out of the haze and, my soul from the devil, it was the mirror of Great Blasket's White Strand, but ten times bigger. What a comfort that was to see. I raised my eyes, blessed by God's mystery as I gazed into the great expanse of His sky or, as Old Conn the Poet would say, 'the airy skin that holds the world together and makes it one'.

The next moment, the *General St Clair* was tying up to the pier and I saw that cheerful oaf of a brother down below, shoving ahead of everyone else to greet us, arms raised and shouting like a foghorn, and at the sight of his great head I felt a surge of joy and hope in my heart, despite that Oscar had been puking for three days and my legs were weak as feathers. My eyes were this wide when I stepped ashore that morning. The town might have been a dwarf compared to what it is today, but Chicago seemed to me the largest, finest place in the world as we left behind the crowds on the pier, traveling like English lords in a shaky old wagon Mochta had called with a whistle and snap of fingers as if he did it every day. Despite the tribulations of the voyage, I felt as lively as a trout. Mochta directed the wagon to go first down this street, then down that one, so we could admire the line of glittering stores and hotels and coffee houses, with painted signs and fine ladies seated near the windows drinking out of china cups, and all manner of people walking about and hawking wares, and snorting horses that pulled wagons and carriages all fighting for space and, wisha, it was magic I shall never forget, because it was like arriving in paradise, and nobody can do that twice.

Mochta told the wagon to stop outside a market square, and had a spat with the driver about the fare. The scent of spices filled the air, of mint and ginger and marjoram, and many others I did not know. When you've been living on hard biscuits and oatmeal, and drinking water that stinks, a market makes your stomach growl. We passed stalls packed with every foodstuff you could imagine, tables piled with fresh loaves of bread, bags of sugar and salt, tea and coffee, dried fruits and flour. We saw butchers beating flies off great sides of pork, and fat, plucked chickens and juicy cuts of beef.

While Mochta talked with a fishmonger, I compared the catch with those on Great Blasket. There were bass and perch and a browner shade of trout than I had ever seen, slithering about in full baskets. *They must be easy to catch*, I thought, *as easy as those mackerel off Beginish three summers past*. As we walked on, I said to Mochta: 'Now I know why it's a grand job you've found me.' I could already imagine our canoe pulled up on those dunes that looked like the White Strand, but ten times bigger. 'It will be the same as in the old days.' There was no reply. My brother was talking to Oscar. Maybe that was why he did not hear me. Was I afraid? Never. Dingle might have been a minnow compared to Chicago, but why worry when Mochta was with me? You never saw a man more at ease, my trunk under one arm and Oscar under the other — he had adopted the boy at first sight — and greeting half the people we passed, though whether he knew them I could not say. He was that kind of man, who had a cheery word for everyone, friend and stranger alike.

We stopped at a food stall and were soon eating off plates piled high with batter cakes and beans, our glasses brimming with ale. It was the best meal I had ever tasted in my life and I felt the world was back in tune. Church bells were ringing somewhere, and each stroke was like a chime of freedom. The Great Master had indeed brought us to the Promised Land. I was convinced of it, seated with Mochta that morning in the middle of the market. Oscar looked better already, and was holding down a bowl of bread and milk.

My brother did not bide to start his questions. We became lost in the lives of our far-off Island as I gave news of every member of the family, and of the friends we had left behind. What exquisite pleasure that conversation gave me. How much I had longed for this moment when we two brothers would be reunited somewhere beneath God's 'airy skin'. And how wonderful that we needed no ships or long, perilous voyages to transport our hearts back to the Old Country, for that past was private and particular, it was in us and of us, ours and ours only.

Yerra, that would be the first and last time since I came to America that I've heard any bells of freedom chime or fairy music go a-playing in my head.

———

After the welcome at the pier, and the celebration in the market, there were no more wagons. No canoe was waiting for us on the lakeshore. Mochta did not have lodgings in Chicago. He was not even 'settled' there. He bought a loaf of bread and some dried fish before announcing that we had to walk. Off he strode, with Oscar now hoist on his shoulders, merry as a bottle of the best, whistling with the joys of life. He did not tell me how far we had to go.

After leaving town we followed the cutting for a new canal and were seated on the towpath, taking a rest as we fought off blackflies big as hurley balls, when Mochta described the 'fine job' waiting for me. We were to dig out sod for this same canal, armed with only a pick and shovel, starting another fifteen miles along the line. When he saw my disappointment he tried to froth the truth, saying we could earn enough in a few months to buy a canoe. So the rascal had heard me, when I talked about a canoe. That changed my mood. We could soon be out at dawn, hauling our nets through that fish-filled virgin Lake. But who shall care for Oscar? I asked. The cook's wife, he said, 'who has a boy the same age'.

And how much would we be paid for this work? $17 a month, he said, minus the $3 they deduct for food and lodging. I did not know the cost of things in those days. It seemed a grand sum, but it wasn't. We worked from dawn to dusk, every day but Sunday. In summer, you can imagine the hours. But 'the newcomer sees only the sun', as Old Conn used to say. I was happy. I slapped Mochta on the back, and spoke another line from Old Conn, for good measure: 'honest labor feeds the belly, an honest heart feeds the soul'. He smiled, but he did not smile much. I thought I understood why. He had never given the Old Poet the respect he deserved.

It was dusk when we arrived at the camp. The rain was coming down and we were soaked. My feet had come up in blisters. For the first time since stepping off the steamer, I felt the stirrings of despair. I had never seen a place more desolate than this. There were a dozen leaning shacks knocked together from old planks, each one marooned in a pool of mud. The rain fell in flurries as we squelched towards the shed Mochta said was ours. The door hitched open. Half-a-dozen men were inside, four playing cards, each one looking glum and red-eyed from exhaustion as he took his turn and swore and swatted at mosquitoes, two more racked out asleep on splintery wooden bunks. There was a stench of feet and sweat. The roof was leaking. The earthen floor was covered in spit and stains, another burst of rainfall struck the roof like gunfire, and we had missed supper. Oscar began to bawl.

Mary Virgin! I have run away with myself. You want to hear about Mochta, not about the whelp and me. But we had to reach the canal, in any case, because that's where the story happened. It started like this. One day, a foot beneath the surface of the soil, we hit a bedrock ...

Yerra, if you insist. Before I tell you about Mochta and the bedrock, I'll describe the work we did each day, though I don't know I have the words to do it justice. At dawn the ganger, Mr Krumpacker, clanged the bell loud enough to shatter the deepest dreams, and we'd rise in clothes dried and stiffened while we slept and grope about in darkness for our damp, rotting boots. I'd shake Oscar awake where he lay beside me. There'd be yawns, and curses as we got in each other's way. My fingers caked with yesterday's soil, I'd feel for the swell of new mosquito bites (I was known as 'walleye' for a while, for the number of times the overnight bites bigged up sideways on my blinkers) and after a breakfast of bacon strips and cold potatoes washed down by a mug of lukewarm coffin varnish (as we called that version of the beverage), we would be marched off to the worksite. I'd leave little Oscar with the cook's boy, Dermot.

There were about eighty or a hundred of us in the camp, working in teams of eight. Each team had three picks, three shovels, two wheelbarrows and one plank. The plank was used to run a full wheelbarrow up to the top of the ditch and take it past the towpath to dump the soil. Mr Krumpacker also used the plank to avoid dirtying his breeches when he came into the ditch to measure its width and depth. The canal was forty feet wide at the top, six feet deep and twenty-eight feet wide at the bottom. He barked out the numbers, over and over again: 'Forty, sechs und zwenty-eight! Forty, sechs und zwenty-eight.'

The first part of the day seemed the longest (though it wasn't, according to the clock) and it was the worst. Our bones jarred from the day before, and with every movement muscles ached and old pains came out of hiding. The bottom of the ditch was underwater. Our feet were always wet and numb, the skin wrinkled and blue and swollen, and we lived in constant fear of gangrene. Time moved like a snail. It seemed impossible, in those first few hours, that we could survive another day. Everyone had bites, blisters, cuts and bruises. Everyone was sick, some more, some less. In those summer months, the mosquitoes and blackflies were the happiest hunters and we hated them for it. The only thing bad as their bites was to strike a hidden rock with the pick. Every nerve in the body jumped.

After the cook had brought beans and bread, our minds slowed down and the body's exhaustion numbed the pain and the heat of the day lashed down and we stopped with the idle chatter and our mouths became parched, and it wasn't long before we stopped thinking at all. Our shirts clung to our backs, but we dared not remove them for the mosquitoes. We were too tired not to drink our own sweat as it rolled off the brow. Even if we had set off that morning with an idea of where we were, raising another shovel of soil somewhere in America, the notion had passed. We no longer knew where we were or why, or how it started and whether it would ever end. Our bodies kept working only because they knew what to do and there was no choice. If they stopped, Mr Krumpacker would notice soon enough and come swanking across to flick at us with his cowhide whip. He had a mean little *pus* to him and a buck goat's wiry bush cut to a triangle beneath the chin. And those boots on which he swaggered were soled high off the ground, as if he lived a step nearer to God than the rest of us. He liked to pick on the weakest among us, and if that doesn't show the coward, I don't know what does.

The top boss wasn't Mr Krumpacker. It was Mr Goodman. He held the contract from the Canal Commissioners for the section between Saganashkee Swamp and Lockport. At least, that was how I understood it. When the canal was finished it would run from Canalport in Chicago to La Salle in the west, and join Lake Michigan to the Mississippi River. It sounds grand, when you say it like that, but there was nothing grand about the way we dug it. We'd never seen or heard of Mr Goodman till one morning we hit a bedrock one foot beneath the surface that made our picks spark. We'd dug out rocks before, and big ones too, a curse because of how they slowed us down and put Mr Krumpacker into a temper. But this was a shelf of rock, stretching nearly two hundred yards in front of us. And that meant the canal would either have to change direction, or we'd be told to drive our way through.

Mr Krumpacker must have sent urgently for Mr Goodman because he arrived the next day, a hard-eyed Yankee on a white horse who spat and swore at that cussed rock, as if the rock had no business to be there. He was the same as an English landlord because that was the only time we ever saw him, if you follow my meaning. A few days later, Mr Krumpacker (the landlord's bailiff) came to the site with a bag of black powder.

It probably won't surprise you that Mr Krumpacker did not like Mochta. He never dared to leather him and we all knew why. The ganger was no dwarf, but that brother of mine was a giant, the biggest man in the camp, and probably Chicago too. So when

Mochta took breaks to smoke his pipe, the German would pretend not to notice, and whenever he raised our spirits by leading a song in the Irish tongue (only English was allowed on the line), Mr Krumpacker would ride his horse in the opposite direction until we had quietened down. In little ways like this, Mochta whittled away at the anchor line of Mr Krumpacker's authority. And I don't doubt this was behind what happened next.

Mr Krumpacker chose Mochta to lay the charges and set them off. You might think this was a job that needed nimble fingers and caution and experience, and you would be right. Life and death was a lottery for all of us in that camp. Every week another soul was lost to fever. Whenever dysentery or typhoid struck, a cull took place. It was wretched and a tragedy. There was no comfort in suffering like that, but at least we could say we had equal chances, to live or die. But when you blast your way through rock with black powder and a fuse, there is only one man at risk, and Mr Krumpacker knew it.

Mochta, the great fool, rejoiced in his new role. He always liked to be at the center of things. He never recognized a risk in anything, and explosions were no different. It thrilled him to pack the powder into the cigar-sized holes we had taken turns to chisel out of the rock at one-foot intervals. That's no easy work, neither. The chisels were blunt, my blisters burned, and however hard we worked it was never quick enough for Mr Krumpacker. Mochta would lay the fuse and, always with a wink towards the rest of us to make sure he had our attention, he'd strike the match and light the taper and as the flame fizzled fast in one direction, Mochta would hurl himself in the other, laughing like a maniac as if he were charging along the White Strand in the final game of hurley against the Dunquin folk in Christmas week. We were at a distance, crouching with our hands over our ears, our backs turned as the powder exploded and shards of rock went flying and black smoke belched out and our breath choked on that metallic-stinking cloud, while Mochta continued to cry out in a kind of ecstasy, as though the blast had revealed to him a mystery the rest of us could not see.

This went on for weeks. Mr Krumpacker ordered us to collect the broken rock and chip it into slabs because the absent Mr Goodman had decided they must be used to build locks to manage the canal's descent to the river. That's right, it was the Des Plaines River. In the end, we would build four of those locks: four locks and, as I'll explain shortly, a clochan.

Mochta became the expert of how to break the rock to best effect. Whenever he was cut by slivers before he had time to get away, he laughed it off, as if it was nothing. You'd likely be thinking the same as me, that the number of those accidents should have gone down, the more experienced he became? They didn't. They increased. They increased because the quality of Mr Krumpacker's black powder decreased. In cheap black powder, Mochta told me, the ingredients were either mixed in the wrong amounts or they weren't pounded tight enough. The result wasn't only weaker, it was more unpredictable. It exploded too soon and scattered too far. Was Mr Krumpacker saving money for Mr Goodman, or was the extra going into his own pocket? When there's a shoal of guilt to be shared, everyone's net is heavy.

Although Mochta liked to play the hero, he was no fool either. He complained to Mr Krumpacker and when the powder didn't improve, he refused to lay any more until it did. For a while it did get better, but then, just before the end, Mr Krumpacker began to save his pennies again. The powder was the poorest Mochta had ever seen. And that was why he lost his right eye.

And this, my young scribe, is where the story about that great rogue of a brother really begins. I won't tell you what pain that lost eye caused him, how if affected his balance, the private distress it caused him. He never complained, neither in public nor to me. It was his fate, he would declare, and there was nothing more to be said. If that does not tell you what kind of man he was, nothing will. 'I'll get my chance one day,' he would say to me, 'whenever the Great Master decides.' And by that, I guessed, he meant a chance to take revenge on Mr Krumpacker.

Sad to report, since the loss of that eye and wearing the patch, Mochta became more taken by the drink than I'd ever seen him, until his dollars were all drowned and he was sinking mine in whiskey too. It was as if he were intent on courting oblivion and an early grave. Every Saturday, after work was finished and we had coins in our pockets and a whole day lay ahead of us without sight or sound of that stinking muddy ditch, 'Mr Whiskey' would arrive at the camp with a crate full of bottles. He'd been a brewer from County Cork in the Old Country, so he knew his mix well enough. Mochta had never been able to turn the back of his hand to a pot, but the state of him now became a fright to see. He tossed off the whiskey like water. He'd have drunk the stuffing out of a saddle. It went too far.

Yerra, I swear to you it did. And that was why one late summer evening I lost my temper and said too much. Was he so thick-skinned he couldn't see we needed money for Oscar? Hadn't he noticed the whelp was so weakly there was no telling when he might hear the final call? And what about the canoe he had promised? What kind of no-good was he, that he could waste everything on whiskey? Was he trying to kill himself?

It was true that Oscar had been up and down ever since we made the crossing, but it wasn't true about the money because I've always been the frugal kind, and I was squirreling away what I could, buried safe in a tin near the camp. Anyway, may the Devil take me, I didn't stop there. I ranted and raved at my brother that night as I'd never done before. Hadn't he promised me a fortune when I came to America, and wasn't that a dreadful lie and wasn't he ashamed of himself for bringing us here to a life more wretched than anything we'd ever known on the Island? On and on I went until my throat was sore. I blamed him for everything, which was neither fair nor honest. The truth is that I was only sorry for myself, and that's an ugly thing to be. I can see that now.

Well, Mochta — and may God remember this when the Scales Up There are weighed — stopped drinking at once. He stopped that very evening, as if he'd seen an angel. And maybe he had too. Yerra, maybe he had.

He loved Oscar, you see. And Oscar loved him back. By my cloak, how he loved him back. Sometimes I had to bite my tongue, when it seemed Oscar was loving his uncle more than he loved his own father. I told myself Mochta always had that effect on people, young and old, inside the family or out. You're puzzled by that? How do I describe what made him different to one who never met him, except to say that when the troubles of life were rolling in your wake he had the gift to smooth them into tiny ripples, to put you on an even keel, to send those ripples back to where they'd come from. Sometimes he didn't even need to open his mouth. In those moments, he was transformed from Mochta the Clown into something rare and fine. He'd give you all his attention and listen to every word, as though there was nothing he wanted to do more, and when you were finished with your fears and worries, he'd lean forward and, the smile quite gone from his face but with eyes full of light, he'd touch you on the shoulder with his large, rough, hard-worked palms. The touch was gentle. Yet it was strong as a laying on of hands. Yerra, I swear my brother could pass the spirit on like a priest, though it be a blasphemy to say so. And it wasn't only me that felt it.

Mochta was always playing with Oscar. He told him stories about growing up on the Island that made it sound like a country of magic and miracles. He taught him fighting songs like 'Ye Men of Sweet Liberties Hall' and 'Dunlavin Green' which the boy still sings today when I've told him off for this or that. And their favorite outing was to the prairies on a Sunday, often taking with them his friend

Dermot, the cook's son. Mochta made hurleys out of local furze, and they'd practice tossing a ball for hours at a time, the same as he and I would do on the White Strand when we were young cubs.

I went the first few times, but I could see I wasn't needed. Oscar had a good strike and could run too, much better than Dermot. 'Fly like a bird, Oscar!' his uncle would shout, and the boy would tear around those prairies fast as a comet on the turn. And then they'd laugh when Dermot tried and tripped over himself in the attempt. No wonder it's a baseball hero Oscar always wanted to be. Go ask him how that started, and if he tells the truth you'll hear it was because of hurley on Sundays with his Uncle Mochta. He'd come back flushed and happy, and full of secrets. Oscar never cried when he was with Mochta.

But it was me that fed and clothed and cared for the boy, sitting wakeful by his side each of those long nights he was sick. *Mochta has no child of his own*, I told myself. *No wonder he's trying too hard with mine. No wonder he spoils him.* The sum of the matter is that my fits of envy never lasted because Mochta's heart was wide-open. There was not a shred of jealousy to his character, and that's why he couldn't imagine it in others. You see what I'm saying? He had no idea how I felt, and I never told him.

And then, a few weeks after the drinking stopped, Oscar did fall sick. Very sick indeed. It began with a fever, he stopped eating, his skin came out in rashes and he grew thin as a conger. We thought he was about to make his last farewell, and the only way to save him was to seek help fast as we could from a doctor in Chicago. Mochta knew a doctor who was also a 'good friend' he said, and he would take him there at once. Maybe I should have gone too, and things would have turned out differently. But I didn't go. We needed all the money we could get. One of us had to keep working the ditch. So I dug up my buried tin of savings, gave Mochta every last cent, and he set off for Chicago, with Oscar strapped to his back like a babe.

I have never known days worse than those that followed, not even on the crossing, not even when my wife was taken away that night off Inishtooshkert and I found myself alone again in the world, one tiny heart beating in the big silence. Each day drifted into the next. I woke up, I dressed, I ate, I worked and then I tried to sleep. I had no appetite. I did not notice my aches and pains, blisters and bruises. I started talking to myself. My thoughts were always with Mochta and the boy. The more I worried, the more I feared Oscar was with the angels and Mochta was drinking himself into a stupor. A dozen times, I nearly started off myself for the town, but what would I do when I got there? Who did I know? How would I find Mochta?

And then one day — O my eternal thanks to the Great Master — they returned. Oscar was on his own two feet, still weak but getting better. The doctor, I heard, had put him in isolation, treated him with broth and special syrups and bloodlettings. At first, I was too overwhelmed with joy to ask how much this treatment cost and Mochta did not mention it. But when eventually I did, he said he had found the best doctor in Chicago and I should be pleased about that. Indeed, I was, I said. But had he brought back any change from our savings? No, he had not. It had cost all our savings? Yes, all our savings, he said. And, he added with a sheepishness that alarmed me, there was also a bill to pay. A bill? I cried out in dismay. Yes, a bill, he said, scratching his big head as though it were as puzzling to him as it was to me. Begorra, only Mochta could have charmed a doctor to treat Oscar on the promise of paying for most of it later, just as only crack-toothed grinning Mochta would have agreed to such an outlandish price. It was a bill for $200, one that would take the two of us a year's labor to pay off, even if we pared everything else back to the bone. 'Are doctors in America paid like millionaires?' I raged.

I fumed, not because I was stingy and would have tried to save a cent where Oscar's life depended on it, but because I knew that big oaf had been bamboozled by his 'good friend' the doctor. Mochta apologized. Oh, how he apologized. But for the first time in my life I would not forgive him. For days I gave him the cold shoulder, as I had never done before. Yerra, I wanted to hurt him, and that was a terrible thing to do to your own brother, whatever his mistakes. And hurt him, indeed, I did. But how much I hurt him, how guilty I made him feel, to what tragic end I would push him, and how profoundly his passing would forever weigh down my conscience and my soul — of these things I had as yet no inkling.

Life returned to its miserable normality. The summer passed and the fall weather began to take hold. The days were shorter, which was a blessing, but the cold began to bite. We had been forgotten, that was how it felt. No longer human beings, but beasts of burden, condemned to a lifetime of hard labor. There was frost on the ground in the mornings, the earth hardened, and our meager rations of bacon strips, potatoes, coffin varnish, beans and bread did not vary. I feared what the winter would do to us. It would be our first here, and I had been warned that the cold would freeze the very blood in our veins. I was afraid for us all, but mostly for Oscar. He was big for his age (he found ways to make the cook feed him extra) and he seemed to be recovering well, but there is no telling what misfortunes lie in wait for us, hidden in the deep.

It was in the midst of this despair, when I caught my first glimmer of Mochta's outrageous plan. Strangely, it was I who had — without realizing — prompted it. Back in the summer, shortly after Mochta lost his eye, we were down in the ditch one day, working the picks side by side, when he remarked that though there was more turf in the land of sweat (by which he meant America) than the world would ever need, the turf here had no magic, not like in the Old Country.

I quoted Old Conn the Poet, from a song about beating off the bailiffs. 'All turf on earth is sacred,' I said, 'it's older than Adam and belongs only to God'. But Old Conn wouldn't have sung that line about this poor turf, said Mochta. Yerra, he was right. I don't know why it was as rough as it was. Maybe because it lacked a salty breeze to soften the clods, a mistful rain to loose its clumps, sheep and cattle to turn it dark and fertile, or maybe it was just too recently formed in the earth to burn bright and hot. I'd dreamed often enough of journeying into the prairies to search for sod to cut like the sod of Great Blasket that would keep us warm in the evenings. 'By the Breviary!' I declared, 'Old Conn would have seen magic even here, in this miserable turf. He'd have found a way to store it in the clochan.'

You're frowning. Because that's the second time I've said 'clochan' and you think I should tell you what it is. Be patient and bide, my friend. We have all night, and there's a bottle here that needs draining to the last drop, though I shouldn't be talking like that, not in view of the terrible things that have to be said. I'll tell you what a clochan is when the time is right.

Back to the misery of those fall days, as we headed into winter weighed down by a doctor's bill as heavy as an anchor stone. One day, Mochta was pushing a wheelbarrow of turf up the plank when Mr Krumpacker arrived to make one of his inspections.

'I've been thinking,' said Mochta quietly when he saw him coming, as if communing only with his own soul, 'that it might be a good idea to be treating this turf inside a clochan.'

Mr Krumpacker stared at him.

Meek as a Blasket lamb, my brother apologized for speaking aloud and pushed his barrow to tip the soil.

On the way back, Mr Krumpacker stopped him. He was in a good mood that day. You could tell from the way he stood rocking on his heels, hands stuffed beneath his oxters. And surely, even a man as hard as he must have felt some sense of guilt about Mochta's eye. He asked what Mochta had been talking about.

Oh, it was nothing, said Mochta. Only an idea, really. It was just that where we came from, turf the same as this turf he was tossing away, was worth its weight in gold. Because on the Island, just the same as on the prairies, there were hardly any trees to be found. That's why he knew something of the matter. 'We are made experts by necessity, as Old Conn the Poet used to say,' he said, a sly touch from that big dolt. Despite his lack of respect for the Poet, at least he understood that quoting Old Conn lent weight to a man's words. If this turf was treated the Blasket way and it worked, there would be no need to float timber downriver for fuel. 'Ten slabs of this turf,' he said, 'could burn for as long and hot as a whitewood tree.'

'And how this turf you treat, Mucker?'

'In a clochan, sir.'

'What is this clochan?'

Mochta pretended to reconsider. He looked at his feet. He was trying to look embarrassed. 'Oh, I don't s'pose, sir, I should be saying, now should I?'

'Mucker?'

Mochta looked down at us in the ditch, still pretending embarrassment. And when he spoke, he mumbled. 'A clochan's a kind of kiln, sir. You fire the turf like bricks, though it's a book more complicated than that.'

This exchange between them had dragged us away from our drudgery and, by the Virgin, we must have managed to keep our faces straight enough, for otherwise the joke would have ended there and then. The clochan was no mystery to us, you see.

Yerra, I'll put you out of your misery. Clochans are shelters that you find all over the Island. We use them for sheep, or for storing turf. Nobody could ever use a clochan as a kiln. Well, you can imagine how difficult it was for us to stop from grinning. We were all beavering our brains to imagine what might happen next. Who would girliggle first and break the spell? And when they did, what punishment would Mr Krumpacker devise for us? For that was his way; one man's failings became the cause of every man's punishment. Would he go on a spree with his whip? Or would Mochta the wag step forward to plant two wet kisses on Mr Krumpacker's puffed up cheeks? Stranger things had been known to happen.

What did happen was stranger still.

'By the Devil's pulleys, I'm sorry!' exclaimed Mochta, slapping his forehead as he rolled the empty wheelbarrow down the plank into the ditch. And he now made an apology to us in English so simple that Mr Krumpacker could not misunderstand its meaning. And though we had been ready to collapse with laughter only a few moments before, and even if we couldn't possibly have divined his scheme, we understood well enough what we had to do. With our blackened faces, holding our tools still for just a moment, we bestowed on Mochta looks as grave as the judge in Dingle would use to sentence a prisoner in the dock.

Mr Krumpacker clapped his hands and told us to get back to work. But you could see he was intrigued. And we were greatly cheered. We had never known such entertainment in the ditch.

For the next few days, Mochta pretended to be in disgrace with the rest of us. There were no songs, no Irish chatter, only lowered eyes and hard work. I knew he must be up to something, but he refused to say what. And when I said I could see no possible good in this doffing-the-cap to Mr Krumpacker and speaking of clochans, he clapped me on the shoulder and — by the Cross — he quoted Old Conn at *me*! 'Neither luck nor good fortune,' he said, 'ever came to anything that runs in people's talk.' And then he added: 'We'll pay that doctor's bill before Christmas, Dubhaltach.'

'And how shall we do that?' I said. 'Raid a bank?'

Oh, that was cruel, I know. But I'd heard these kinds of big words from him so often before that I knew exactly how much weight to give them.

Let me put what happened next in a nutshell, so that you can glimpse the mad trajectory on which my brother had determined. Back in the summer, after we'd had that talk about the poor turf in America,

Mochta — without telling me — asked a friend who knew his ABC to send a message to the Blaskets, requesting that they send him a box of Blasket sod. Only after that box arrived, did Mochta begin to spin his tale. He told Mr Krumpacker that a friend of his had built a clochan on the other side of Chicago. Would he like him (Mochta) to test some prairie turf in that clochan? Yerra, said Mr Krumpacker, why not? And that, my friend, was all it needed. Once he had seen that Blasket sod burn in the hearth, Mr Krumpacker was on the hook.

Each turf block, Mochta explained, was made by pressing the right mix of clochan-fired soil and shredded prairie grass into a wooden mold. Once you had the right blend, it was as easy as making bricks. You put them in the clochan, fired it up, let the turf bake overnight, and by morning you were ready to make your fortune. Mochta could begin at once, he said. All he needed was permission to use some of those rocks he'd been blasting from the canal — and $4500. Yerra, $4500 was a grand sum, wasn't it? A fortune, no less. The *spezialist* who built that clochan on the other side of Chicago would then build one for Mr Krumpacker too. Only a *spezialist* could build a clochan because it was like a factory, Mochta explained, with *spezial* holes at *spezial* points at *spezial* angles for a very *spezial* ventilation.

In the beginning, I refused to help Mochta with his clochan. Each Sunday he would go to work on it. He told me he had chosen a site hidden in a dip between two ridges, an empty place, about a mile from where the first canal lock would be positioned. I've never built a clochan, nor seen anyone else build one either. They were done before our time. But I knew it wouldn't be easy to do. He would need persistence, patience and hundreds of flat stones. It begins with a layer laid in a circle on the ground. On top of this layer goes another, but this one must be set a little more inward than the one below, so the overhang is pointing always towards the center of the circle. Layer is placed on layer. In this slow way a thick round wall is built, and the circles grow ever smaller until the central and the highest point of the dome is reached, which stands at more than the height of a man. From a distance, it looks like a beehive, though that might give the wrong idea. A clochan is one of the most solid buildings on earth.

Each week Mr Krumpacker would hand over bills to Mochta, hidden in a roll of newspaper. Presumably, he went to check on progress before he did so. I often wondered how a ganger could find so much money, however much he'd stolen from us. Probably from investors. At least, I think that's what they called them. If that was true, I hoped they were as crooked as Mr Krumpacker so there was no sin in taking it away from them. In any case, Mochta would bring every single dollar straight to me. I was to handle all the money, he said, because I was good with it. As soon as we had $200, Mochta went to pay the doctor.

There was one major problem with Mochta's madcap plan and it bewildered me that he would not see it. 'What do we do,' I asked him, 'when Mr Krumpacker discovers he's been taken for a fool? He'll send his thugs for us, and we'll be lucky to escape with our lives. Then we'll have to hand back the money, including the $200 we don't have because you've paid your good friend the doctor. We'll be out of work, and likely as not in jail, with half our limbs broken into pieces. What would our parents say, Mochta, if they could see us, gone to jail in America? Is that what we came here for? And tell me this, what happens then to Oscar?'

Mochta always answered, when I look back at it, too calmly. 'This agreement is between me and Mr Krumpacker, Dubhaltach, not you as well. Remember this. He doesn't know we are brothers.' That, at least, was true. Mr Krumpacker knew nothing about anyone. 'He doesn't know you have the money for the clochan. You and Oscar don't have to worry about a thing.' And then he'd add: 'Trust me. I have a plan.'

'And what's your plan?' I'd say in exasperation. 'Have you found the seven seers inside your head? Is that why you're suddenly so clever?'

Not another word could I get out of him. I had to trust him when he said he had a plan, and that was that. I feared he had no plan at all, that this was simply Mochta taking one more foolish risk that would bring danger to all three of us.

And then, one day, I realized what the plan must be, and I was furious. We were simply going to take the money and run. 'You great bosthoon!' I raged. 'You think America is so big we can hide in it? We're not thieves. And I'm not going to spend the rest of my life running from the law.'

I had got it all wrong, he said. Nobody would be running anywhere. 'Trust me, Dubhaltach. Just this once, trust your own brother.'

One Sunday, when he told me the clochan was nearing completion, I offered to help him and what a surprise I got. It was the most beautiful clochan I had ever seen. He'd built it with such perfection, such a grand choice of stones, that all the admiration I used to feel for him as a boy came rushing back. Only Mochta could have done this.

It was a glorious day, that last day we would spend together. It felt as though we were back in our own small world on the Blaskets, without anyone to tell us what to do or how to do it. We were two brothers, alone in the world, who loved each other. The clochan seemed to emit a spiritual interferingness into the air, like a veil of Blasket mist. We competed to find and lay the best stones we could. And although we did not talk much, there was an ease come between us that had been lacking these last few months. I felt ashamed of how I had blamed him for everything that had gone wrong, and I vowed I would find a way to make amends. All day long, the only noise in that little valley was the clinkity of stones and the occasional cries of wild geese that passed across the slit of prairie sky.

I reminded Mochta of how Old Conn would chant: 'The Fenians

of old sang hymns of praise when monks sat in their clochans.'
Probably, I should have told you this earlier. All the clochans on the
Island are ancient. That's why none of us had ever built one before.
Although we've turned them into sheep shelters and storehouses,
they used to have a higher purpose as temples where monks would
fast and pray on their way to the Blessed Isles.

'Old Conn said something else about them too,' said Mochta,
to my surprise. 'He who lays the crow stone shall be blessed in ways
miraculous, and his fortune assured forever.'

Indeed he did, I said, with a smile. Ah, if only I had known what
he meant.

The next Sunday, the clochan would be fired. Again, I asked Mochta
about his plan, and again he would say only that he had one and
I should not worry. And so did I let that jester pull the wool over
my eyes one last time. It has always been my failing, to be too 'easy
come, easy go'. When Oscar grew up he said he'd take a very different
path to mine and by God's bright sake he did, though he never visits
his father any more to tell him of the life he leads. How I wonder if
he thinks of me sometimes, and of his poor lost mother, and of his
Uncle Mochta too, for haven't we all had a hand in giving him his
start in America?

That final Saturday night, there was a mood in the camp like
on St Patrick's Day. When Mr Krumpacker rode off to his family
in Chicago, the same as every Saturday night, Mochta announced
that on the morrow he would fire a clochan to make sod for burning
in the hearth for Mr Krumpacker and everyone was invited. The
whiskey, as you can imagine, began to flow.

Begorra, you know how it is with the Irish at times like this.
We'll drink and dance until the knees collapse, and when the dapple
of the next day's dawn peeks into the sky we'll be found horizontal

somewhere or other on God's earth, crooning about the Old Country, weeping like babes. Mochta, for the first time since that day he stopped, was drinking with the rest of us and I couldn't blame him. I even began to believe, the more I drank, that the clochan might work. That's what a lush I'd become.

It was an early Fall day with only about an hour or so of daylight remaining as we gathered at the site. Oscar was whining. All day, without a break, he'd been pestering me about when we'd see his Uncle Mochta. It was beginning to get cool and a wind was pushing off the prairies, but I didn't notice these things because my throat was still well-wrapped in whiskey.

When Mr Krumpacker arrived on horseback, his buck-goat bush trimmed neat and wearing his best duds, we were already collected on the overlooking ridges. He was not pleased when he saw the crowd that had come to welcome him. And no wonder, from the way we clapped our hands and cheered. One other point he probably grasped was that although nobody was fighting, none of us could stand too prettily on our legs. And our singing was not in any tune a sober man would recognize.

What a mistake it had been to bring his wife and youngsters, even if his daughter didn't understand the shame of it. He seemed to have given her permission to crawl inside the entrance of the clochan to look at the *spezial* mix of soil and prairie grass piled up inside that would soon be turned into magic turf. And what a mistake to invite some friends, or maybe those were his investors? He looked around anxiously. Where on earth was Mucker?

Mr Krumpacker wasn't the only person worried about Mochta's whereabouts. When I had seen him in the morning, he was a shipwreck. But he promised me on the Virgin he wouldn't touch another drop till sunset. Then he disappeared again. Don't worry, Dubhaltach, the others told me when we set off from the camp. Mochta's gone ahead. But I had still not seen him.

When the little girl emerged from the clochan, she ran back towards Mr Krumpacker, wrinkling her nose and shouting. She didn't tell him it was very dark inside, or that it stank, as she might have done. She was screaming so loud we could all hear what was on her mind: 'A ghost, dada. There's a ghost in there.'

I should have thought about what she said and kept a close eye on Oscar, but I wasn't in my ordinary mind, and was no more steady on my feet than anyone else.

Mr Krumpacker began to shout. 'Mucker?' he cried out. 'Mucker?'

That was a signal for all of us to join in, and we were soon making a great hurly burly. 'Mucker!' we yelled, laughing ourselves to tears, as if it was the best joke we'd heard for years. Yerra, for my sins, I was a part of it. 'Mucker! Mucker! Mucker!'

I don't know when I first realized Oscar had disappeared. Did I turn to the side and see him gone? Or did I spot him only when he was already scrambling into the clochan? At any rate, I flung myself downhill as soon as I understood he wasn't there. I slipped and tumbled and went head over heels. When I righted myself, I saw him tugging at a massive pair of gray pantaloons I knew only too well. He was helping Mochta squeeze out of that little entrance to the clochan, backside first. As soon as I saw them I set off again, hurtling their way fast as I could. Once upright, my brother swayed and hoisted Oscar high onto his shoulders. The boy was gazing around with pride and happiness while Mochta waved. I was frantic, shouting at the top of my voice for the boy to be put down at once. But my words were drowned out by another round of cheering and applause. Next, Mochta was greeting Mr Krumpacker, and the daughter too, with a low bow that almost toppled the two of them, both him and my son.

'Ladies and Gentlemen,' he cried out in words that slurred. 'I shall now ...' He made five or six attempts to find the word he wanted, which was a complicated and slippery creature. I think it was 'inaugurate', or something of the kind. 'I shall now inaugurate the clochan.'

Somebody produced a burning torch and a cheer went up. He turned to wink at us, to make sure we were all watching, before plunging the fire into the hole out of which he had recently emerged. There was no turf in there, of course, for it wouldn't have caught and there'd have been no spectaculation. There was only some timber we had loaded inside the day before. The cheering grew louder. They were waiting for the flames to take hold.

And Mr Krumpacker? I have a picture of him in my mind, standing at a distance, trying to smile as though he hoped this was normal. But I don't know whether this was real, or whether it's only in my imagination. If it was real, I do know it was the last time I ever saw him.

Oscar — thank God — was standing back, no longer on his uncle's shoulders. I pulled him away to safety. And because I was so concerned for Oscar, I did not look to see where Mochta was. He had already clambered halfway up the outside wall of the clochan before I realized. That great oaf was using for steps the corbel stones that jutted out at *spezial* intervals. And what reason could there be, you'll ask, for him to climb up there?

He had not yet laid the crow stone.

The crow stone is the last piece to be set on top of a clochan. It is laid across the central hole above the highest circle and is no ordinary stone. It is the flattest, largest piece in a clochan, and the nearest to God. We believe it to be sacred. Mochta must have spent days searching for it, because I never saw one more perfectly round and smooth.

You might have expected to hear the crow stone had to be hauled to the top by two men and a donkey, using ropes and pulleys. But if that was in your imagination, I am a poor teller of tales because you still haven't understood the gigantic strength of my brother, even when he was awash with drink. That noble brute held the crow stone under one arm, easily as the likes of you probably carries a pile of books. All he had to do was drop it in place on the top and come back down the same way he'd gone up. In theory, God willing, it was still possible that nothing would go wrong. But he would have to be quick about it.

Perhaps if I had gone to reason with him, there would still have been enough time for him to jump away before it was too late. It's easy to know afterwards what you should have done at the time. Well, I didn't reason with him, did I?

There came a moment when even Oscar went quiet. Indeed, a stillness fell over the scene. The cheering and singing stopped. Everyone was staring at Mochta in amazement when they saw what he was doing. People were either rooted on top of the ridge, or staggering down to get a better look. My heart was gripped by a horrifying fear that we had already passed the tipping point and there was nothing to be done. For isn't this always the case, that when the celebrations have peaked we have to go down the other side and slide towards the wake, which is the final truth for all of us?

The timber inside the clochan had caught. Smoke was beginning to filter out of the ventilation holes. And at the very moment when he laid that crow stone on top of the clochan to cheers from every one of us ... yerra, at the very moment when the clochan reached completion ... at that same moment I realized what his plan had always been. He must have squirrelled away some of Mr Krumpacker's bad gunpowder. That's what he must have done.

Because the clochan exploded.

Black smoke smethered out of the ventilation holes and flames leaped through the hole where the crow stone should have been.

Mochta was changed out of recognition. Begorra, he was! And the reason he didn't look like you and me any more was because he was being swept up in the Great Master's final mystery. I'm certain of what I'm saying. I know I'd been too friendly with the bottle but a shock like this quickly sets you straight. Mochta glowed and shimmered. I could no longer see any brother of mine on top of the exploding clochan. What I saw was the flying eagle with six wings about him rising to the jasper stone of Heaven in the Book of Revelation, the same as the priest would read aloud to us in Lent in a voice of thunder, the words watering his eyes.

I gazed up at the bright, swirling colors of holy fire and vapor that were consuming him. In his new robes of sacred flames, Mochta stood astride the raging furnace, and a rainbow of violet and indigo, of emerald and jacinth, formed about his head and his face shone as if it were the sun, a thousand times more brilliant than the lonely rock of Teeraught, and his feet were pillars of fire, and he opened his mouth and roared like a lion and seven more explosions there came in answer, and when in time they passed we heard another voice that came from Heaven itself with orders that everything uttered should be sealed up for eternity and never written down.

Mary Mother! King of the Angels! God of the Miracles!

We dropped to our knees and prayed. Even the day's setting sun fell down dead in the little valley and bled all over the terrifying brightness of the clochan.

So be it, I am done. My tale about Mochta is over and the bottle is empty. You can put down what I've told you as you will, and I'll be none the wiser. But I tell you this. When brothers are torn apart, the one that's left behind has to go on alone and so it's been for me. I've spent half my life dragging the weight of the world behind me, for the loss of that great ruffian has never left me, nor will it ever, even if I live to be a hundred.

The money went into the bank in Oscar's name. I never dug another ditch in my life. It is almost like the old days, except that I'm on my own. And, believe me, no man was ever born to be that. I rise early in the mornings to fish, but I don't go on the spring tide to Inishvickillaun to hunt seals or drag my seine net for shoals around

Inishtooshkert. Instead, I paddle across the waters of Lake Michigan in search of brown trout and king salmon. And I think endlessly about what I drove my brother to do, and what it was for.

I know that if anything good ever comes out of this tragedy, it must come from Oscar.

You've not yet heard enough? You want me to speak of Oscar too? Then you'd better bring out another bottle, my friend, and hoist this old man on the pig's back because that's another bitter tale to tell.

1850

The Lobbyist

(Extract from *Chicago: An Alternative History 1800–1900* by Professor Milton Winship, University of Chicago, A.C. McClurg & Co., 1902)

As we continue our leisurely journey through the century, I suggest we slow down at the mid-point to consider how close Chicago came to being as unimportant as, say, Peoria. But how, I hear you ask, could Chicago have failed? Was its population not continuing to grow at an astonishing rate? Had the I&M Canal not opened at last, enabling ships to cross the continent from the Great Lakes to the Gulf of Mexico? Did Chicago not hold an unassailable position at the center of the continent's trade routes?

It might surprise the reader to know that the answer to that last question is 'no'. If we take high population growth as a measure of whether a town is thriving (and my favorite booster, Mr John S. Wright, always argued that we should) then it was no mean achievement for Chicago to have taken just half-a-century to develop from a handful of log cabins into a community of nearly thirty thousand souls. It wasn't, though, much of a place to look at, with its acres of cheap frame houses and muddy streets. Indeed, Chicago paled in comparison with St Louis, its much better established rival in the West, which eighty thousand people called home. And there were already six cities on the North American continent with populations of more than a hundred thousand: New York had in excess of half a million.

It is understandable, when you belong to a place, to imagine everyone else must consider it to be as important as you do. But the truth is that by mid-century, Chicago was just another rough little frontier town with its destiny as a great American city not even remotely in prospect, despite the exaggerated claims of its boosters. One thing, and only one thing, would change its fate forever.

Permit me one brief aside, to put this event in context. My fellow historians like to claim that 1848 was an *annus mirabilis* for the city. Now, I accept that we all — myself included — have a predilection for this kind of game. With the benefit of hindsight, we fiddle about with our material and look for patterns. I don't deny that in 1848, in addition to the opening of the I&M Canal, there were other important 'firsts': the telegraph line reached Chicago, the Chicago Board of Trade was established, the first cattle yard was built — a modest little place called the Bull's Head — and a rudimentary steam-powered grain elevator went into operation. It was also the year in which Chicago's first railroad opened, all eight miles of it. But if I were using hindsight to proposition an *annus mirabilis*, it would not be 1848. My choice would be the half-century mark — 1850. And this is the reason why.

We are going to position ourselves, like proverbial flies on a wall, inside the palatial North Side mansion of Mr William Ogden one bright afternoon in early April 1850.[1] Mr Ogden, who had served

---

1 I am indebted to Mr Quigg, secretary to Mr Ogden, for providing me with an excellent account of what took place that afternoon, to which I have occasionally added some informed guesswork.

as the first mayor of Chicago, was the richest and most influential businessman of his day. Now in his mid-forties, he was a fit, handsome fellow, dark-haired with two beetling eyebrows, a nose as sharp as a blade and a formidably solid jaw. He exuded confidence, intelligence and cunning. His agile mind, eloquent tongue and sophisticated manners were said to command everyone's respect.

Shortly after two o'clock that afternoon, Mr Ogden's secretary, Quigg, knocked on his master's second floor study door to announce the arrival of a visitor. Mr Ogden rose to his feet and tapped the embossed leather surface of his desk three times with the knuckles of his right hand. He had once explained to Quigg that he did this for luck. His father used to tap the kitchen table of their little Walton townhouse, once before opening a transaction and once after it closed. 'But my father, Quigg, was a poor businessman. So do you know what I do? I tap three times instead of once, and it has never let me down.'

Mr Ogden was already in the hallway by the time the front door was being opened.

'Welcome, John,' he said to his visitor. 'Come in, come in.'

The doorway was filled to its entirety by 'Long John' Wentworth, a man so tall he would always incline his head on entering a room, just in case. Though he was no stranger to the house, there were still moments when Quigg found himself taken aback by the man's stature. Indoors, he looked larger than ever, the archetypal giant of a fairytale, with his broad, rangy shoulders, his ruffled mane of hair, the sumptuous beard and sideburns, the florid hands that enveloped yours, the slouch hat wide as a wing chair and the vast black cloak that fell from his back like a theatre curtain.

On entering the vestibule, Long John paused to admire Mr Ogden's new painting, hung in pride of place on the right hand wall. 'Now I reckon this one must have been painted a few feet from where I'm standing,' he said. 'I recognize the humble lodgings, William, with those Corinthian columns and porticoes.'

Mr Ogden seemed surprised Long John had noticed, doubtless because that gentleman was better known for his boorish side than for his appreciation of fine art. Mr Ogden explained the scene. Set in England in the 18th century, *Lady Strafford's Vision* showed the Lady on horseback in front of her mansion.[2] 'Look at the quality of the color and brush strokes, the extraordinary crimson shade of her gown,' he said. 'And the flowerbeds are gloriously bright and detailed, all the way down to the ornamental lake.'

'And that's a shrine she's on her way to?'

'I'm not sure. I wonder whether it might be a hermitage.[3] I believe it was popular, in those days, for a big house to have a resident hermit.'

'Looks like that curious thing the Irish working on the canal built a couple of years ago. Then some drunken fool blew it up and killed himself, and they tried to turn him into a saint or a martyr or something. Dirty bog trotters, up to their usual barbarity.'

Mr Ogden was quick to change the subject. Quigg had noticed that his master's relationship with this particular acquaintance was regularly characterized by reticence, especially when Long John brought up the Irish and the punishment he would like to mete out to them. There were probably things Mr Ogden judged it better not to ask of Long John, so that he did not need to know.

'Walk around the painting,' he said. 'Observe Lady Strafford from different angles. See how the eyes never leave you.'

Long John did a turn. 'Darn it, you're right. You should be careful, William. Ain't good for a man's constitution, to be watched like that by his wife.'

As they climbed the stairs to the main reception room, he

---

2 The reader will remember that this painting had been a favorite of Chicago's founder, Pointe de Sable, and that he named his horse after Lady Strafford.

3 Pointe de Sable believed it to be an oracle. As mentioned on page 18, he believed Lady Strafford to be a worried lady. The times were changing, trouble lay ahead, and she wanted to find out from the oracle what would happen to her property, to her horses and her hunting dogs, to herself and to her family. Precisely the questions, of course, that Pointe de Sable was forced to ask himself.

explained how the painting had come into his possession. 'It was Quigg here who was responsible. Back in the summer, he brought to my attention a lengthy letter in our friend Mr Wright's *Prairie Farmer* journal ...'

'No doubt it was authored by him?'

'No, on this occasion it was a lengthy letter written by someone else. After much preamble, it transpired that it was advertising a sale by auction of paintings in St Charles, Missouri. There then followed descriptions of each piece. At the very end, the author mentioned that some of the works might once have had a connection with Chicago. I was due to be in the vicinity that day, so I decided to take a look. It was a very interesting collection.'

As they entered the salon, Mr Ogden told Quigg to prepare two whiskey juleps, indicating that he should put more whiskey in Long John's glass than his own.

'And is there a Chicago connection?' asked Long John.

'If so, it's a tenuous one. The auctioneer said he'd bought them in one lot from a lady who had inherited them from her grandfather, and the grandfather used to live in Chicago. But he had no idea who this grandfather was.'

They clinked glasses before sitting across from each other on the cushioned banquette that ran around the oval window overlooking the garden. Mr Ogden was fond of pointing out the features of his garden to visitors. It was a well known refrain of his that horticulture was a mark of refinement and Chicago needed a lot more of it. It was also his way to let visitors settle in and feel at home before he made his first move.

'The crocuses are out already. That bodes well for the summer.'

Long John grunted and brought out a pipe, which he began to fill with tobacco.

Mr Ogden persevered: 'You see those little blue and white flowers? Those are grape hyacinths. The first year I've tried them.' He told Long John it was important to plan gardens so that different parts were in bloom in different months, and he urged him to build a keeping house too. 'I can help you with seeds. Grow your own exotics. Grapes, apricots, oranges, figs.'

Long John, his vision doubtless impaired by his energetic production of tobacco smoke, said that if he ever planted a garden he would make sure to ask for advice. He took a long draught of whiskey julep.

Mr Ogden delayed no longer. 'I assume you saw John Wright's latest piece in the *Boston Courier*, advising Easterners to put their money in Western railroads?'

Long John swallowed hard before popping his eyes and mimicking John Wright's breathless way of speaking: 'Men of the East. Railroads are the path to Glory. Follow me to the Promised Land and make your fortune!' He shrugged, shaking his head. 'Yes,' he said. 'I saw it.'

'I grant Mr Wright can seem over-excited at times.'

'The man's a raving lunatic, William. Admit it.'

Mr Ogden admitted nothing. 'You concede, do you not, that thanks to the influence of his *Boston Courier* column there will soon be three times as many railroads running to New York and Boston than go to Philly and Baltimore?'

'Doesn't change my view that the man's touched. And he's a liability to anyone with whom he comes into contact. You never know what crazy scheme he'll come up with next. And as a businessman? Those Bronson lots!'[4] Long John guffawed, and the banquette shook. 'You know he already went under once, back in '37, and in my view it's only a matter of time before he does so again.'

---

4 In 1848, John Wright bought two properties from a Mr Bronson for a price of $82,000, said at the time to be more than double the rate he should have paid. They were considered foolish, improvident purchases. But a decade later, without even taking into account the value of the buildings or the substantial amounts of rental income he would have received, the land alone would be valued at $400,000. In other words, it would prove to have been an excellent investment.

Mr Ogden's demeanor, while his friend savaged their mutual acquaintance, did not betray his thoughts. He listened politely. He indicated that Quigg should refill Long John's empty glass. Then, rubbing his hands together (an indication that he was keen to move things along), Mr Ogden asked Long John what he thought the prospects were for Mr Douglas's Amendments.

Let us pause for a moment, because it is important to understand what Mr Ogden meant, when he referred to 'Mr Douglas's Amendments'. Mr Stephen Douglas represented Illinois in the U.S. Senate. At the time of this meeting in Mr Ogden's Chicago mansion, the contents of a Central Railroad Bill were being debated in far-off Washington. Included in this bill was the proposal that the Illinois Central Railroad should build their trunk line across the state from Galena to Cairo. If my readers have a map to hand, they will see what this meant. The line was to bypass Chicago, and favor the city's fiercest rival — St Louis. Enter, at this moment in the story, the amendments. Mr Douglas had proposed two changes. The first was that the national government should, for the first time in American history, cede public lands to the State to help fund the construction of the railroad, as it had been persuaded to do for the I&M Canal. The second was that a 'branch' line be built from Chicago to Centralia. Mr Douglas, Mr Ogden and Mr Wentworth were certain that, as long as this 'branch' line was built, the business they could bring to it would guarantee its future. The 'branch' would soon become the 'trunk'. That was why they had already purchased the land through which the 'branch' line would run.

Long John, on being asked by Mr Ogden about Mr Douglas's Amendments, shifted in his seat. He admitted that he was troubled.

Was it true, as he had heard, that some powerful voices in Washington were being raised against them?

Mr Ogden said that it was indeed true.

'In your opinion, the amendments won't be passed?'

'It seems unlikely.' He swirled the almost-untouched whiskey in his glass. 'I fear those gentlemen in St Louis must be rubbing their hands in glee.'

For a moment, Mr Ogden said nothing more. He let that message strike home. Long John's dislike for anything to do with St Louis was legendary. Together, in silence, they contemplated an exceedingly gloomy future.

Over by the drinks cabinet the silent Quigg was intrigued. He knew his master must be leading this conversation in a particular direction, but he had no idea where.

'I did have one thought,' said Mr Ogden quietly.

Long John raised his head. In his rueful visage were signs that hope had been rekindled. He inhaled a mighty lungful of smoke. 'I am all ears, William.'

'Shall we step back from our current difficulty, and consider how Chicago has addressed these kinds of challenges before? Take the canal. Of course, many of us were involved in backing the canal, but if we had to name one person who did far and away the most, would that not also be the same person who secured from Washington a land grant for the I&M Canal very similar to the one in the proposed amendments?'

Long John's face, in which hope had briefly flickered, returned not to its former crestfallen state, but to one of indignation. He tried to interrupt, but Mr Ogden begged that he hear him out. In his corner Quigg, once he had gotten over his surprise, began to worry that Mr Ogden might have overreached himself.

Long John would be silenced no longer. 'I'm sorry, William. You know I have the greatest respect for you. But I thought I had made it clear that I will never again have any dealings with that ... that ... with Mr Wright.' He swallowed back his drink in one.

'I understand. And, believe me, I share your concerns. But would you agree with me, that if we could find a way of keeping him at a distance — and I think dispatching him to Washington would achieve that for us — he would be ideally qualified for the task? Nobody — not you nor me, not even Stephen Douglas himself — has better contacts in Washington than John Wright. Can you imagine how it would discourage our brethren in St Louis if they heard he was at the Capitol, lobbying on our behalf?'

Throughout this encounter, Mr Ogden had remained courteous and reasonable. Long John was sulking. He stared out the window at the garden he did not want to look at earlier, he repeatedly cleared his throat, he sprayed tobacco on the floor as he refilled his pipe.

'Even if we did,' said Long John, 'and I'm not suggesting that we should, he would want his pound of flesh.' He looked with baleful eyes at his friend Mr Ogden. 'If you think, for one moment, that I'm going to let Mr Wright have a single square foot of my land ...'

'And what would you say,' asked Mr Ogden, 'if we could engage John Wright without paying him a penny?'

Long John bestowed on Mr Ogden a look of bewilderment, as he took delivery of a fresh glass of whiskey julep from Quigg. But before he could hear the details of Mr Ogden's extraordinary proposal, a carriage and horses came *clippety-clop* into the front yard. Moments later the bell downstairs went *ring-a-ling-ling*.

John Wright strode into the room like the embodiment of a strong west wind. He was a tall gentleman with striking blue eyes and curly hair that hair tonic, it seemed, could not tame. Though smartly dressed, there was an appealing air of homely dishevelment about him. His shoes were muddy, his pantaloons were creased and it looked as though he had spilled coffee on his shirt. These signs of wear and tear gave the impression of a man who had already done two dozen different things since rising from his bed that morning.

'What a magnificent house,' he said. 'And this room is the icing on the cake. This oval window reminds me ...' He recounted an anecdote about a window in the White House, at the same time as he greeted Long John with great cordiality. Long John did not budge from his banquette. 'Are those grape hyacinths, the little blue and white ones?' asked Mr Wright, looking out. Mr Ogden confirmed that they were. Long John scowled. 'We used to have them in the garden in Williamstown when I was a boy. But that's the first time I've seen any in the West.'

He would prefer coffee, he said, to whiskey, which was another thing that probably did nothing to endear him to Long John.

There was no doubting Mr Ogden's disapproval of the way in which Long John failed to return to Mr Wright the same courtesy that was extended to him. For his part, he made Mr Wright welcome, saying how grateful they both were that he had made the time to join them.

Long John, at this last comment, appeared to choke on his pipe smoke. He was presumably still roiled by the fact that Mr Ogden had forgotten to make mention of Mr Wright's visit beforehand.

The conversation that followed, though centered on Chicago's prospects, was steered away from the matter at hand by Mr Ogden. It was a discourse, reports Quigg, marked by flattery and cunning on the part of Mr Ogden, surliness on the part of Long John, and a refreshing candor and good humor on the part of John Wright. His ease and wit and cheerfulness had such an uplifting effect that there were moments when even Long John's ingrained hostility towards him appeared to founder.

But Mr Wright, it emerged, was also susceptible to Mr Ogden's flattery. In Quigg's dispassionate view, he was overly susceptible. He seemed dazzled by the splendor of Mr Ogden's mansion, and when he was invited to go upstairs to the observatory, he accepted with boyish enthusiasm. Perhaps this was where his charm lay, in the fact that he did not try to dissemble.

Long John declined the invitation to join them in the observatory. After pouring him another whiskey julep, Quigg was required to take more freshly brewed coffee to Mr Wright. A circular staircase led to the timber platform at the top, an area measuring about twenty-five square feet, on which there stood a table and two chairs. Both gentlemen, though, were on their feet near the railings when Quigg arrived. It was an unusually clear, still day. From here, one had an excellent view of the Lake, the port and the town. They were watching the arrival of a steamer whose smoke trail hugged the Lake's flat, silvery surface. Mr Wright held Mr Ogden's telescope to his eye.

'Judging from the numbers on deck,' said Mr Wright, 'I'd say that must be another hundred new arrivals.'

'You can see why I like to come up here, Mr Wright. The best measure of Chicago's growth has always been the number of ships coming into port —' Mr Ogden paused '— though I hope there might be a still better measure in the very near future.'

Mr Wright lowered the telescope. 'You are thinking of the canal?'

Mr Ogden shook his head. 'No, not the canal. Though I agree that will help.'

At this point, Quigg went back downstairs. He had forgotten to bring sugar for Mr Wright's coffee. By the time he returned, it was clear that Mr Ogden had made considerable headway.

They were still on their feet, looking towards the town's sprawl of dirt streets, ramshackle roofs and smoking chimneys. 'I agree with you, that we should congratulate ourselves on how far we have come so quickly. But we must also be honest. If the railroad does not come to Chicago ...' Mr Ogden did not finish the sentence. He turned to

Mr Wright, placing a hand on his wrist. 'You understand what I am saying, John?'

Mr Wright seemed to like that familiar form of address. He said he understood, that of course he understood. 'We can and must be so much more than this.'

Mr Ogden smiled in a way that Quigg recognized. It meant he knew he was succeeding. 'There is only one person in Chicago who can take us from here ...' With his hands he described first a small circle, then a much larger circle. '... to here.' He paused, clearing his throat with an admirable show of emotion. 'I realize the immense personal sacrifice this will entail, John. Rest assured that I would not ask this of you, were you not my only hope. That is why I am beseeching you to join the cause. Without you, believe me, we are lost.' Previously, Quigg had seen Mr Ogden use all manner of persuasive tactics, but had never witnessed such a personal appeal as this. 'Will you do this for me, John? Will you take up the fight? Will you transform the town we love into something magnificent? Will you make me a city?'

When they came down from the observatory, Mr Ogden and Mr Wright were in high spirits. They joined Long John on the banquette. Mr Ogden tapped the seat three times with the knuckles of his right hand.

'I am deeply touched by your faith in me, gentlemen,' said Mr Wright. 'I give you my word that I shall not return from Washington until the President has signed the amendments into law.'

Long John stared at Mr Ogden.

'Chicago will owe you an incalculable debt,' said Mr Ogden, finally drinking his whiskey julep. 'And although it is a noble gesture on your part, to say that the signed amendments will be the best possible compensation you could receive, Long John has suggested another small way in which we might show you our gratitude, and I am in full agreement with him.'

Long John did not look as though he had suggested anything.

Mr Ogden smiled. 'Shall we go downstairs?'

The three men stood in front of the painting of *Lady Strafford's Vision*. The idea had come to Mr Ogden when he heard that Mr Wright had bought his wife — an Eastern belle said to be considerably above his station in life — the most expensive Arabian mare ever sold in Chicago.

'George Healy will be coming to stay with us next week,' said Mr Ogden.

'You mean G.P.A. Healy?' asked Mr Wright. 'The portrait painter?'

Mr Ogden nodded. 'You've heard of him?'

'Of course. You must be delighted. If one of the greatest painters in America can find time to come to Chicago, we can surely bring a railroad here too. Will he be painting a portrait of Chicago's first mayor? And of course ...' he turned to Long John, '... of our esteemed congressman?'

Mr Ogden smiled at Long John who, this time, did his best to smile back.

'We shall have to see. More importantly, we were hoping you might allow us to commission a portrait of your wife as a small gesture of our appreciation, indeed of Chicago's appreciation too, assuming that your wife were also agreeable to the notion? I thought the portrait might be modeled on this painting of Lady Strafford? Although Mr Healy is noted for his portraits, I hope he might also be persuaded on this occasion to include your wife's fine Arabian mare.'

Mr Ogden indicated to Long John, with a look, that he would take care of Mr Healy's remuneration.

And on that happy note, Quigg records, the afternoon's meeting came to a close. Mr Ogden had got his way and Long John was mollified because it would cost him nothing and require no contact or association with Mr Wright. In a day or two, John Wright would board a steamer to begin the first leg of his journey to Washington. He would spend five months there, advising, cajoling and promoting the urgent need for that 'branch' line to Chicago. Finally, on September 20, 1850, he would be able to send a telegraph to Mr Ogden in Chicago reporting that President Millard Fillmore had signed the Central Railroad Bill, including those two amendments, into law.

I puzzle over what to make of Mr Wright. Often depicted as an overly ambitious businessman, this affair shows him prepared to work on behalf of the city. He comes off well when compared with those two titans of industry, Messrs Ogden and Wentworth, who decided that a pat on the back and a portrait of his wife by G.P.A. Healy would be sufficient compensation for bringing the Illinois Central Railroad to Chicago.

Mrs Wright was said to have been delighted with her portrait, despite some minor disagreement with the artist over her decision to wear headgear that looked more like a helmet than a riding hat, in what appeared to be an attempt to mimic a Greek goddess. We have no record of Mr Wright's opinion.

1851

Truth Facts

(Excerpt taken from *Reminiscences of Early Chicago*, A.C. McClurg & Co., 1898).

THE DIARY OF HANNAH (ANTJE) VAN VOORHIS

Since a few days I decide to keep a diary. The first thing to put in my diary is the true story I wrote for Miss Trumbull about the school visit to the Indian camp.

She said the story was wrong and did not give it back to me. I was rather flabergasted because I do not think my story had very greivous mistakes.

Even Karin stopped walking home with me after that and this was very sad. Karin is my best friend. We have done many things together, like the hooping cough and toothache.

I am not popular with Miss Trumbull. I asked her if everything we learned in history was true or made up presumpsushly the same as poetry. History is truth facts she said with her nose in the air and nothing else but truth facts.

Because I am rather curius by nature I asked Miss Trumbull who keeps all the truth facts because I cannot comprihend how one person can know everything since Adam and Eve.

My father and my mother (step) often argue horsely about what happened or did not happen. Maybe one of them is right and the other is making up the past presumpsushly. But if they are both mistaken, where is the truth fact now? This is the big ridle my story will solve.

I should think up some more to say for my diary so that when I am grown up it will be nice to read again if I am in a remembering mood.

I am eleven years old and this is the first year of the second half of the nineteenth century. My name is Hannah Birgit Van Voorhis and it is not a bad name but my father calls me Antje which is Dutch for little Hannah and I like that more.

My mother is not my real mother but a step. My real mother was also called Hannah Birgit Van Voorhis but she passed away in New York when I was two years old before I remember anything.

I am still dispressed about that. I think everyone should be allowed to remember her real mother. In the portrait she looks very beautiful. Her name is the only relick I have inherited because I am not particulerly beautiful. My ears stick out and I have freckles on my nose.

My father is called Isaac Van Voorhis and he is a doctor the same as his father was a doctor the one that died in the Revolushunry War. We risided in New York until I was eight years old and then we moved to Chicago. I never saw my grandmother (fathers mother). My father says she is too exentrick.

I think exentrick people are interesting and they are trajic as well even if not always. I have met a lot of exentricks since we came to Chicago like Mrs Daly who only has one lung and lives on sugar and cabbage and sings even during the sermon which keeps me awake. Karin sits in the same row and we conduct

Mrs Daly with our fingers and when she sees us, she gives a dainty smile.

Then there is Mr Church who never goes to it and he swears in a snappy tone at his oxen and wears a black patch over one eye and a yellow straw hat on his head like a basin tipped on its side. Karin and me always run past his house.

But after Miss Trumbull did not care greatly for my true story I went home on my own and this time when Mr Church called me for a bevrage I went for a stop. I was so heart broken it did not matter if I died now though it was dispressing not to have time to bid a fond farewell to my father and my brothers (own) and sister (own).

But Mr Church did not slay me. He gave me a sweet lemony drink and when I enquired him about the black patch over his eye he laughed which he never did before. His eye had a very serius tussel with a meat hook at the factory he said. I said I was sorry about the tussel but he said I was not to greive too much because the other eye worked.

Suddenly I had one of my ideas that seems less clever after I say it. Maybe he could get another eye because our Natural Science teacher Mr Raven brung into class the eye of an ox one day and he cut it in pieces and showed us it was the same with our eyes. Mr Church laughed again when I said that and told me to come back again for a sweet lemony drink because he liked me. But I do not think I care to.

I have introduced Miss Daly and Mr Church as the prologue in my diary because the ancient Indian Majic Man is the most superior exentrick I ever saw. I cannot think of anything more to write about myself so I will now record for posterity the true story Miss Trumbull said was wrong.

'True Story About an Ancient Majic Man in an Indian Camp' by Hannah (Antje) Van Voorhis
Wednesday April 16, 1851

I had never espide real Indians before so I was rather exhilerated to be going to the camp. Our convayance was a prairie skooner and in our party was 17 young ladies (school girls) and 3 teachers escorted by two (2) sentries with guns.

Miss Trumbull said we would spectate a special Indian Dance for Spring. I asked if the Spring Dance was like the Dance of Departure she told us in our history lesson when the Indians left Chicago many years ago.

The Dance of Departure was dispressive, she said, but the Spring Dance is happy because of new crops. Is it always sad to leave I asked. She said it was. I said I think it must depend on what you are leaving and where you are going. Suddenly Miss Trumbull looked purplexed.

Our skooner sped speedily past the Lake which was shining green with purple ripples. I asked Miss Trumbull why the color always changed but she got on her high horse and told me to resist from any more questions. She is not very geniul to me. I whispered to Karin that I thought the color changes because there is a majic man living under the lake.

Karin and me were still best friends so we made up stories presumpsushly about the majic man all the way to the Indian camp. When we saw smoke messages in the sky we cleverly decifered what they said. And our majic man made birds wear hats and run on four legs and grasshoppers sing and flies stop buzzing and mosquitoes stop biting.

Suddenly the great moment had arrived and we were jumping actively out of the convayance in front of the Camp. The mist was oozing from the ground but the heaven above was blue. We held hands, two by two, as we walked towards the Camp. I never did see such strange homes in all my born days.

They are portly rectangles in shape with walls made from poles covered in bark. The roofs are very high and airy. Inside the house there are pots and baskets and mats on the floor. Maybe the mats were majic. Maybe tomorrow the Indians would fly away forever. And that made me sad to think about. Maybe I will also fly away forever one day but I hope not.

The Indian ladies are called <u>squaws</u> and some had babes tied to their backs or little ones at their feet and they were sweeping daintily or making baskets. The men were ancient with red eyes and blankits around their shoulders, playing with beads and smoking.

Everyone in Indian camps moves like the tortus while everyone in Chicago runs like the hair. In the story the tortus beat the hair but I do not remember why. Only the other Indians (not ancient) did not move like tortuses. They were racing gallantly on their horses.

While we were strolling geniully two lady squaws hailed each other in high voices and Miss Trumbull said this was rude. I enquired her why it was rude because ladies and gentlemen in Chicago shout the same way too. Miss Trumbull did not care for my question. She did not reply, and gave me a speaking look instead.

The squaws were admiring us politerly and making us welcome and come here into my house please miss. But Miss Trumbull told us to stay close and hold hands until we reached the prayed ground for the Spring Dance.

I got lost from Karin and the other 15 young ladies (school girls) when we had to duck our heads and pass between some dripping blankits hung on trees. I do not know why Miss

Trumbull took us that way but there were too many blankits and it was like amaze.

I stopped holding Karin's hand and maybe I doordled and that was when a vishus dog came barking at me so I dashed away in terror with the wild beast biting at my heels.

When I was almost out of breth the dog collapsed on its paws near a portly house where an old lady squaw was cooking in a big black pot. Her face was brown and creasy and she waved with her hand saying to please come to eat with me miss.

I said yes thank you because since breakfast was a long time and I felt hungry. The old lady squaw stirred inside the pot with a long wooden spoon. The broth purspired actively. I sat next to her on her mat and another dog (friendly) came to sniff and put his head on my knee.

Take your seats please, ladies and gentlemen. Lend me your ears. Because suddenly the great moment of my story has arrived.

The old lady called like a bird and momently from the darkness of the house an old man strolled out even slower than a tortus. He was top sized and straight and his chest was shiny. I knew immediatly he was a majic man even though I had never espide one before.

His skin was very dark and silky. He held one hand at his heart and in the other was a fur bag with his spells inside. He oozed goose grease and fish oil. I counted the lines of red paint across the tops of his cheeks (five) and purple (three).

His gray hair was playted down to his shoulders and deckerated with a silver fether. He was as ancient as my grandfather if he did not die in the Revolushunry war and the most beautiful ancient majic man I ever saw and better than a picture in a book.

And he had the trajicest face I ever saw. The cheeks were like old leather and bended in where tears had run like a waterfall

173

to make them smooth. His mistick eyes were orange brown like leaves in the fall.

He bestrode his hand on my head and made a spell, speaking the majic words very perlitely in a deep voice. I was not scared because his hand was warm and it sounded like a good spell. Then the majic man lowered himself in a seemly manner to the ground and laid his legs out flat beneath him like a pancake. There was no doubt he was the correct article.

Suddenly he began to speak to me in quear English. I was very purplexed at first because I did not expect this. He enquired me my name and where I came from and who was my father. So I told him everything and then I asked him questions too.

Why did they live in a camp with portly houses that can blow away? Where did he come from in the beginning? Where was he going tomorrow? Why were white people and Indians not friends? And why did Indians not have their own land like white people?

He watched me in a gallant way but did not speak a word. He lapped up the soup in the bowl and I was perterbed he might be angry.

The soup was bitter (sour) with hard pieces (meat) but the old lady squaw was smiling. She showed me how to soak flat bread in the soup until it became soft with only pips left.

The ancient majic man finished eating and began to make a spell in a rarther pious way with one hand at the heart. I knew it was a spell because it was very long and musikle and never even braked for breth. I shut my eyes and when the spell was finished I opened them again and the majic man looked even more top sized and shinier than before.

While his eyes were spectating the sky he spoke again in his quear English. Those eyes were teliskopes and his voice was like a river running from the highest mountain.

This is exactly what he said in his superior way the best I can remember. <u>The Great Spirit has brung little Antje from Chicago. She has asked me about the white mans land and the land of our fathers. This I say in answer. The Great Spirit gives the land to all his children.</u>

I asked him to repeat that please nobull sir because I had never heard anything so beautiful. <u>The Great Spirit gives the land to all his children</u> he repeated. <u>The Great Spirit gave them the land to share together geniully for growing corn and for hunting and for living on and for dying on when their last breth comes.</u>

It was a long speech. I cannot remember the words exactly so I will not underline them but I promise they are true. This next part is the most greivous that did bring my tears streaming.

The white people came from across the seas and because they were visiters from a far place we perlitely said welcome. But then the white people made dainty picture maps of the land given by the Great Spirit and divided it into pieces and said they wanted to perchorse this part and that part and all the parts.

Our people had never seen picture maps before or played this perchorse game. The white men gave our people whiskey and said they were our friends. And then they said with their noses in the air that we lost the game with picture maps and must leave the land and go away forever.

When the majic man stopped the speech and my tears were streaming I said I would tell our history teacher Miss Trumbull immediatly what trick was played on his fathers because it must have happened since a long time and that was why nobody told her.

Suddenly a shiver flustered down my spine. I realized like a flash that I had found the answer to the big ridle. <u>History was since a long time and very mistick.</u> That was why Miss Trumbull did not care for my question if history was like poetry. Because she already knew the truth that only majic men could see all the truth facts from the days of Adam and Eve.

It must be trajic to know everything that ever happened and that is why I hearby declare the majic man a superior exentrick to the one lung Mrs Daly or one eyed Mr Church. I was greatly oared by this news and wanted to tell Miss Trumbull at once.

The ancient majic man said one more quear thing. He said I am fortunate that the Great Spirit has sent little Antje from Chicago because she gives me hope. I said please nobull sir explain yourself. Not hope for myself he said because in a few moons I shall follow my fathers to the shades but hope for the land.

I was still purplexed because I did not know how to give hope to the land so I asked the ancient majic man please to make a spell on me so I could understand. He bestrode one hand on my head and waved his fur bag in the pious manner and the spell was long and musikle with no brakes for breth and I knew in my heart that its power would preside in me forever.

Suddenly the 16 young ladies (school girls) were there and I was in very greivous trouble with Miss Trumbull because I did not go to the prayed ground for the Spring Dance.

When I told her perlitely that the ancient majic man was the best historian because he knew all the truth facts from the days of Adam and Eve she mountered her high horse. She did not care to listen but gave me a speaking look.

I turned around to bid a fond farewell to the ancient majic man and was dispressed to see he had already flied away forever.

1852

The Automaton

John pulls the bell chord. A few moments later, there is a knock at the door and his manservant sets a basin of warm water on the stand.

'Good morning, sir.'

John has drawn back the curtain and is opening the window.

'It certainly is, Seamus. Another splendid day. I shall take coffee with my mother.'

He leans out the window. The sky is the deepest early morning blue. A ship's horn blows in the distance, while a carriage passes by below. Wabash Avenue is still quiet, with only a few people about, the road deserted but for the four or five broughams drawn up, each one waiting outside one or other of the identical three-storey brownstone buildings that line the street. He likes being high up, on the third floor, from where he has sight of the Lake. He can often see ships pass by, masts glinting as they come in and out of view.

He takes a deep breath. The early morning air is pleasantly cool, though already soured by wood smoke and horse dung and the swampy fetid aroma that periodically comes off the Lake. It could be worse, he thinks. Indeed, later on in the day he knows it will be worse when the temperature rises and the colourless miasma from the stockyards starts wafting across, just as he also knows that Kitty will find an opportunity to bring this fact to his attention. But consider what a fine house we have on what a fine street, he hears himself argue. To which she will reply, with hauteur, that Chicago is hardly Virginia, and that Number 36, Wabash Avenue is not, absolutely not, the family mansion at Blakeley.

He sighs with a sense of defiant pride. Making a city is not a genteel process, Kitty, he would like to say. Chicago will sometimes forget its manners. If the beginning has been a little unruly and boisterous, we should not be surprised. Because unlike you, Kitty, I did not grow up in one of the most privileged households in the land. Unlike you, I did not consort with presidents and senators at Mount Vernon as a child. Unlike you, I do not describe the soldier Mr Robert E. Lee from Arlington as my 'uncle'. Number 36, Wabash Avenue may not be Blakeley, but for Chicago we could not do much better.

Enough of such thoughts. He washes, dresses quickly and goes down to the second floor where he creeps past the children's room and taps gently on his mother's door. He enters without waiting for a response. She is always up early too. But this morning, to his surprise, he finds her still at prayers. She is kneeling beside her bed, hands clasped together, eyes closed, lips moving.

He waits until she has finished. After his own bedroom, this is his favourite place in the house. Everything speaks of who his mother is. The room is always brightly lit and discreetly scented with a violet fragrance. On top of her bookshelf are her teaching books. Next comes her collection of Greek and Latin classics and English literature. On the bottom shelf are a mixture of more modern texts about politics. On the pine bulletin board that hangs above the bookshelf she has pinned clever or amusing notes from past pupils. The old kitchen table that followed them from Sheffield to Williamstown to Chicago has become her desk. That was where he used to do his homework. The wood is cracked and warped in places, and he recognises some of the ink stains as old friends. The desk is tidy. Her Bible lies in the middle.

Pen, ink and blotter have been wiped clean. Her diary is closed. Above the desk hangs a portrait of his father Deacon Wright, looking stern and inscrutable. And on the wall opposite is her picture of Christ driving out the moneychangers from the Temple, entitled: 'My House Shall be Called the House of Prayer.'

She says 'amen' aloud and rises to her feet. He steps across to kiss her. 'Extra prayers for someone today, *Mater*?'

'Yes,' she says, with a smile. 'For my eldest son.'

'Even though your eldest son is the one you don't need to worry about?' How often has he had to rescue one or other of his younger brothers? 'Have you slept well?'

'Thank you.'

She looks, though, wan this morning. The light shows up her wrinkles and blotchy hands. Only at odd moments like this does he remember she is growing old. She remains so active. She is still teaching at the State Road school ('Behind my back they call me Beaky, the little imps'), she is still a member of all kinds of associations and societies, she still insists on walking everywhere she can. But she is sixty-six years old. The doctor has told her to slow down and do less or she risks having another of those fainting attacks. And the next time it could be more serious, he warned. Not for the first time John vows to speak to her about this.

There is a knock at the door and Seamus brings in the coffee. Its scent gives John almost as much pleasure as the taste. If he has any weakness, or addiction, it is for good coffee. Seamus pours a cup for them both and adds sugar for John.

'Will you be taking breakfast with Mrs Wright this morning, sir?'

Seamus means Kitty. John tells him he will not be taking breakfast at all.

He puts the saucer aside and takes short, rapid sips from the cup. Kitty hates it when she catches him doing that, and says it is bad manners. He likes to drink his coffee hot and fast.

'I was hoping you might have a chance to talk to Kitty before you left this morning,' says his mother.

'I'm afraid I have an early appointment. That's why I don't have time for breakfast.'

'I see.'

'I have,' he insists.

'I'm sorry to say this, John, but I do think you should put your foot down this time.'

'Very well. I shall talk to her again tonight. But you know how she is. I don't think ...' His voice tails off.

Kitty is due to depart tomorrow for Virginia. Augustine, poor Walter (deceased) and Maria were all born there, and Kitty sees no reason why their next child should not have the same 'advantage'. When he tried to persuade her to stay this time in Chicago, she reeled off the same reasons as before. In Virginia, she is assured of the best doctor and the best care, the air is more healthful, the climate is more temperate, levels of cleanliness and hygiene are vastly superior, there is less risk of infection etc. etc. And you can sneer at Chicago from over there, he thinks, far away from your husband and mother-in-law.

He claps his hands and smiles. 'Anyway, *Mater*, listen to this. My appointment is about a most intriguing new business proposal.'

'But I thought you already had a new business.'

'The wool company is hardly new.'

'Six months is not new?'

'It's already doing very well and amounts to little more than managing a warehouse. This new proposition is very different indeed. It's about making something useful.' His mother has always chided him for not doing enough serious 'useful' things ('In the final analysis buying and selling real estate is nothing but gambling, John. It's un-Christian.').

'I worry when you take on too much,' she says. 'You know what can happen.'

'I learned my lessons the hard way, *Mater.*'

She nods. 'But don't forget that other people get hurt too.'

'That's a long time ago.' His mother never lets him forget that when he went bankrupt in the crash of '37, the people he employed lost their jobs too. 'This business proposal is based on what sounds like a very clever invention,' he says.

His mother sits up straight. She peers at him over the rim of her cup. 'Is it another machine?' she asks suspiciously.

'This won't be like the last one, I promise,' he says. 'I'll tell you about it tonight, when I know more.'

He lost over $10,000 on the failed bread-making enterprise and she has still not forgiven him. John loves and admires his mother, but the older she gets the more conservative she becomes. She has a particular aversion to machines that take over what she believes we should do ourselves. 'Making bread is a human ritual,' she argues, 'and once machines start taking over our rituals, what do we have left?'

'Whatever you do,' his mother says, 'don't rush into anything. Your father always believed in thinking things through first.'

John knows he has a tendency to be impulsive, but his instincts are usually right. His father's problem was the opposite. He thought things through for so long, he never did anything.

He kisses her again and wishes her a good day.

'You won't forget about Kitty?'

'I'll do my best.'

'You know I try not to interfere. But I do feel that just this once it's important.'

He pauses at the door when he hears the strain in her voice. He comes halfway back towards her. 'I love you, *Mater*, you do know that, don't you?'

She sighs. 'Of course I do, John.'

———

181

Outside, he jumps into the waiting brougham and tells his driver to make haste for the intersection of Washington and State Road, where he has agreed to meet Mr Albert Sage. He adjusts his topper and sits back. His earlier excitement about the day ahead, dampened because he had let his mother ask the wrong questions, returns with a vengeance. How he loves the city in the early morning, with its noises and smells and never-ending activity.

At this very moment, there will be the scramble of steamers, scows and clippers at the docks fighting for space with the fishing boats as they slap down their catches on the pier. He can as good as hear the yells and whistles, the thump of grounded cargo and the squeal of straining ropes, smell the addled sweat of the Irish and Negro dockers, their shirts plastered to their backs as they haul the cargo ashore without pause, cursing life and their lot and America.

They will already be offloading lumber, wheat, wool, cement, sugar, salt, crates packed with fine pieces of china, sack-wrapped rosewood and mahogany furniture with marble table-tops and turned bedposts, huge rolls of carpeting and Persian rugs carried ashore like logs on the shoulder, cartons loaded with finely crafted boots and shoes and fashionable clothing imported from the East. Into the warehouses they'll be going — the warehouses that make up the frontage where there is not an inch of space to spare between each unit (he should know — three of them are his). What better sign of progress is there, than the range and quantity of goods now needed to satisfy the citizens of Chicago?

Over on the canal, ships and barges will be arriving, pulled by teams of mules on the towpath, their holds heaving with all manner of fabric and foodstuffs, with molasses, cocoa, spices and tropical fruit that have travelled from across the Caribbean sea. And most important of all, just a few blocks away on La Salle Street, a locomotive would shortly leave for Joliet. When the line is completed it will, like the canal, connect Chicago to the Mississippi. And in the other direction, trains will soon be running from Chicago to Boston and New York. Every train that comes from the East will end up in Chicago, and every train that comes from the North and South and West will also end up in Chicago. Chicago will be the beginning and the end of every railroad line in America. And all because of a certain 'branch' line.

The brougham pulls up at the intersection of Washington and State. These are extraordinary times, he thinks. Wonders never cease. If the invention described to him last night by Mr Sage performs as promised, it will change the life of farmers all over the world. And he, John S. Wright, will make that happen.

The man in question is waiting at the corner. Mr Sage is a short, stocky gentleman, with stooping shoulders and washy eyes and a thick half-moon droop of a moustache that is bristling, this morning, with breakfast grease and crumbs. John does not know him well, only that he owns a reputable hardware store on Madison from which John has, in the past, bought building materials. He is reliable, honest and, frankly, a bit dull. Their conversations have always been confined to general business affairs. It was therefore a surprise when Mr Sage's presence was announced at his home the previous evening. The poor man had been in quite a fluster, apologetic for having called on Mr Wright like this but he hoped he would not consider it an impertinence etc. etc.

Mr Sage steps up into the carriage and removes his hat; John latches the door shut.

'And Mr Atkins' address, Mr Sage?'

Mr Sage gives a number on Kinzie Street, the driver goads the horse and they rattle off and turn onto Lake Street, which might be a mistake because the morning traffic is already considerable. They are soon weaving their way through the flow of carriages and carts. Stores are opening. Awnings are coming down, doors are being unlocked, signs are going up in shop windows, paper boys are yelling at the tops of their voices. He likes the noise and the traffic, and watching people rushing here and there. The sidewalks are thronged with labourers in scuffed clothes and flat caps on their way to work.

John stops the carriage outside a bakery and buys two doughnuts, one for each of them. Hopping back in, he eats fast. He must have been hungry. As he dusts the crumbs off his coat, he remarks to Mr Sage that he first came to Chicago about twenty years ago. 'There was one inn, about a dozen stores, and a few hundred people.' He gestures outside. 'And look at it now. We haven't done badly, have we?'

Mr Sage agrees they have not.

'Now tell me, Mr Sage, how did you become acquainted with Mr Jearum Atkins.'

Mr Sage is not much of a talker. He explains that they both grew up in Vermont, and have known each other since childhood.

'And you say you are his assistant?'

'I help him make models of his designs. Only in my spare time, of course.' He clears his throat. 'There is one other matter I should warn you about, Mr Wright, that perhaps I should have mentioned last night. Mr Atkins is confined to his bed.'

'You mean he is ill?'

'No, sir. Mr Atkins has to lie on his back.'

'He has had an accident?'

'Yes, sir. About ten years ago.'

'You mean he's been lying on his back for ten years?'

'Yes, Mr Wright.'

'Then how on earth could he have invented anything?'

'He invents in his head, sir.'

They pull up outside a dilapidated-looking one-storey frame house on Kinzie Street. John is an optimist. But he also knows himself well enough to realise that this would not be the first time he has misjudged a man's character. Mr Sage has always struck him as polite and sensible. Now, as he adjusts his topper and straightens his coat, as he picks his way through a scrabble of hens pecking at potato peelings in the front yard, he feels the stirrings of disappointment. Some things sound too good to be true precisely because they are too good to be true. He can imagine his mother's face, were he to admit this to her, the sense that she could have told him so.

As Mr Sage makes for the front door, a goose comes hurtling around from the back of the house, squawking and flapping. It goes straight for his legs and he freezes, cowering against the door. 'Sir?' He looks imploringly at John.

John drives the goose away with his cane. He should leave at once. He has a dozen better things he could be doing.

'Thank you,' says Mr Sage. 'I have never been at ease with geese.'

The door opens. An attractive young lady stands there, dressed in a green silk pelisse with a matching bonnet that barely holds in her luxuriant dark curls. From her attire, she is a lady who looks more suited to the Exchange Coffee House on Wabash Avenue than this modest dwelling on Kinzie Street.

Mr Sage introduces him. John tips his hat. 'May I present Miss Aureka Atkins,' says Mr Sage. 'She is a cousin of Mr Jearum Atkins.'

With lowered eyes, she addresses him. 'I do apologise for the goose, sir. As Mr Sage knows, I have tried and failed to teach him good manners.'

John smiles. This visit might be a waste of time, but Mr Atkin's cousin is a charming surprise. 'It would be no small achievement if you could. You look as though you are leaving, Miss Atkins,' he says.

'No, no, sir,' she says, colouring slightly. 'You are most welcome. Please come in.'

He removes his hat as she leads them into a small, dark kitchen with two doors leading off it, both of which are closed. There is an earthen water pot in the corner, some embers on the hearth, a blackened kettle sitting lopsided on top. A pile of logs is stacked to the side. Peeled potatoes lie in a basin of water. The room is stuffy, and smells of smoke and cabbage. Beside a shuttered window two upright chairs are pushed beneath a small table. It is dismal. The most noteworthy item in the room — and it looks out of place — is a handsome chamber set with a blue porcelain basin for washing.

'I'm sorry, sir,' says Miss Atkins, 'I was not expecting visitors.'

John tells her there is nothing to apologise for, and remarks on the basin. 'I have one identical to that at home. It is very pretty.'

She holds her arms down in front of her, fingers intertwined. 'Thank you, sir.'

Someone shouts from behind a closed door. 'Who is it?'

Miss Atkins answers. 'Mr Sage, mother.'

'Coming for breakfast now as well, is he?'

There is a moment's awkward silence. John wonders whether this is a second misjudgment of Mr Sage. Is he also the kind of man who exploits another's hospitality? Mr Sage looks embarrassed, as does Miss Atkins. She taps on the other door and pushes it ajar. 'You have visitors,' she calls out.

'I'm busy. Tell them to come back later.'

'I think it would be better,' John tells Mr Sage, 'if we returned another time.'

'It's Mr Sage,' Miss Atkins explains through the door, 'and a gentleman.'

'Albert? Why didn't you say so? Tell him to come in.'

John, following Mr Sage inside, looks around the room in astonishment. He has never been anywhere like it. True, there are some familiar enough features. There are items of furniture: a bed with a big board table beside it, a couple of upright chairs and what might be a chest of drawers, over which a large horsehair blanket has been thrown. An open window looks out onto the street, but the room is still smelly and airless. He catches an unpleasant whiff from the chamber pot. But that is where the resemblance to any ordinary room ends.

The walls and the ceiling are covered by drawing paper. All the pieces pinned up are perfectly aligned. On every sheet is a geometrical design, many with symbols and sums and numbers at the bottom. They are drawn in pencil, their subject matter ranging from the most futuristic-looking machines with arms or wheels and even wings, to simpler diagrams that show only a section of something, a valve, a mechanical joint, the arch of a building. Dotted around the room, like sculptures on show in a museum, are half-a-dozen wooden models of strange contraptions. At first glance, John has no idea what any of them are supposed to be. Arranged on the table beside the bed are some tools — a file, a hammer, a chisel — and a pile of timber offcuts. Residing at the centre of it all, propped up on pillows and lying on his back in bed, is Mr Jearum Atkins. He is a severe, pale-looking gentleman with frizzy ginger hair, a straggly beard and, if John had to guess at his age, he'd say he was probably, like him, in his late thirties. He is writing with his left hand on a large sheet of paper pinned to a board propped on a stand that, rather ingeniously, leans over him.

'I'd like to introduce,' says Mr Sage, 'Mr John S. Wright.'

Mr Atkins tilts his head towards John. His gaze is intent, and his voice sounds strange. It takes John a few moments to realise that he uses almost no intonation. His speech is flat and expressionless. 'Who is he again?'

'Mr John S. Wright,' repeats Mr Sage.

John steps forward and, awkwardly, shakes his hand. He says he is delighted to meet Mr Atkins and what marvellous creations these are. He gestures around the room.

Mr Atkins' eyes narrow. 'You know about mechanical things, Mr Wright?'

'I am not myself an engineer,' he admits, 'but I know men who are. I own a factory that manufactures the Hussey reaper.'

'You own a factory,' he says, 'but you don't understand how its products are made?'

'Naturally, I have a broad understanding but my point is that I am not, by training, an engineer.'

'Then may I ask what you have trained in, Mr Wright?'

Mr Sage intervenes. 'Mr Wright's Hussey reaper competes with the McCormick.'

'That's correct,' says John, exchanging a glance with Mr Sage. 'We compete very hard with him.'

'Remember how Mr McCormick laughed when I showed him the iron man, Jearum?' adds Mr Sage. 'He said it wasn't possible.'

Mr Atkins takes a moment to reflect on this while continuing to eye John suspiciously. At length, he says: 'Do you want to see the iron man, Mr Wright?'

'That is why I am here.'

'Albert?'

Mr Sage crosses the room and pulls the blanket off what John had assumed to be a chest of drawers. It is, though, another curious contraption that stands about four feet high and resembles a toy reaper. But if it were really meant to represent a reaper, surely the blades to cut the wheat would be behind the wagon? This one has the blades attached to the side of the driver's seat, beneath a platform. Above this platform is a baffling assortment of metal limbs.

'Will you be the horse, Albert?' says Mr Atkins.

Mr Sage moves the worktable away from the bed. He wheels the model over and scatters wood chips on the platform at its base, to represent the cut grain.

'Ready, Mr Wright?'

John watches in amazement as, from his prone position, Mr Atkins pulls a lever and the simulacrum of a human arm descends, complete with a joint at the elbow. In place of a hand are two pincers that, when they near the platform, bend like fingers, scrape the wood chips into a pile and lift them up in a bundle.

John claps his hands. 'Extraordinary,' he says.

'The iron man can do the work of two human beings, Mr Wright,' says Mr Atkins. 'And where reaping is concerned, it will be quite as fast and efficient as a McCormick.'

What a boon this will be for farmers. What a sensation. John can already imagine the kind of sentences he will write. *As every farmer knows, it takes two men twice as long to rake and collect the grain as it does to cut it. This is hard, back-breaking labor. As farms are hit by the continuing exodus of our young men to California, let us welcome with cheers and outstretched arms the 'iron man' that has come to our rescue.*

He sits down on a chair. He feels quite emotional. Miss Atkins has brought coffee.

'I arranged for a friend to bring a McCormick reaper here,' Mr Sage is saying, 'so that Jearum could study through the window how it worked.'

'And then?' asks John, still not really comprehending.

'That's all,' says Mr Sage.

'If it will not work here,' says Mr Atkins in his monotone, tapping his brow, 'it will not work anywhere.'

John gestures, rather helplessly, around the room. 'So all this, everything here, has to work first inside your head?'

Mr Atkins nods.

'I see.' He is feeling distinctly strange. Mr Sage told him earlier that Mr Atkins had rarely gone to school because his parents could not afford to send him. And yet he has done all this and who knows what else too? He is struck by a sense of his own inadequacy, of the frivolity ... how that word grates ... the frivolity of his existence. He hears his mother's voice. *Why can't you put your energy into doing something serious, something useful, John?* In front of him lies a man to whom the ordinary pleasures of life he takes for granted have been denied for the last ten years. Mr Jearum Atkins, forced to suffer whatever indignities being bedridden must involve, has nevertheless designed a machine that will transform the lives of farmers across America.

Then may I ask what you have trained in, Mr Wright?

There is only one other person who has made him feel inadequate, though in a different way, and that was many years ago. Miss Eliza Chappell was also someone of strong will and a sense of purpose. Maybe his mother is right. Sometimes, it feels as though he is always flitting from this to that, on to the next new thing before he has finished the last one.

The moment passes. He returns to business.

'It is important, Mr Atkins,' he says, 'that the name of any new machine should not only seize the imagination but also convey a sense of its unique and remarkable capability. This is the secret of marketing in today's world. I would therefore suggest that your invention be sold as The Automaton. This captures the way in which the iron arm simulates the workings of its human equivalent. Or perhaps, better, it should be the Atkins Automaton.'

'You have trained in marketing, Mr Wright?'

John laughs that away, and says that one day people really might be trained in marketing. His factory, he pledges, will make a working model of the Automaton in time to demonstrate at the first important agricultural exhibition of the season in Geneva, New York, opening on July 20. He also commits to taking the model, in person, to all the other major agricultural shows. He will file for a patent for the Automaton in their joint names, and will replace the Hussey reaper in his factory with the Automaton. When he finally leaves, he has no idea how long he has been there. He feels quite exhilarated.

That evening, after he has played with Maria and read another Potawatomie myth to Augustine, John spends the first part of the evening with Kitty, making the final arrangements for her departure in the morning to Virginia. As promised, he makes one last attempt to persuade her not to go, but he cannot put his heart into it. He knows it will make no difference.

When she prepares for bed, he calls in to see if his mother is still awake. She is seated in her armchair near the open window, strands of grey hair escaping from her bonnet as she leans forward to catch the light from a kerosene lamp. She is sewing buttons onto one of his shirts.

She looks up and smiles when he comes in.

'I don't know what you'd do with yourself,' he says, 'if I stopped losing buttons.'

'Or if I were caught again, putting them on.'

'And were then caught ironing the shirt as well.'

They share a look. There was a heated argument the last time Kitty found her doing her own sewing and ironing. That was what they had slaves for. 'What would Molly think, if she knew what you were doing, Mrs Wright?' Molly is Kitty's favourite slave, who came with her from Virginia, and the laundry is her responsibility.

Slaves, and Kitty's insistence on keeping them, has always been a keen source of unease to John. He has managed to keep only an Irish coachman and his butler Seamus, who are both paid and treated as servants. The rest of the house, to his chagrin, is run by Kitty and her slaves.

'Does she still insist on travelling to Virginia?'

'I tried, *Mater.*'

His mother sighs. He knows only too well how she feels about her daughter-in-law's refusal to find anything good about Chicago. 'I don't know what your father would have said.'

'He would probably have prayed.' Deacon Wright has been dead for over ten years. He finds it touching, and a sign of her deep affection for his father, how often she wonders about his reaction to things.

She nods, smiling thinly. 'Yes, he would have prayed and said not a word to anyone about what he thought. Not the most forthcoming of men, your father. But a very good and thoughtful one.'

'He was, *Mater.*'

'I think he would have found a way to get along with Kitty,' she says. 'Yes.'

He is not so sure he would, and he is not sure his mother really believes this either, but it is something on which they like to agree. He knows she does not believe Kitty is right for him, though she would never say it.

She lets the shirt drop to her lap. 'I am afraid we had a disagreement today.'

'Oh?' Kitty has said nothing to him about it.

'She accused me of being "one of those awful Republicans" because I support abolition.'

John puts his head in his hands. Not that again.

'She said she knew what I was thinking, but she would never allow me to take Molly away from her. Didn't I remember what happened to poor Molly when she arrived in Chicago?'

John shakes his head. 'I'm so sorry, *Mater.*'

It is one of Kitty's favourite anecdotes. Some Abolitionists 'threatened' Molly in the street when she first arrived in Chicago by telling her she was free. Poor Molly was petrified. Of course, she was. 'Leave me be,' she told them. 'Miss Kitty owns me.' Did those horrible Abolitionists ever give any thought to the plight of the poor Negroes? How on earth would they survive if they were freed?

'She is a little on edge at the moment,' says John, 'with the baby due, and the journey.' He hates himself for making these excuses on Kitty's behalf.

'It's just that sometimes I feel she's being allowed to get away with too much,' says his mother. 'Do you know what I mean?'

He nods. 'I do, *Mater.*' He knows exactly what she means but he does not want to engage in this conversation. He can guess where it will go. From slavery they will move on to the question of schooling. How could he have agreed to send Augustine to a private school at

Lake Forest instead of a Normal school? Did he no longer believe that an equal education should be made available to all children, regardless of their background? She had fought for this principle all her life, and so indeed had he.

And from there, it would not be long before she found a way of mentioning the horse. It couldn't just be any thoroughbred for Kitty, could it, but the most expensive Arabian mare in Chicago. And from the mare, she would move on to the portrait. It couldn't just be a regular portrait, but a vast affair that took up one wall of the main salon downstairs. It does not help that he also finds the portrait vulgar and pretentious. Nor is he proud of the fact that he has never admitted to his mother that he approved of the idea himself. Indeed, he has found it easier to say: 'You'll remember I was in Washington at the time, *Mater*', as though it was a surprise to him too, the way it turned out. Once, he had tried to argue that the portrait was modelled on a masterpiece by a famous English painter, a painting that Mr Ogden had on display in his North Side mansion. But she remained unimpressed. Next would come the expense. 'I do not dare to imagine how much it must have cost you.' It does not matter how often he tells her it was a gift from Mr Ogden himself and didn't cost him a cent. She pretends not to remember or not to hear or not to believe him.

Oh yes, he knows what his mother is like. He does not want to give her the chance to start talking about abolition or education or the Arabian mare or the G.P.A. Healy portrait.

'I had a very interesting meeting this morning,' he says, to change the subject.

But she is not listening. She is now asking him about something else entirely. 'Whatever happened to Miss Eliza Chappell,' she says, out of the blue, 'after she married Reverend Porter? I've often wondered.'

'I don't know,' he says.

'I liked her.'

'Yes.'

'She knew her own mind, but she was never proud or unreasonable.'

'No.'

There is a moment of silence.

'Promise me one thing, John.'

'Of course, *Mater.*'

'Don't spend the rest of your life trying to please her.'

Later, he does tell her about the Automaton and how useful it could be for farmers, without admitting that he has committed to anything. 'Believe me. It would be hailed as an agricultural breakthrough, a sensation, a remarkable curiosity. And, *Mater*, one more thing. Remember that nothing would exist, not even Chicago, without farmers.' He recites the passage from the Lord's Prayer about giving us our daily bread, which is perhaps foolish, given the demise of his bread-making machine. He hastens on. 'And for that reason alone you can be sure it would provide for a very safe, staid business for many years to come.'

He did not mean to go that far. She is silent, and to his alarm he sees tears welling in her eyes. Without looking at him, she says, in a voice with almost as little intonation as that of Mr Atkins: 'You've already committed to it, haven't you? Even though the man has nothing but a drawing, you've already told him your factory will drop everything else to make this new machine. It's no good pretending you haven't, John. I can tell.' He tries to interrupt, but she raises a hand. 'Promise,' she says, 'that you will concentrate on it.'

'Of course.'

'I mean by that,' she says, enunciating carefully, 'that you mustn't allow yourself to be distracted by anything else.'

He kneels beside her, and speaks gently. 'I am quite certain this will work, *Mater*. If you had seen this man Mr Atkins, you would have believed him too. You could see it in his eyes. He is not just an engineering genius, he is also a man of conviction.'

His mother pats the back of his hand, before wiping her eyes. 'Good,' she says. She picks up her sewing. 'I'd better get these buttons finished.'

'Good night, *Mater*.'

John tiptoes upstairs to his bedroom and spends some moments looking out the window before he retires to bed. It is a warm, sultry evening. Lights burn in some of the windows opposite. A lone carriage passes by below but otherwise Wabash Avenue is silent. The sky looks more purple than black. In the distance, he can see some tiny bobbing lights on the Lake. Chicago is preparing for sleep. And up above the city a new moon is rising, which is the best of omens for a new venture.

1856–1857

1856

The Last *Stim*

The ground was soft now that the morning frost had melted. The mulch was a deep dark brown. Gus picked his way through the undergrowth, following the contours of the land. There was not much up and down. The earth was flat and boggy. Old tree stumps furry with moss were masked by undergrowth. He moved fast, and only occasionally did he feel his boots sink. The river boomed, as if in constant echo, masking every other noise. Where only two weeks ago, sluggish water had moved in silence hemmed in by a layer of ice, there was now a raging torrent. Its downward rush was like a dance of freedom. The long hard winter was over and spring had arrived. It was time to escape.

At the bend in the river, Gus paused and looked back. As usual, he had been sent ahead to search for possible bottlenecks. Shading his eyes he saw the first logs in the distance, already beginning to darken the river's silver gleam. As he watched their approach he was removed, momentarily, from the horror they represented. He saw only the beauty of their onward rush.

It had been the hardest, most exhausting, most wretched four months of his life. He was young, strong and healthy, but he had found himself pushed to the limit. Often, on the verge of collapse, he had kept going fuelled only by stubbornness, a refusal to submit, and a burning ambition for his future in America.

The river's exuberance this morning inspired him. The sparkling waters thundered down like a train over the tracks, steaming with spit and foam beneath the freight they carried. This misery would soon be over. Never again would he endure a winter like this. Never again would a permanent layer of cold sweat lie like scum between his skin and his shirt. Never again would he suffer from the bouts of diarrhea and colds that lasted for weeks, the nights of confinement in a cramped stinking drafty shack, surrounded by the worst kind of American. Never again would his muscles recoil as the axe blade jarred against cold timber first thing in a morning. Never again would he climb to the top of a stack to straighten them up, and have to look over the edge.

A few days ago, one of the old lumbermen pushed him as the cook was handing across his breakfast plate of salt pork, beans and potatoes. He lost most of the food, which made everyone laugh, except Paddy the Irishman. He retaliated with a series of three punches that left the bully gasping in a crouch. Gus did not act out of anger, nor did he feel it. It was the only way, in that world, in which he could seek justice.

He continued to gaze at the logs, at how they shimmied downriver. All roads led to Chicago. Once this drive was over, he would go where they were going. He would make a new life for himself. In Chicago, he would become more American than the lumbermen, as American as if he had been born here. With renewed hope, he shielded his eyes against the glare of the pale March sun. The mass of logs, in the passion of their approach, reminded him of a *stim* of gigantic fish.

The memory was fresh, of how he'd hide his fear from the other boys, of how his stomach rebelled at the sight of the drop and of how he would close his eyes before taking his turn to jump. That was the only way he could make himself do it. But the fear, always, was more in the anticipation than the act. Once he broke the surface, he forgot how terrifying it had been and he'd find he could hold his breath and swim for longer underwater than anyone else. After the first shock of cold, he would open his eyes. The Holjeån River was clear as glass and, more often than not, he'd see a *stim* swirling in the shallows, a sight that felt like God's reward for confronting his fear. He would gaze at the *stim* for as long as possible before coming up, gasping for breath, amazed. Those *stim* were the most beautiful things in the world. It wasn't their brightness and colour that affected him most, but their motion. How did they swim without a leader, without bumping one into another, in order and yet without order, as if every little fish were one part of a single body, controlled by a single mind? Ah, the wonder and safety of Småland. How far away that was now.

The logs, suddenly, were upon him at the bend. He cursed himself for daydreaming. There would be trouble. The river here was too narrow, the turn too sharp. Some of the timber in the lead had failed to make the turn and pummelled into the far bank. Within seconds, a curving trail of splayed tree trunks, glistening and upended, marked the line of the river.

He hurried back to alert the others to the bottleneck, and as he did so it crossed his mind that a real *stim* would never have got stuck.

The boss was called Jack, he'd been a lumberer all his life, and he let you know it.

'I want you out there, Gussie,' he barked. 'Now.'

This came as no surprise. Jack always gave him the dangerous jobs. 'You're the youngest, Gussie' or 'You've got no aches and pains yet, Gussie' or 'You've got no wife and kids, Gussie'. He never said, 'It's because you're a Squarehead, Gussie'. Nor did he tell the other truth, that 'Gussie' (his English might be poor but he could hear the insult in 'Gussie') was the only man who could do it. Nobody else had the footing or the eye, the sense of balance and the will. He was only seventeen years old but he had already proved he was as strong as any of Jack's regulars. He had muscle and they knew it. He could swing the longest axe and pull the heaviest load. He never ducked his share of the work. He suffered from no long-term hacking cough, his shoulders weren't crabbed, his hands might be blistered from the axe but the fingers were not yet permanently crooked.

'You want to feckin' kill the boy?' protested Paddy Mohan. 'Nobody should go out there, not with logs backed up like that, and not this near to the Falls. It's feckin' suicide. Don't do it, Gus.' Paddy was probably about thirty years old, new to the country too, and the only other outsider. He looked out for Gus, and there was nothing more to it than that, though to hear the filth talked about the two of them you wouldn't have known.

Jack shoved Paddy backwards and told him to shut his mouth. He yelled at Gus, panting and slew-eyed. 'Get out there. Now.'

Gus stood his ground. He said he would not do it.

'One rule of my camp, Gussie boy, in case it's passed you by. Nobody disobeys a fucking order, especially not a kid like you.'

'He just did, didn't he?' said Paddy, from a distance. 'And I tell you this, nobody has the right to send a starvin' mutt into that mess, never mind a youngster.'

Jack raised his fist. 'Stitch it, bog man, or I'll bust you open.'

'I stop this jam,' said Gus, 'you give me one V.'

Jack seized him by the collar, almost throttling him. 'I hope my ears are playing tricks, Gussie boy, and I didn't hear that correct?'

'I do this thing you asking for one V,' he said, right into his face.

Some of the old loggers were sniggering, but they didn't step forward to say they'd do it. They never did. The boss told them to shut it. Gus was glad he understood so little of what they were saying, though he didn't care much either. He was sure most Americans were not like these ones. It was the logging that knocked the sense out of you and turned you into a brute. He had felt it happening to him too, in just a few months. These men had been doing it for years. There was no time to think beyond the next tree, the next break, the next food, the next sleep. Your body worked, and while you watched it work your mind dulled and grew bitter. Yes, he had felt the same, and the feeling was dangerous.

'Don't you dare do it,' warned Paddy. 'Not even for five Vs. It's feckin' madness and the Boss knows it and I don't doubt you do too. You're no brickbrain, boy.'

Gus did not think it was madness. There was risk, and it would be the biggest jam he had ever tried to break on his own, but it was not impossible. And he wanted to show these Americans, that while they might be scared to death, the Squarehead wasn't. Pride, though, wasn't the most important reason for doing it. His mother needed those five extra dollars. Since his father passed away, it had been up to Gus to keep his mother and sister alive, and he had done it. He was already imagining himself as he handed over the V, and the gratitude that would come into her eyes and how good that would make him feel.

He also knew it was worth holding out. Jack was desperate for those logs to start moving. The early winter freeze had blocked the Great Lakes and cut off supplies to Chicago. It was a fine opportunity to break into the market. But they were already running late, as Jack kept telling them, even before this jam. There would be some very unhappy people downriver, he said, and some very unhappy new customers in Chicago who couldn't wait any longer for their white pine, no matter how young and green it came in. They were not interested in snowfall or sledways or ice melts down there in Chicago. They neither knew nor cared how the timber arrived, just as long as it did.

Business people in Chicago meant nothing to Gus, but the money he could take back to his mother meant a lot. So he held out for his five dollars. Jack was mostly mouth, as he had worked out by then.

He swore at Gus, he called him 'the stupidest fuckin' Squarehead in the State of Michigan', and then he agreed. Break the logjam and he would be paid an extra five dollars.

The rock from which Gus decided to start was flattish and aligned with the centre of the jam. He laid down the pike pole, stripped off his shirt and handed it to Paddy who gave him the tin of goose grease. He rubbed it into his chest, arms and legs. He put the shirt back on, and told himself to ignore the cold.

'Don't do it, Gus,' Paddy urged him again. 'You don't need to make of yourself a martyr for this pissproud mob.' He was shouting, to make himself heard against the rush of water.

Gus concentrated on the logs. He scanned them, searching for the spot, willing himself to ignore the bitter wind that whipped across his back. The spray stung like hail. It was a source of pride, how he had learned to steel his mind against cold and pain. There would be no shivering, no distractions; he would allow himself to feel no fear. After all, he told himself, he was not about to climb a log pile. One false move at the top of a log pile, and everything underneath would disappear. It would not be like diving into the Holjeån. From his earliest days, this was what had terrified him most, the thought of slipping from on high when you couldn't help yourself, the thought of dropping through the air like a stone.

Jack was on the bank now, shouting instructions and pointing, but Gus took no notice of him. He narrowed his eyes against the freezing spray and looked only at the logs, shoving at each other as the water roiled around them. He felt the cold streaming through him and, despite his best intentions, he was afraid. Even if he did not drown out there, he would freeze to death. Paddy was right. This was too dangerous. He should go back.

He prayed for strength, and the moment passed.

He resumed his search for signs, for the spot where they were choking, the destination they were all trying to reach, the point of greatest pressure, the bottleneck. One of the Americans — it was a voice he recognised but did not bother placing — shouted that Gussie boy should get on with it and stop standing there like a Nancy because some of them had real work to do. He spat and drew in a deep breath. His eyes were fixed on a point about twenty yards distant, not quite halfway across the river. He had been watching the way in which the build-up formed, looking for little signs of readjustment and displacement that were the clues he needed. It was not the centre he would strike, it was the centre's flank. All he had to do was to find those few logs that were at the heart of everything. Maybe they were stuck beneath a rock or wedged in a sandbank. There was always, in everything, one last point of resistance. This was the trick, and the lesson. Find it, break it, and the rout would begin. He decided where to make the first attempt. If he was wrong, if there was no sign of movement, he would withdraw and choose again. Speed and decisiveness were everything now. If he hit the mark first time around, he planned to be back on this rock in the blink of an eye, collecting his V.

Jack handed him the rope.

'Don't forget it's for your waist, Gussie boy,' shouted the same American, 'not your neck.'

'One more word out of you, you scum,' retorted Paddy, 'and you'll be taking a swim.'

Jack told them to cut it out. 'And hold that fuckin' rope tight or you'll be the next.'

To Gus, these words seemed to be coming from a great distance. The water was drumming furiously against the horde of blocked timber. Freedom, he told himself. Break the jam, and freedom would return. The shifting wood creaked and scraped and thudded. He bent down to pick up the pike pole. He weighed it in his numb hands.

Raising one foot, then the other, he tested the spikes in his boots for their hold. He unknotted the rope Jack gave him and let it fall away. It would be more of a hindrance than a help. Jack started yelling again but his voice was small and faint and unimportant. He took a deep breath, readied himself and sprang off the flat rock towards the first log. Above the blind percussion of the water, he heard Paddy shout one last time, telling him to 'come back in one feckin' piece'.

Water was bucketing over the logs; a frost of ice stuck to his legs as his eyes smarted and retracted. He could not feel his feet. No thoughts troubled him. There was only then and there. He was not conscious of who he was or how he got there or how long it had taken or how he fixed the pike pole to hook the handful of logs that were the key to everything. There was only that instant, that instant before everything began to shift and the whole crooked edifice on which he was standing would rumble and creak beneath him; there was just that instant when Gus felt invincible, the master of nature, triumphant. It was only an instant, because the sensation of triumph was caused by the same telltale shift that marked the moment of true danger. But he had done it. He had found the point of least resistance, he had broken it, he had won.

Now he had to get back.

He leapt onto the next log and then the next as he made for the bank. He knew he only had seconds to get there, before the resurgent logs knocked him out or over or under, before they hauled him downriver towards Chicago and crushed him to death.

He abandoned the pike pole. He jumped onto a huge trunk that was already beginning to move away from him, landed badly, and was thrown onto his back. His hands stung. As a wave burst and smothered him like a snowdrift, he swallowed a mouthful of icy water. He gasped in pain. It seemed to burn his throat. His legs were up and in one piece but it made little difference. He was now being driven downriver, logs grinding beneath him as they churned and bumped and tossed him along. He could be trapped between them in an instant. The bank, the bank, he had to reach the bank. He must find his feet and face forward. At least this was a big log, more stable than some of the others, less liable to be knocked sideways.

And by God he managed it; he dropped into a crouch and held fast as his log smashed at a diagonal into a smaller log and mounted it. He was raised up, swinging from side to side, so that for a moment he was held aloft as the two trunks slid onwards together, towards the frothing chute of water in the centre. And that was the moment when he first noticed them. It was a roaring, a rumble, a booming, and it was growing stronger. Moving water is sound, he told himself, blind sound. It could not harm you. Until this moment, he had deliberately not thought about the Falls.

But that was where he was being taken. He looked up long enough to glimpse where the water's horizon vanished into thin air. There wouldn't be enough time to reach the bank even if he could see a way to do it. Timber was everywhere, slick brown logs fighting, crashing, pounding into each other. The water was silver and freezing. He needed to be a flying fish, like one of those he saw jumping in front of the ship, when they made the crossing to America. He hung on because there was nothing else he could do even though he knew, now, that he was going to die.

He imagined the news being brought to his mother. Paddy would do it, wouldn't he? He could see his mother's surprise when he appeared, and then her alarm as she saw his face. 'But where's Gustaf?' she would cry out. Paddy would break the news, and his mother would sit down rigid on her chair and not say a word and hold her apron to her eyes, and she would weep. When his father passed, she wept all night. And now, in less than a year, she would have lost him too. He thought of his sister Ingrid and his uncle Mr

Swanson in Chicago, whom he had been planning to ask for work. Too late for that now.

At least he would never again have to find sleep on a hard bunk in that stinking shack, reeking with the stench of feet and sweat and urine, while he picked lice out of his hair. At least there would be no more blisters on his hands, no aching back and shoulders, no more cuts and bruises. No more of those endless dishes of cold beans and half-cooked potatoes. No more days when time would not stop. No more feeling he was less than human. Yes, at least he would never have to go through any of that ever again. These thoughts took no time. They came to him in a flash, as though he had them all at once.

He was on all fours now, digging in with his feet even though they were so frozen he could not feel them. What really held him up was the stub of a branch to which he was clinging with his fingertips. He was trying, Lord knew he was trying. But he was only managing to keep his balance and stay afloat. He was going to die, and he couldn't stop it, and that made him furious. He was too young to die. And for what? To make some businessmen in Chicago happy? Was that all his life was worth? It was only a few months since God took his father. *And now you're taking me too? What kind of cruel, heartless God are you?* Rage renewed his strength. Don't think, God, that I shall go quietly.

He made a frantic last attempt to reach the bank. He even saw Paddy jumping up and down, waving, and that filled him with hope and he wanted to wave back but he could not because he was slipping and sliding in the rushing water. A wave hit him full in the face, hard as a plank. It knocked out his breath, and he tasted the metallic tang of blood. *Change your mind, God, and surprise me. Give me a rock to mount, give me a branch to grab, strand me on a sandbank. Dear God, give me one of your miracles.*

Gus had no more thoughts, at least not in the ordinary sense. In the last few seconds, when he was neither fully alive nor fully dead, his mind was filled instead with pictures of his life. An ordinary mind would have tried to look at them one by one, and put them into sequence. But at the last moment, Gus's mind changed into something else. It expanded and found remarkable, unimaginable new powers. That was why his life, at the moment of its imminent demise, turned into a magnificent *stim* of pictures.

———

The Detroit Evening News
March 29, 1856

Swedish Immigrant finds a Watery Grave at St Clair Falls

A sad accident which resulted in the going out of one life at St Clair Falls Tuesday morning. A logging team led by Jack Stone, comprised of eighteen men, were engaged in a drive down the St Clair from their camp four miles upriver. We understand that all was going well until a logjam built up a few hundred yards before the Falls. A seventeen-year-old Swedish immigrant named as Gus Swanson, working his first season with the team, volunteered to break the logjam. It seems that the young man, having achieved that aim, was swept off balance and carried towards the Falls. Mr Stone reports that despite repeated attempts from the rest of the team to pull him to safety on the succor rope, their efforts were to no avail. Swanson was observed flying off the edge into the seething rapids, clad only in shirt, pants and caulk boots. In a poignant touch, we must add that according to fellow logger Paddy Mohan, who observed the fall, Gus Swanson had his eyes 'tight shut' when he was driven over the edge to his doom. No body has yet been found, but pieces of his clothing have been discovered on the lumber. This is the first such accident to have occurred in St Clair this spring, and it is indeed an unhappy beginning. Incidents like this occur with appalling regularity and yet any number of men are prepared to try their luck, even though the wages decrease with each passing year. One lumberman who has served three years in the army, as well as run these Falls in all stages of water, says he would rather take his chances in battle. There is particular urgency this Spring to drive as many logs as possible into the boom due to unprecedented demand from businesses in Chicago whose customary supply lines for timber were disturbed by the early freeze on the Great Lakes. St Clair logging companies hope to take advantage of this situation, not only to make up Chicago's current shortfall but also in the expectation that this will lead to additional business in future years.

1856

People from the Past

John is preoccupied this morning, saying little to Augustine on the slow journey across town from their Wabash Avenue home to the factory on the north bank. It rained heavily overnight, the streets are still flooded and the traffic is heavy. He answers the boy's questions about what this or that building is, or what it's going to be, but not with his customary enthusiasm. He would have preferred not to have brought Augustine along today, but he has been promising for such a long time that, even after what happened, he decided he could not put it off.

As they clatter across the Rush Street Bridge and onto the north shore, Augustine wants to know why the water is red and greasy. That is because there are stockyards, tanneries and distilleries upriver, he explains, and they have nowhere else to get rid of their waste. The boy thinks that is silly, to throw everything away into the river. And why does it smell so bad and what is this barge taking where, and where is that clipper coming from and if two boats are heading straight into each other how do they not crash?

He tells Augustine that most of the boats are carrying grain, and will be coming from elevators at the railroad terminals. What are elevators and how many are there in Chicago and how big are they and how much grain do they hold all together? Normally, these kinds of questions would have delighted John, and he would have explained the purpose of the elevators in detail. Today, he merely answers the questions. There are a dozen elevators in Chicago. The biggest is the Chicago and Rock Island Railroad's, which has ninety bins and holds up to seven hundred thousand bushels of grain. The city's elevators can store over four million bushels at any one moment, which is more than St Louis can ship in a whole year.

'What is a bushel?'

'A quantity of wheat that weighs sixty pounds.'

'How much does a pound weigh?'

John feels numbed by hurt. The only good thing to be said is that his mother did not live long enough to witness what happened earlier this morning. For her, it would have been the last straw. She was always telling him he should not stand for it, and that Kitty ought to show him more respect. In other words, that he needed to put her in her place. It is perhaps his greatest failing, he thinks, that he never has. And it's too late now.

Perhaps it was foolish to have confronted her in the way he did. She was bound to retaliate. On the other hand, does she not deserve it? John swallows. Yes, she deserves it. But even as he reassures himself, a little voice asks him what right he has, to cast the first stone? What about his own transgression? Yes, but she knows nothing about it, and it was only once, and it was a mistake.

Kitty has never loved him. But can he say that he has ever loved her either, *truly* loved and worshipped her as he once, in his youth, loved and worshipped Miss Eliza Chappell? No, he was temporarily infatuated with Kitty. That was all.

He cannot get it out of his mind, how she stood in front of the giant portrait of herself, hands on her hips, a lock of red hair shooting out of the bonnet at each ear, her narrow face pinched with fury. She acted as if *he* had betrayed *her*. He had been snooping on her, she said.

He explained to her what must have happened. She had dropped the letter. One of her slaves had picked it up and assumed it belonged, not to her, but to him. It was therefore put on his desk. He could not be accused of snooping, could he, for reading a letter left on his own desk?

But she was not interested in listening to reason, or to anything else he had to say. Did he not see how he had ruined her life? Was he not ashamed? Everyone knows he only married her for her money and her position in society. 'If only *you* had joined the Army, you wouldn't have turned out the way you have.' She should never have agreed to marry a man beneath her station and condemn herself to a life in this 'filthy backward city'.

They are nearly there. As they turn onto his private road, and the driver hisses to the horses, pulling on the reins to slow them down on the curve, John leans forward and tells him to stop in front of the gate. The wrought iron signage over the top marks the entrance to *The Prairie Farmer Works*. He shades his eyes to look up. It's a cloudy day, but the sun is working its way through. The italic lettering style is excellent. He had insisted on it.

'Look, Augustine. What does it say?'

Augustine reads the words aloud and then asks why he is not calling the new factory after the Atkins Automaton, if that's what he is making there.

'A good question.' He pats him on the shoulder and gives him an affectionate squeeze. He is proud of the boy. 'If you want to be ahead of everyone else, Augustine,' he says, 'you must look not only at what's happening now. You must also prepare for the future.' When he still looks puzzled, John explains that the site is much bigger than they need to build the Automaton. 'That's why your father had to pay $72,000 for it.'

'But why did you do that, if you don't need it?'

'What did I just say, Augustine? About the future? How often have I told you that Chicago is growing faster than any other city in America? Remember those old charts I showed you last week, the ones your father drew a long time ago, when the Indians were leaving? What did I tell you made this place special?'

'The Romans would have liked it.'

'Yes. And why would they have liked it?'

'There are no mountains. And it's flat.'

'Exactly. There are no limits on how far and wide this city can go.' This time the boy seems satisfied. 'And even if we do nothing with the extra land, in five years' time it will be worth double what it is now.'

Augustine makes another face, and takes a five cent coin from his pocket. 'Does that mean this will be worth ten cents in five years' time, if I don't do anything with it?'

John laughs and tells him to put it somewhere safe because if he loses it, it won't be worth anything at all. 'Location, availability and need, that's what makes real estate different from the coin in your pocket.'

He steps down from the brougham and swings the boy to the ground. For a moment, his private worries disappear as he enjoys Augustine's astonishment at the size and scale of the factory. 'Is it really all yours, father?' John is proud of what he has built. How happy his mother would have been to see this. She always wanted him to have a safe, steady business. The solid brick frontage soars three storeys high. Above, two chimneys are pumping out plumes of grey smoke. The double doors are open. From beyond comes the noise of manufacture, the grind and hammering of iron, the squeal of metal and the rasp of timber being sawn, sounds that from a distance fill John with another wave of pride. He has made all of this activity possible, activity that is changing the lives of farmers all over the country, because — four or five years ago — he dared to believe in the revolutionary ideas of a man who is a bedridden genius.

He asks one of the foremen about the whereabouts of Mr Jenkins, the factory manager, and is told that he's most likely outside at the far end, where the new steam drying kilns have been installed. Taking the boy by the hand, John leads him inside. Within the building, the competing sounds of the foundry, the metalwork and the carpentry benches are magnified, echoing back and forth as though not a single sound can escape. The noise is deafening. The air is hot and reeks of iron and oil. John rarely feels self-conscious, but walking through his own factory always unsettles him. There are not many places where he has a sense of not belonging but, ironically, this is one of them.

Perhaps he is feeling more vulnerable than usual because of what happened earlier. Normally, he can shrug off the sense of inadequacy he feels when he sees a labourer do something he could not do himself. Put one of these rough, uneducated men with their knotty muscles and callused hands on a desert island like Robinson Crusoe, and they would soon find a way to build a shelter and catch food and make fire. He, though, would be dead in no time. The thought recurs more often these days: what have I achieved to equal what a labourer in my own factory can produce with his bare hands? What have I achieved that compares with what Jearum Atkins, confined to his bed, has achieved? How would Miss Eliza Chappell have judged me?

He tries to explain the manufacturing process to Augustine, who has gone silent since they came inside. The boy looks overawed. They start at the near end, where two finished Automatons are standing on blocks as wheels are being rolled into place. John walks around and stands in front of one, touching a rod here, a blade there, trying to make it look as though he knows what he is looking for. They proceed down the middle of the two lines of work tables that run half the length of the factory. He stops to chat with one or two workers, as he always does, but feels particularly conscious today of his silk top hat and boiled white shirt and soft, clean hands. He does not ask about what they're doing, but where they're from and how long they've been in Chicago and whether they have family. Mostly, the employees are Irish and German, with the odd Englishman and Swede.

At one workbench they are sawing and planing lengths of timber that will be used to build the Automaton's frame. But the workbenches nearby, he notes with alarm, are empty again. Dai Jenkins had better have a good explanation for that, a very good explanation indeed. Where is the man? He hurries on. Augustine, annoyingly, insists on watching the welders. Clad in apron and gloves, they push rods in and out of the furnaces. One glowing orange-yellow lump is being withdrawn. It is hammered into shape. Sparks fly.

'Shade your eyes, Augustine.'

The boy is full of questions again. 'Do they have a rest?'

'Of course.'

'How often? It must get very hot. How much do they get paid?'

'About a dollar a day.'

'Can I be a welder when I grow up?'

'That's enough, Augustine. Come along now.'

They find Dai Jenkins outside. He has worked as John's manager since the doors first opened, six months ago. He is a young Welshman full of energy and good intentions, but he has never run a factory before. At first, John hoped it did not matter because he seemed to be a quick learner. But he is becoming more and more skeptical about Dai's ability to meet production targets. John needs a minimum of three thousand Automatons this year, up from twelve hundred last year, but they have not yet made five hundred. At this rate, they risk missing the season altogether. New problems always seem to be cropping up. 'Don't worry Mr Wright,' he likes to say, 'we'll be back on schedule in no time.'

Dai wipes his hand on his coat before bending down to shake Augustine's hand. 'Good morning, young sir,' he says.

'The timber benches are idle,' says John. 'Are the kilns still not working properly?'

'The kilns are working, Mr Wright, and I can promise you that very soon they'll be working exactly the way we want them to. Just a few more tests to run to be sure. The thing is this. It's no good taking only ninety per cent of the moisture out. We need a full one hundred per cent.'

'At ninety per cent the timber will warp?'

'Not necessarily. But I'm not prepared to take the risk. Every Automaton that leaves this factory must be perfect.'

'Do you understand, Dai, what it means for this business if Automatons do not start rolling out of here at once?'

'We're nearly there, we're very nearly there, sir.'

It looks as though virtually all the lengths from the first two consignments of pine John has bought at great expense from mills in Michigan — after exerting enormous pressure that they be given priority — are still stacked up, the same as they were a week ago. Dai promised that the new kilns would be working last week, and that they would dry the wood in a matter of days.

'Come along with me,' Dai says to Augustine. 'Let me show you how a kiln works.'

John hears Augustine say, unimpressed, that it looks like a big oven.

'It is. But it's a very special one.'

'But if it's an oven, doesn't the wood just burn?'

'No. We steam dry it instead.' Dai Jenkins explains that the oven creates heat that draws moisture out of wood that was still part of a tree somewhere in Michigan only a few weeks ago. 'Isn't that a wonderful thing? A tree one day, inside an Automaton the next.'

'If only,' thinks John. He curses silently. Why this year of all years, did the Great Lakes have to freeze early? If they hadn't, there would have been no need to build these kilns and buy green wood because the seasoned pine he'd ordered months ago would have arrived. He has made big claims about those three thousand Atkins Automatons being on the market this summer. If they can't produce them, he will be a laughing stock and the financial consequences don't bear thinking about. Mr McCormick will sweep up his unfulfilled orders and claim that John S. Wright and his Automaton are nothing but hot air.

———

That evening, after saying goodnight to the children, he goes into his mother's old room and closes the door behind him. Molly has informed him that Kitty is not feeling well and has retired to bed early. When his mother died, he ordered that her room be kept exactly as it was. Kitty objected and on a number of occasions during the first few months, she insisted it be opened up, cleared out and used. The children could make it a play room, or Molly could store the linen there and do her ironing and sewing. John snapped back that that was one thing Molly would never do there. In any case, argued Kitty, it was a waste of a perfectly good room. Strangely, even though he knows that for once she is right and that it is an odd battle to fight, he has refused to back down. The room has become his sanctuary. Kitty would never come in on principle, and the children know to leave him be.

He stands for a moment by his mother's ironing board, which is supported on two trestles and covered by the old blanket she always used as a base. On top is the flatiron itself and her sewing basket, with its little compartments for thread, scissors and pins. How she loved her sewing and ironing. *It calms me down.*

At the bookcase, he runs his fingers along the spines. He feels exhausted. Will Dai Jenkins ever get those kilns working properly or not? If so, when? And there is everything else too. The sale of the old Searcy lot has fallen through, and that means he has no choice but to mortgage Kitty's properties on Clark Street if he is to pay off the outstanding loans on the factory. The *Prairie Farmer* is owed over $10,000 as a result of subscriptions not being paid. Nobody seems to have any cash, and Eastern pens are beginning another spiteful campaign to denigrate the West. He loosens his collar and undoes the top two shirt buttons. The third button pops off and lands somewhere on the floor. 'Sorry *Mater*,' he says aloud.

How long is it since he has had time to sit down and read a proper book? The only reading he does is to the children before bed. They don't like the Bible and he is sick of Potawatomie myths. He pulls out a tome at random. Another one on the Potawatomies but at least it's not myths. This one is *A History of the Potawatomie Tribes in the Great Lakes*. His mother probably used it in class. She has inscribed her name on the flyleaf. He flicks through the pages before replacing it on the shelf. On the board above the bookshelves, where she pinned notable essays or letters from some of her pupils, he happens to see one phrase in a curious letter from a student asking 'Teacher Wright' whether, in the course of her long life, she has had any 'snakes in the long grass'. The expression has been underlined, in ink, presumably by his mother. She would do things like that, whenever she came across something she liked. The gist of the letter seems to be that the pupil wants to know whether it is true, as she has been told, that all older people have some 'bad secrets'. She goes on: 'Is it true that in every old life there are snakes in the long grass?'

For a moment, he simply stares at the words. He can even hear his mother saying them aloud, asking him the question directly.

He sinks down into her old armchair and folds his arms.

We now know Kitty has a snake in the long grass. What about you, John?

He wonders how long Kitty has been carrying on. Months? Years? While she was still bearing the children? Could it have been going on ever since their wedding? Has this ... this Southerner been a frequent visitor at Blakeley when Kitty takes her three-month annual trips there? Do the children know him? Or do the two of them meet somewhere else? He wonders whether there have been clues that he has failed to notice and he thinks back to the few times when she has seemed embarrassed about something. He ponders what he should do now.

Above all, he decides, there must be no scandal. The children can never know. Nor can anyone else in Chicago. He realises it is her deception that hurts most, not the knowledge that she has actually made love with this Southern soldier. Their physical entanglement leaves him unmoved. He has not slept with Kitty since before Maria was born. Does he demand that she tell him everything? Would she? Is it better not to know? And even if he does ban her from ever communicating with this man again, would she abide by that? What if she challenges him? It is not inconceivable that she would go on the offensive. Has he ever betrayed her with another woman? If she asked, would he tell the truth?

He wakes up in the middle of the night still seated in his mother's chair, cold and stiff, and at first he cannot think where he is. Moonlight is streaming into the room and words are repeating themselves in his head.

In every old life there are snakes in the long grass.

He stands up, lights a candle, takes the blanket off the ironing table and wraps it around himself before returning to the chair. He realises he has been dreaming of Aureka Atkins again. At times when his confidence is low, that shame comes back to haunt him. Is it always thus, that when business is bad he is forced to look into the gaping hole at the centre of his life?

It occurs to him that his mother must, in her way, have helped him paper over it. With her gone, the hole is back, more profound and empty than ever. The fact is that his own heart remains a mystery to him. He ruined the one true chance he ever had. That is why, at the age of forty-one, he still yearns for love.

As he sits in the silent room, haunted by the benevolent spirit of his mother, his other problems begin to resurface. The cash squeeze, the failed land sales, the debts. And what happens to the Automaton sales if those drying kilns do not work? His mind bestirs itself, as it often does when he cannot sleep. And gradually, while thinking about the problem of those kilns, his mood begins to change. He knows, deep down, that whatever Dai Jones says, they will probably never work properly. He should therefore make a virtue out of necessity. His mind, in a spirit of liberation, seeks all manner of different and unusual ways in which to confront the problem. And that is how an idea comes to him, one of those transformative ideas that seems obvious only once it has been had.

He stands up and paces around the room. Let dawn come quickly, he thinks. In the morning, I shall tell Kitty I have forgiven her and nothing more is to be said about it. She is to break off communication forever with her Southern lover. She must never see him again. In the morning ... he can feel his heartbeat begin to race ... in the morning, I shall announce new plans for branch offices around the country where Automatons can be assembled with local supplies of timber and where repairs can be made. They will be in Dayton, Baltimore and Harrisburg. It will mean transportation costs are reduced, parts can be bought locally, the backlog in the factory will be cleared and, on top of that, a local presence always increases customer confidence which, in turn, increases sales. By doing this, he will have wrongfooted Mr McCormick again.

And, while walking back and forth, another idea comes to him that is so daring and brilliant it seems Heaven-sent. He has to sit down again and catch his breath. The Lord doth truly work in ways mysterious. That must be why, only last week, he happened to hear her name mentioned. A few moments later, he mutters aloud: 'It may be a small town, but it makes commercial sense. Yes, I am decided. I will open a fourth branch office in Rochester. And that is where I shall travel first.'

It would not look planned. And if nothing comes of it (a voice of reason warns that nothing will) what harm will have been done? He feels giddy at the prospect — albeit only a faint prospect — of bringing succour to his wounded heart, even as he saves the Automaton.

He begins to make a mental list of the people he must contact. There will be an enormous number of meetings, but it can and must be done at once so that this season's sales are saved. He goes East at once. In fact, he will leave so early in the morning there will be no time to see Kitty in person.

He takes the candle to his mother's desk. Before he begins to write, he pauses to pass his hands across the gnarled surface, thinking back, once more overwhelmed by memories. Melancholy and nostalgia make him uncomfortable. He has always considered them to be signs of weakness. If there is one mantra he has always preached, it is that one's gaze should always be on the future. There is no point in looking back. And yet, at the moment, he seems to be doing little else. Perhaps this is what happens as you get older.

Is not this very room, by his order, frozen in the past? And does not this desk mock his 'don't look back' mantra too? Was it not here where they sat down to eat as a family when he was a boy? Was it not here where he studied Greek and Latin? Was it not here where his mother prepared her lessons and read her Bible? He is not sure what to make of the feelings evoked by these reminiscences, but he cannot pretend they do not exist.

He picks up his mother's pen and begins to write. He has little idea of time passing. But when he comes to the end of his letter to Kitty the candle is no longer needed. Daylight is seeping into the room. He pushes back the chair and looks up at the portrait of his father. He wonders what Deacon Wright would have done in his position, before deciding he would never have become involved with Kitty in the first place. His mother, he thinks, as he looks down at the pages in front of him, would have approved of the letter he has written. *About time*, she might say.

A Visitor From Long Ago

Rochester, NY

March 20, 1856

My dear F_____,

You must wonder at my silence since arriving back in Rochester with little Robert. He is a sweet child, perhaps the sweetest of them all, though I grant that may be the clouded judgment of a mother inclined to dote on her youngest, especially when he is in poor health. The truth is that I am equally blessed by all my children. But I am glad to say the boy is making a good recovery, and though I greatly miss my husband and my duties in Green Bay, I have no doubt that to come here was the correct decision.

The reason I have taken so long to write is because I have wished to compose myself first. I do not know whether I am more angry or saddened by what I have to tell you, nor whether my judgment in this matter too is clouded, after a manner of speaking. I have received a visitor from long ago. Nobody likes to be reminded of painful chapters in their past, as was I last week. I have been left feeling upset and irritable.

Perhaps you can divine of whom I speak? There was no warning. Nor do I know how he discovered my whereabouts, but you can imagine my surprise when my sister announced a visitor was come to see me, by the name of Mr John Wright. I have since calculated that we had not set eyes on each other for twenty-one years, not since that time the reverend was raising funds for missionary work in China and I was offering for sale a watch that Mr W. had given me. Just as Mr W. arrived on that occasion without warning, so too he was suddenly at my sister's door in Rochester, asking to see me.

It surprised me, to see how little he had changed. He seemed to have aged much less than he should have done, though I reminded myself that he is some years younger than I (seven or eight?), which must put him only just past forty. Yes, he has more girth and wrinkles, but his hair remains thick and curly, and he has the same boyish smile, head slightly tilted to one side, and his eyes are still a remarkably brilliant blue.

In the beginning, I was almost persuaded he was telling the truth when he put this visit down to a series of coincidences. He was in Rochester on business, my name happened to be mentioned, so he thought it an opportunity to become re-acquainted. Was he often in Rochester on business? I asked. His answer was less than direct. He was looking, he said, for someone to be a distributor in these parts for a machine that rakes wheat. I don't believe he is the kind of man to tell blatant falsehoods, but he always did have a way of imparting only what he wanted you to hear. On further inquiry, it emerged that this was his first visit to Rochester, and when I asked why he had chosen this town in particular, and which person it was who had mentioned my name, he became embarrassed.

Despite this, I cannot say I was displeased to see him. For me, those unfortunate indiscretions that occurred when we were young and untested is water under the bridge. True, they have always served as an important reminder of my frailty, but I hope I have long since learned from my mistakes.

My sister served coffee and biscuits. Mr W. drank his coffee quickly, and kept refilling his cup until the pot was empty. His news, at first, sounded bright. Married for ten years he is the father of three children, of whom he is evidently fond and proud. It was no surprise to hear he has his finger in a lot of pies. He is involved in a variety of businesses, from wool to railroads, but his main interest still appears to be property speculation. He was keen to stress, though, that he also does many things for what he calls the 'public good'. For example, he founded the *Prairie Farmer*, a newspaper that brings advice and news to all those living in rural areas. And he has devoted much time and money, he says, to the establishment of Normal schools. Recently, he has established a 'Scientific University'. The list went on.

Mostly, though, he wanted to tell me about his new machine — the Atkins Automaton — which he manufactures in a factory in Chicago. This Automaton, in a way I don't understand, reaps wheat and then collects it into bundles. He claims it represents a revolution in American farming. I confess his energy and enthusiasm for the project made me smile. He was always like that. 'And you will never believe it,' he said, meaning that I would have to, 'but the Automaton was invented by a bed-ridden genius.' He added: 'God moves in mysterious ways.'

He does indeed, I agreed.

'And Reverend Porter?' he asked at last.

A strange look crossed his face when I reported that the reverend was busy and well. It was fleeting, and he recovered himself quickly, but I had noticed. The point, dear F_____, is that I detected in that look a hint of disappointment. He was greatly surprised to hear that our Lord has blessed me with no less than nine children, of whom eight are alive and well. In fact, he paid a compliment as to my appearance after so much childbearing that I blush to remember. And when I told him I had given birth to Robert only four years ago, at the age of forty-four, he was amazed. After a moment's reflection, he began to laugh. Had he not always said the registrar's pen must have slipped when recording my date of birth?

Strangely, I do remember him saying that. I responded by remarking on his own shortage of gray hair, which seemed suspicious to me, and I wondered whether he had a good macassar oil to recommend. Our conversation proceeded for some minutes more in this surprisingly easy and familiar manner.

I asked whether he had any news about our mutual acquaintances from those days. He knew that Mr Mark Beaubien, who managed the Sauganash Hotel (which is no more) has removed to Kankakee with his family, but he had no information about our old friend Mrs Eulalie. I often think about her, and wonder what became of her, and whether she was ever re-united with her son. Do you remember all the letters we shared about her? I still don't think she unburdened herself of all she should have done. Maybe, if she had, we could have avoided that terrifying incident during the Indians' Dance of Departure. I pray that she may have found the Lord.

'In the end, she left that picture behind,' Mr W. said of Mrs Eulalie. 'You remember the one? Of the old mansion? I have it hanging in my office.'

If Mr W. had stood up at this point to leave, and if I had not inquired about the health of his mother, it is probable the unpleasantness that was to come would never have happened, and there would have been no need to disturb the memories I had preserved of a charming and articulate young Mr W. who would surely, one day, find his true calling in life.

But he did not stand up, and I did ask after his mother. She had passed on after suffering from a bout of pneumonia, he said, two years before, at which news I expressed my sorrow for I remember her as a pious lady of strong character, and an enthusiastic supporter of Normal schools. He said he missed her greatly. And then, after a brief pause, he added in a different tone of voice: 'She never did think well of Kitty.' Kitty is the name of his wife.

I tried to move the topic of conversation elsewhere for it was quite improper of him to raise a matter of such intimacy in front of me. But to no avail. He insisted on talking about her.

In brief, the story he told was as follows. The lady he married was born the daughter of a big plantation owner in Jefferson County. But she was raised in Virginia by her aunt, Mrs Jane Washington. Mrs Washington had inherited the Washington family's Mount Vernon Estate in Fairfax County, and this was where Kitty spent her formative years, meeting any number of notables, not least because it was customary for the President and Cabinet to dine there at least once a year. She was, we can conclude, quite a catch for Mr W. and considerably above his station in life.

Mr W. and his wife became only modestly acquainted, he said, before their marriage and it was not long before what he called his 'mistake' became apparent. 'From the very beginning she showed me little affection,' he complained, 'and I have now found out why.'

He had recently discovered (by accident he claimed) correspondence that showed his wife was in love with a Southern gentleman in the United States Army. This gentleman was not a recent acquaintance. He had been suitor to Kitty immediately prior to her marriage to Mr W. Mrs Washington, though, disapproved of him, not least because he had a weakness for liquor. She forbade the match unless he abstained from alcohol for a period of one year. Allegedly, his resolve held until the very last night before they were due to marry. The wedding was duly canceled. On the day of Kitty's marriage to Mr W., this broken-hearted soldier-lover shot himself. But he was only wounded. It is this same gentleman with whom Mr W.'s wife is allegedly in love.

I interrupted. Though I was tempted to point out that his wife's story of her Southern beau sounded too melodramatic to be true, I held my tongue. Instead, I expressed sympathy for his circumstances before pointing out, politely but firmly, that his marriage was no business of mine and I wished to hear no more about it. I stood up in a way that indicated his visit was at an end.

He did not, though, budge from his seat. His earlier mood had been cheerful enough, as I have indicated. It was now considerably altered. He sat hunched over, wringing his hands, and I sensed he was trying to find the courage to say something intensely personal. *Some people change so little*, I thought. It was behavior that reminded me of his awkward younger self, who was as confident a man as you could meet until it came to matters of the heart. I assure you, though, I had no desire to hear whatever secret it was, that he was struggling to impart.

'There is nothing between Kitty and myself.'

'Mr Wright, I implore you not to speak to me of such matters.'

'Don't you see?' he murmured, his eyes fixed on the floor.

Only now did I have a terrible premonition as to what he might want to say.

'My mother was right. She said she had met only one woman in my life who ...'

'Stop this, Mr Wright,' I insisted.

I opened the door to the parlor and indicated he should leave. He rose reluctantly and with immense languor. 'My wife's story is much embellished in her imagination,' he admitted. 'I made inquiries about her lover. He never abstained from drinking. No suicide was ever attempted. He is still alive and still in the army and' — he paused — 'I suspect they have continued a liaison throughout her marriage to me. Nor do I believe anything will stop them now.'

'Why are you telling me this, Mr Wright?'

There was a pause. And then there was the truth I did not want to hear. He swept at the air with his hands, as though swatting a large, slow fly, a distraught expression on his face. That look transformed him. The happy father of three and the successful man of affairs was replaced by a lost and confused soul, consumed by regrets.

'I wanted to explain how I feel about you still,' he said, 'even after all these years.'

'This is absurd.'

But he would not be quietened. 'There was no single moment,' he said, 'when I understood I had lost the greatest opportunity of my life. But maybe a man can never see who he is until he has enough years behind him on which to look back.'

I shall not burden you with all that passed between us, dear F_____, nor could I claim to remember it with any great precision. It was distressing beyond words. The more he spoke, the more I came to see that this impulsive visit was similar to a last throw of the dice by a desperate gambler. He was trapped in an unhappy and unsuitable marriage. Beneath the facade of the wealthy businessman and proud father, a demon was running riot. This demon was clutching at straws in his past, of which I happened to be one. I don't doubt there were others. My suspicion was this, that the younger version of myself he had once known, unwed and childless, had surfaced in his daydreams. He dared to imagine my marriage had also been a failure, or perhaps that my husband was no more, that I might offer him a second chance, and that everything could go back to how it had been twenty years ago. It was the thinking of a creature with the body of a man and the mind of a child. I'm afraid I had to tell him so.

When I did, he responded in Latin. At first, I did not realize what it was he had said.

'You don't remember? Not even that?' From the pocket of his waistcoat he brought out a silver watch on a chain and turned it around to show me the inscription on the back. His face was a picture of melancholy.

I remembered it, of course. It was the silver watch he gave me, which he then bought back at the auction to raise funds for missionaries in China. 'Meanwhile it is flying,' he said, 'irretrievable time is flying.' He replaced the watch in his pocket. 'I always carry it with me.'

I said I did not see the relevance of either the watch or that quotation to our conversation. We were acquainted for a short time many years ago. Our lives had taken very different paths and our responsibilities had multiplied. There was no useful purpose to be served by the kind of reminiscences in which he seemed bent on engaging. I reminded him how it is written in Ecclesiastes, that everything has its due time: 'To everything there is a season, and a time to every purpose under the Heaven.'

I confess I was beginning to lose patience with him, especially when it emerged that in spite of boasting about his work and support for Normal schools, his own children were being educated privately. How could that possibly be, I demanded to know? Because his wife, he admitted shamefacedly, had insisted.

'And I suppose your wife also insists that you keep slaves?' For a moment, he said nothing. He stared at the floor. I repeated the question. Slowly, reluctantly, he nodded his head.

You can imagine how angry this made me. 'Are you telling me, Mr Wright, that you are a man who keeps slaves in your home, after everything that was said on that matter between us? After all the promises you made?'

After saying this was indeed another concession he had made to his wife, he sheepishly owned up to a further act of unparalleled vulgarity. Some years ago he paid $40,000 to buy a ship that would take to Liberia all those slaves in the employment of Mrs Jane Washington (his wife's aunt) who wished to go there.

'Then you are a colonizer too?'

He looked down, wringing his hands. 'I had to tell you,' he murmured.

That was the moment when it struck me he might be seeking my forgiveness (but why mine?) as though he were a Catholic at confession and I was his priest. In your opinion, is this a possibility, dear F_____? You were always so much more attuned than I to the peculiarities of human behavior. I recounted for him the tale you already know, about how my husband risked his life and reputation when he kept secret in the belfry of his church for four days and nights a family of slaves seeking freedom in Canada. 'You cannot have it both ways,' I told him. 'We all have to take a moral stand.'

We were both seated again by now. He looked dejected, and at this point I went further than I should. It is one of my great faults, dear F_____, with which I seem to make no headway, that my tongue will often outrun my tact. 'I always hoped,' I said, 'that you were one of those people who would make a significant impact on the world. The reverend and I play our little part in our little corner, and with that blessing we are content. But I always thought you, Mr Wright, had the ability and ambition to go much further. I tried — and perhaps I tried too hard — to alert you to what I still consider, twenty years on, to be the greatest problems of our time because I hoped you might take them up as causes of your own. I knew you had the wit and the energy to achieve almost anything ...' I fear I may have paused at this point, as if I were raising the hammer to take one last blow '... if only you had the will.'

Our talk was interrupted by a knock at the door. You know my sister is the kindest soul, and a dear aunt to little Robert, but she is also an insatiable gossip. Doubtless, she was eager to know why we were engaged in such animated conversation. Her pretext was to ask whether Mr W. would like more coffee but before he could say anything, I thanked her and told her he would not. I indicated, with a look, that she should leave us on our own. The door closed behind her.

Mr W. took to his feet again. His mood was altered. He spoke differently now, with eerie composure and a distant look in his eye. 'You are right, Mrs Porter,' he said, 'as you always were.' He apologized if his visit had caused me distress and expressed admiration for my husband's courage and resolve. 'Before I go, though, there is one more matter for which I would like to offer my regrets.' He cleared his throat. 'That afternoon, a long time ago, when it was raining ...'

As it happened, rain was at that very moment beginning to spit against the window. And as he talked, I could not stop myself remembering. The vividness was horrifying and I was filled anew with shame. What could have possessed me to behave as I did in that Chicago schoolroom? Such was my distraction that I heard little of Mr Wright's apology. He was shuffling his feet, a nervous tic of his I remembered from long ago. He had often wondered, he said, how his life might have been nobler and more fulfilled, had he only been worthy of me.

'Mr Wright!' I pleaded.

'But I know I was never worthy enough to share your life, Mrs Porter,' he said. 'My mother in her heart knew that too, however much she would have wished otherwise. I have no doubt it was for this reason that the Lord judged it fit and proper to send us out into the world on our separate paths.'

I did not know how to respond to that.

'Goodbye Mrs Porter,' he said. 'My greetings to Reverend Porter and your family. May God be with you all. I apologize for this visit, which has clearly been upsetting for you. I should not have come, and I swear I shall never trouble you again.'

He put his hand on the doorknob, and turned his head my way. His eyes were clear but distant. 'You are right, Mrs Porter,' he said. 'I fear I have never believed profoundly enough in anything that really matters.'

I stretched out an arm towards him. 'Wait!' I whispered. 'There is something I want to say.'

I had been unfair, and for this I wanted to apologize. Nobody has the right to speak to another as I had just spoken to him. He had already achieved more in his life than most of us, and I should have had the grace to commend him for this. I wished to tell him I would always remember him with great affection, that I was as much to blame for what happened that afternoon as he was, that I was glad to have had a chance to see him once more after all these years, that I hoped one day the Lord would finally grant him true happiness, that I would always include him in my prayers, that we were all imperfect before the Lord but he should rest assured I knew — as well as anyone perhaps — that he had always been, in his heart, a goodly, generous man.

Mr W., though, had not heard me. He turned the doorknob before I managed to say any of these things. There was the noise of my sister stumbling on the other side. She had been eavesdropping again. The moment was lost and I said nothing of what lay in my heart.

Your sister-in-Christ,
Mistress Eliza Porter

You Can Be Anything You Want

There is such a high tide on the Lake today that parts of the road are flooded. Wave after wave surges ashore, striking the land in a cascade of surf. Further out, thousands of white crests skim the swaying water. A strong, warm wind whips ashore. As his brougham careers along the lakeshore in the direction of Evanston, swinging from side to side, John removes his hat and lets his hair fly loose. He has told his driver that the other wagon can come along at its own pace. He wants to take the road at a good clip. He has always enjoyed the sensation of speed. He sprawls across the leather seat, hanging on with one hand, rolling with the bumps and relishing the breeze on his face that comes tinged with the occasional whiff of horse. A few thin clouds are racing across a blue sky. Normally, fine windy days like this fill John with hope. They are a reminder from nature that we should never fail to move on and refresh ourselves, because the alternative is stagnation. And how many times has he warned readers that it is stagnation, not money, that is the source of all evil? Don't just seize the day, my friends, seize the future.

Today, though, the wind and the blue sky fail to work their magic on his spirits. The foaming, churned up Lake, as it bucks and spits, reminds him of one of the Potawatomie myths Augustine has insisted he read to him again. In this story, a monster that lives beneath the Lake creates a storm whenever man's behaviour becomes offensive. The shipwrecked are taken underwater and never seen or heard of again. If only that were to be the fate of those spiteful Eastern pens that have spent the last three months talking up a depression in the West. Their lies have been repeated with such frequency that people think they must be true. In contradiction of all the facts, a depression has been created out of thin air. And what motivates those Easterners to do this? Their envy of Chicago is so deep-seated, they will do anything to try to undermine the city. That is what this is all about, and John takes it personally.

As they draw close to Evanston, the road narrows and winds inland and he feels the dust thickening on his throat as the horses slow their pace, trotting past ruined fields of dry, shrivelled wheat. Who could have predicted that, on top of all the other problems with the Automaton, there would be a drought this year? Everyone agrees it has been the driest summer in living memory. He is reflecting on this, and on the fact that however hard you try, the world will sometimes throw its weight against you, when he sits up straight and grips his temples, screwing his eyes tight shut. From nowhere has come a shuddering jolt of pain. It feels as though a nerve inside his brain has snapped. His eyes water. He holds his head tight until the pain begins to subside. His sight, for a few moments, is starry and blurred.

He has not had an attack like this since New York. He should see a doctor again. *Anxiety*, he tells himself. *That's what it must be. Too little sleep and too many worries.* He is not himself. He knows he's not, and that should put him on his guard. When on edge, he feels vulnerable. He is liable to let his emotions get the better of him.

They are nearly there. But how pleasant it would be if the wind could blow him past Evanston, deep into the prairies, into the middle of nowhere. And when it died down, he would stretch out on the hard warm earth, close his eyes and fall into forgetfulness. By the time he woke up, he would feel rested, his problems would have vanished and he could start over. He would leave Kitty. She could have whatever was left from this mess and he would then have a clean slate and the prospect of a fresh beginning. He has always been at his best, at his most daring and visionary, when there is everything to go for.

He claps his hands. What balderdash, he tells himself. You don't run away at the first sign of trouble. Pull yourself together, John S. Wright.

The brougham comes to a halt in front of the Sage and Atkins residence. He replaces his hat and steps to the ground. Pausing, he does his best to collect himself by taking a moment to admire the house, with its one-and-a-half storeys and steeply pitched roof. He found the site for them, and Jearum then designed it after the manner of some colonial buildings he said he had once seen as a boy in Cape Cod, Massachussetts. John has not been here for some time. He had forgotten how striking it was. The slope of the tiled roof is like a hat pulled down low, shading the house's brow. Dark brown gables overhang the tall windows and the walls gleam with whitewash. The Automaton has done well, he thinks, in providing them with this splendid house. That is one fact Jearum will not be able to challenge.

Aureka opens the door. The moment he sees her, he feels a tightening in his chest. One of the things he has been contemplating on the way over is whether he should try to clear the air between them. A crisis in one's life is not all bad. Imbalance can create new perspectives. Those old cupboards, where embarrassments and failures are hidden, can be opened up. In all these years, they have never talked about what happened. What would there be to lose in apologising to her, now that it is all in the past? Although the awkwardness that once prevailed between them is over, the fact — or perhaps it is the memory — of their liaison lies beneath the surface of every word and look they exchange.

Their eyes engage briefly before she glances away.

'Good morning, Mrs Sage. I am sorry. You were not expecting me.'

She raises her hands, still white with flour. 'I was baking. You are welcome, Mr Wright.'

He wonders what she thinks when she sees him. He had been relieved by how quickly she recovered afterwards — if that is the right word — and put him behind her. Her marriage to Mr Sage, which seemed hasty at the time, appears to have prospered. She has matured and gained in confidence. Gone is the shy, apprehensive look in her eyes that he remembers. She has filled out and become almost matronly. Self-possessed, she is the mistress of her own house.

He follows her into a small, bright parlour. There is a mirror on the wall, two or three rather gaudy landscape paintings, and some easy chairs around a low rectangular table on which stands a vase of freshly cut flowers. Everything seems a little too neat and in its place, as if the mistress is trying hard to impress. He positions himself with his back to the window.

'You are well?' he says.

'Quite well, sir.'

'And Stephen?' He had glimpsed the boy when the door opened. 'He has your looks. More of you in him than his father, I'd say.' She blushes. The truth, though, is that he rarely gets it right. People say Augustine is more like Kitty than like him, but he cannot see it.

'And the baby?' Her name eludes him.

'Mildred is growing and in good health.'

'And Mr Sage?'

She hesitates. 'He is well, given the circumstances.'

'He runs a fine store. I am certain ...' he says, before adding with emphasis, 'I am quite certain that he will pull through.'

'Thank you, sir.' She looks down. 'And you, Mr Wright?' she asks.

'I ... er ...' His first reaction is to say, as he always does, that things are not nearly as bad as some people claim and that they will soon get better. 'Darn it!' he says, shaking his head. 'You must have heard what's happening over there.' He juts his chin in the direction of Chicago. 'A few months ago, everyone was behaving normally. Now they're running around like headless chickens.' He is about to say more, to start raging against Eastern pens and spineless bankers, but he stops himself. He has no right to inflict such a tirade on her. He takes a deep breath. 'A false depression is under way, but there's nothing to be done about it now.'

She looks straight at him with a boldness that disarms him. Her voice is low, but clear. 'If anyone can stop it, Mr Wright,' she says, 'surely you can?'

He is rendered momentarily speechless. A clock ticks. A baby — Mildred, he remembers — yells in another room. He is trying to analyse what she has just said, and the tone in which she said it. 'Well. I thank you for your confidence in me,' he says, 'but I fear it is too late now, Aureka.'

Her first name hangs for a moment in the air like a secret between them. He has not called her that for years. She bites her lip before turning abruptly. He cannot tell whether she is more discomfited by the response he gave, or by the little gesture of intimacy.

At the door, she says: 'I shall tell Mr Atkins you are here.'

Who does she see, five years on? Someone who took advantage of his position to seduce an impressionable young woman? Or a gentleman with whom she had been on respectable, friendly terms until, one day, things went too far? Might she still, distantly, feel something for him? Not in any sexual way, but might she remember fondly — as does he — some of their exchanges in the cramped little house on Kinzie Street, whenever there was a moment's peace from her insufferable mother?

She was miserable then, as he was often miserable himself. Looking back, he can see that his behaviour demonstrated only his own weakness. It comforted him, after another battle with Kitty, to have a pretty, admiring and sympathetic female ear in which to confide. He began to buy her little gifts and enjoyed too much the pleasure she took in them. Yes, but he brought gifts for Jearum too, didn't he? Indeed, he did. He also, though, told Aureka more than he should have done. And he complimented her in ways that overstepped propriety. In short, he encouraged her to believe that she might be able to mean more to him than she ever could. But did he behave like that because he truly intended to make something happen between them? After all, he had a wife and three children at home. He was nearly twice her age. It would have been quite wrong of him to try to seduce her.

Aureka. He is reminded of the one and only time she ever addressed him as John. It was that same fateful afternoon. He was searching for his underclothes, fallen somewhere to the floor beneath her mother's bed, dazed by what had happened and wondering, in the aftermath, whether he should apologise, though he sensed this would be a foolish and hurtful thing to do. That was the moment when she drew him back towards her. She sat cross-legged on the bed, the sheet pulled up to her breast, waves of hair falling over her naked shoulder. He still had his shirt on. From the other room, Jearum — who had no idea that John was in the house — was calling for her. He pointed in that direction, indicating that she should respond. She took no notice. On her face was a serene, contented look that unnerved him. One small hand tugged at his, bringing him close, until his shoulder pressed lightly against her breast. For some time, she inspected his hand, tracing it with a fingertip. It was a beautiful hand, a kind hand, she murmured. Then she slid the fingers of her other hand through his hair and placed her lips close to his ear. 'I love you, John,' she whispered.

He tiptoed out of the house a few minutes later like a thief, full of remorse. What had he done?

Now, he waits alone in Mrs Sage's parlour, feeling unutterably strange, almost as though he is standing apart from himself. He lowers himself into a seat. The room is too warm. A gust of wind rattles the window. He closes his eyes. He sees himself floundering in the middle of a storm-tossed Lake, waves breaking over him, each line of spume representing one more debt. He is bankrupt and drowning and the shore is too far away to reach.

A noise draws him out of this unpleasant reverie. He goes into the hall and finds the door to the kitchen ajar. Inside, young Stephen is visible. He is on his knees, crouched over a book, deep in concentration. A pencil is in his hand. He is drawing something. John had once dreamed of being not a painter, but a musician. How much more fulfilling a life that would have been. Equipped with art, he could have scorned the turbulence of economics and the need for profits. He leans over the boy. It is a strange drawing, more of an abstraction than a real picture. He admires the boy's absorption in his task.

John finds Jearum reclining, propped up by cushions, on the serpentine-back sofa with a book-stand set up in front of him. With help, he can now make that transition from bed to sofa. His drawings are pinned up on two large bulletin boards that flank the sofa. Beside him is his work-table, covered in papers and books and pencil stubs. The sofa is positioned so that he can look down to the Lake. The back garden is a mix of a chicken run, a line of recently-planted poplars and a sorry-looking vegetable plot, thirsty leaves drooping (it occurs to John) like Mr Sage's moustache. Through the open door comes only the chatter of cicadas and the *tap tap tap* of a woodpecker. Chicago, with all its problems, could not seem further away.

'The *Scientific American* again?' says John cheerily, sitting down on one of the upright chairs. 'It was always too technical for me.' He feels intimidated, as he always does, in Jearum's presence. He is reminded not just of his own good fortune, but of something more troubling about himself, that relates to his character and achievements. Jearum is sprucely attired in a fresh white shirt and is wrapped, from the waist down, in a blue cloth. His ginger beard is now flecked with grey, and his gaze is intent and suspicious.

'*Again*, Mr Wright?' he says without warmth. He will insist on continuing to address him as Mr Wright instead of John. 'That makes it sound as though you were here only last week.'

'I'm afraid I've been very busy.'

'Yes, of course. I read the newspapers.'

John smiles uncomfortably. He wonders how much he has read, and how much he knows. He can sense Jearum is waiting for him to say more, but now that the moment has come, he has a desire to put it off. 'Anything interesting?' he asks, indicating the journal.

Jearum looks as though he has neither listened to the question, nor has any intention of answering. His stare remains direct, and disconcerting. 'You are involved in real estate, Mr Wright,' he says, in his flat nasal tone. 'So you will know about the problems of building on Chicago's subsoil. Nothing down there but mud, sand and clay. The article I have been reading poses a question. How does one construct a tall building that requires deep and solid foundations on a subsoil as fickle as this? The traditional method of sinking concrete piers is inadequate.'

'And you have found a solution?'

'Not yet, Mr Wright.' He narrows his eyes. 'Not yet.'

'Oh, I'm sure you will. But you know what else you should do? Invent something for the railroads.'

Jearum's eyes do not even flicker. 'Tell me why you are ... finally ... here, Mr Wright?'

Before he can respond, there is a patter of little footsteps.

John swings around and scoops up a wary Stephen. 'My, how you've grown!' He sets him on his knees. 'Is the drawing finished?

Do you want to be a painter when you grow up?'

He's shy. Very different from Augustine at that age. 'I want to be an inventor like Uncle Jearum,' the boy whispers.

'An excellent idea. And there's no reason why you can't be. Now listen to me. You can be anything you want when you grow up, Stephen, as long as ...' he adds with emphasis, '... you want it enough.' He looks at Jearum. 'That's right, isn't it?'

Jearum does not reply. He addresses Stephen. 'You have something to tell us?'

'A wagon's come, sir.'

'Has it indeed?' says John. 'And did you see what's on the wagon?'

'Furniture, sir.'

'And not just any furniture.' John lowers his voice. 'I'll let you in on a secret, Stephen,' he says. 'In the old days, when there was no city and Chicago was nothing more than a few houses, there were only two buildings that were beautiful and important. One of them was a fort. Oh, what a magnificent stockade it was. Fort Dearborn was as big as a castle, made from lengths of fine old seasoned oak, each one as thick as this.' He spreads his hands wide. 'In those days, the fort was full of soldiers.'

'Why was it full of soldiers?'

'To protect the village from enemies.'

'Were they Indians?'

'Some of them were, yes. Anyway, the fort is not needed any more.'

'Because there are no more Indians?'

'Because there are no more enemies.'

'What happened to the Indians?

'They moved away.'

'Why did they move away?'

Stephen was now behaving more like Augustine. 'Because they wanted to go somewhere else.' The boy does not look satisfied. 'And the other important building was even more beautiful than the fort.

It was the house built by the first man who ever lived here.'

'What was his name?'

John did know it once. 'It's not important, Stephen. Do you know what your Uncle Right did, when he heard the first house and the old fort were being taken down so they could build some new buildings in their place?'

'Why do they need new buildings?'

He chuckles. 'In a city, three things are always needed. New buildings, more railroads and more people. And that, Stephen, is one of the most important lessons you can ever learn.'

The boy looks puzzled. 'Why?'

'Because that is how you make a city, and one day very soon, because of its new buildings and its railroads and its people, Chicago will be as big as New York.'

'Why does it need to be as big as New York?'

He gives Jearum a knowing smile, which is not returned. 'It's our destiny, Stephen. Now listen. When your Uncle Right heard what was happening, he bought that special old timber.'

'Why did you do that?'

He is beginning to wish he had not started this. 'Because it's our history,' he says. 'And I wanted the best carpenter in Chicago, a man called Mr Joseph Meeker, to use the timber to build some marvellous furniture for my friends.'

Stephen is wriggling. He lets him go. The boy goes to stand beside Jearum's bed.

He addresses Jearum. 'Mr Meeker has made you a reclining chair with wheels so that you can move yourself around, and a drawing board attached to a bracket that swings across when it is needed.'

'Please, sir?' asks Stephen. 'Can I go see it?'

Jearum says he can.

The boy runs towards the door but then stops. He looks at John, his head slightly on one side, squinting his eyes. 'How will Uncle

Jearum be safe on a piece of fort? There'll be ghosts of Indians, won't there, from the old battles?'

'Don't worry. His chair is made from the timber of the first house, not from the fort.'

He runs off.

Jearum tells him to take the reclining chair with wheels back to Chicago. 'I don't want it.'

'But I've had it specially made. It's a gift.'

'One that I don't wish to accept.'

John stands up, and goes towards the window. At first, he is genuinely puzzled. The timber is of a fine quality. All the furniture he has commissioned from Joseph Meeker is bespoke. On reflection, though, it strikes him how this might look to Jearum. 'It's not what you think,' he says. 'I commissioned it months ago, before all this ...' Before all this what?

'Mr Wright? I am waiting to hear you explain what has happened.'

John can see a woodpecker, digging into one of the poplar trees. Its labour and determination seem admirable, especially in this heat. He fishes out a handkerchief and wipes his brow. 'I expect things to get better soon,' he begins, 'but ...'

When he closes the door behind him, John stands for a moment in the cool of the hallway, leaning against the wall, hands over his ears. He closes his eyes. His head is hurting again, not in the sudden, violent way it did earlier, but with a dull, prolonged ache. Jearum's accusations keep running through his head. What hurts most is the charge about his trip to the East. *Oh, I don't doubt you went East, Mr Wright, but for what purpose I don't know except that it can have had nothing to do with the Automaton. Because if it was to set up branch offices for us, where are they? The fact is that you bought a lot of green wood in a hurry from Michigan, left a man without experience in charge of drying kilns that never worked, and spent three months in the East. And during those three months, not a word was heard from you.*

He was tempted to tell Jearum the truth, that he had been ill. But he did not want to invite any more questions about the trip. Even now, it pains him to think about what happened after he visited Eliza Chappell. The next three months, despite their intensity, are mostly lost to him now. He went straight to New York and spent his days ensconced in libraries. He was pursuing a new idea he had about slavery, a truly great idea, an idea that would solve the problem that was dividing the country once and for all. It was simple in concept, but fiendishly complicated in execution. He intended to prove, by citing the greatest religious and philosophical authorities in history, that slavery was not only a sin before God that condemned to Hell anyone who upheld it, but also indefensible in every branch of ethics, morality and justice. If he could provide such all-encompassing proof and lay it before the government in Washington they would be obliged not only to ban slavery in the new Western states but also in every other State in the Union where it was currently being practised. And this transformation would be achieved, not through abolitionist movements or partisan publications like *The Liberator*, but in that loftier sphere where the twin forces of religion and philosophy could be harnessed to provide a final, irrefutable verdict.

For those three winter months, he read avidly. He made copious notes on the Bible, he consulted and dismissed the views of Aristotle and Plato, he devoured the works of Thomas Hobbes, John Locke, Francis Hutcheson and Jean Jacques Rousseau before moving on to other lesser-known philosophers. In a quest of such magnitude no stone could be left unturned. He read on and on, his notebooks multiplied and his health deteriorated as he became ever more convinced that this great work, to be titled *The Definitive Explanation: Why Slavery is Immoral, Unlawful and Sinful*, by John S. Wright, would change the course of history. Armed with this book, he would lobby Congress, the Senate and the President himself until slavery in America was banned. And he would inscribe in the flyleaf of the copy he sent to Eliza: 'To Mistress Eliza Porter, with the author's admiration for the example she set and his deepest gratitude for her encouragement in this venture.'

That was when he had the first attacks. It felt, for the few moments they lasted, as though his brain was being scorched. He became so ill that he had to return to Chicago with only the first few pages of the book completed. By the time he had recovered, the Automaton crisis was at its height and, thanks to those invidious Eastern pens, fears of a recession were already beginning to blow through the boardrooms of Chicago. Later, when he looked back over all those notes he had made, he could make little sense of them.

'Mr Wright?' he hears Aureka ask. 'Are you all right?'

He follows her to the kitchen.

It is a bright, cheerful room that smells of cake and coffee. Through the open window, sunlight spans the solid oak table where he takes a seat. He is vaguely aware of Aureka moving around, adding wood to the stove, taking things out of cupboards and giving instructions to her maid. He remembers how his mother would move around the kitchen while he sat there as a small boy, doing his homework. They only had an open fire in those days. Their clothes and hair and books always stank of smoke. A copper kettle and a large charred pot would hang suspended on an iron pivot, filled with soup or potatoes. He can see himself bent over his books at the end of the table, staring into its grooves and ink stains as he memorised verb conjugations and algebraic formulae.

Aureka is at his shoulder. He watches an arc of steaming coffee, the same colour as her hair, fall from the pot's spout into the matching cup and saucer set she has placed in front of him. Her hand is steady. Not a drop is spilled. She moves away and puts the coffee back on the stove before returning with a sugar pot and another plate, on which sits a piece of cake, its pale sponge speckled with pieces of cherry.

'My favourite kind of cake.'

'Yes.' She turns towards the door. 'If you need more coffee, please ring the bell.'

'Mrs Sage,' he says, his voice curiously hoarse. 'Please stay.'

She looks at him, in a way that indicates it would be improper.

'Just for a few moments,' he says, 'while I drink the coffee.' He stirs in some sugar and takes three or four rapid sips before realising that he has burnt his tongue.

She takes a seat at the far end of the table. It strikes him as a little unnecessary, this affectation of propriety. They are hardly taking coffee in the Tremont House Hotel.

He does, though, feel the old urge to confide in her, in a way he would never think of doing with Kitty. 'I was just thinking,' he said, 'how differently my life has turned out, from the one my mother wanted for me. I used to do my homework at a table like this. She thought I was a child prodigy. She always said that, at three years old, I could already read Greek. But her true desire was that I should go into the church.'

'I am sure you would have been a good preacher,' she says. 'And did your father want that for you too?'

'My father never talked much, and not in that way. He wasn't ambitious. He was a small merchant, and never a very successful one.'

'Then he would have been proud of what you have achieved.'

He gives a grim smile. 'Not if he judged me on today's results.' He takes more sips of coffee, and wonders what old Deacon Wright would really have thought. 'He never approved of me much.'

'Fathers often don't,' she says.

He looks at her, vaguely recalling something she once told him about her own father, or rather the lack of him. If he remembers right, she never even knew him.

'And Stephen,' he asks, 'what do you want him to be?'

She shrugs. 'I think it's too early to be thinking about that.'

'And his father?'

'Mr ... Mr Sage?'

'Yes. Does Mr Sage want him to take over the store?'

'I dare say that would make him happy, yes.'

They lapse into silence. He eats the cake. She looks at her hands.

'Is it very serious, Mr Wright,' she asks, 'for the Automaton?'

'I have told Jearum that I shall have to close the factory.'

There is a sharp intake of breath. 'I see.'

'I also told him to take the patent straight to Mr McCormick.'

She looks up in surprise.

'I've never liked Mr McCormick. He's a bully and a cheat. But he's been wanting to get his hands on that patent ever since we filed it.' He waves an arm. 'Once McCormick starts manufacturing the Automaton, which I'm sure he will, this will all be quite safe.'

He finishes the coffee in one gulp. His headache, he realises, has gone. Aureka stands up and returns to the stove to refill his cup.

She sits down again, watching him drink it.

'And you, Mr Wright?' she asks in a small voice. 'Will you be all right?'

He feels drowsy, and more than a little odd. He cannot shake off the feeling he has had all day, that the world is out of kilter and he is teetering on the edge of something, liable to lose his balance at any moment. Surprisingly, perhaps, it is not an unpleasant feeling. This warm, friendly kitchen is an island of sanity and peace compared to what awaits him on his return to Chicago. They say the Bank of Commerce is about to fold next. One by one, goes the rumour mill, all the banks will fail and the city will be back in the Dark Ages. Nobody has any cash, and nobody will give any credit. Not for anything, not to anyone.

But why? Because of lies. From the perspective of this solid table, with its cherry cake and coffee, with Aureka seated opposite, what is happening in Chicago seems nothing but a bit of humbug. How did she put it earlier? *If anyone can stop it, Mr Wright, surely you can?* She's right. He will fight those charlatans in their own coin. He will write them into the dust. People will see reason, confidence will return and this nonsense will be put behind them.

The notion, once he has it, seems urgent. He must leave at once. There is just one thing he would like to do before he goes. He removes the silver watch from his waistcoat pocket, and unhooks the chain. 'I bought this watch a long time ago,' he says, 'at a jeweller's that had just opened in Chicago, called J.H. Mulford. It was intended as a gift for someone I admired and whose company I valued, but in the end our lives would go in different directions, as lives often do. I recovered the watch and have carried it with me ever since.' He reads the engraving on the back. It is still, just, legible. 'I had something inscribed in Latin on the back. There was a time when I could have told you where it came from. Ovid? Virgil? Horace? I don't remember, and it no longer matters. In English it means *meanwhile, time is flying; irretrievable time is flying*.' He sits back. 'I have always liked the reminder,' he says, 'that there is not a moment to lose ... and that nothing ever comes back.' He grins, as though the idea has revived him. 'It also makes the present seem less important than it often seems.'

He slides the watch towards her, inviting her to hold it.

Sunlight glints off the worn silver surface. Gingerly, she picks it up and strokes the top. 'It's beautiful,' she murmurs, turning it over, looking at the inscription. 'But why are you telling me this, Mr Wright?'

'Because I want you to have it.'

She frowns. 'But I couldn't possibly ...'

He insists. 'It would make me very happy,' he says, 'if you would accept it.' He clears his throat. 'You don't have to keep it. It must be valuable by now. An antique.'

She shakes her head. No, she would never sell something as beautiful as that, no matter how bad things were. The point, though, is that she cannot accept such a gift.

He smiles. He has been expecting her to object. 'We both know there is something important we've never talked about,' he says, 'and it is my fault. But it has been much on my conscience. It is cowardly of me. I should have said something long ago.'

She raises her head slowly, the watch enclosed in the palm of her hand, trailing the chain. Her expression, on the instant, has changed. Her eyes are wide, her mouth is fallen half open. 'You mean you know?' she gasps.

John has no idea what she means by that, but he is alarmed by the sudden change in her mood.

She rises from her seat. The emotion in her voice is palpable. She is choking on the words. 'You knew,' she says. 'You must have always known. Oh, what a fool I am.'

He is on his feet too. 'Mrs Sage? Aureka?'

She swivels around, and there is a desperate, pleading look on her face. 'You mustn't tell him, you understand? You must never tell him. It would ...' She begins to sob. 'It would ruin everything for them both, if they ever knew. Promise me, John. You must never say a word.'

'Oh dear God,' he says, slumping back into his seat as, finally, he understands. 'Yes, yes, of course. Stephen. Why else?'

Aureka puts a hand in front of her mouth, as though she would like to take back what she has just said. Her eyes look past him. She tries to wipe away the tears in her eyes.

Stephen's small voice comes from behind him. 'Why are you crying, Momma?' The boy runs around the table and throws himself into her arms.

Whenever there is a smooth patch of road, John tries to make notes for the article he will pen as soon as he gets back. He invokes history and common sense, he cites the good news that is being ignored, and he prepares a string of pithy attacks against the Eastern detractors.

He curses the twenty-five miles and almost two hours it will take to reach his office. These arguments need to go into print as soon as possible. He can still make tomorrow morning's papers. He will speak to Joseph Medill at the *Chicago Daily Tribune* — Joseph owes him a favour — and he will demand two columns on the front page. Once those columns have been read and digested, people will begin to see sense again and disaster will be averted. It is not too late.

In this way, by immersing himself in what must be said and the challenge to be taken on, he suppresses the sense of vertigo that has had him in its grip all day. The only way to avert disaster is to challenge it head on. The city will not fall apart, and nor will he. He shivers. Dear God, though, what has just happened? For a moment, he wonders whether she might have made it up. But then he recalls the desperation in her voice and he sees the boy in his mind's eye — the curly hair, the blue eyes, the Roman nose — and he tries to remember and work out the dates. And on top of that there is the name.

But then again, he reflects a little later, perhaps there is no great harm done. After all, nobody need ever know, not even the boy himself.

The carriage comes to a halt at a crossroads. He writes notes. *Submission and Surrender begone. The Path to Glory is paved by Bright Visions of the Future. Stagnation is the Root of all Evil. Learn from the Waters of our own Lake Michigan. Learn from the Wind that Blows, the Waves that Roll, the Tides that Turn and Know that Chicago will be Forever Rising.*

1861–1871

On the Up

(Extract from *Chicago: An Alternative History 1800–1900* by Professor Milton Winship, University of Chicago, A.C. McClurg & Co., 1902)

John S. Wright's valiant efforts with the pen to head off the Depression of 1857 would come to naught. Over the next few months, more than two hundred businesses in Chicago went bankrupt with debts amounting to over $10 million. Illinois currency lost its value, and the use of 'wild cat' bills became commonplace, notes so depreciated that they paid only sixty per cent of their face value. Tradesmen and retailers regularly had to issue 'promises to pay' and 'shinplasters'. By 1860, just one free bank in Chicago — the Marine — had survived intact. In 1861, Congress began taking steps to resolve the crisis and this would lead to the issuance of the first greenbacks in 1862. By then, of course, the Civil War was underway.

Once again, as had happened to John S. Wright twenty years before, he went bankrupt. He had unwisely mortgaged much of his wife's property to fund his business activities, in particular a new factory for building the Atkins Automaton. This must have caused much ill-feeling within the matrimonial home even before the schism created by the Civil War. Mr Wright supported the Union; Mrs Wright supported the South.

At this point, as the Civil War begins, we take our leave of Mr Wright. I do so with regret and unsated curiosity: regret because I have grown fond of him and unsated curiosity because in spite of my attempts to explore who he really was, I feel I have only scratched the surface. He would live for a good number of years yet, and his pen was by no means still, but as far as the history of Chicago is concerned, he has played his part. As he aged, the more volatile elements of his character would come increasingly to the fore. People began to give him a wide berth, his commercial judgment was distrusted and the biblical fervor of his prophecies were looked upon as the words of a man who was likely touched.

My subject is Chicago, not the Civil War. Much has already been written about Chicago's contribution to the Union cause and I do not plan to add to it. Cook County sent twenty-two thousand young men from different ethnic backgrounds to fight, most of them from Chicago. The city's lively politics during the war, and the trouble whipped up by Lincoln's opponents in the wake of his amnesty proposal of December 1863, have been ably dealt with by my fellow historians. My interest is in how ordinary people pursued their lives during the War. Perversely, it was a time of growth and prosperity for Chicago. Local companies won contracts for the supply of equipment and food to the soldiers. There were more jobs, immigration increased, new buildings went up. The city consolidated its position as the nation's leading market for oats, wheat, pork, beef and lumber. In all respects, then, during those war years, Chicago was once more on the up. And that included the very ground on which the city stood.

You read that correctly. The very ground on which Chicago stood, like everything else in the city, was 'on the up'. To understand why, let us pause to introduce another colossus of Chicago who, like Mr John S. Wright, has not been given the accolade by history that is his due. Who, today, speaks of the city's pioneering sanitary engineer, Mr Ellis S. Chesbrough? Mr Chesbrough's first act, when appointed chief engineer in 1856, was to tell the Chicago Board of Sewage Commissioners to raise the city. Yes, he said, he meant the whole darned city had to be raised — roads, houses, hotels, shops, stations, churches, you name it. The flabbergasted commissioners were told that unless Chicago stood twelve feet higher than nature had planned, the city's devastating sewage crisis would never be resolved.

Reluctantly, and with many powerful voices raised in opposition, the City Council declared that streets near the lakeshore should be raised between eight and ten feet, and the rest of the city should be raised between six and eight feet. Did the councilors avail themselves of the public purse to make this happen? No, they did not. It was, as usual, every man for himself. Officials, armed with the new city ordinances, took to patrolling the streets. I have my own memories of these self-important functionaries. *You, sir, want to put up a new building on that lot? Then you'd better make dang sure its foundations are laid at the higher grade. And you over there? You own the shack down that hole? Land sakes, when was that privy of a house first stuck together? You know what you gotta do, don't you? Either knock it down or climb on out. And there's only one way to climb, ain't there? Raise the foundations, throw in fill, lay new footings, and make yourself an eight-foot high cellar in the process. You don't like what I'm saying? Heck, you'd better watch your lip because the law's on our side.* And what they claimed about the law was true. Whenever some chuffy citizen dared to bring a suit against the authorities because they wanted to stay down in their hole at the original level, the Council's legal cavalry came charging over the horizon.

Inevitably, Mr Chesbrough was not the most popular man about town. Given the size of the city and the scale of the problem, it was also impossible for the conversion to take place overnight. People, anyway, had different reactions to those ordinances. You know how we human beings are. There's the law-abiding folk who'll do whatever they're told, the crafty ones who try to blink the question, the crooked ones who bribe officials to turn a blind eye. And then there's the rantankerous, the idle and the poor. Some of them can afford to do it, some of them can't. Some of them want to do it, some of them don't. Some of them object on principle (*the City Council should pay for raising every last inch, given those extortionate taxes they make us pay* or *nobody tells me what to do with my own goddam home*). Others don't give two cents one way or the other.

The result was that for nearly twenty years, Chicago would be a city that was lived on two levels, until the law had dealt with all the protesters and the land was filled and the old was replaced by the new. I guess this is always the way, that the old has to cede to the new. It certainly is when we're talking about Chicago. As Mark Twain put it in 1883: 'It is hopeless for the occasional visitor to try to keep up with Chicago — she outgrows his prophecies faster than he can make them. She is always a novelty; for she is never the Chicago you saw when you passed through the last time.' Well put. Thank you, Mr Twain. Because that was as true in 1861 as it was in 1883.

I hope my readers will permit me to draw on my personal experience in describing what Mr George M. Pullman falsely claims was the first brick building to be raised in Chicago. Being seen to be first in whatever he does has always been very important to Mr Pullman. He was the first man to build a luxurious railroad sleeping car, the first man to build a whole town for his employees and he has recently become the first man to make a profit out of a tragic incident in our collective past by charging visitors to view what he calls 'The Massacre Tree', a sculpture erected on the site of the 1812 Potawatomie victory over American troops in retreat from Fort Dearborn. This knack for profiting from adversity is reminiscent of his sleight of hand in arranging for the corpse of President Lincoln, on its return to Chicago in May 1865, to travel the last stage of the journey in his 'Palace Sleeping Car'. The irony probably escaped Mr Pullman, that his 'Palace Sleeping Car' was first advertised to the nation as a first-class hearse.

To the matter at hand: the Tremont House Hotel was lifted up to its new level over five days in February 1861. Mr Pullman's erroneous claim that this was the first brick building to be raised in Chicago (the Briggs House Hotel was raised in 1857) is not the only example of his faulty memory. He also likes to recall how he marched up and down Lake and Dearborn Streets, blowing his whistle and yelling 'Heigh ho!' as the Tremont made its graceful ascent. The truth is otherwise. Mr Pullman wasn't anywhere near the Tremont in February 1861. He had left for Pikes Peak, Colorado, where there was talk of a gold rush. His brother Albert was in charge of raising the Tremont. And how do I know this? Because I was there.

In those days, I was a student at the Old University of Chicago, still uncertain about what career I wished to pursue and very short of money. I was a strong boy, brought up on a farm and unafraid of hard physical labor, so to finance my studies I would look for short-term work. The hours were usually long and the pay miserable, but I was young and capable of taking a few knocks.

The raising of the Tremont was an extraordinary feat. In those days, it was the largest, most luxurious hotel in Chicago. Two hundred and sixty suites were arranged on five floors, with a capacity for two thousand guests. The Pullman Car Company needed approximately twelve hundred men for the job. That was why subcontractors were used. I was hired by one of those subcontractors — Swanson & Co. — who were responsible for a two hundred foot section abutting the hotel's main entrance on Lake Street. Mr Swanson divided us into teams of five, and in each one there was a mason, a carpenter and three unskilled laborers. The mason and the carpenter in my team were both Swedes, and the two laborers with whom I worked were of Irish extraction.

We had to dig holes beneath and into the foundations around the circumference of the Tremont at one-foot intervals. Our team was responsible for five of them. Into our holes, we drove heavy timbers, each one supported by an iron jackscrew. All around the building other teams were doing the same thing, so that by the time we were ready to start lifting, there must have been over a thousand jackscrews in place. When the whistle blew, we made one simultaneous turn on each jackscrew. That raised the timbers a few inches beneath the existing foundations, enough to insert a new brick footing in the gap beneath. Mortar was then added. In this way, inch by inch, the building began to rise.

Arranged on the plank boards behind us we kept a supply of bricks, sacks of Portland cement and buckets of water. We fetched fresh water from the Lake, prepared the mortar, stacked the bricks and, at the foreman's whistle, made those turns on the jackscrews. The days were cold, but the working hours were relatively short, and the labor itself was not too hard. I had done worse. Over the next five days, the Tremont would make its slow, gradual ascent, until it stood about eight feet higher than before. We had to build temporary new plank steps at the hotel entrance as the level rose, so that guests could continue to go in and out as though nothing was happening. There is no doubt that it was a spectacle. Sightseers came every day to watch the show.

The mason was our foreman, and a fine example he set for us all. He was also, I would come to learn, the nephew of the boss. His name was Gus. He was probably about the same age as I was. Gus was a perfectionist. Although his English was slow and halting, his passion for the work shone through in everything he said and did. He explained to us the first morning that to lift a building of this size depended for its success on everyone doing exactly what was expected of him. If we were late turning a jackscrew, or gave him too watery a mix of cement, or were too slow with the bricks, we risked causing a crack in the hotel walls. A crack could quickly spread and jeopardize the whole project. It was monotonous work but what Gus said inspired me. I liked the idea that we had to go beyond the next turn of the jackscrew, and see the project as a whole. History is like that too. The details are essential, but the bigger picture to which they contribute is what's important.

I fear that to my two Irish colleagues, Oscar and Dermot, this was nothing but a load of flapdoodle. I am not even sure they were listening. They were more interested in whistling at the fine ladies parading up and down the steps of the hotel. It annoyed me, because I liked Gus and wanted to do a good job for him. Oscar and Dermot were often behind in mixing the cement filler and its consistency varied. They handled the bricks carelessly, which meant some of them had to be thrown away. They were late turning the jackscrews.

Maybe it was partly because they were a few years younger than I was, still more juveniles than adults. But more likely, that's simply how they were. At first, I covered for them if I could, until I realized they did not care, one way or the other. Oscar, I remember, was the big mouth and the ringleader, Dermot merely his suggestible accomplice. Finding different ways to irritate 'the Scandi' was one of the boyish wagers they held between themselves. Who could make one of the ladies turn her head with a whistle, who could creep up on the Scandi and make him jump, who could break wind the loudest. They complained about the stiffness of the jackscrews, about blisters on their hands, about the hours they had to work without a break, about the $1.50 a day wages they were earning, about the weather, about everything. And, worse, when they weren't passing judgment on the hotel's female guests they were making remarks about their 'Squarehead slave driver', disguising their insults with the thickest of

Irish accents. Gus would not have understood what they were saying, but its import must have been clear.

I used to spend my lunch breaks with Gus. While the Irish boys went to buy hot food at one of the stalls that had set up across the road, we would make a seat out of bricks on the plank boards and take out our packs of pork and cheese sandwiches, prepared for us by our landladies. That was how I learned something extraordinary about Gus, an anecdote worth sharing because it provides a reminder of how redemption may come from confronting one's deepest fears. The revelation came about more by chance than by any burning desire of his to share it with me. He was reserved by nature and although he would speak with enthusiasm about the art of building, teaching me useful rules I have long since forgotten, he did not talk easily about himself.

On the second or third day, as we ate our sandwiches in a companionable silence over the lunch break, a heated argument got underway. The windows of a top floor room, right above our heads, had been flung open and a gentleman sat on the sill, legs swinging. He was threatening to throw himself to the ground. This incident, I am pleased to report, would end happily enough when the gentleman was persuaded to return inside. But a curious exchange then took place between Gus and myself. I said that I could not imagine a worse way to end one's life than by falling from a great height, with all that time before hitting the ground. To which Gus replied: 'It is not that bad as you think.' I asked him to explain what he meant, but at that moment the whistle blew and we had to go back to work.

The next day, as we ate our lunch, I asked him again. It turned out that when Gus arrived in America, he had settled with his mother, father and sister on a prairie lot near the town of St Clair, in Michigan.[5] The lot belonged to his uncle, the Mr Swanson of

5 This was the same St Clair where Jean Baptiste Pointe de Sable once worked for the British at The Pinery, before he moved to Echicagou.

Swanson & Co. For a few months one winter, he worked in a logging team, something he said he vowed he would never do again, even before he had the accident that is the subject of this anecdote.

One day, he was given the job of breaking a logjam and, though he managed to do so successfully, he failed to make it back to the riverbank. Instead, he was driven over the nearby Falls. (He is telling me this, I should add, in the most matter-of-fact way.) He knew there was no chance of survival. But, he said — and this was the reason for his comment about the gentleman falling from the window — he did not feel afraid.

These are the notes I made that evening in my journal, in which I tried to capture — no doubt inexpertly — something of his halting English:

I am having much time for think before I go over. I don't explain this. Only that time, it is slow. I am not thinking and nothing to worry. I see beautiful pictures to my life from when I am born to when I am die. The pictures are having no order or number one two three. They are like a *stim*. Now I am learning you Swedish. Maybe this is a new work for me! The Swedish say one *stim* is many fish together. This is how the pictures are. One big picture to my life from many small pictures together. Not too much fast, not too much slow.

I am so interesting in the pictures. Even some are happy and some are sad it is no different. I am seeing Lake Holjeån and Liverpool and flying fish and St Clair house and my mother and father and Ingrid, she is my sister, and each mile to America from outside the train window. And I am interesting most in the pictures to my grandfather's house. This is the house when I am born. Not like to houses in America built from nails and two-by-fours that fall down in five years, ten years. My grandfather's house stay for three hundred years. I am the small boy to the pictures my face pressed to the walls. The timber is smooth. Deep gold color. Even in the joins they are having no holes or gaps. It is beautiful like a palace and strong like a rock. When I am seeing these pictures I decide if I am born a second life I want to build houses like this to last for three hundred years. Then I can leave behind something special to the world.

In one picture I go to the roof of the house. It is made in shingles of birch bark. There has sedum on the sod. The sun is shining bright. I am the small boy to the roof and I fall asleep. When I wake up I am sliding over the edge. I drop like a stone. And for the first time in my life when falling from a height there is no afraid in my heart.

How did he survive? That was a miracle nobody could explain. By sheer luck, he said, he must have landed not just in the deepest part of the pool, but in the only fraction of it that was momentarily free of churning logs. For the next three days he was sheltered and cared for by the farmer who had fished him out of the water five miles downriver, still clinging to a log, barely conscious. It had always been his greatest fear, he explained, to fall from a height. The accident at the St Clair Falls was a blessing because it cured him of that fear forever. He now knew that if he were ever again to fall from on high, it would be neither a painful nor an unpleasant way to die.

The whistle blew, and the lunch break was over. I reflected on what he had told me, and how much stronger we all might be if, like him, we were forced to confront our greatest fears. Sadly, I never had a chance to ask Gus any more about the experience because the next day's lunch break would be interrupted in a very different way, one I also noted down in my journal, but which I have decided not to put into this book. The incident has no direct bearing on the history of Chicago, although its inclusion in these pages would cast one of our participants in an even more unfavorable light.

On that sensitive matter, I proposition to beat about the bush no longer. No doubt there will be readers, in any case, who have already put two and two together. The young Oscar with whom I worked for those five days, raising the Tremont, would become Alderman Oscar 'Burner' Brody. I will have plenty to say about him later. But on this occasion I will spare the rod. In any case, I have probably made enough derogatory comments already for the Alderman to sue me — or worse. Suffice to say that Oscar Brody did not come off well in a confrontation he engineered the next day with Gus Swanson, our Swedish foreman.

The Tremont House Hotel was one of the earlier brick buildings to be raised in Chicago, thanks to the initiative of Mr Ellis S. Chesbrough. While the Civil War divided the nation, caused immense suffering and claimed the lives of over six hundred thousand young men, fomenting deep splits within families such as that of John S. Wright, the city of Chicago prospered. It remained literally 'on the up' during the War, through to and beyond the Great Fire of 1871. Sadly, though, the Tremont House Hotel that I helped to raise, in my own small way, would be one of the thousands of buildings that failed to survive the greatest conflagration in the city's history.

1861

The Masoner

(This chapbook was believed to have been in private circulation in Chicago during the 1890s. Who transcribed the monologue, and when, remains unknown. The trustees of the Chicago Historical Society have declared it to be an artifact of cultural importance. It should be noted, by way of introduction, that more Irish immigrated to the United States during the 1840s, when the potato famine was at its height, than any other nationality.)

Yerra, my friend, you want to hear about Oscar when he claimed to be learning masonry? I shall do my best, though it is a tale that brings me no joy to tell. And I shall drink only a little more of your nectar for it hits the throat as fierce as the westerlies blow off Inishtooshkert on the spring tides, and the story I must relate has need of a careful tongue.

We lived on Archer's Avenue at number 361, a house we shared with the cook, his wife and the boy Dermot, that was Oscar's friend from the canal. Our ward boss was 'King Mike' McDonald, a rascal worse than Mr Krumpacker for the swaggering on him and the hurt he meted out to those who least could take it. In the Gaelic tongue, he was a *bradacha*. When I heard Oscar had been working for King

Mike, the news cut me to the marrow.

I talked to the boy. I reminded him of sacrifices made for his schooling and I urged him, by the saints, to use what he had learned from Father O'Connor to make a better life for himself. So I was happy when, one day, he told me he was training to be a masoner. Masonry is a noble trade. If there had been a great city like Chicago on Great Blasket, instead of little Dunquin and Dingle across the way, Old Conn would have had something to say about it. For it is masoners, is it not, that make a city? Wisha, that it had been true, what Oscar told me.

On the fourth day of work, it was past the midnight hour and Oscar and Dermot were still not home. When I heard their drunken crowing in the street, I rose from my bed and waited. The gate was kicked open, followed by a search for keys. In they swayed, Dermot in the rear looking sheepish. I unleashed my tongue. I knew he had been consorting again with that villain King Mike. I told him plain and simple, he should be ashamed of himself. A man's nature arrives when he's a cub, and hadn't I done my best to drive the Devil from him? I parleyed too long, and said more than a father should ever say to a son, whatever the cause. Ah, how painful it is to speak of what lays heavy on the heart.

Oscar pushed me hard against the wall, one hand like a vice on my throat. He would not end up like me, he said. He would be a big man in Chicago one day, not a penny-hoarding fisherman who pushed out a canoe each morning, praying that the fish would bite. He squeezed me like one possessed. I was beginning to wonder if the Great Master had decided my time down here was done when, letting go, he collapsed onto a chair, his head in his hands.

'By God and Mary, Oscar,' I gasped, 'you'll say you're sorry.'

He raised his head. 'A real man,' he said, 'would fight back.'

'With his own son?' I told him some truths. He thought life was easy, did he? He thought he could make the world bend whichever way he wanted? One day, he would learn that nothing is easy, and that anything too easy cannot be honest. He should listen to what Old Conn said about that. But he was not listening to anything. He was snoring in his chair, and nothing would rouse him. That was why I spoke about Mochta in the way I did. I wanted his attention.

'What?' he groaned. 'What're you sayin' about Uncle Mochta?'

'Ah,' said I. 'I thought that might be awakin' thee.'

I should have stopped there, and said no more. But at times like this the tongue runs swifter than the brain. I told him about his Uncle Mochta, and the fortune that awaited him.

'What money? How much?'

'Begorra,' I snapped. 'Don't think you'll know how much, nor that you'll be getting your hands on it, not until you stop behaving like a lout and turn into a man. There is something broken in you, Oscar, and ye need to be afixing it.'

That silenced him. His eyes began to fill with tears. After a while, his aggression passed and the apologies began.

This is the problem. I love Oscar, whatever the badness he does, and he knows it.

He pushed himself onto his feet, searched for balance like a drowning man, and lunged across the room towards me. He arrived on his knees, his face a picture of penitence. 'I'm sorry, father,' he said. 'I'm shamed, the same you're sayin'. I promise I'll change my ways.'

After more apologies and more pleading, I yielded. Uncle Mochta had left him $4500, I told him. It was locked up in a bank, and would be released on his twenty-first birthday.

It was Dermot, after I pressed him, who told me what happened the next day, though I don't know why I am sharing this shame with you, my friend, to put on that page of yours. My son woke late. Then there was a problem with the train from Bridgeport so he jumped out at the corner of State and 12th Street, and because the omnibuses were full, he decided to walk. It was another cold, gray February day. I know what Oscar is like. His head would have been spinning with that $4500. He'd have seen himself seated at a mahogany desk in a big office with soft leather armchairs, his black overcoat on the coat stand, a bowler on the hook. He'd have seen himself walking the aisles of the Potter Palmer Dry Goods store on Lake, ordering merchandise with the flick of a finger as liveried staff scraped and bowed and called him 'Sir'. Once he inherited the fortune from Uncle Mochta, he'd start a business, a huge business. Yerra, that would have been the kind of nonsense that filled his head.

According to Dermot, when Oscar turned the corner onto Wells, he climbed some steps towards a line of shops built at the new street level, full of fancy signs and gas-lit windows. He must have known he needed to brisk up, but something caught his eye in the window of a Gentleman's Haberdashery. A long-sleeved white shirt was on display next to a pair of dark pants like the ones used by the Union baseball team. He'd always dreamed of playing for the Union team. He would have stood there before that window and imagined dressing up in the colors, with a pair of spiked shoes and cap to match. After all, why not have an office with a big mahogany desk *and* play baseball for the Union team?

A wind was beating off the Lake as he set off again. It was a bitter morning, colder than a Presbyterian charity, he later cracked to Dermot. I grin, despite myself. He always had a likely tongue on him, the rascal. When he turned the corner at Dearborn and Lake, he ran into the crowds come to watch the raising of the Tremont. He bludgeoned his way through, probably still lost in his baseball daydream, yelling, 'Clear the way for a home run.' I reckon that boy — the son I raised and love — instead of being worried about arriving late, was more interested in pretending to be the hero in the final between Union and Excelsiors, the last man in, making the home run that would clinch it and oh how he gripped the bat tight, and with the ball hurtling towards him how wide he swung to strike — the same as we'd do on the White Strand against the Dunquin folk in Christmas week — and there was a thwack of leather on wood as the ball soared into the outfield, and he cleared first base, second base, third base ... the crowds were roaring 'Oscar! Oscar! Oscar!' and in his daydream he heard Uncle Mochta's voice — 'Fly like a bird, Oscar!' — and the bat in his hand wasn't straight but curved like a hurley and the outfield was open prairie and he was astride his Uncle Mochta's shoulders as the crowds chanted his name.

See, how I've got carried away myself, in the imagining of it. I don't know if that's what he was really thinking. But I do know he arrived late, and was shouting 'Home run, home run.'

During the lunch break, their foreman (Dermot insisted on calling him 'the Scandi') sat eating sandwiches with another laborer, a young American they didn't like: not because there was anything wrong with him, as Dermot admitted, but because he worked too hard. Those two sandwich-eaters were sensible, to my way of thinking, not throwing their pennies overboard on stale pies and weak grog from a stall. Oscar and Dermot had one of their wagers — when the whistle blew, whoever reached the stall second had to pay. Oscar won (he probably always did) but he treated Dermot in any case. He couldn't wait to talk about his fortune-in-waiting.

This is where my tale saddens me to the depths. To take a swipe at your own family can be pardoned. We all commit that unkindness, once or twice in our lives. But to swipe a stranger without provocation? Imagine this. Their pies and grog are finished, and they're stamping their feet to keep warm, with their hands shoved beneath their oxters.

'So what shall you do,' asks Dermot, 'when you git the 'heritance?'

At that moment, they're distracted by a lady coming out of the hotel entrance. The bellboy holds the door open for her. She is tight in furs and scarves and her hat is pulled down low, but it's clear that she's a beauty. The whistle blows but Oscar does not move. 'We shall stay at the Tremont House, Dermot, to celebrate,' he says. 'And we'll find for ourselves two young cherries, just like that one.'

Dermot blushed when he told me this, and no wonder.

'Brody?' It is the foreman, calling them.

Oscar leads the way across the road back to the site, but he's in no hurry. The opposite, in fact. The foreman is waiting for them, hands on hips.

'You know why I didn't fire you before?' says the foreman. 'Because an Irish was helping me one time. I was to pass on the favor, by helping an Irish in trouble.'

Without saying a word, Oscar punches him.

The Scandi doubles up and groans.

'The mutt wasn't expecting that, eh, Dermot?'

How it hurts me to talk like this but now I have started, I must go to the end. Oscar spits on his knuckles, and slaps Dermot on the back. 'I've been wanting to do that for a long time.' Then he kicks over a pile of bricks, and says it feels grand to do that too.

Everyone has stopped work to watch. A whistle is blowing somewhere. Foremen are shouting. But nobody's moving. Nor does Oscar seem to have noticed that nobody's cheering.

'If you want a fight,' says someone, 'fight on equal terms.'

'Fair fight,' shouts someone else.

The Scandi is struggling back to his feet.

Everyone takes up the cry. 'Fair fight, fair fight.'

Dermot has started to retreat into the crowd. There's nothing he could have done, he claims.

The Scandi is showing his fists.

I heard all this later, after I'd tended Oscar's wound above the eye with a dose of carbolic. He was in a poor way. Over and over, he repeated a story about how he fell from the first floor when the wall collapsed beneath him, and of how he'd always worried the Tremont foundations looked unstable but nobody ever listened.

Later, when Dermot told me all he could remember, however much I wanted to believe otherwise, I knew in my heart it was the truth. I was left to wondering if Oscar managed to land a single blow on the foreman before that gentleman knocked him out cold. My boy fell sideways, and cut his head on one of those bricks he'd kicked over.

Dermot took him to a quack on LaSalle Street who pulled and tugged at his forehead as though he were a baker kneading dough before putting in stitches that felt, reported Oscar, 'tight as knots and thick as cord'. He vowed that one day he would get his own back on the 'Scandi'.

I told him to look inside himself instead, and learn to be a man. 'This wound will take some time to heal,' I added.

'It stings,' he said.

'Yerra. That's a good sign,' I told him. 'Old Conn said the sting of an honest wound earns the respect of all mankind.'

That is where this tale ends, my young friend. I am weary and the hour is late. Write down what you will, I shall be none the wiser. But I tell you this. A father has grand dreams for the future of his son, but he can only do so much. The day comes when he must cast him loose, and leave what follows in the hands of the Great Master.

1867

The Haunted Tunnel

This short story, set in 1867 and written by Thomas Hunter, was published by A.C. McClurg & Co., Chicago, in the March 1896 edition of *The Dial* magazine. Thomas Hunter's wife is the journalist Antje Hunter (née Van Voorhis) of the *Chicago Daily Tribune*.

I give you, dear reader, fair warning. The story I am about to tell you is mostly true, even though it may not have happened. My role is merely that of amanuensis. I have transcribed the story on behalf of its narrator as faithfully as I can, a man who (I believe) had his own reasons for wanting the tale to appear fantastical. Where I have made additions, they are of a purely descriptive nature, putting more flesh, if you will, on the bare bones of what happened, or what may have happened. I invite anyone who is skeptical about the existence of spirits or monsters to read this tale as a straightforward ghost story that will, I hope, prove entertaining. But for readers who accept there may indeed be more things in Heaven and earth than are dreamt of in Horatio's philosophy, I offer a word of warning: beware.

The events I describe take place on the night of a full moon. Our protagonist, an Engineer, tells his wife he is going out for a walk.

He doffs his top hat, takes hold of his cane and steps onto Clybourn Street. In terms of appearance and age, the Engineer is a tall, broad-shouldered and unremarkable gentleman of fifty-three years. He looks well fed, fit and strong, and his attire is smart without being ostentatious. He walks with a mild stoop, typical of a man whose life has become more desk-bound than it once was. The casual observer might assume he is a respectable, successful man of affairs who, like many a resident on a hot summer night, is trying to escape the unholy stench from the Union Stockyards that has hung over the city all day. If we search for clues to his character we might find one in the striking gray beard he wears — it is longer than fashionable and, on close inspection, does not look to have been groomed for some time — evidence perhaps of a man who keeps up appearances but without much enthusiasm. We might also note the intensity with which he observes the world about him. This is a person who, despite his advancing years, finds it difficult to relax and enjoy the world for what it is. He must always know what it is made of and how it works. Oh, and there are his hands, of course. They are the big, strong hands of a practical man.

Tonight, he is in an odd mood, a very odd mood indeed. In fact, he is not at all himself. He walks without apparent purpose. Indecisiveness, as it happens, is a charge his detractors unfairly make against him. At some point, he finds himself in a park where the foul city air becomes pleasantly sweetened by the scent of honeysuckle and clover, and the grass is soft beneath his feet. As he passes between the trees, he absent-mindedly forgets what they really are, pausing to speculate on the nature of their foundations, to tap their trunks with his cane, and to look for the joints and screws that must be holding such tall, thin structures upright. He chuckles, with self-conscious embarrassment, when he realizes his mistake. He continues towards the Lake.

He steps into a rowing boat, and plies the oars. The pale yellow moon is massive and rising. All along, it has been drawing him on. He knows where he is being taken. There is a misshapen hulk, out in the Lake, that looks like a shipwreck. This hulk is called the Crib. The boat slips through the still water. The Crib looms larger and larger. Fear begins to tickle his thoughts. For it should be acknowledged that, underneath, the Engineer can be an anxious fellow, a weakness he has to work exceedingly hard to hide. He says he inherited that trait from his Welsh mother — long since departed — who, despite employing dozens of tricks to ward off evil, always feared the worst. What if the Crib, thinks the Engineer, is not really the Crib? What if it is a hideous monster? What if it is alive?

But the Crib is not alive and is indeed nothing more or less than the Crib.[6] A watchman is leaning over the rail, a lamp in his hand. The Engineer wonders why he knows everything there is to know about the Crib. Then he remembers that it was he who dreamed it up in the first place, just as it was he who dreamed up the Tunnel that runs beneath the bottom of the Lake, connecting the Crib to the shore.

The watchman's face, when he catches sight of his visitor, turns a deathly white, as if he has seen a ghost. 'G ... good evening, Engineer,' he stutters.

While he ascends the ladder to the deck, numbers come to him, a stream of numbers whose arrival he finds deeply pleasurable, even though he cannot remember what they are for. Numbers are everything to the Engineer. It is with numbers that he makes sense of the world even if, in this curious mood, he can no longer tell whether these numbers refer to feet or inches, planks or nails, tons or gallons, miles or dollars. They come and go, flashing like fireflies.

---

6 I do not intend to denigrate the real Crib's size or ingenuity or purpose, but it was a very familiar structure to the narrator, which was doubtless why he chose not to describe it. The Crib was pentagonal in shape, stood forty feet high and was ninety-eight feet in diameter. Inside, it was divided into fifteen separate watertight compartments where the pumping equipment was housed, and at its center stood a shaft that went down to the bottom of the Lake. It will be down this shaft that the Engineer descends.

One number — by far the biggest — recurs again and again.

'Fifty-seven million what?' he asks the watchman.

'That would be gallons of water, Engineer.'

'Every day,' he says, remembering.

'Yes, Engineer. That would be every day.'

The watchman is proffering his Davy lamp, which signals to him what he must do next. He says he is going down, that he has to check something urgently — the flow rate or the water quality or a stretch of the Tunnel's brickwork where cracks have been reported. 'I shall be down there for some time,' he says.

'Y ... yes, of course, Engineer.'

A sticky black fog fills the netherworld beneath the surface of the Lake. The Engineer, who suffers from a phobia of being buried alive in one of his own underground tunnels, proceeds cautiously down the first ladder, staring intently at everything illumined by the lamp. He is alert to each small sound, notices each infinitesimal shift in The Crib's foundations, recoils from each drop of condensation as though he has been stung. In this slow, halting fashion, he descends the shaft, inching past the architecture of silent pumps and pipes that he knows best as lines, angles and elevations on a chart. The air is stale and damper than a mildewed cellar. Indeterminate whiffs of decomposition come his way.

The further he goes, the more the Engineer becomes suffused by a sense of dread. Why is he tormenting himself like this? Why not go back now, before it's too late? The weight of water is immense. More gallons lie in the Lake than can be conceived of in the human mind. What if his calculations are wrong? A strident Irish whisper, worryingly familiar, fills his head. *You in't a janius, then, you's a murd'rer. A murd'rer ... murd'rer ... murd'rer.* The last word will not stop. It comes back off the chamber walls. He fears he could, indeed, be that murderer, but he cannot remember why.

The shaft narrows the deeper he goes. The dankness is seeping into his clothes. His shirt and breeches are too tight. The world seems to be contracting. He fears imminent suffocation. Might he be losing his mind? He panics. He wants to get out, he yearns for light and air and dry land. He tosses his top hat into the darkness, he tears off the collar at his throat, he cries out 'let me go', but no sound emerges from his lips. The shaft swivels on, and swivels down.

Perversely, the numbers in his head grow clearer. But they are no longer pretty fireflies. They glow in the shapes of bright, malevolent grins.

84 steps.   3 ladders.   19 feet below.

5 ft diameter   2 miles long.

2 ft slope per mile.   4 miles per hour ...

They are my numbers, he thinks, numbers I made. And those numbers have come back to taunt me. The tunnel is reached by 84 steps, down 3 ladders. It lies 19 feet below the bottom of the Lake, it has a 5-foot diameter, it stretches for 2 miles, slopes at 2 feet per mile, and the water travels at 4 miles per hour.

Before he can dwell any further on the treachery of his numbers, he stops, mid-step, in alarm. He has heard a strange, unearthly cry, that seems to be coming from somewhere in the very bowels of the earth. It is an enraged, tormented sound. That must be how a werewolf, he thinks, howls at the moon. There is another outburst, identical to the first. Then there is another. He holds his breath and listens. He listens until the cries have stopped and the echoes have dissipated into nothing. Maybe it was indeed a werewolf howling at the moon. Maybe they came from above, not below. But in his heart he knows the truth.

When he takes another step down the ladder, his legs feel shaky. There is a rush of warm, rancid air. He holds out the lamp, but all he can see is a trickle of condensation running down the brickwork. How did the watchman put it? *That would be gallons of water, Engineer.* 'Would be.' Does that mean the Tunnel is not yet finished? But surely it <u>is</u> finished. Surely it has been finished for a long time. Hasn't someone already declared the Tunnel 'the wonder of America and the world?' How could it be called a 'wonder' if it was not yet completed?

He feels angry. Angry that he is here, angry that there is no way back, angry that he cannot understand what is happening. The full moon brings many things. It brings lunacy, it brings murder and pregnancy and nightmares and sleepwalkers and werewolves. And it brings ghosts. Yes, above all, the full moon brings back the dead.

He drops the lamp and falls off the ladder. For how long does he fall and fall through the under-Lake darkness before he is falling no more? He finds himself on his feet again, the lamp back in his hand. And he hears new sounds. A hubbub of thuds and thumps and scrapes. The sound of digging.

Ahead of him, he can make out a boat. This one, unlike his rowboat, is a narrow, flat-bottomed vessel. A shadowy figure — the oarsman — is waiting aboard. Everything, finally, falls into place. The Tunnel is finished, but it will not be opened until tomorrow. Yes, not until tomorrow will it be called the 'wonder of America and the world'. He does not know how he knows this, but he does. He is about to carry out the final inspection. That is why this boat is waiting for him. And the hubbub of thuds and thumps and scrapes? Some workers must be out there, doing their last minute repairs.

He steps aboard. The boat is stocked with tools — picks, trowels, drills, hammers, a heap of sand, a bag of cement. There is also a stretch of copper piping. He places a hand on the arch of bricks overhead to hold himself steady. The bricks, damp and cold against his palm, reassure him that this is real.

The oarsman propels them forwards. The Engineer, holding up his lamp, inspects the brickwork reflected in the leaky yellow light. The thuds and thumps and scrapes of the workers' picks grow louder. He hears their shovels heaping the clay earth onto trolleys. The Engineer begins to feel apprehensive, but he does not know why. He raises the lamp, and looks ahead. The air is changing. It is being filled by a stench like the Union stockyards. He can make out the emaciated shapes of diggers at work. They move in silence. Only the shovels scrape as they lift their loads of clay, only the trolleys groan and squeal along the tracks, only the piercing whistles of the foreman echo back and forth through a gloom that is neither day nor night. It is hellish, awful, unbearable. Their phantom bodies, bare to the waist, are coated in grime and sweat. Eyes flash in the lamplight, unseeing, red with dust and hurt. And beyond he sees masoners bricking up the newly excavated space, racing to prevent its collapse. There is the slop of water, the grind of mortar, the *slap slap slap* and scoop of trowels.

The Engineer cannot understand why they are here.

Suddenly, he is in the middle of them, encircled by wraiths armed with picks and spades and shovels. They are staring at him through hollow eyes. He is spattered by drops of deadman spit and sweat. He strikes out at the sea of gaunt, accusing faces. But it is like striking thin air. A voice calls out, the same Irish voice he heard before, the one he recognizes but cannot place, and he understands this voice is speaking for them all: *You're no janius, like they say, now ain't that so? I tell ye this and I tell ye true. We ain't be savidges the way you think. A dollar a day ain't jistice in Archer's Avenue, nor in this Tunnil neither. Seven Irish workers dead as donkeys ten fath'ms deep when the roof fell in. You're no janius but a comm'n murd'rer … murd'rer … murd'rer.* Dear God, the calculations must have been wrong. He strikes out ever more desperately at the wraiths, to try to find that voice and silence it. *To that seven, add one more. One more, one more, one more is yet to die. Murd'rer … murd'rer … murd'rer.* The voice fades and as their boat moves on, the phantoms begin to sing. The Tunnel is flooded by a great chorus of Irish voices, rich and sweet as angels. The voices rise and fall and rise again, full of rage and despair at their own deaths.

One more is yet to die. The Engineer knows what he must do. He must prevent that final death. But who is it? Which one is he, of those hundreds that have worked in the Tunnel?

He has no time to think because another bloodcurdling howl rings out. The oarsman brings the boat to a halt. The Engineer crouches and, the lamp held high, stares into the darkness. Only a creature not of this world could make such a hideous sound.

How long do those ferocious cries echo through the Tunnel? How long is it before the oarsman begins to push them forwards again? The Engineer wants him to turn back, he wants to return to the safety of the Crib, but he can issue no instructions. No words will come out of his mouth. The oarsman stands erect, driving them forwards. All the Engineer can do is watch.

The air is changing. It is unnaturally warm and ominously rotten.

Another howl breaks out, this time so close and loud that the Tunnel shakes on its foundations. The din comes thundering towards them like an express train. There is an onrush of hot, moldering air and they are plunged into darkness. He must have knocked over the Davy lamp, but they are still moving forwards. What does the oarsman think he is doing? Why doesn't he turn back? Oh, how he would rant and rave, what a reprimand he would deliver, if only he could speak to the man.

The reverberations of one more tormented bellow are followed by a rush of putrid air that comes spinning towards him with the force of a whirlwind, around and around the tightness of the Tunnel. He is knocked backwards, into the water. The world turns black.

But though he might wish darkness and oblivion to be the end, it is not. He does not die. His eyes are wide open. He is forced to watch as his oarsman propels the boat forwards, towards a dark shape that fills the Tunnel, towards a shape that looks grotesque, towards a shape that looks alive. Two beams of light are its cold, green eyes. The face is that of an enormous cat, whiskers stiff as ship's cordage sprung from each side of a head clad in bedraggled gray fur. In front, the brute rests on two giant paws, padded by clumps of more fur, bristling with long, curved nails that taper to a point. But the body of this fiend is not that of a cat. The Engineer catches a glimpse of its cumbrous slithering bulk when the colossus shifts its weight, to reveal a heaving wad of slimy, misshapen copper-colored scales.

Opening wide its mouth, the monster seizes the boat between its jaws. The Engineer wants to do something. He wants to fight, he wants the oarsman to get out of harm's way, he wants this to end.

But it does not end.

He watches a set of gnarled, yellow teeth grind the boat to splinters, spitting out the debris in dark-flecked spume. He watches the oarsman, erect and fearless to the end, thrust his pole deep inside the creature's cavernous mouth, which roils with foul saliva. He watches the pole snap like a twig. He watches the ogre heave itself laboriously, clumsily, gracelessly around the confines of the tunnel. He watches the scales shift like giant links of chainmail on a tail that narrows to a solid tip the width of a stout club that, with one short flick, knocks the oarsman over. The massive paws, their tufts of gray fur stiffening and the scimitar-shaped nails drawn to their full extent, stamp him to death.

And that is when the awful truth comes to him. The oarsman was the man he had to save. The oarsman was the eighth man, and he was always there, in front of his eyes. But all the Engineer has done is watch.

The beast turns, it slams a paw against the roof, the Tunnel trembles as bricks fly down. The Lake rushes in and fills up the Engineer like a bottle.

AUTHOR'S NOTE

I thought it might be of interest to readers to hear of how I came upon the material that inspired me to write this story. Late in his life, I had the privilege of becoming acquainted with Chicago's great sanitary engineer, Mr Ellis S. Chesbrough. On one occasion, I asked him about the famous Crib and Intake Tunnel he built to solve Chicago's chronic problem of polluted water in the 1860s. Even in old age, he had a remarkable grasp of the details of their construction, about which I took copious notes (without ever imagining I would actually make use of them).

The next time I saw him, he was keen to speak again about the Crib and Tunnel. He wanted to tell me something, he said, that wasn't 'entirely factual'. He proceeded to recount details of 'a recurring nightmare' from which he said he continued to suffer. It is this nightmare I have recorded in 'The Haunted Tunnel'. Nightmares are not, generally, promising material for a story. They have neither the craft of myth nor the psychological accuracy of truth. Also, a recurring nightmare is usually influenced so much by the life of its recipient that it is rendered incomprehensible.

After finishing the story, I asked my wife — Antje Hunter — to read it through for me. As a reporter she is more concerned about facts than I am, and the story prompted her to do some research in the archives of the *Chicago Daily Tribune* on the subject of Mr Chesbrough's Crib and Tunnel. Two small items she unearthed may be of interest to readers of this story. I should stress, though, that 'The Haunted Tunnel' was written before I saw these reports and it is presented here with not a word added or changed. Whether or not these cuttings have any bearing on the story, I leave to the judgment of my readers.

The first extract is taken from the *Chicago Daily Tribune* of March 7, 1867. It reports a disturbance said to have taken place in the Tunnel the previous evening.

Nobody saw the cow enter or leave the Intake Tunnel, but it is presumed the breach must have occurred because a gate to the new pumping station on the lakeshore had been left open. The chief engineer, Mr Ellis Chesbrough, was carrying out a final inspection of the brickwork before the Tunnel's opening when he and his team heard the cow 'mooing furiously'. They went to investigate. The cow, doubtless maddened by its confinement, kicked out with such savagery at the oarsman, Mr Michael Molloy, that the attack brought about his demise. Cracks were also sustained in the Tunnel's brickwork that have since been repaired. Mr Molloy's death brings the number of lives lost in the building of the Tunnel to eight.

The second item Mrs Hunter found was written many years later, in the early 1880s. I suspect she brought it to my attention more for my sake than hers, in that its news element was slight.

Strange goings on were reported last night inside the Intake Tunnel that feeds fresh water into the Waterworks at the foot of Chicago Avenue. It appears that a large unidentified animal may have entered the Tunnel and become trapped inside. The night watchman reported that, around midnight, he heard sounds consistent with 'a distressed beast' coming from somewhere inside. A rescue team was dispatched but, although they confirmed hearing an animal's cries, they failed to find one inside the Tunnel. They did, though, discover a section of damaged brickwork. This led rescuers to speculate that the beast, thinking itself trapped, may have tried to force its way out. The mysterious visitor, then, appears to have entered and exited the Tunnel without detection.

Whilst baffled officials continue to pursue their enquiries into the incident, it is perhaps worth mentioning in this context an old Potawatomie myth. According to the Potawatomies, a creature called Nambi-Za lives beneath our Lake. Nambi-Za is one of the most terrifying creatures in Indian mythology. A large beast, he is said to have the face of a cat and the tail of a dragon. He lives underwater. His realm encompasses the Lake and the lakeshore, and he punishes intruders and those he considers to have 'abused Nature' by luring them beneath the water, from whence the victims' bodies are never recovered.

For worried readers who fear they might become Nambi-Za's next victim, there is protection to be had. The creature's scaly dragon tail, the legend goes, is made out of copper and the dragon would never attack anyone it perceived as one of its own. Wear a copper charm and you will be perfectly safe. And one more piece of advice. Avoid the Lake on nights of a full moon. That is when Nambi-Za is said to be at his most active.

1871

The Perils of Compromise

Ellis struggled to get to sleep and, when he did manage to nod off, he had the nightmare again. He woke to find himself standing by the window, short of breath. His nightshirt was damp. The last moments were achingly vivid. All at once, the doomed oarsman thrusts his pole down the beast's throat, the Tunnel brickwork cracks open and the Lake comes rushing in. He wakes up drowning. The details of the dream varied, but that was how it always ended.

In her bed, his wife stirred. He heard her turn over. 'Ellis?' she murmured. 'Are you all right?'

'Quite well, dear.'

She was soon asleep again, snoring gently.

Ellis lowered himself onto the edge of the bed. A shiver ran down his spine, even though it was a warm, humid morning. Why had that dream started to recur? Was it anxiety that, despite preparing for every possible contingency, something had to go wrong at the last moment because something always did go wrong? Was the dream a warning? In which case, should he do what his mother would have done and go out to find a haystack he could stare at for good luck? Staring at haystacks was her remedy for everything. It was an old Welsh custom, she said, that never let her down. Even if it did not give her luck, at least it always gave her courage.

He lit a candle and went downstairs to the water closet. Mrs Molloy insisted on closing the window at night. He flipped the latch and enjoyed the feel of fresh air against his face. Leaning over the basin, he turned the tap. There was a gasp from somewhere in the pipework, like a clearing of the throat and then, after a moment's delay, it came. The pressure was strong. Water slooshed into the basin. He stopped the flow when it was half-full. Bending forwards, he inspected the clarity. There were little particles, visible even in this poor light. He sniffed. All summer, the smell had been getting worse. Today, he thought, today that would change.

He took hold of the soap and worked up a strong lather. As he plunged his hands into the basin and washed his face, scrubbing vigorously, the anxiety that had kept him awake began to feel overblown. Through the open window came the sound of birdsong. To his surprise, a warbler was singing to the new morning even though its natural habitat was no more. As a boy, that was the sound that would wake him on the farm in far-off Baltimore County. He sighed at his own contribution to the razing of the warbler's habitat. How much simpler life was, without cities. Well, it was too late now. The bird's final call was interrupted by a distant squeal of brakes, the city's answering cry. That would be the first train coming through on the Milwaukee line. He used to travel it himself when they lived out that way. After Fullerton, the train would cross North and Division and Chicago and come to a final stop at the station on Kinzie. At this time of day, it would be packed with labourers on their way into the city looking for a day's work at one of the construction sites in the downtown area.

Some of them might even be his own Canal workers, though most of them came from the shanties on the South Branch of the river near Bridgeport. He paused his ablutions. The soap slipped out of his hands, and he did nothing to stop the trickle of water down his beard. Eight men, including Molloy on the final inspection, had died in the building of the Tunnel. He remembered the words of his early mentor, Mr Stephen Long. *The death of the few will always be justified by the improvements we make.* The Tunnel had worked in the beginning, and would work again — would work again from today — once the Canal extension was opened and the sewage driven away from the Lake. Even so, wholeheartedly accepting Mr Long's argument had always troubled him. Mr Long used to say something else, too, about the duty of an engineer, but Ellis preferred not to think about what that was.

He picked up the soap. He thought and worked in numbers all the time. But people were different. Could he really be absolved of responsibility on the simple basis of an arithmetical majority? And how robust did it look now, when they found themselves back at square one? He dried his face. Eight men had died building the Tunnel, but he had no idea how many had died in the construction of the Canal extension because the contractors deliberately hid the information from him, and from everyone else too. Ten, twenty, thirty? Even if the Canal did exactly what it was meant to do, could one say the death of the few justified improvements made for the many? And if the Canal did not work? That did not bear thinking about.

In the dressing room, Mrs Molloy had prepared his clothes. His best black coat, satin waistcoat, pantaloons and a boiled white shirt were waiting on hangers. On top of the chest of drawers were his bowtie and a folded white handkerchief for his top pocket. He would be too hot, but he had no choice. He hated attention, but today it could not be avoided. They would all be there. If it worked, the city boosters and bigwigs and politicians, most of whom had criticised him for taking so long to put forward his proposals, complained at the expense and dismissed him as a 'well-meaning but impractical dreamer', would forget their hostility and pretend they had always been behind him. Fuelled by beer and bourbon, they would use big, fine-sounding words. And he would have to stand in front of the crowds and pretend he felt honoured by their attention. God knew what exaggeration they would find today. Mayor Rice had used an excruciating expression, the day the Tunnel was opened, back in '67. *The wonder of America and the world,* he had called it.

He went downstairs into the dining room. On the table, there was an apple on one plate, two thick slices of bread coated in butter and ham on another. He could hear Mrs Molloy moving about in the kitchen, muttering to herself. There was the welcome smell of freshly ground coffee. He called out a greeting, sat down and pressed the two slices of bread together to make a sandwich.

She was talking even before she came in. 'And it shall be a gran' day iv speechin', an' hailin' ye a janius, Mr Illis, that it shall. I tell ye everything, an' I tell ye this. Wurruk is the enchantriss of a janius, now isn't that so?'

The coffee pot struck the mat and she took up her usual position, standing on the opposite side of the table, arms folded, watching. She wore a faded apron and bundled her hair in a net to 'keep itsilf to itsilf'. Woe betide should he fail to retrieve every last crumb off the plate. She would remind him of the war years, and the starving soldiers she had seen when she was cleaning for the Union troops at Fort Pickering. With Mrs Chesbrough, Mrs Molloy was a great deal more reticent.

In the four years she had been with them, he had never seen Mrs Molloy smile, but he did not put that down to grief. Ellis wondered what their life had been like together. Mrs Molloy peppered her speech with references to her husband that revealed nothing. So even now he hardly knew anything about Molloy, other than the feel of his limp, wet body in the dark of the Tunnel. He remembered how tightly he'd held on to the poor man, arms underneath his shoulders to keep his head above water as if there were a chance he might still be alive. His corpse had seemed heavy, as though waterlogged, and he was surprised to discover that Molloy had, in fact, been short and slim. Of how he actually dragged him back to the Crib that night, he had only the vaguest recollection.

Mrs Chesbrough had been opposed to their taking Mrs Molloy into domestic service. He said it was their duty. She asked whether it was their duty to take on the wife of every man who'd been unfortunate enough to lose his life while working on one of his projects? That struck him as a cruel thing to say. He insisted Mr Molloy was a special case, and that his decision was final. Sometimes, though, he wondered if it was pathetic, this attempt to assuage his sense of guilt by employing the dead man's wife.

Even though the house was small, Mrs Molloy bustled in and out of rooms and up and down stairs as though short of time. She slammed doors and dropped plates and did everything with more noise than was necessary. She might irritate his wife but Ellis tolerated her behaviour benignly. Her puzzling contradictions amused him. You never knew whose side she would take. She would either love the Irish for being poets in their hearts 'evry list one of them', or hate them for being lazy, drunken dreamers. One day she would be against Republicans, the next day against the Democrats. Even in religion she was a puzzle, a devout Catholic on Sundays but prone to moments of outrage during the week against a God that could permit so much evil to go on in His Name.

She asked if he had planned his speech already because there were some things she thought he should say. He was saved from her suggestions by the cries of the paper boy. 'It'll be the *Chicago Daily Tribune* then, Mr Illis?' she said, as she always did. Without waiting for an answer, she disappeared, the front door banged shut and he could hear her telling the boy that if he knew what was good for him he'd bring a newspaper for Mr Chesbrough, fast as greased lightning.

Her return was slower. She would be trying to read the article that he knew would be in there. She was not a good reader. She 'hidn't the patience for letters'.

'Frint page, no less, Mr Illis. Three columns or I'm a leprechaun.'

'Thank you, Mrs Molloy.' He took it from her. *Chesbrough versus Nature,* read the title.

A battle of giants will take place today at noon when the South Branch of the Chicago River meets the Illinois and Michigan Canal. At a cost of $3 million the Canal has been deepened and extended, and is now powered by the largest pumps ever seen in the West. It will be the crowning achievement in the illustrious career of chief engineer to the Chicago Board of Sewerage Commissioners, Mr Ellis Sylvester Chesbrough (or 'Mr Sewage' as he has come to be known) if the River does indeed change direction and flow back into the Canal, heralding a new era of safe, clean water for the city.

'And will ye be takin' bacon 'n eggs this mornin', Mr Illis? It shall be a fine long day, ye kin be sure, and ye don't know the nixt time ye might find the good Lord's fodder.'

He thanked her, but he would not.

'As ye will. Now don't be forgittin' to tell them that if it wasn't for ye, we'd all be living like savidges in this city.'

He turned over the paper. 'Oh, now I think that's an exaggeration, Mrs Molloy.'

'Is that so?' She looked at him defiantly. 'If we left it to politishins and bisnessmen, where would we go? I'll tell ye. Back to the bottom of the fens. That kind don't care for nothin' unless it's a rattlin' inside of their purses and I don't mind who tries to say different. Tell me this, Mr Illis. Tell me if ye ever seen one of that kind walk straight. No, you hav'int. And ye know why?' She stamped her foot. 'Because only hon'rable men put the right foot in the right boot, only hon'rable men like you, Mr Illis.'

'I fear I may not be quite as honourable as you think.'

Mrs Molloy stared at him. 'God preserve us! What are ye saying? If you isn't an hon'rable man, Mr Illis, will ye be tellin' me who is?'

'There is something I'd like to tell you.'

She folded her arms, a quizzical look on her face.

'Your husband,' he began, 'was a brave man.'

Mrs Molloy listened in a moody silence as he told her about those aspects of his dream that seemed relevant, though he took care to refer strictly to a cow when he reached that moment in the story. The truth, he said, was that he could not really remember the sequence of events because everything had happened so quickly, but there was one matter that had long been on his conscience. He should have been quicker to go to Mr Molloy's assistance, and that maybe if he had been quicker he could have …

Mrs Molloy put her hands over her ears. 'I don't belief in this kind of talk, Mr Illis, and neither should ye. It is the divil's wurruk and no mistake. It was God and only God that took Mr Molloy that night … may he rest in peace. And leave conscience be. Give that worm any excuse, and it finds a way into even hon'rable men such as ye. I never heard such nonsinse about what happen'd that night. Have ye forgott'n the way you looked yoursilf when you came out? Bruised and cut to pieces by horns and hooves. It's lucky you lived to tell the tale. And I tell ye this and I tell ye true — God be my witness — if you had been tak'n in place of Mr Molloy, this city would be much the worse for it.'

'Mrs Molloy, I don't think you should say things like that.'

Mrs Molloy picked up his plate. 'I'm sure ye know best, Mr Illis.' At the door, she stopped. 'But the truth is the truth, and I do belief it will always find a way out in the end.'

Ellis felt shamed, not for the first time, by the frankness with which she spoke. It was entirely without artifice, or fear of consequences. No shield existed between her feelings and her tongue. Was it also true, then, what she said about that night? He frowned.

Had he really been hurt and, if he had, how could he have forgotten? To his surprise, a faint memory did indeed begin to stir in which there were bandages and wounds and a lotion that stung.

'I bin telling people,' Mrs Molloy said when she came back in, 'what ye shall bring to pass today and they din't belief it. They says it could niver wurruk in a month of Sundays. They says nob'dy bit God Above can make one of his own rivers go backwards. I tell those Thomases it's Tuesday today, not Sunday, so He's not lookin'. And even if He does, He'll see the good in it, ye can be sure.'

In anyone else, that might have been a joke.

She looked at him expectantly.

'Don't worry, Mrs Molloy,' he said. 'It will work. As long as ...' he added, with a tremor in his voice he could not suppress, 'there are no surprises.'

She nodded, satisfied. 'That's all right, then,' she said. 'Because I know nobody niver bicomes a janius without seeing all the surprises coming. So when they do arrive they're not a surprise any more, not in the least. That's what makes ye a janius, Mr Illis, isn't that so?'

The buggy clipped briskly down Clybourn, took a left turn and crossed Clark before heading south on State. They could have stayed on Clark, but he preferred State even though it was a longer ride. He was still puzzled by what Mrs Molloy had said. Did he try to save Mr Molloy? Had he buried the memory of the attempt simply because he failed? His father had spent his life failing, and he had vowed to be different. Was it fear the Canal would not work that had brought the nightmare back, not fear that he might once have acted like a coward?

He looked out at what had become Chicago's widest street, following its purchase by the millionaire Potter Palmer. Even though he disliked the values represented by the imposing new edifices that had been erected — four storeys, finished in Athens marble, fake porticoes — he could not deny they were a spectacle. They were nearly all stores that had transferred here from Lake Street when Potter Palmer suggested it would be a good idea if they did. Mr Palmer was like a few other prominent gentlemen he could name whose word was more powerful than a city ordinance. Ellis did not like these men, he resented the fact that they looked down on him for his lack of education, but he had learned that if you wanted to do anything here, you had to get them on your side.

It was not long before they were passing Potter Palmer's own hotel, on the northwest corner of Quincy and State, with its vulgar mix of neo-classical pillars and fake turrets. Three or four porters in blue-gold uniforms and peaked caps stood at the front entrance. If all went well, they would try to bring him here afterwards to celebrate with French champagne and canapes and drunken speeches. In which case, he would make his excuses. He had been inside once before and was appalled by its extravagance and ostentation. It struck him as grotesque to build a marble palace like the Palmer House Hotel in a city where most of the population still lived in wooden shacks, without clean water or covered sewers. How many gallons of water, he wondered, does this hotel consume every day for its lawns and fountains and private suites?

When he reached his office, he did not sit down at his desk. He went to the window, from where he had an uninterrupted view of the Waterworks. Two black columns of smoke drifted across the sky, dwarfing the massive brick-built counterparts from which they emerged. In the comparative silence of the early morning, the churn of the engines that turned the fly-wheel was as regular as the slap of waves against the lakeshore. It was a solid, reassuring sound. As the numbers came to mind — 4 engines, 3000 horsepower, 2750 gallons of water at each turn of the 26-foot diameter fly-wheel, 57 million gallons a day, 270 miles of water pipes serving 150,000 people — he allowed himself a moment of self-congratulation.

Perhaps the quandary over lives lost could, after all, be resolved numerically. A stranger visiting Chicago would have to conclude that, in almost every area of life, the fortunes of a small elite had been bettered at the expense of the masses. But the same could not be said for water supply and sanitation. For a moment, he tried to imagine how the Waterworks, with its floors of throbbing pumps and pipes, would look to a poor farmer from the prairies on his first visit to Chicago, a man still gathering water in pails from a well and measuring out each precious drop. He would surely marvel at the way in which nature had been bent to man's will. And he would gaze in wonder across the street at the water storage tower with its vast, elevated tank.

He was about to go to his desk and deal with paperwork — it would be a good way of distracting himself from the events to come — when a carriage pulled up below and a familiar figure stepped out. As the man crossed the street, there was no mistaking his brisk, purposeful steps. There was no reason for him to be here, and certainly not at this time in the morning.

He opened the door. 'Good morning, Dr Rauch. This is a surprise. Do come in.'

'Mr Chesbrough.' Dr John Rauch, with whom he sat on the Board of Health, acknowledged him with the curtest of nods as he removed his hat. A lean, wiry man, his sandy hair was cut unfashionably short. 'It will not work,' he said without preamble, hardening each 'w' in a Germanic inflection.

Ellis had not even had time to close the door. 'I don't follow your meaning, sir,' he said, annoyed by both the intrusion and the man's manners, despite being used to them.

'The Canal,' said Dr Rauch. 'What else would I come here to talk to you about today? The Canal will not turn back the River.'

Although Ellis did not like Dr Rauch, he had a grudging respect for his integrity. At times, indeed, he found himself admiring the doctor's single-mindedness and refusal to compromise. He was one of those few Public Health officials who campaigned, as Ellis liked to think he did himself, to put the welfare of the general citizenry above that of any powerful, private interests.

'In my calculations, I have anticipated the worst, Dr Rauch.' He took time to settle behind the desk and draw up his chair, glancing at his visitor as he did so, wondering how he could send him quickly on his way.

'The same as you anticipated the worst for the roof of the Waterworks?'

'I fail to see any connection between the two,' he said, barely managing to disguise how much the reference irked him. Ellis had insisted the roof be constructed of iron. If anything else were used, the whole building was liable to go up in flames if a fire ever took hold. But the Council would only approve the project if the roof were made with much cheaper — and highly combustible — timber and slate. In the end he had conceded, but it was a compromise that always rankled. Perhaps the Council had only been bluffing. Perhaps he should have put his foot down.

'You will see the connection,' said Dr Rauch, 'when you go to Mud Lake.'

Ellis was no longer prepared to play at being civil. 'And why would I need to go to Mud Lake, wherever Mud Lake is?'

'Mud Lake is past Bridgeport.' Dr Rauch paused. 'Halfway between the Des Plaines River and the South Branch of the Chicago River.'

Mud Lake, the doctor seemed to be telling him, was close to the course of the Canal. An inner voice began to crow. *It doesn't matter how good your calculations are, something will go wrong because something always does go wrong.* 'What,' he asked in a voice that failed to mask the concern he felt, 'don't I know about?'

———

A few minutes later they boarded Dr Rauch's brougham.

'Along the Blue Island line?' he heard the driver ask. Dr Rauch gave some instructions but Ellis was not attending. He was annoyed with himself for having agreed to do this, despite the doctor's refusal to elaborate.

'You must see this for yourself, Mr Chesbrough,' he had insisted.

'Why are you only telling me about this today?'

'I myself was only informed by a little bird late last night. They must have paid to keep it secret until after the opening, so they don't ruin your big day.'

'Who are "they" and what have they done? I demand that you tell me.'

He could demand as much as he wanted, said Dr Rauch with maddening *sang froid*, but he was a doctor, not an engineer. 'If you were to tell me you had evidence a friend of mine was on his deathbed, would I take your word for it or would I seek to examine the patient myself?'

So here they were, he and Dr Rauch, travelling together across the city towards Mud Lake in the early morning of Tuesday, July 18. Ellis sat in one corner of the buggy, and submitted himself to its rolling fits and starts. What danger could a small lake near Bridgeport pose to the project? And what person in his right mind would want the Canal to fail? Success would mean that the whole city was better off. Everybody, from the richest businessmen to the poorest labourers, would benefit from the river being turned back. The businessmen, in fact, whose factories produced most of the toxic waste that ended up in the Lake, stood to benefit most of all. There would be no further point to Dr Rauch's noisy campaign to make them take responsibility for their own waste. Everything undesirable or dangerous would be taken far away from Chicago, in the direction of Joliet and the Mississippi, and along the way it would be deoderised. By the time the water reached the Gulf of Mexico, it would long since have been purified. As Ellis always said: 'the solution to pollution is dilution'.

The driver cajoled the horses and cracked the whip as they sped along an almost empty Wabash, the grind of the carriage wheels over the macadam surface amplified in the early morning quiet. It was a fine tree-lined paved street with gas-lights and iron gates and wooden walkways. This was where the wealthy lived. The lots were spacious, the houses built of brick, and faced with Athens limestone. There were stables to the side, and gardens to the front. They were extravagant, built with a pot-pourri of European influences. You could see hints of a French chateau, an attempt at a Gothic tower and even one would-be English castle with little turrets on each corner that resembled those on the Waterworks. He looked away. There was no desire on his part to live in such grandiose surroundings or to associate with those that did.

Dr Rauch leaned out and pointed, as they drove past four identical brownstone blocks on three storeys erected side by side. 'Those are apartments, New York style. How much rent you think, every month?' It was not really a question and, even if it was, Ellis did not intend to answer it. 'And you know who are the landlords? The Founder of Chicago,' he said, 'and the city's never-ending congressman.' Dr Rauch regularly employed sarcasm, though it did him precious little good in a committee meeting. 'Why, Mr Chesbrough, you surely know who I mean, don't you?'

'Of course I do,' snapped Ellis. Good Lord, the man could be irritating.

'They'd do anything for a profit, those two.'

Ellis had often heard Mr Ogden described as the Founder of Chicago and Long John Wentworth had been a congressman for as long as he could remember. Cunning, powerful and extraordinarily wealthy it was also true they were misers where public funds were concerned. They had both opposed the Canal scheme when he first proposed it in Committee on grounds of expense. In the consultation period, when the two of them pressed him to make an adjustment to the route, he thought it must be a ruse to stop the project altogether because of the extra costs the diversion would entail. In the end, though, that was the route they approved. Long John was now such a keen supporter of the Canal that he had made a point of taking the credit for it in his re-election campaign. Both Mr Ogden and Long John would be at the opening today, showering him with praise and compliments. Ellis smiled grimly to himself. Sometimes, to get things done you had to make concessions that went against the grain. He guessed Mr Ogden and Long John owned the land through which the adjusted Canal route now passed. Dr Rauch, had he been in his position, would doubtless have refused to make the alteration, and the project would never have seen the light of day. That was the difference between them.

The landscape changed when they turned their back on the Lake. If someone wanted to try to understand Chicago, thought Ellis, he need only see how suddenly the downtown area ended south of Wabash and Michigan, and how abruptly the real city began. Brick ceded to timber, large shrunk to small, order turned into chaos. The road deteriorated and narrowed. Everyone was on foot, labourers in caps and dirty shirts on their way to town, hand carts on their way to market. Every so often they passed a cluster of workshops. Blacksmiths and bakers were busy. The sky was beginning to fill with streaks of early morning smoke as the city awakened.

A few stray sparks in a strong wind, and the whole place would go up in flames. They were all timber frames, huddled close. The yards were small. Some of the buildings leaned precariously, others were tight up against each other like conjoined twins, two to a lot, one in the front, the other in the alley. There were open sewers with no sign of lime, that led into swamps of brown sludge. It was a miserable way to live. A lot of these shanties had probably been erected for a few dollars a long time ago on ground that was prone to flooding and subsidence. Ellis put his handkerchief in front of his nose, and was not surprised to see that Dr Rauch was doing the same.

'It's a disgrace,' said Dr Rauch. 'We need bricked sewers and health officers in every part of this city. We need cleanliness and education. Prevention is the best cure.'

Ellis agreed, and it angered him that the aldermen did so little, but he had no intention of provoking another lecture from Dr Rauch. They passed through Bridgeport and then, at the end of a rutted street that started out like any other, the landscape returned. It was as if they had emerged from a long, dark tunnel. They were in open prairie again, so flat and endless that at the borders it became indistinguishable from the sky. There were a few homesteads and cultivated fields, but mostly the land was empty. When Ellis looked back in the direction of the city he could see the cut in the land made by the Canal. It was unmistakable, as fixed as a line of ink on a page. But they were not, as he had expected, going towards it.

'How far is it now,' he demanded of Dr Rauch, 'to Mud Lake?'

'That's it. Over there.'

Ellis shaded his eyes. If he was looking in the right place, Mud Lake was dry.

They set out to walk the last stretch. The sun was higher now, making him only too aware of how overdressed he was. After the uncomfortable drive, with its stark reminder of how most people still had to live, he should have enjoyed the freedom of being able to stretch his legs. He should have been happy. They were in flat, virgin prairie. Tall grasses were rustling in the wind. The land was alive with dense patches of purple and yellow flowers. It was summer, a time of harvesting and celebrating the earth's abundance. Nature was kind and at her most alluring, despite the lack of rain. Dr Rauch had fallen silent. Yes, surely Ellis should have been happy. But he was not. He had just seen what it was they were walking towards. He broke into a run.

How long had he been standing there, coat flung over one shoulder, sweating and wheezing for breath, staring into the newly dug channel as though he had never seen one before ... how long had he been there before Dr Rauch caught up? Ellis was bent double, unable to utter a word even if he had known what to say. He was a mild-mannered man. He prided himself on being polite and reasonable. Now, he was incoherent with rage.

The channel was about twenty feet wide and five feet deep. The banks of fresh earth piled up on each side were being hauled off in donkey carts and dumped further away. The working area was shrouded by a veil of dust. Thirty or forty men were down there with picks and shovels, pushing wheelbarrows up and down plank boards, moving about like the wraiths in his Tunnel nightmare.

There was no mistaking the channel's direction. It was coming from the Des Plaines River, and it was going towards the Canal, a total distance of about five miles. When finished, it would connect the two. In the spring runoff, if not long before, the force and volume of the water that would be diverted from the Des Plaines — he made some calculations in his head — would be stronger than anything they could pump through the enlarged Canal. The river would revert to its old course. On top of that, sediment would be washed from the Des Plaines into the Canal. The build-up, unless it was regularly dredged, would create blockages.

'Well, Mr Chesbrough?' Dr Rauch was out of breath too, but he wore the same smug smile he saved for moments in Committee meetings when he was about to utter some truth he knew would outrage many of those present. 'What is the engineer's perspective on this?'

Ellis's sight was blurred with sweat. His chest was still pounding. His shirt was damp. He rounded on Dr Rauch and focused all his anger on the cocky, self-righteous, tactless little man standing in front of him. He seized the lapels of Dr Rauch's coat — Ellis must have stood nearly a foot taller — and he shook him, back and forth. 'Happy now, are you?'

'Mr Chesbrough?' pleaded Dr Rauch. 'Please let me go.'

But he would not let go. He pulled his face close. 'Why did you let them do this?' The notion had come to him that Dr Rauch was responsible, that he was in league with the perpetrators. 'Tell me which of your friends is doing this and I will personally ... I will ...'

'My *friends*?'

The look of astonishment on his face began to bring Ellis back to his senses. He released his grip and staggered away. What was happening? What was he doing?

Dr Rauch was moving off, adjusting his collar, eying him warily.

A whistle blew. A man was approaching. 'I'm the foreman here and you're trespassing, gentlemen,' he called out. 'This is private land.'

'It is private profit,' Ellis retorted, 'and it must be stopped.'

The foreman stared at him, a puzzled frown on his face. 'Are you Mr Sewage, sir?'

Ellis caught up with Dr Rauch and they walked, side by side, towards the road.

'I'm sorry,' he said.

'Don't mention it, Mr Chesbrough. I often feel like that myself.'

'Can we stop them?'

Dr Rauch shook his head. 'I'm afraid it's too late now.'

There has to be a way to stop this, thought Ellis. 'You go on ahead,' he said. He wanted time to think and he had spotted a field where the hay was already cut and stacked. He needed all the help and luck that superstition could bring. And if there was none to be had, at least it might give him courage.

———

A brass band was playing, though it was hard to imagine how they could cope. Ellis, handkerchief alternately swatting at flies and pressed over his nose and mouth, took his place in the centre of the black-coated top-hatted dignitaries already gathered on the bridge. It was furiously hot, the insects were intolerable and there was not an inch of shade. He made no attempt to look at ease, as some of the others were doing, for the sake of the onlookers. There was nothing pleasant about this. He was already glued to his shirt and pantaloons, and his beard itched. It was impossible to stand there and breathe normally without feeling nauseous, and yet breathe in some form he must. The cotton handkerchief was a weak filter, and was soon poisoned by the noxious fumes that rose off the sludge below.

He leaned over the rail. Six feet beneath him, the water barely stirred. Large black flies mulled over the murky surface like a room full of elderly gentlemen after dinner, slow and ponderous, hissing contentedly, licking their lips. In places, the water shone yellow, like a rash. In other spots, it was a tarry black. He focused his gaze on a patch of solid mulch, brown and glutinous, that lay partly above the surface like a quivering jelly. Lumps like that, he thought, once they had been caught by the Canal, would have been pushed south for miles and miles, and the sheer volume of water would have deoderised them, breaking them first into smaller bits, and then smaller still, until by the time the residue reached the Gulf of Mexico there would have been nothing left. Ah, the magic of water. Yes, that was what would have happened.

The stench was palpable, filling the air like a thick, toxic mist that stained everything it touched. When he got home that night, even after he had scrubbed himself down, there would still be traces left. Mrs Molloy would have a battle on her hands at the washboard. Dr Rauch nudged him, offering a boiled sweet. He sucked hard, but it did not help much. Its sweetness was smothered by the odour of raw sewage.

The sooner it was over the better. Crowds were gathered on both banks, with the ladies accommodated on benches to one side beneath a covered stand. Most of them were waving fans and held handkerchiefs before their faces. People were complaining. Why can't they just break down the dam and see if it works? Then we can all go home. Why wait for the Mayor? Where is he, anyway? On his high horse, you can be sure of that. Why is he always late? The stench alone could make you ill, never mind the heat. And the mosquitoes. Ouch, that's another one ... (*Slap*) ... D... you! It was a mistake to have come here in the first place. Whose idea was it? I think I'm going to faint. It'd d...d well better work. Or we know who's to blame, don't we? Mr Sewage. Look, that's him over there.

Ellis ignored the chatter.

They had said little on the way back from Mud Lake. Ellis felt ashamed of how he had seized hold of Dr Rauch like that, and for the absurd accusations he had made. He did not know what had come over him.

'I'm glad to see you angry,' Dr Rauch had said.

'I should have been more suspicious,' he said, 'when they pushed for an adjustment in the route of the Canal. They don't need it, Dr Rauch. That's what I don't understand. They have more wealth between the two of them than anyone could spend in a dozen lifetimes, never mind one. Why do it?'

Dr Rauch shrugged, as if it were no mystery to him. 'Because they can.'

They walked on in silence. 'I feared something was going to go wrong,' he said. 'I just didn't know how.' He swatted a fly. 'You know what my maid says? A genius is the man who can see surprises before they arrive.'

Dr Rauch chuckled. 'That explains why there are so few of them in the world.'

'Until that channel opens, I think the Canal will work. When it backs up, what if I simply tell the truth, that this is because of the new channel that's been dug? The channel should therefore be blocked.'

Dr Rauch pursed his lips. 'They own the newspapers. They will say they had permission for the channel, though they won't think to add that the permission came from the Committee they control. Mr Sewage, they will say, miscalculated.'

Ellis knew he was right. And that meant three years' work and $3 million had been spent on a project that would fail. There would be no clean water for Chicago. 'I don't even know,' he said, 'how many lives were lost in the building of this Canal. And for what?' He clenched his fist. 'For what?'

'You did what you thought was right.'

'But doing what you think is right is not always enough.'

For a while, they contemplated the turgid mess below in silence, holding their handkerchiefs tight over their mouths.

At last, a black landau could be seen approaching along the Bridgeport road, pulled by two white horses. It drew to a halt near the bridge, the gold-embossed door opened and out stepped Mayor Mason, followed by Mr Ogden and Long John Wentworth. They were handed little Stars and Stripes by schoolchildren as they stepped towards the bridge. The brass band struck up again. Nobody seemed to care any more that they had been kept waiting. There was applause. Long John moved like a great sea creature through waters that parted before him, never halting his pace, somehow managing to grip shoulders and slap backs and bellow greetings as he advanced. The big black slouch-hat aslant on his head stood a foot higher than anyone else's. A cigar was wedged in his mouth. He held out both hands to greet Ellis, and enveloped him in a hug, growling in his ear that he planned to recommend a bonus of $10,000 be paid by the City in recognition of his achievement and he already had Mr Ogden's approval. Oh, and the Mayor's approval too. Before Ellis could respond, Long John had moved on and Mr Ogden was greeting him. 'The City is in your debt, Mr Chesbrough,' he said, tapping the rail three times with the knuckles of one hand. 'I do that for luck,' he explained.

Ellis barely listened to the speeches. He was conscious of his name being mentioned from time to time, and every so often the speakers asked that he be given a round of applause. The loudest demand came from Long John, who called him 'St Sewage', which everyone thought was a fine jest.

Eventually, the Mayor gave the order that the temporary dam dividing the Canal and the River be broken down. Even now, as the anticipation around him reached fever pitch, Ellis could summon up no enthusiasm for what was about to happen. He did not watch the fuses being lit, and barely flinched when the dynamite exploded and the timber wall supporting a thin crust of earth gave way, allowing the Canal and the Chicago River to begin their tussle for supremacy.

People began to drop leaves and twigs and bits of paper off the bridge into the water. Ellis could have explained that a large mass of water is not unlike a big steamer. It takes time to turn. It would be a few more minutes before the Canal could force the river back onto itself.

He asked the Mayor for the speaking trumpet.

He was no public speaker. His voice did not carry, he felt self-conscious, and he lacked the rhetorical skills of the men who had gone before. Normally, he would have felt nervous. But today he did not care.

'Very soon,' he began, 'you will see the river change direction.' There were cheers from the crowds on the banks and a chorus of 'here heres' from the bridge. 'But in a few months' time,' he continued, 'the river will revert to its old course and the city's sewage will once more pollute the Lake.' This statement was met by a bewildered silence. 'And when that happens, everyone will assume that it was the mistake of Mr Sewage.' Ellis realised that his voice was carrying better than he had thought it would.

He explained how, ever since he arrived in Chicago twenty-five years before, he had tried to improve the city's sanitation. He loved Chicago. He thought it had the potential to be the greatest city in America. (*Relieved cheers.*) He had tried to be pragmatic. 'Sometimes this has meant making compromises with businessmen and civic officials that braver and more honourable gentlemen, such as Dr Rauch, would not have agreed to make.'

There were calls for the speaking trumpet to be taken away from him. He heard Long John's voice. He was making a d...d fool of himself. Ellis knew he had to speak fast. Dr Rauch cleared a path for him as they pushed their way across the bridge. All the time, he bellowed into that speaking trumpet at the top of his voice. He told the truth, as Mrs Molloy would have told it, as Dr Rauch would have told it, without tact and without obfuscation and without caring about the consequences.

He told them what Mr Ogden and Long John Wentworth had done. 'They claim to serve the city, but the truth is that they're only interested in their own profit. They do not, as the Irish say, put the right foot in the right boot.'

Those were the last words he managed to utter. The next moment, the speaking trumpet was seized. Long John had him by the arm. He was swearing. He would have him fired. He would have him locked up. He would run him out of Chicago. He would ruin him.

Mr Chesbrough pushed him off. He felt quite indifferent to his threats, just as he felt indifferent to the cheering and applause from the bridge that drowned them out. Leaves, petals, pieces of paper, twigs were being dropped like confetti into the river. It was official. History had been made. The Chicago River had been reversed.

That evening, when the civic leaders repaired to the Palmer House Hotel, Ellis went home. He slept late the next morning and woke up feeling refreshed. If he had been dreaming, he could not remember what it was about. When he went down to breakfast, he found that Mrs Molloy had already placed a copy of the *Chicago Daily Tribune* beside his plate. The speeches by the Mayor, Mr Ogden and Long John Wentworth were reported at length, followed by a description of the moment when the river was first observed to be moving in reverse. There was no reference to his intervention. The article ended with the news that, at an elaborate ceremony at the Palmer House Hotel that evening, where civic and business leaders gathered to celebrate the achievements of 'Mr Sewage', it was announced that the City Council was awarding a bonus of $10,000 to Mr Chesbrough in recognition of his outstanding contribution to the water and sanitation infrastructure of Chicago. Thanks to his efforts and ingenuity, the city was now entering a new era of 'safe, clean water'.

He put the newspaper aside in disgust. He could no longer ignore the other point always made by his early mentor Mr Stephen Long that had been troubling him. Mr Long used to speak not only about the primacy of the *improvements we make* where lives are lost in an engineering project, but also about the duty of the engineer to *set the rules by which the work is done*. Ellis decided he would today begin an investigation into the identity of every man whose life had been lost in the building of the Canal. He would interview every contractor, and he would insist on interviewing their employees too. He would consider their working conditions, and publish a report with recommendations for improvements. And when he was satisfied that he knew who and how many victims there were, he would distribute the $10,000 among their nearest relatives. He was under no illusion that this was an attempt, perhaps as pathetic an attempt as his employment of Mrs Molloy, to assuage his sense of guilt. But since there was no numerical comfort on offer, since it could not be argued that the lives of the masses were going to be improved, it was the best he could think of doing. He wanted no more nightmares.

The Background
of a Salesman

Certainly, sir. I'd be happy to return the compliment and tell you something of my own father, though he was from a very humble background by comparison. Might I suggest we try those satin breeches with this midnight-blue smoking jacket? Yes, imported, sir. Tailored by Henry Poole in Savile Row, London. My father was a fine man, as I best remember him. Honest, capable, salt of the earth. He had real craftsman's hands. There was nothing he couldn't make with them. One quality above all, sir? If I had to choose just one, it would be this. My father was a perfectionist. Everything had to be on the nail or it was not worth doing at all. It mattered not one jot how long a job took, he would never leave anything half done. It's only my opinion, sir, but I do think the beige overcoat and midnight-blue go together quite well. And another curious thing about him, if you'll bear with me: had it not been for my father, nobody would have ever heard of Mr Jearum Atkins. Yes, Mr Atkins the inventor. Exactly, sir, the one they wrote about in this month's *Scientific American*. I'm proud to say he's my uncle. Well, not exactly my uncle, but very close. He's my mother's cousin. Yes, sir, I couldn't be more in agreement. He is indeed a genius. More patents to his name than there are departments in Field

& Leiter! The Safety Valve Regulator, the Locomotive Smoke Stacks, the Hydraulic Steering Apparatus, the Mechanical Calipers. And, best of all, the Self-Raking Harvester. You have five of them on your estate, sir? Well, I'm blessed! No, no, I promise it's absolutely true, sir. Mr Atkins has often said in my hearing: 'If my friend Albert Sage had not made those models of the Automaton, we would never have found someone to manufacture it.' That's right, sir. The Atkins Automaton, as it said in the article, was the name for the Self-Raking Harvester he invented before Mr McCormick took over the patent. No, no, that's my pleasure. I'll put the jacket and breeches to one side. You should feel free to browse as long as you like. No need to buy a thing. Actually, he was in the hardware business himself. Just a small concern. The Sage Family Hardware Store. You remember it, sir? Yes, that's right. It was on Madison, near the corner with State. How extraordinary. No, I'm afraid the store is no longer there. But it prospered for a long time, even in the bad years and the Depression, when everyone else was closing their doors and declaring bankruptcy. The way he managed that small enterprise was one of the most important lessons I ever learned from him, even though I didn't understand until I was older and went into sales myself. My father had loyal customers and plenty of them. They could always rely on Mr Sage to give them the right product at the right price. It was well known that nobody need have any fear of being honey-fuggled in the Sage Family Hardware Store. Well, thank you, sir. Most kind. Yes, I suppose you're right. He was something of a gentleman, in his own small way. Anyway, that's the story of my father, and I don't mind admitting that he probably influenced me in ways I have yet to discover. Understanding one's parents is a way to understand oneself. Isn't that what they say? Now, sir, would you care to try this rather fine combination of a pink cravat and russet brown waistcoat? They are a rather daring combination, I agree. It's only my opinion, and the choice is entirely yours, sir, but I do think they might suit you like a dream.

Yes, sadly, that is true, sir. I'm afraid the store had to close when my father passed on. No, no, I don't mind talking about it. It's a long time ago now. We lived in Evanston. You've never been? Oh, it's a pretty place. You'd probably find it rather backward, sir, but that's the price we pay these days, isn't it, for some peace and quiet. It happened without warning. I went to school that day as usual, and probably spent most of it staring out the window. I'm afraid I wasn't much of a student and never got on well with books. I think a page full of words from top to bottom rather intimidated me. The only thing I really liked to do was draw. Funny, when I think back on it. What false signals our beginnings can send to our futures, though I hasten to add I'm sure this wasn't the same in your case, sir. I don't think anyone, certainly not I, could have imagined I would end up here, working in the finest dry goods store on State Street. For one thing, I never wanted to live in the city. And I was too quiet as a boy, I wasn't good with words, I was one of the shy ones. That looks capital, sir. In my humble opinion, a very pleasing tension is created by those contrasting colors. Well, when I got home that day I found a strange buggy outside the front door. We lived in a pleasant house on its own lot. Nothing grand, but built in the colonial style, with a steep roof and tall gabled windows. Normally, there was always someone about but on that particular day, the house was quiet as a mouse. As I stepped inside, a frightful sound emanated ... if that's a nice way of putting it ... from the direction of my parents' bedroom. Off I rushed to find out what was happening, only to be stopped at the door by my mother. She wouldn't let me go inside. What is it? I cried. I knew, of course, it must be my father making the terrible noise. I told her I had come to help and it was unfair not to let me see him. I'm afraid I threw a rather regrettable tantrum, sir. Things that should not be repeated, not even in confidence. Perhaps, if you still have reservations about that rather lustrous pink, we should try a more sober combination? How about this pearl gray? That would be more appropriate for the occasion? Excellent. The point is that I think I was always more of a father's boy. You were too, sir? It's an honor to be in such good company. Well, my mother was in shock too, of course, poor woman, though I was too young to understand. We'd both said goodbye to him in the morning, the same as always. There was no reason to suspect today would be different from any other day. I was still fighting to get inside the bedroom when the door suddenly opened. An old man came out who said he was a doctor. He ruffled my hair and spoke to my mother in a church voice. I can still remember what he asked for. Boiled water, damp cloths, carbolic soap, vinegar. He told me my father needed peace and quiet. Then he could get better. How do you know he'll get better? I asked. The doctor did not have a reply for that. So I took my chance and ducked beneath his arm. And that was how I saw my father for the last time. Yes, I think that's a perfect match, sir. Very becoming. Splendid. And do you know what question that final sighting of my father always raises in my mind? Why on earth did it take the city so long to clean up its sewage system? That's what I ask myself. How many people had to die before they built the waterworks and the new Canal? Excuse me, sir. I should never have got started. You're very understanding. Thank you. Let me say this, though. The strange thing about cholera, apart from the frightening speed at which it arrives, is what it does. I don't just mean the ... er ... excretory effects. The worst thing, sir, was seeing how his skin had turned blue. And those craftsman's hands had become covered in wrinkles, crumpled up like paper. And his eyes had retreated deep into their sockets. A few hours, that was all it took. Just a few hours. You're very kind, sir. Well, might I suggest one of these new cotton handkerchiefs as the perfect accompaniment? Yes, they are indeed from Paris, correct sir. Paris, yes, Paris, France. Strange, the memories that won't go away. I remember how his eyes flickered when they saw me. And there was a quiver in his throat that gave me hope he was about to speak. But he never did, at least not before I was dragged away, never to see him again. The coffin was carried from the house that same afternoon. There was no grave, just a lime pit somewhere outside the city. I'd read about that happening in Europe. But that was back in the Middle Ages, not the nineteenth century in America. Oh forgive me, sir. I've gone too far. Yes, I think I might just take a moment, if you don't mind. I shall be back in a minute. Perhaps you would like to peruse the display cabinet over there? We have an exquisite new range of pocket watches, just arrived from Switzerland.

Not at all, sir, I think I know exactly what you're asking. In other words, how did a country bumpkin like me happen on such an enviable occupation as this at Field & Leiter? The truth is that I had connections, sir. My mother knew someone, and that someone knew Mr Field himself. A gentleman called Mr Wright, sir. Mr John S. Wright. You haven't heard of him? Well, I understand he was quite well known in his day. In fact, it's a funny thing, but he was the first manufacturer of the Self-Raking Harvester we were talking about, before Mr McCormick took over. He's now, shall we say, past his prime. No, I hadn't seen him for a long time, not since I was a youngster. My mother took me to see him in his office at the *Prairie Farmer* newspaper. Well, it's not really an office. He hasn't worked there for a long time, but he still keeps a room in the building where he goes to write. No, it's a book he's working on. I believe his subject is Chicago. He calls it *Past, Present and Future*. Now if I could suggest taking a closer look at this one here, sir. The case is pure gold, twelve carat, and it features a remarkable keyless winding mechanism. The creation of a jeweler called Patek Philippe. I am told he was originally commissioned to design it for a Hungarian countess. Anyway, Mr

Wright asked me what I wanted to do with my life and I said I had no idea. Of course, I did have some ideas but I didn't dare tell him. Really, sir? Well, do you remember I told you earlier I liked to draw? My dream was to become a painter. Anyway, I'm pleased to say Mr Wright made me see sense. He told me I should go into sales. He said that was the way to get ahead in life, that once a man knows how to sell, he can do anything. Chicago has the best salesmen in America, Stephen, he said, and the best of the best is Mr Marshall Field. You agree, sir? Ha ha. That's very kind. Now, if I could assist you with that chain. There. I think it's a perfect fit. Very *à la mode*. Shall we proceed at once to the looking glass? So, as I was saying, Mr Wright wrote a personal letter to Mr Field and here I am. No, I've never spoken to Mr Field myself. But he often comes round the store, checking on merchandise. You approve? Excellent. Will that be all today, sir? No, no, of course there's no need to pay at once. Let me arrange for a slip to be made out for you. Yes, indeed, I do wear a watch as well, but mine is rather old-fashioned. And it's silver, not gold. That's right, yes. How did you guess? It is indeed a family heirloom.

The Great Fire

Sundays were Stephen's day off. He usually spent them in Evanston, which meant leaving in the dark on the first carriage for the two-hour ride into Chicago on Monday morning. His mother would wake him and, after gulping down a bowl of porridge dipped with biscuits, he would hurry towards the junction. On this particular morning, when he first became aware of her attempting to rouse him, he was reluctant to wake up. His body was telling him it was too early. It would be cold outside. A wind whistled through the eaves. He was warm and comfortable, and in the middle of a dream. 'Get up, Stephen. Get up.'

It was the edge of terror in her voice that convinced him to bestir himself. Perhaps something had happened to Uncle Jearum. Maybe the house had been robbed. Had the wind blown the roof off? He turned onto his back. Or was the house on fire? Hardly a drop of rain had fallen for the last three months. Everybody was talking about the risk of a stray spark setting something off. He opened his eyes. The room was filled by a faint, flickering light. The light was neither the grey of dawn nor the crimson of sunset nor the glow of a candle.

'Mildred,' said his mother, with blank, staring eyes.

He sat up. Something had happened to Mildred? He was close

to his sister, closer now than ever before, and he was responsible for her. But he was confused. He saw her only yesterday ... no, not yesterday, it was on Saturday morning ... before he left for work. They both had rooms at Mrs Creeley's boarding house. He had arranged the lodgings for her when she began, just a few weeks ago, to train as a nurse. Unlike him, her Sunday had not been free. She was still in Chicago. What could possibly have happened to Mildred, that they were learning about it here in Evanston, in the middle of the night?

He jumped out of bed at the same moment as his mother drew back the curtain. 'Look,' she said. Tears were welling up in her eyes and she made no attempt to wipe them away.

That was how he first saw the Fire, at some hour before dawn, through the window of their house in Evanston. He had seen pictures of volcanoes erupting, but they did that out of mountain-tops. This was the flattest land in the world. The effect, though, was the same. It was a horrifying, unnatural sight. A smoke cloud had spread so high and wide it hid the moon. Beneath it, the city was burning, ragged and enraged, tongues of flame leaping from a bright orange core.

He let his mother lean her head on his shoulder.

All day, they waited at the carriage stop in the village. There were all kinds of awful rumours about where the Fire had reached, how it had left nothing in its path, how some of the most fireproof buildings in the downtown area had been destroyed. Train stations, hotels, banks, churches, the big central Court House and the Post Office had all been swept away. And if they had gone, what else could have survived? Bridges had gone up in flames, or collapsed because of the weight of people trying to cross. Women with their clothes on fire had been seen jumping into the river. Looters were ransacking any building not yet burnt down. The firefighters had run out of water.

Nobody knew how many people had been unable to escape in time. Hundreds, maybe thousands.

Late in the day, Stephen saw a colleague from the Field & Leiter store on a carriage passing through Evanston on its way north. He was quite certain, said his friend, that the whole of State Street had been flattened. 'If the Palmer House Hotel has gone — and it has — you can be sure Field & Leiter went too.' Stephen found it hard to imagine, those six vast floors, filled with everything from Persian carpets to French furniture to the finest New York jewellery, going up in flames. Later, he overheard someone else saying that the Waterworks building had also been destroyed. Sheer rumour-mongering, he decided. He had once walked around it, and he knew the place was built like a castle. Even from outside its solid stone walls, you could hear engines ceaselessly pumping water into the huge elevated storage tank across the road. If the Waterworks had burnt down, they might as well start believing in the fairies.

Whenever a vehicle pulled into the village, there were chaotic scenes. Stephen saw more pitiful sights, in those few hours, than he had ever seen in his life. People alighted, cut and bruised, their clothes torn and blackened by soot and ash, clutching a few belongings wrapped up in a cloth or bedsheet. They looked dazed and frightened. Everybody had lost someone.

Their overwhelming anxiety, of course, was Mildred. With the appearance of each carriage, their hopes were revived as they pushed forward to see the new arrivals. And when she was not there, he would try to console his mother and assure her there was every chance she would be on the next one. They questioned everyone they could, trying to understand how far the Fire had gone and whether it had reached the Sixth Ward. Some said it had, others said it hadn't.

All day, he kept trying to imagine a good outcome. Mildred was a light sleeper, she would have woken as soon as an alarm was raised. Her room was on the second floor. It would have taken her no more than two minutes to dress and leave the house. She would have gone south, not north. She must know her way around well enough by now to recognise the difference. Anyway, Mrs Creeley and the other lodgers would have been there too. And by going south, how could she possibly have found a carriage headed to the north? If, that is, she had been able to find a carriage at all. From what they'd heard, drivers were charging extortionate fares.

They were wasting their time, he assured his mother. Anyway, Mildred had a friend who lived on Adams Street. That's where she would go first. 'And one more thing,' he added, 'the Fire would have had to cross the river to get to the Sixth Ward, and what are the chances of that happening?' By the time it began to rain on Monday night, they had been waiting for roughly fourteen hours, and there was no word of her.

It was a mostly sleepless night. He finally nodded off in a chair in Uncle Jearum's room, where they all waited together until the early hours, in the hope that there would be a knock on the front door and they would open it to find Mildred standing there.

The next morning, Stephen took the first carriage he could find going into Chicago. His mother gave him a package of sandwiches. 'You've made a lot,' he said, thanking her.

'She'll be hungry,' she said.

'Yes,' he said. 'Of course.'

He let her hug him. 'Be careful, Stephen.'

This crisis had renewed feelings of tenderness in him towards his mother. His relations with her had never been easy. She could be overbearing. She expected too much of him. She wanted to know everything. And she was always putting on airs. But as they waited in vain for Mildred, he found himself desperate — but helpless — to protect her. He could not imagine what might happen to them all, if she were to lose Mildred too.

———

The carriage would go no further than a point on North Avenue. Stephen stepped out and observed a world so altered, he could hardly make sense of it. The air was swirling with ash, and he could already feel the heat. He narrowed his eyes, put a hand up to shield his face. The houses were blackened with soot, a layer now firmly imprinted by the overnight rain. The sky was a limpid grey. The sun must be somewhere in the background, but it was hard to tell how much of the grey was smoke, and how much cloud.

He crossed what felt like a border. Beyond, lay nothing but ruins. The ground was soft and warm, layered with ash, the horizon cluttered with blackened masonry and a few surviving timbers grizzled to silvery charcoal. In what must once have been a house, an old iron clothes mangle lay twisted and deformed, a sewing machine congealed into a lump. Stretching out into the wasteland ahead, for as far as he could see, staggered the remnants of whatever buildings had once lined the street. A few tumbling walls, broken and charred, stood like broken teeth. For no obvious reason, the odd building was still standing, almost untouched.

Trees burnt down to jagged stumps sometimes gave the best clue as to where a street had been. Smoking embers, in all directions, littered the wasted landscape. Heat came off the earth in flurries. Occasionally, there was a burst of new flame. But mostly there reigned a silence almost as profound, at times, as a fall of snow.

He passed people walking the other way, hollow-eyed, faces streaked with grime and soot, children crying. Sometimes they were alone, sometimes in bedraggled groups led by militia. They were on their way, he learned, to an emergency camp set up to the west of the city for all those who had been made homeless. *Perhaps*, he thought, *that is where I should go to search for Mildred, if Mrs Creeley's — please, no — has been burnt down.*

He kept a wary distance and avoided eye contact with men climbing over rubble, kicking things, and poking with sticks. Maybe some of them were former residents but more likely they were looters. From time to time, he saw a hog or wild dog rooting through the debris. With their fur greyed by ash, they looked like hideous phantoms. And once, in a vision that brought him to a halt, he saw a hand. It was a small hand, perhaps a child's or lady's hand, protruding from underneath a pile of charred bricks. He repressed the urge to retch. He glanced again, furtively this time. Maybe it wasn't what he thought it was. But it was. Should he try to do something, or pretend he had not seen? What could he do? Life had long since left that hand. And there was no time to waste. He had to find Mildred.

He got lost. In places, it was impossible to tell where one street began and another ended. The sidewalks had all been obliterated. So had any streets whose surfaces were laid with pine blocks. Over the last three years, he had come to know the downtown area well. But the Fire had devastated the new brick palaces as comprehensively as the old timber frames. There was only fallen rubble, piles of blackened bricks, occasionally part of a wall still standing. That was why he even struggled to recognise the ruins of State Street. Field & Leiter had vanished.

He had been using occasional sightings of the Water Storage tower — that, at least, was in one piece — to guide himself south. This was how he came upon the Waterworks itself. What he had heard was true. Even this great building had gone. He stood, gawping at the massive scene of destruction. Only one corner wall was partly in place. Smoke drifted off the tangled iron remains of its engines. What looked to have been a giant wheel lay on its side, fractured, one rim sticking up. Two men with a fire trolley were directing a hose at an outbreak of flames.

He was not the only person who had stopped to look. Militia were stationed at the perimeter, keeping people away. He watched as three gentlemen stepped gingerly around the great wheel that lay upended, apparently inspecting the damage. Stephen found himself standing next to one of the firefighters. The man was sweating, wiping his forehead with an elbow. His eyes were red. He swigged from a flask. 'The older one in the middle with the long grey beard is the chief engineer,' the man said, 'probably cursing himself, that he didn't see it coming.'

'How could this burn, though,' asked Stephen, puzzled, 'with all that water inside?'

'How do you think? We've been telling them for years,' complained the fireman. 'Roofs should be made from iron, not timber. If you don't, all you've done is create a sockdologer of a firetrap. One live ember on a dry timber roof, and up she goes. But oh no, the Council won't have it. That would mean more rules and higher taxes. Do that, and you'd drive business away, wouldn't you?' He spat. 'Pisspot politicians. See what they've done?'

'I'm sorry, sir. I didn't mean to ...'

'Oh, ease off, son. Unless you're one of them? No, you look too young for that kind of nonsense.'

Stephen assured him he was, and then checked for directions towards the Sixth Ward. 'Do you know, sir, if the Fire went that far?'

The fireman gestured with his chin. 'There's no telling where this one went. Probably landed on the darned moon.'

Stephen set off again.

The man shouted after him: 'Good luck, son. Hope you find who you're looking for.'

He quickened his steps. The closer he got, the more inevitable it became that Mrs Creeley's house would not have escaped intact. Here, south of the downtown area, almost nothing at all had survived. Fires still burned. The heat was scalding and the ground treacherous. He picked his way through. There were few relics of stone walls or twisted iron. Everywhere, here, lay scorched smoking earth. He must have become inured to the stench because he hardly noticed it any more. When he blew his nose it was black, his eyes were sore and weeping, and his lungs felt dry as tinder. The package of sandwiches his mother gave him, which he had not once thought of opening, was covered in soot. He paused to take a careful sip of water from the flask he carried. He did not know how long it would have to last. The further he went, the less believable it became.

When he reached the South River bank he finally knew where he was. It had been stripped virtually naked. The remains of what might have been a lumberyard were still smoking, miraculously a warehouse still half-stood, its roof capsized. But everything else — the other warehouses and coalyards and grain storage depots — that had lined the river when he passed here on Saturday, were gone. The river itself, the water littered by charred driftwood, was crowded with boats and skiffs, some loaded only with people, others packed high with household goods that had been rescued. The scene was frantic and upsetting. The boatmen were bargaining hard, the prices they quoted absurdly high. Everybody was pushing to get aboard. The boatmen, he thought, might be the only people to benefit from this disaster.

He had to pay five cents, double the normal rate, to get across in a leaking skiff. The Fire had indeed crossed over the river too. He found Mrs Creeley's, or at least he thought he did. It was impossible to be certain about exactly where it had stood. Nothing on that street was there, nor on the street in front or behind or beyond. Stephen began to imagine the worst. There was no warning, Mildred was fast asleep when the flames, fanned by that evil wind, whipped along the street. The houses fell like dominoes. She did not even have time to get downstairs ...

Pull yourself together, he told himself. *Mildred is fine. She's probably back in Evanston already. But what if she isn't?*

He began to wander aimlessly, wondering where to look next. Should he try to find that camp in the prairies to the west, where they said homeless people had been taken? There was no point trying to find Adams Street, even if that still stood, where he told his mother Mildred had a friend. He had made that up. He was beginning to feel a touch light-headed, as if intoxicated, as he trod the ash and cinders, bombarded by the kinds of big questions he rarely put to himself these days. Who was he? What was he doing here? Why was he alive? What for?

He asked a couple of patrolling militia for directions to that camp on the prairies. He was told to head west, and was making his way there when he came across a crowd, gathered around a wagon. The wagon had been turned into a makeshift platform. There must have been twenty or thirty people listening to the man speaking. Behind the speaker, daubed in red paint on a banner stretched between two stakes, were the words: *Chicago Will Rise Again*. He was going to walk straight past until he was pulled up short by the voice. A chill ran through him. It was a voice he thought he recognised. He edged closer to take a look.

Mr Wright was on the platform. He had the pale, ghostly appearance of an Old Testament prophet. His long white hair blew in the wind, his torn black coat was mottled with ash, and there was a piercing intensity to his darting gaze as he harangued the crowd. He was gesticulating, urging them to have faith in the future in a voice that rang out with eerie clarity in the stillness of the ruins. 'In five years' time,' he declared, 'Chicago will have more men, more money, more buildings, more railroads, more business than it would have had WITHOUT this Fire.'

Nobody applauded.

Stephen watched with a mixture of pity and shame, glad his mother was not there to witness it.

'I shall make a prophecy,' raved Mr Wright. 'One day we will be grateful for the opportunities this Fire has created. Where I am standing now, we shall build a bigger, better and more magnificent church than was here before. And what is true for our church, is also true for the city. I shall say that again, my friends. What is true for our church is also true for Chicago. Chicago will be bigger, better and more magnificent than it could have ever been without this Fire.' He threw back his head and raised both hands high in the air. 'CHICAGO WILL RISE AGAIN.'

Stephen lowered his gaze and once more turned towards the west.

1873-1874

Browse for as Long as You Like

(The following article, written by Annie Borne, was published in the *Chicago Daily Tribune* on June 7, 1873. Annie Borne was the pen name used by the newspaper's food and fashion correspondent, Mrs Antje Hunter (née Van Voorhis). Please note that all items marked in square brackets [ ] were removed by the copy editor prior to publication.)

Ladies, their sales campaign begins before I have even set foot inside the lavishly decorated five-story marble palace at the corner of State Street and Washington. A young porter, trussed up in a dark-blue uniform that shines with enough brass buttons for half-a-dozen ordinary bellhops, greets me with a smile. 'Welcome to Field & Leit-er,' he says, 'the largest dry goods store on earth,' as he makes a low sweeping bow and with a seemingly Herculean effort casts open the heavy glass-paneled doors over which he stands guard. With that portentous greeting ringing loud and clear in my ears, I step inside.

Dear readers, discerning ladies of Chicago, believe me when I say that these front doors represent the gates to a magical, elect kingdom wherein are gathered a host of unimaginable wonders. With what a sense of awe will you first glimpse the spacious lobby, with its recessed ceilings and cascading chandeliers, its gaslit displays of sparkling jewels, the warm, colorful frescoes dominating the walls that lure the mind towards notions of sunshine and leisure, and prepare it to adopt the spendthrift mood of a vacation.

To anyone who witnessed the devastation caused by the Fire that struck two years ago, the speed with which State Street is being revived is little short of a miracle, an inspiring testament to the thousands of laborers working in its reconstruction as well as to the deep pockets of our city's business titans. [On this occasion, let us hope those illustrious titans have adhered strictly to the new fire regulations. Because, ladies, is it not a fact that building is a man's world? And is this not the embarrassing truth about the Fire which dare not speak its name? That, however much we admire and respect our dear menfolk, it was *their* build-

ings, not ours, that burned to the ground, causing such terrible destruction and loss of life?]

In the grand lobby, the air is pleasantly temperate and scented with an artificial flowery sweetness. Beside banks of dark walnut display cases filled with gemstones and exotic curiosities stand the drilled legions of clean-shaven greeters and salesmen, dressed as if for dinner, in white tie, top hat and tails, each man (for they are all men) bearing a silver-handled cane, embossed with the Field & Leiter coat of arms. None of them shows any surprise at the arrival of a lady on her own. Indeed, rather the opposite. We are given an even warmer and more respectful welcome than those ladies or gentlemen accompanied by their spouses. 'Browse for as long as you like, madam,' they say, 'and remember there's no need to buy a thing.'

Apparently, there are three rules of human behavior at work here. The first is that we ladies, whether on our own or in a company of other ladies, must feel safe when we visit Field & Leiter. The store is the most respectable of establishments, a destination for only polite, well-bred customers. The second is that a lady will be more amenable to making a purchase if there is no overt pressure to do so. The third is enough to make us blush. Avert your eyes, if you would prefer not to know the truth. It is we ladies, rather than the gentlemen, who spend the most. And, o pinnacle of shame, we are even more extravagant when we shop without them.

Today, as if our senses might not have been sufficiently stimulated already, there is an added extra. Messrs Field and Leiter are here in person. In what I understand to be a reprise of the original opening ceremony for the pre-Fire Field & Leiter store, we are directed to stand in line like guests at a wedding, and on our arrival before these two business magnates, we ladies are presented with a red rose, while the gentlemen receive a Cuban cigar.

Regular readers will know by now I like to have my fun. I decline the rose, and prepare a place in my handbag for the cigar instead. It is not, I regret to report, forthcoming. Rather, I am greeted by the very perceptible rise of Mr Field's left eyebrow. Ladies, I tried.

Acres of newsprint will doubtless be written in praise of the extraordinary enterprise of Messrs Field and Leiter. Much will be made of its scale, of the inexhaustible range of products on offer, of the guarantee that any item can be returned for a full refund, with no questions asked. But the sales approach goes deeper still. Providing your deportment and dress (i.e. your purse) is deemed satisfactory, you can ask for an official slip of paper that will allow you to take an item home on approval without paying a cent. Imagine, for example, that you find a rather delightful Persian rug, but are uncertain how well it will match the other furnishings in your boudoir. Simply ask one of those nice gentlemen wielding a cane for a slip and you can take the rug home, with no obligation to buy. Should you decide you don't want it, simply return it at your convenience. The same applies to anything else, whether it be a Saratoga trunk, Staffordshire crockery, Sheffield cutlery, a Zouave jacket or (my own weakness) the latest Dolly Varden outfit.

It sounds too good to be true, doesn't it? And yet, ladies, this purchasing bonanza is not yet over. You may be exhausted, your feet may ache, your bank account may be wilting, but the Field & Leiter sales effort has still further to go. Let's say you don't fancy carrying that new Dolly Varden outfit home and would much prefer to take high tea at the Palmer House Hotel. 'Your wish is my command,' says the salesman. (Forgive me, I made that up. But the sentiment is accurate.) The point is that the store *will* deliver the outfit in its Field & Leiter wrapping to your front door, *at no extra charge.*

Dare I suggest that there is something inherently false in this approach? Dare I suggest that in taking such measures to extract dollars from our purses, there might be something at work that borders on the dishonest? Dare I suggest that the artificial scents which lighten one's mood, the curtained windows that confuse one's sense of time, the lack of clear signs towards the exit that delay one's departure, are evidence of some underhand sales techniques at work?

Of course I would not dare. I would not even dream of daring! In any case, those who know more than I about merchandising affairs tell me it was our chief titan Mr Potter Palmer who pioneered these sales techniques in Chicago, and that he learned them in no less a country than France. If Mr Potter Palmer was behind them, and if a country with such a rich cultural heritage as France can sell with such *élan* and fervor, who on earth is Annie Borne to question such techniques?

[Who, indeed, dear ladies? And yet I ask you, for a moment, to indulge me. Let us reflect on some of the consequences of creating 'the largest dry goods store on earth'. What kind of society are we creating, what kind of city is Chicago to become, when the greatest ambition of its citizens and their most valued form of entertainment, lies not in the pleasures of an art gallery or a visit to the theater or a stroll in the park but in an afternoon spent walking the make-believe aisles of the gigantic Field & Leiter temple to luxury and consumption? I fear it may be an illusion, ladies,

and a deceptive one. For what ordinary citizen could ever afford to
buy anything but a handful of the
multitude of products on display?
What does this say about the age
in which we live? What will future
generations say about us and our
achievements? What of the arts,
what of good taste, what of education, what of our nobler aspirations,
what of our benighted souls? And
how many of the products so cun-
ningly presented on the six floors
of Field & Leiter are pure fripperies
that will have been forgotten by
next year, when others take their
place? What kind of world are we
creating for our children? How
long will it be, I wonder, before
we forget there are farmers on the
prairies without whose wheat and
meat and milk, without whose oats
and hens and vegetables, we would
never have been able to live in this
city in the first place? The seduction
becomes absolute, does it not, when
products from all over the world
can be found in a single building on
State Street?

Yet I confess that] as I wandered
up and down and around this vast
emporium, I found myself un-

able to resist its charms [entirely].
Like you, ladies, I have an eye for
fine linen, for the cut of a skirt,
for bright, bold colors. [If only the
salespeople — and once past that
imposing entrance many of this
tribe were of the female sex too
— had been a little less fawning
in their behavior.] For example, I
found a shawl I liked, and I [would
probably have] bought it [had I
been left to my own devices. 'Now
it's only my opinion, and the choice
is entirely yours, madam, but that
paisley shawl suits you like a dream.
I swear the gray matches your eyes
and makes you look like a princess
in a fairytale.' I point out that my
eyes are green, not gray. 'Either
way, you look like a princess, in my
humble opinion.' And like a princess in which particular fairytale?
'Oh, whichever one you like, madam.' Flatter, flatter, flatter, seems
to be the Field & Leiter approach
to sales, and though I grant I may
not be their most impressionable
customer, how irritating it can be.
Ladies, you have been warned.]

We must, as always, end on the
happy note of my weekly tip. I shall
give no prize to my regular readers

for guessing in which department we shall end our visit. Even so, I cannot explain precisely *where* the lady's fashion garments are to be found. I suspect that, the better to tempt us, the Field & Leiter sales geniuses might have chosen to place them in more than one location. Suffice to say they are easy to find and hard to get away from.

I began by casting my eye over the latest offerings of *haute couture* from Paris, which seem to be dominated by morning dresses much in fashion two years ago. Whether they still are, I leave to my readers' discretion. Personally, I find the French desire to set off a dark-colored satin dress of a low neckline and flounces beneath the knee, with a brightly-colored ribbon at the neck and matching sash at the waist (cut into streamers at the back), a trifle *insipide*. I understand that the style is much favored by the French *nouveaux riches* and between you and me, dear ladies, they are welcome to it.

Much more interesting is the gay offering of Dolly Varden-style hats, scarves and skirts. As I have mentioned before in this column,

it serves as an advantage in my own household that Dolly Varden began life in a novel by Charles Dickens. My husband is the most generous of gentlemen who, despite my best efforts, continues to demonstrate no eye for style or fashion. But because his life is devoted to the study of literature, it is much in my favor when I can say that my new purchase ('yes, I am afraid it was not the cheapest, my dear') was conceived not in a house of fashion, but in the mind of a novelist.

It is the patterns and bright shades of the Dolly Varden collection, designed to lighten the mood and put a smile on the face of even the dourest of matrons, that attract the eye. There are plenty to choose from, and I do not deny that some of them try too hard. Nobody wants to look as though they are wearing, at one and the same time, a clutch of wild animals, an aviary of tropical birds and every garish summer bloom imaginable. My own favorite is a more subdued style, featuring a floral chintz pattern on the polonaise and a silk petticoat with arms finished in a satin piping of apricot and white. The apricot and white piping is repeated also in a *foulard* sash and in the ribbon around the straw hat (which must be worn, of course, at a slight forward tilt). An elegant parasol, in matching colors, can also be bought as an accompaniment.

And, I am glad to report, this particular Dolly Varden has not been cut and sewn by seamstresses in far off Europe, but by our fellow citizens in the northwest district of Chicago. Best of all, having carried out inquiries, I am pleased to report that the conditions under which this dress has been made are not those of a common sweatshop. It comes from the most enlightened modern garment factory in the city. I shall therefore, satisfied on all counts, now return to the largest dry goods store on earth and buy that Dolly Varden outfit at once providing that you, dear readers, have not already beaten me to the purchase.

1873

It's Pointless to Look Back

Aureka likes the way the overskirt of her new Dolly Varden outfit, bought last week with this visit in mind, swings behind her as she walks towards the main door of the hospital. She has always enjoyed wearing fine clothes. It makes her feel stronger in herself. How little time it took John to see that side of her. Today, she needs all the strength she can find. She is apprehensive, unsure whether what she is trying to do has any sensible purpose.

This is a much larger institution than she was expecting. She stops to gaze up at the soaring layers of brick. To her left are three separate frontages on four floors. The windows are fitted with iron bars that make the place look more like a prison than a hospital. At least the bright August sunshine lends a sheen to the walls which makes them less forbidding than they must be at night, or on a cold winter's day. It is only when she reaches the main door that she sees the sign.

Her first thought is that she must have misread it, the second that she might have come to the wrong place. She tries to recall exactly what the two men in Finns said. They just called it a hospital, didn't they, an ordinary hospital? But that is incorrect. This is no ordinary hospital. In which case, Stephen had not been exaggerating when he described him as a 'crank'. She has come, she reads, to the *Northern Illinois Hospital and Asylum for the Insane*.

She went to Finns to buy Stephen a hat for his birthday. He was about to turn twenty-one and she remembered how disappointed she had been on her own twenty-first birthday because nobody remembered it. She was inspecting a black silk stove-pipe when she overheard two men, farmers by the look of them, talking about a mutual friend who had just gone to 'that Elgin place'. It was for the best, they agreed. The doctors up there were good, and they were sure he'd be cured and back home in no time. They talked for some time about their friend, how lonely he had found life on the homestead, especially after his wife died.

Aureka was already at the counter, enquiring about the price of the stove-pipe, when something they said made her freeze.

'You know who else is there?' said one of them. 'The man who started the *Prairie Farmer*, now what's his name?'

'Waite?' said the other.

'No, more like White, I think,' said the first.

She left the counter and walked up to them in a daze. 'It's Wright,' she said, 'It's Mr John Stephen Wright.'

They looked at her in surprise, but were grateful to be corrected. She asked them where the hospital was and how to get there and once she had the information, she left without buying the hat. She walked the streets for an hour or more before taking refuge in the new Exchange Coffee House, rebuilt on the site of the old one, where she used to meet Mr Wright before the Fire.

Those meetings began after he helped Stephen get the job at Field & Leiter. He would always be there first, and she would see him as soon as she came in the door, seated at one of the corner tables, hunched over, writing. It made her proud that she should know a writer and a gentleman. She enjoyed watching him at work. Only when he had reached the end of a page would she place a hand on his shoulder and begin the process of drawing him away from his words. She knew he was not in good health — he complained of frequent headaches and sleeplessness — and his conversation could take some very strange turns, but she attributed that to the brilliance of his mind and his high education, of which she had always been in awe.

She did not say much when they met. He liked to talk, and she liked to listen. They provided each other with pleasant companionship. He was lonely. His wife lived apart from him, somewhere in the East, and she, of course, only had Jearum for company. Mr Wright would drink coffee with sugar while she sipped tea. He always asked about Stephen, how it was going at Field & Leiter and whether there was anything else he could do to help him. That would evidently not be help in a monetary sense. His circumstances, she understood — and she could tell this from his appearance too — had declined. He mentioned that he was fighting with his brothers over the rights to some property. A few times, he asked whether she might bring Stephen along with her, but she never put the question to Stephen himself.

Once, Mr Wright asked her whether she was sure it was for the best that Stephen did not know the truth. Yes, she was quite certain. He had loved Albert, she explained. It would be devastating for him to find out he had not been his real father. Even so, she could not deny she sometimes had an urge to tell him. 'In my heart, I would like him to be proud of you, and who he really is,' she said once. 'But I'm afraid that can never be.'

He talked about many things in those coffee-house meetings, and sometimes when he got distracted he would mix Aureka up with another lady who was called Eliza, but she always forgave him, especially when he told her that Eliza had been an acquaintance of his when he was very young, who had gone on to marry a preacher. She liked it best when he told her about his plans for the future. Most men of his age would surely seek a quiet life, but not John S. Wright. He was planning to open a University of Chemistry in Chicago because that was where the future lay, or he was importing a new kind of cereal grain from Mexico that would double farmers' yields, or he was raising funds to buy a swath of prairie land that skirted the city because one day, when Chicago was five times the size it was now, that land would be worth a fortune. It felt a bit like the old days in Kinzie Street, when he would sit down in the kitchen and confide in her. In spite of everything, she would never regret what happened between them.

The Fire put an end to those encounters. Stephen had spent two days searching for Mildred who, unknown to him, was already back in Evanston. She had managed to escape from Mrs Creeley's boarding house with the other residents before it was razed to the ground. On his return, Stephen told Aureka what he had seen and, though she was glad to know Mr Wright had survived, to hear her old friend referred to as a 'crank' distressed her more deeply than Stephen could have guessed. Since then, she has not heard from Mr Wright.

There is a noise behind her. She did not notice them before, but a line of four or five people are seated in armchairs underneath the trees in the garden. They have their backs to her. None of them, she decides, resembles Mr Wright. A man is on his feet. He starts to dance, except that the dance is not really a dance. His movements are contorted and become increasingly frantic. It is distressing to watch. An attendant in a white coat hurries across the grass towards the group. He is shouting, telling the patient to sit down again. The man's movements only grow faster. He drops to his knees, shaking uncontrollably, beating his head against the ground. The attendant grips him underneath the arms and begins to drag him back, an unwilling, struggling hostage, towards the building.

She eyes the bell chord at the door. It was always going to be unnerving to see him again. A part of her had been thinking it might be best if they refused to allow her in. That way, she could at least have consoled herself with the fact that she had tried. But what is the point of seeing him at all, if he is in such a state? She turns to leave.

At that moment, the front door swings opens and a young nurse in a long black dress, white apron and frilly cap, rushes out. The nurse trips over something, reaches out to Aureka for balance and almost knocks her over. She apologises profusely. 'Oh dear, sorry, that was silly, I'm afraid that's not the first time I've done that. They say I must take things slowly but I'm not like that. I'm new here,' she says. She is short, stout and wilfully cheerful. 'Nurse Agnes,' she says. 'Can I help you?'

Aureka, even though she's decided against trying to see him, mentions John Wright's name to justify her presence. Before she can say any more, Nurse Agnes has taken her by the arm and is propelling her down the steps. 'Oh good, you're here at last. Come along, come along. The poor man's been expecting you. He'll be very happy. I'll take you straight over.'

Before Aureka can explain, she is being led across the lawn. It is hard to keep up. Nurse Agnes takes short steps, but she takes them fast. She chatters as they go. 'Oh, what a different world it is inside these gates. You meet all sorts, if you know what I mean. Some of them are quiet enough and you wonder what's wrong with them until they say something cuckoo, and then you remember they're only here in the first place because their minds are in a loop. The things I've heard, and I've only been here for two weeks, but I could write a book of nonsense already.' It's true there are some violent ones, she says, and you have to be careful with them. But most of them aren't too bad. Because they suffer from fits and spasms does not mean they're violent. 'Your Mr Wright, though,' she says, 'now he's one of the nice ones and I'm not just saying that because he's your father.'

'I'm not his ...'

Nurse Agnes does not let her finish. 'You did sign the book, when you arrived?'

'No, I'm afraid I didn't see a book.'

'Oh dear, that's another thing for Matron to get upset about, if she finds out. Could you sign it for me before you leave, ma'am? It would save me another rap on the knuckles!'

Aureka gives up trying to say who she isn't. Yes, she will sign the register before she leaves.

'Thank you indeed, ma'am, thank you. And here we are.' Nurse Agnes points towards a big oak tree near the high brick wall that marks the limit of the grounds, beneath which a man is seated on his own, bowed over a small wooden table. Aureka stops, her hands go cold and she's aware of a shortening in her breath. That posture is so familiar. It is him, she thinks. It is really him. He is wearing a top hat. His hair flows out from underneath, long, curly and white.

'Writing away as always,' says Nurse Agnes, 'as though there aren't enough words in the world already.' She leans over him. She says that his daughter is here at last to visit him.

There is still time to stop this. Aureka can simply walk away. He hasn't yet looked up. In fact, he's taking no notice of the nurse. His pen is racing across the paper.

Nurse Agnes turns to her and shrugs. 'I'm not surprised,' she says. 'You should see what we give him every day. I sometimes wonder if it doesn't make them more confused than they were in the first place.'

Aureka steps forward and places a hand on his shoulder. Through the coat, she can feel him trembling. 'Mr Wright?' she whispers in his ear. 'Hello John.'

His pen slows. He turns his head and looks up. His fine blue eyes are set in a cloudy film. He seems to be trying to focus, to put her into context, but it is a battle he loses. 'Eliza?' His mouth is lop-sided and his voice slurred.

'Aureka,' she says gently, leaving her hand on his shoulder. She gives him a light, affectionate squeeze.

'Don't worry,' says Nurse Agnes. 'He's always doing that, ma'am, muddling people up. I'm Eliza sometimes. Even your mother, she was Eliza when she was here. Probably that's who he's writing to now.' She rolls her eyes. 'No Eliza ever came here. And I don't imagine they ever will. I don't think Eliza exists, except up here.' She taps her head. 'Now I must be off. Remember to ring that bell if you need help. An attendant will be over at once.' She leans forward again. 'Now you be nice to your daughter, Mr Wright. She's come a long way to see you. And she looks just like you, doesn't she?'

Nurse Agnes sets off across the lawn.

In all this time he has not looked away from Aureka. Purple pouches lie beneath each eye. His white whiskers are raggedly cut, as though he allowed someone to start shaving him, and then changed his mind. Lines furrow his brow. He looks anxious. He also seems unbearably shrunken and diminished. The sight fills her with an inexpressible sadness.

'Hello John,' she says again. 'I'm not really your daughter.'

His mouth falls into a smile. 'I know you're not.'

'We're both getting older,' she says.

'I'm glad to see you, Aureka.'

She smiles in relief and gratitude. She starts to explain how she happened to overhear the conversation in Finns. But she stops herself. 'It's been such a long time,' she says.

His pen is still in his hand, but he seems to be concentrating closely on everything she says. 'The Exchange Coffee House.'

'Yes,' she says, taking his other hand in hers. 'I miss those days.' She runs her fingers over the back of his hand. The skin is wrinkled, the veins prominent; the nails are bitten down. He is still looking at her. 'The basin,' he says. 'Do you remember?'

She chuckles. 'Of course I remember. The blue porcelain basin of my mother's that I broke, and you paid for a new one. That's what I was thinking of too. How did you know?'

He taps his forehead. 'It's still here, my dear, whatever they tell you.'

She bites her lip. 'I think you look very well.'

He regards her suspiciously.

'I do,' she insists, as forcefully as she can.

He lays down his pen and frowns. 'And ... and how is ... you know?'

'Jearum?'

'The Automaton,' he says. 'No, not him.'

'You mean Stephen?'

'Yes. Stephen.'

Aureka tells herself it is not his fault, that his mind is damaged, that he is being given all kinds of medicines, but the fact that he needs help to remember Stephen's name still hurts.

'He is well,' she says.

'My children don't listen to me. They think I've lost my wits, which is why they had me locked up here. Stephen has spirit. I would teach him not to make the mistakes I made.'

Aureka nods. She squeezes his hand. She does not know what to say.

'And he mustn't look back, my dear,' he says, as some confusion seems to come into his eyes. 'We must never get sucked into the past. It's pointless to look back.'

She has heard him say that many times before, and she has never given it much thought. He is, after all, the educated one, the wise one. This time, though, the argument sounds flawed. The past has far more meaning for her than the future, and it grieves her to see it slipping away.

He picks up the pen again, and looks down. 'Three years from now,' he says, 'in 1876, on the Fourth of July ...'

He tries to continue writing but she takes hold of that hand too,

341

and encourages him to drop the pen. That, though, only makes him hold on to it more tightly.

'You always had such beautiful hands,' she says.

'Does Stephen know?' he asks. 'About me?'

She shakes her head, fighting back the tears.

He nods in a way that seems to say this is a pity.

Silence falls.

She breaks it with talk about Stephen. She praises Stephen, and then she hears herself tell a lie. 'One day,' she says, 'I have decided I shall tell him that you are his father. It will make him very proud.' The fantasy of telling Stephen the truth is one she has often entertained. She talks about the ways in which Stephen resembles him, in his looks and behaviour, she talks about the silver pocket watch — *his* old silver pocket watch — he always carries.

At first, John seems to follow her and he even asks some questions. Where is Stephen now? Could she bring him to visit? And when she mentions the watch, he quotes something in Latin, which he says was once on the back of it. She can see that what she is saying makes him happy. And it makes her happy too. Even if she is only speaking about how it might have been, to share that possibility with him is a relief. There is no shame involved, and there are no unpleasant repercussions. For a moment, she can dream that the truth would make Stephen happy, that he would forgive his mother. And that would mean there was nothing left to hide.

John's attention, she notices, has strayed. His eyes have wandered off. He looks worried, taps the table with his fingertips. 'There is so little time left,' he says. 'So little time. The printers close at noon. This must be with them by then or we are lost.' He stares, a pleading look in his eyes. 'You know I must do this for Chicago, don't you? Otherwise the country will fall into the hands of villains and cheats, into the hands of the judges and the juries and those cursed brothers of mine. Who will speak, if I don't? The common law is an abuse of God and Nature. There is only One who can make laws and His name is God.'

Aureka wipes her eyes. She did not even know she was weeping. She stands up and places her hand on his shoulder for what she knows will be the last time. How fiercely he is trembling. His words are becoming more confused. He is talking again about the Fourth of July, 1876, and about the government in Washington.

'I mustn't delay you any longer, John,' she says. 'You are very busy. I will be leaving now.'

He pauses again to look up at her. His eyes struggle to come back from where they have gone.

'Goodbye, John,' she says.

She wonders if he will remember that she was ever there.

1874

In Memoriam

(Published in the *Chicago Daily Tribune* on October 2, 1874)

John Stephen Wright
(July 16, 1815–September 26, 1874)

At twelve noon yesterday, in the tranquil surroundings of Rosehill Cemetery, a somber group of settlers from Chicago's earliest days gathered to pay their respects to Mr John Stephen Wright, who passed away on September 26, aged 59 years.

Chicago clocks, some wags have claimed, must be running faster than any others in the Union. How else do we explain the frantic pace of change? It was your writer's reflection, during the proceedings in question, that the same principles might apply to our collective memories. How few are the names that survive when history is written. No doubt Chicago will keep forever its Kinzie and Ogden and 'Long John' Wentworth and Potter Palmer, but what about Mr Wright? How carelessly we consign significant lives to oblivion. The name of John Stephen Wright, alas, is probably unfamiliar to most of our readers. And yet how many touching stories were told yesterday of the role played by Mr Wright when this city was but a flickering light in the American firmament.

Mr Wright arrived over forty years ago, when Chicago was nothing more than a frontier settlement of log cabins and Indian wigwams, set in swamps that stank of wild onions. But from the moment he landed, he never had any doubts about Chicago's glorious prospects. John Wright helped George W. Snow build the very first balloon-frame house. He trained himself to make maps and gained such a reputation for excellence that his work was adopted by the Government Land Office. One of the pallbearers yesterday was Mr Philo Carpenter. He recalled how he and Mr Wright would strike out into the untracked prairies with their surveying equipment to measure land — some of which is now prime real estate in the heart of the city.

The achievements of the deceased were too numerous to list in this brief notice. But to mention a few: Mr Wright was one of the key voices behind the building of the original Illinois & Michigan Canal, and by lobbying in Wash-ington he did more than anyone else to bring the Illinois Central Railroad through Chicago. Thousands of farmers across the country will be grateful to him for founding the *Prairie Farmer* newspaper. One speaker recalled that it was Mr Wright who led the campaign to use the Osage Orange plant to fence the prairies, long before the invention of barbed wire. His early support for the Atkins Automaton self-reaper revolutionized the way in which crops are harvested.

In particular, Mr Wright was applauded for being the finest booster this city has ever seen. This was true to the end. Even after the Great Fire, three years ago, it was Mr Wright who immediately saw the potential offered by that tragedy. While others were bemoaning their losses, he could look only to the future. There had never been a better time, he claimed, for investment in property. 'Five years,' he wrote, 'will give Chicago more men, more money, more business, than she would have had without this fire.' The city was not 'burnt up' it was 'only well blistered for bad ailments, to strengthen her for manhood.' Well, five years have not yet passed since then, but his prophecy has already come true.

And so was sadness at the passing of this noble pioneer mixed with pleasant recollections of his achievements. The most touching moment of all came at the very end when a spontaneous address was given by the sprightly Mrs Eliza Porter, a lady with whom I happened to become acquainted during the War when I was reporting on conditions at the front. I met her in Fort Pickering where she did exemplary work for the Sanitary Commission in the most wretched conditions imaginable. Her fortitude in the face of so much suffering and bloodshed as she ministered to the wounded and dying was admirable. While I was at Fort Pickering, I never once saw her shed a tear. I mention this only because it was, therefore, all the more moving to observe with what difficulty she strove to control her emotions as she spoke about her 'old and inspirational friend' Mr Wright. She recalled that conversation with him was like 'gazing up at the aurora borealis, alive with shooting stars. You never knew where the next bright idea would come from.' Mrs Porter said most people would not remember that when she arrived in Chicago in 1834 with the intention of teaching, there was not a single school in the community. 'I would like to put on record,' said Mrs Porter, her voice at breaking point, 'that John Stephen Wright built the first Normal school in this city.' She paused to wipe her eyes, before adding, in a curious turn of phrase: 'In spite of everything, he was a goodly, generous man.'

Mr Wright passed peacefully away in Philadelphia, Pennsylvania, far from his beloved Chicago. He was the most loyal and devoted husband to Kitty, and a kindly, caring father to Augustine, Maria and Chester, who loved him dearly.

1874

The Pennsylvania Asylum for the Insane

Special Report of the Board of Commissioners into the death of Mr John Stephen Wright

CASE SUMMARY

Mr Wright, aged 59 years, was admitted to this hospital on May 17 suffering from acute mania. It is believed he had been a patient in two other Hospitals for the Insane within the three years prior to this one. The first was the Massachusetts Hospital for the Insane in Boston at the turn of 1871/2, after he was found guilty of disturbing the peace. His offense was to have attempted, allegedly with much ranting and raving, to gain entry into private business premises to alert capitalists to the opportunities for building and profit-making in Chicago after the Great Fire that had taken place the previous October.

He was later committed for eight months at the Northern Illinois Hospital and Asylum for the Insane at Elgin on the grounds that he had attacked one of his own brothers with a surveying tool. He claimed this brother had swindled him out of some valuable property. In the courtroom, Mr Wright denied all charges brought against him but was adjudged not to be in his right mind.

The patient was brought to the Pennsylvania Asylum after again being assessed as insane by judge and jury after he attempted to impersonate Bishop Ledimer in the pulpit of the First Presbyterian Church in Philadelphia. After being forcibly removed, he claimed he was only doing what his mother wanted him to do, and what Christian could disobey his own mother? On his arrival here, Mr Wright was received by Superintendent Dr Thomas Kirkbride. The patient's first question of Dr Kirkbride was to ask him where the ceremony was taking place. His son, he explained, had told him they were coming here to celebrate the thirtieth anniversary of the founding of the *Prairie Farmer* newspaper.

On inquiry, it was discovered that Mr Wright's son had indeed brought him here under this pretense. It also transpired that the true purpose of the court convened earlier in Philadelphia — i.e. to assess whether or not he was sane — had also been concealed from him. Dr Kirkbride said: 'Mr Wright, do you not realize you are in a hospital?' Mr Wright was greatly surprised by this, and became very agitated and excitable. He cursed his son for deceiving him and the judge and jury too, for he now seemed to comprehend the subterfuge behind their hearing. The patient then tried to escape through the front door. Despite his declining health, three attendants were required to catch and restrain him, at which point he was placed in Ward B2 under the supervision of Dr Dewhurst.

During the four months he spent at this hospital he was treated, as the case notes indicate, with ever-increasing dosages of bromide of potassium, compound tincture of cinchona and syrup of ginger. His moods alternated between relative calm and high anxiety. When agitated, he would often resort to violence or the threat of violence against other patients and those attendants charged with controlling him. At times, it was necessary to use forceful restraint. The camisole, a stout jacket with long sleeves, was used to confine his arms and hands and, over his final three days here, when his mental and physical fury reached such maniacal levels that they were uncontrollable, he was confined to a crib-bedstead by day and night.

Whenever his anxiety level was high, the case notes indicate he was also treated with hypodermic injections of Magendie's morphine solution (typically in ten minim doses), together with ounces of whiskey for the purposes of subduing him.

The tragic incident that occurred on September 26 seems to have been prompted by Mr Wright's reading of a newspaper report. To put this in perspective, it should be reported that one of Mr Wright's delusions was that the other patients in the Hospital were potential investors in Chicago. He would draw up maps, 'sell' them land and prepare contracts for signature, promising to buy the property back if the value had not doubled by Christmas. At other times he would make strange biblical proclamations, referring to Chicago as the 'promised land'. This is mentioned for the purposes of establishing background and the nature of the acute mania from which he suffered.

Since his arrival in May, Mr Wright had been permitted, at his request, to read the daily newspapers and he would do so with relish. On September 23, the case notes indicate that he read a report in the *Philadelphia Daily News* which warned that the nation's economy was contracting, that factories were closing and the number of unemployed rising, that real estate was losing its value, and that a crash was already underway. Chicago, the writer declared, because it was at the center of the railroads and the grain and meat markets, would be affected worse than anywhere else in the country. Anybody who 'can get out of Chicago and cut their losses, should do so at once'. Reading this report sent Mr Wright into a state of apoplectic rage. He went on the rampage, storming through the wards, yelling at the top of his voice as he denounced the 'poisonous Eastern pens' that always tried to bring down Chicago.

He alleged another patient was the author of this article and, holding the man by the throat, threatened to take him before God to be tried unless he took back his 'd...d cocktail of lies'. Four attendants were needed to wrestle Mr Wright to the ground and during this scuffle he slipped, striking his head against an iron bedstead with such force that he was momentarily concussed. He also received sundry other injuries concurrent with a struggle of this nature.

On recovering consciousness, he began to shake convulsively and spew saliva at the mouth. The rigidity and contraction of his muscles was tetanic. He continued to shout, and though often incoherent, he referred not to the physical pain from which he must have been suffering but to the 'slanderful' article he had read in the newspaper. It took repeated doses of opium and chloral hydrate to subdue the patient. We should observe that this is the first time chloral hydrate is mentioned in the case notes.

From September 23 until September 26, Mr Wright was treated exclusively with opium and chloral hydrate, the first five doses taking place within a time period of only two hours. Dr Dewhurst's explanation for this is that the patient's initial response to the drugs was only a marked increase in fury. 'He kicked and writhed repeatedly on the bed, requiring four attendants to hold him down.' It took a total of fifty minims of Magendie's solution and two hundred grams of chloral hydrate to reduce the patient to slumber. Dr Dewhurst agreed that this was a very high dosage, higher than he had ever administered to any other patient. The Hospital's Superintendent Dr Kirkbride was away at the time in New York, and it was allegedly not possible to keep him informed of developments in the case of Mr Wright.

Over the next three days Mr Wright's cranial bruise stabilized, though it was suspected that internal bleeding was still taking place. He was still subject to sporadic bouts of agitation, but it was judged safe to release him from the crib-bedstead on the morning of September 26 for a walk outside. It was a pleasant morning, and the doctors say they have always encouraged their patients to take fresh air when practicable.

All newspapers had been kept away from Mr Wright since his outburst on September 23. It was unfortunate that when he was walking in the garden under supervision, he passed by another patient who was reading that day's *Philadelphia Daily News*. Mr Wright seized the paper, whose front page contained the following headline: *Will This Crash Be Worse Than The Great Crash of 1857?* An even stronger maniacal attack than the one that assailed him three days earlier now held Mr Wright in its sway. He raced around the garden, wrestling anyone who tried to restrain him as he attempted to climb the garden walls. All the time, he was complaining about the 'poisonous Eastern pens' and he seemed to be suggesting, according to eyewitnesses, that these 'pens' had done the same thing to Chicago in both 1837 and 1857. The doctors described this as the classic symptoms of an aggregate persecution complex. Such patients see a connection with every calamity and place themselves at its center. In this case, Mr Wright deluded himself into thinking that both he and Chicago had been ruined in the crashes of 1837 and 1857, and that this had been aided and abetted by those 'poisonous Eastern pens'.

This is the point at which the case notes become less frequent and precise than one would expect. After Mr Wright had been caught and returned with difficulty to the crib-bedstead, unquantified doses of opium and chloral hydrate were administered until the patient finally calmed down and fell into a fitful slumber. We read that his countenance grew pale, and that his skin and the extremities were cold. It appears that for the next eight hours he passed in and out of slumber, that he suffered from periods of excessive agitation and perspiration and that during this time he was treated with more unquantified dosages of chloral-hydrate together with injections of salt and water, grains of quinine and spoonfuls of beef essence.

At 7.15pm it was recorded that his pulse was regular at 120, and at about this time his bowels and bladder were freely evacuated. The pulse rate would appear to have grown more and more irregular over the next ninety minutes, ranging from 120 to 145. At 8.53pm it is recorded that his breathing suddenly became strained. Before 8.55pm his heart ceased to beat. At 8.55pm there was heard by those in attendance a last gasp.

The probable cause of death, according to the doctors at the hospital, was cerebral congestion. But it must also be recorded that a pale countenance, a coldness to the skin and to the extremities of the body, and an irregular pulse are conditions associated with the excessive ingestion of chloral hydrate.

It is to be regretted that the family of Mr Wright did not order or permit an autopsy to be conducted. One letter placed before the Committee by Mr Chester Wright, the patient's second son, causes us particular concern. It was penned by his elder brother Mr Augustine Wright who was in Philadelphia at the time of the patient's demise. 'All the doctors agreed that Father's mind would never return ... It is better, far better as it is, but it is hard, so hard to part with him. I will send you a lock of his hair.'

The Committee recommends that further investigations are made, that attendants working on Ward B2 are interviewed, and that pertinent records are collected and examined. One objective should be to identify precisely what levels of chloral hydrate were administered, and when. The inquiry should also examine what contacts existed between doctors and family members on September 26 and whether the doctors, in deciding how much chloral hydrate to give the patient, were acting as professionals in an independent capacity.

It is a matter of grave concern when patients of apparently robust health but with reduced mental abilities die in such circumstances. Should it transpire that the cause of death was due to an overdose of chloral hydrate, the Commissioners should consider taking criminal action against those responsible for authorizing those dosages.

1876–1877

1876

The Adventures
of James P. Cloke

At Detroit, an Irishman entered our carriage. He was distinctive as such even before he opened his mouth, looking around indignantly as though everyone else was to blame for what ailed him. A burly creature, he wore a dark cap pulled down too tight over a moist brow, giving the impression of an oyster popping its shell. I would later discover his knitted accoutrement concealed not only a thinning top but also a liverish scar that stretched from ear to eyebrow — proud remnant, no doubt, of a noble brawl. He must have been skimming thirty, a good few years younger than myself. After heaving a trunk beneath the bench opposite, he plumped himself down, eyes glaring like limelight in my direction before they swerved towards the window. There, with considerable effort, they remained fixed. Curiosity: here was a fellow who was trying and failing to appear inconspicuous. 'You remind me, sir,' I said, 'of a dear friend of mine, whom I have not seen in years.'

First, he pretended I was addressing the world at large. Then he gave me another of those fierce stares intended to swat me away. I presented myself. 'I am James P. Cloke,' I said. 'Special Correspondent for *The Times* of London.' His response was to run a telltale forefinger beneath his nose. A man who displays a twitch at the mere mention of authority piques my interest. 'And you, sir, are?' I enquired.

'What business be that of yours?' he demanded, spiky as could be, snorting on his sleeve and spitting out a wad of tobacco on that most convenient of cuspidors, the floor.

'I am merely attempting,' I pointed out, 'to engage you in a spot of conversation.'

'You're English.'

'True it is that I was born English,' I replied.

'I don't like Englishmen.'

'Many people don't,' I agreed. 'Very often with good reason. But ...' I adopted my Irish accent. '... I can also be a Fenian that misses the Old Country, that dreams of his beloved Emerald Isle ...' I paused, to remove a piece of fluff from my coat. '... when I so choose.'

He was staring at me, bottom lip adrift, as if reluctant to believe the evidence of his own ears. Impersonation has always delighted me.

'But I am now — like you,' I continued, 'an American at heart, and I hope that we can forget our differences of birth for the duration of the journey.' I smiled. 'Are you of a gaming disposition, sir?'

He leaned towards me, so close I caught a whiff of his perspiring aura, and proceeded to seize my lapel in a decidedly uncivil way. From behind a palisade of intriguingly crooked ivories, he demanded to know whether 'the Englishman' had ever heard of one 'Oscar Brody'.

'Yes,' I said, trying not to inhale any more of his respiratory aroma than was absolutely necessary, 'I believe I have. Was he not the first winner at Saratoga Springs back in '63?'

'What?' he exclaimed, missing my feeble wit, which was perhaps just as well.

It is one of my greatest flaws, ingrained in the blood of many an Englishman, that I attempt levity at the wrong moment. There are days when I cannot stop myself. 'You're right. My mistake,' I confessed. 'I was thinking of Lizzie W. It was a grand day. I made over a hundred dollars.'

'I'm not talking about a d...d horse, man.'

'No, of course not.'

'I mean —' he leaned even closer, so close we almost rubbed proboscises '— have you heard of a man called ... Oscar Brody?'

It was as though he had hung a sign around his neck. 'No,' I said, 'I don't believe I have.'

My honesty caused the rogue some confusion. Should he be insulted I had never heard of him, or relieved at my ignorance? 'You'll be certain, then, you've never heard of him?'

'I have not heard of him, sir. No. Never.'

I like triple negatives for their impact and, true to form, they put Mr Brody at ease. He grunted, let go of my lapel, re-arranged his bulk on the bench and returned to his contemplation of Detroit's bustling railroad station through the sooty window. Outside a whistle blew, a puffery of smoke obscured the wretched horde of cookie and corn juice vendors, and beneath our feet a magnitude of steel jolted forwards as the railroad chuckers, I surmised, removed the blocks that had been holding us stationary. We were on the verge of departure.

Mr Brody produced a long nine cigar from his waistcoat and plugged it between his lips. Only when his matches failed to ignite did he need to acknowledge my existence anew. I helped him out, at the same time lighting for myself an Opera Puffs cigarita, an exquisite mix of tobacco bought at no inconsiderable cost in New York. My travelling companion's gaze returned to the murky world outside the window as he puffed hard and discontentedly on his coarse cigar. The conductor's whistle blew, we were treated to a percussion of slamming doors, the wheels beneath us creaked and squealed, and the station and the houses and the factories and Detroit itself began to recede from view as open country beckoned and we were finally on our way.

After a suitable pause, I tried once more to oil the engine of acquaintance. 'What takes you to Chicago?' I enquired.

'Work,' he replied.

'And would that be work of a particular nature,' I pressed, 'or work in a more general sense of the word?'

A genial enough enquiry, that prompted one of his hands to ball up into a splendidly bloated fist. 'Why would you be wanting to know, Mr Cloke?'

'I am a reporter, sir,' I reminded him, 'with *The Times* of London. Asking questions is a habit of mine.'

'Even when a man's done nothing wrong?'

'I am not suggesting ...'

'You'd better not be, Mr Cloke.'

Oh dear, thought I. *What rough edges he has.*

Before we go any further, let me recommend an advertisement for our friends in the Pinkerton Agency: 'Ride the Illinois Central railroad'. Believe me, there is nothing like the line from Detroit to Chicago for unmasking society's ne'er-do-wells. I have found that trains can affect people in the strangest of ways. The iron horse is, of course, the greatest wonder of our age: no rutted surface to negotiate, no saddle to chafe the thighs, no doubt about which direction to take. We become lords of all we survey, propelled across the surface of the earth like birds through the sky. Most of us gaze at the grasses of the prairies before falling into a slumber. But there are others, like Mr Brody, on whom the beguiling sensation of forward motion has a very different effect. They can no longer keep their mouths shut. They feel the urge to brag about their squalid histories to any sympathetic listener they can find, safe in the knowledge that once the journey is over, they will never have to set eyes on this stranger again. The locomotive hubbub provides the privacy of a confessional. Only God and his earthly representative can hear the bleating of their prideful souls. And so it would prove to be with us. I was — bizarre to say — cast in the role of Mr Pinkerton; Oscar Brody was my mark.

I have a way with people, I'm told, that makes them say more than they intend. Oscar's 'confession' would warm the cockles of my heart. Worth including is some of the preamble, for what this revealed about the young man's character. How eager he was to speak of the deck being stacked against him. Had he not been brought over to America as a motherless nipper? His father, a Mr Mochta Brody, worked as a digger on the first canal in Chicago, good honest labour (I opine) that nevertheless led many a man to an early grave. Mochta was a giant, crowed Oscar, a hero who did the work of half-a-dozen ordinary folk. Everybody admired him, everybody loved him. One d...d day, though, when Oscar was not yet five years old, a tragedy took place. Mochta was laying charges to blast a hole through some bedrock with black powder of an inferior quality, supplied by a 'son-of-a-bitch Easterner'. The powder exploded before he could get away. And so it came to pass, that the father was consumed by a fireball in plain view of his young son.

I am not, by nature, demonstrative of emotion. It would interfere with my profession. I do, though, know how to act. So I furrowed my brow and produced some affecting expressions of sympathy before, as soon as was decent, urging Oscar to tell me more. It must have been difficult indeed, I remarked, to grow up an orphan. He hesitated when I put it like that. This was the first sign — and an impressively faint sign it was too — that he had not told the whole truth about his father. Despite the blandishments of the Illinois Central, it required a mix of guile and persistence on my part to coax any more out of him. I would eventually discover that there was indeed a conflagration of some kind, but Mochta — the man who went up in flames — was not Oscar's father. He was his uncle. The father is still among the living, Oscar finally confessed, a lowly fisherman eking out an existence on Lake Michigan. At this surprising disclosure, I began to take a keen interest in my interlocutor. The Irishman, it appeared, had brain as well as brawn. Someone who recreates his own past, installing an out-and-out hero for a father in place of a no-account piscatorian, knows where he wants to go.

I flourished a bottle of Old Jake Beam Kentucky Bourbon. 'The very best liquor that money can buy,' I remarked (quite inaccurately, of course) as I handed it across. 'Sláinte!' Oscar was soon partaking with the gusto of a true-born Celt. (I myself do not drink for professional reasons, though it can be pragmatic to pretend to do so.) His reminiscences were soon in full spate. 'You know what I was always dreaming, Mr Cloke? To play baseball for the Union team.' Alas, his gift with bat and ball would never be acknowledged by the masters of the sport. 'They were,' remarked Oscar, while we were passing through the vicinity of _____, 'a bunch of jackeens for not taking me on.'

'Failure to recognise the hidden talent in his peers is the ruin of many a man,' I said, 'And if you don't mind me saying so, Mr Brody, it strikes me that your gifts are by no means limited to baseball. I can see you have potential.'

'You think so, Mr Cloke, do you?' he said, with a touch of his earlier aggression. 'And what *potential* ...' He attempted, unsuccessfully, to mimic my English accent '... would that be?'

I smiled, drew him closer towards me than was strictly necessary, and spoke in the most confidential of whispers. 'Tell me this, Mr Brody ... or Oscar if I may ... could I interest you in a spot of pilfery when we reach Chicago?' I winked.

With the help of Old Jake and the concoction of a few fanciful 'confessions' of my own to balance the books Oscar was soon spilling the beans about his association with a local kingpin of repute known as 'King Mike' McDonald. King Mike, it appeared, was an upstanding citizen of influence, a gentleman under whose protection ordinary Chicago folk could live and work in peace. Of course, such tranquillity comes at a price, and it was Oscar's duty to ensure that the requisite sums were paid.

At this moment he paused, as if fearing he had already said too much. I, though, detected another rich seam of information worth mining. As the next few miles of prairie trundled by, I would extract an excellent confession. Was it any fault of Oscar's that six months ago a cussed 'Squarehead' storekeeper (he seemed to harbour a particular antipathy for former denizens of Sweden) didn't pay his dues? Was it any fault of his that this same Squarehead drew a knife on him, when Oscar roughed him up? Was it any fault of his that, while acting in self-defence, the tip of that knife happened to breach the Squarehead's throat and find entrance to his jugular vein? No, I assured him, it most certainly was not. And what was the name of this Squarehead, I enquired gently, and where was his store, and when was this punishment meted out?

'It was his own d...d fault,' said Oscar proudly. 'And remember this, Mr Cloke. Nobody won't never try that again with Oscar Brody.' There was a pause. His brow creased, he took a long swig of Old Jake, and aired first one damp armpit, and then the other. Perhaps the value of the information thus freely shared was beginning to dawn on him, for he suddenly showed me a resurgent fist. 'And that includes your d...d English newspaper.'

Well! Until he reminded me, I had almost forgotten who I'd said I was. But what an excellent opportunity this presented for a spot of lighthearted recreation. King Mike, after all, sounded like a crook worth knowing. Only someone with genuine clout could disappear a man guilty of a capital offence, and bring him back a mere six months later. And Oscar's fist might come in useful too, as long as it was being wielded in my behalf. I began by pointing out that as a reporter of principle I had a duty to report what he had told me in *The Thunderer*. In which case, I hardly needed to add, there would soon be a noose around his neck. His caddish response was, I am pleased to say, exactly what I had hoped for. Dare to write down a single word of what he had told me, and I would find myself decorating a tree before a single word reached the printer. That's the spirit!

I promised him that, speaking personally, I did not condemn him for what he had done. In fact, I congratulated him. There's no worse affliction to society, I said, than a Squarehead who comes over here and thinks he doesn't have to play by the rules. 'You think so too?' Most certainly, said I. 'Then you won't write nothing?' I confirmed that, notwithstanding the damage it would do to my own career and reputation, on this occasion I was prepared to waive the rules so as to save his skin. After all, we were friends now, weren't we?

I was aware that my tale had turned into an overegged pudding by this stage of proceedings, but I still held out the hope that, sooner or later, he would see through me. The circumstances surrounding the death of the Squarehead would be our little secret, I continued, but I hoped that in return for my silence he might afford me an introduction to King Mike, for he sounded a fine fellow. Oscar observed me through eyes that were now well and truly glazed by Old Jake. After engaging in an extended bout of cogitation, that involved whipping the cap off his skull and mopping his brow with an unpleasantly soiled handkerchief, he finally bared those veterans of many a skirmish — his incisors, canines, molars, wisdoms *et al* — in a magnificently raucous guffaw. 'Yerra, as my father Mochta would have said, you're worse than an English landlord.' He slapped my knee in an unnecessarily familiar fashion. 'You nearly fooled me there, Mr Cloke, with that newspaper baloney.'

His little epiphany was not before time but, to be fair, he had by now drained the bourbon bottle singlehandedly. I shook him warmly by the paw and let him sleep it off. Later, I brought out my deck of cards, fleeced him within an hour for all the cash he had — a little over $30 — which I then returned to him. 'I like you Oscar,' said I, 'but you can't gamble worth a cent. Don't do it again until I've taught you how.'

By the time we caught our first sight of the distant smudge in the sky that was Chicago, rising like a genie from its bottle, Oscar Brody was, so to speak, in my pocket.

———

Chicago is the fastest and most frantic and most higgledy-piggledy upside-down bridge-swinging town it has ever been my good fortune to step foot in. And one should be cautious, by the way, about exactly how one despatches the said foot because many of the houses and streets stand at different heights. Doubt me not. I tend to speak the truth, and almost nothing but the truth, so help me God. There was, I would discover, an unexpected boon to these anomalies of elevation. Time one's walk, and in some places an upward gaze would reveal a lady's underdrawers passing overhead, exposed to best effect beneath a crinoline. I have no shame. Nor, I was pleased to observe, did my friend Mr Brody.

I took him to the best hotel in Chicago. A magnificent establishment on no less than seven floors, the Palmer House was rebuilt after the Fire of '71, its spacious bedrooms adorned with mantles of Italian marble, thick-piled carpets from England, and glossy French landscapes on every wall, from which the paint almost continued to drip. There were speaking tubes and damask curtains lined with silk, rosewood chairs in the parlours, drinking fountains in the halls and, best of all, a bulletin board in the lobby with 'tickers' in perpetual motion, *tap tap* tapping numbers direct from the Board of Trade that represented (I would soon discover) the most important information a man with a penchant for the odds, who happens to be in the midst of a lucky streak, could ever desire. For here, in common ink worth more than its weight in gold, were displayed moment-to-moment, grade by grade, from the markets of London to Philadelphia, from Boston to New York, the most recent prices for pork and spring wheat.

My first act on arrival was to lead my wide-eyed companion into the mahogany splendour of the banqueting hall, lit by two dozen French chandeliers, and treat him to a cocktail — I forget whether

I plied him with a *Claret do* or *Ne plus ultra* or *Tippe na Pecco* — selected from a list as long as a dictionary. I had taken a shine to the strapping and impressionable young Oscar Brody. He was more cunning than he looked, and I saw the potential in him for a useful accomplice. I may have peddled with the idea of going off the crook altogether on my arrival in Chicago, but the truth is that — unlike the great unwashed — I am of that breed who remain true to their calling. And I cannot deny I was titillated by the prospect of an introduction to King Mike.

Oscar could hide neither his awkwardness of manners nor his delight at being accommodated in such plush surroundings. While he disappeared into the hinterland beyond downtown to report his good fortune to King Mike, I began as one must always begin, by making myself look respectable. First, I called in at the hotel barber shop in the basement, a gloriously equipped establishment, its black and white floor tiles embedded with silver dollars. I emerged, an hour or so later, feeling splendid. My hair had been cut and curled and combed and dipped in the best bay rum, and my sideburns and spade beard were as neatly pruned as a picket fence. It was now time to dress for the part too. I made some enquiries and ascertained that Field & Leiter was the store at which a gentleman could sample the very best tailoring. How true that was. By sunset I was in possession of some ready-mades, an elegant claw-hammer coat and a black bowler hat, as well as a go-to-meeting outfit for the daylight hours.

Though playing the odds has always been my passion, I like to spread my risks. Hence, a sideline in pilfery. Pilfery, for the record, is a world away from highway robbery, sandbagging or blowing a safe. When practised skilfully on those in high society who really should know better, I consider it a perfectly legitimate extension of my professional skills. I started that same evening after dinner in the private saloon bar on the second floor of The Palmer House, having briefed my new accomplice, and having dressed him in an ill-fitting shirt, a rude coat and a flat cap. He was to play the yokel, unused to the ways of a grand hotel in the big city. While he kept to the shadows, I stood drinks to a likely looking group and was soon being furnished with an address on Wells Street where a respectable man might engage in a spot of faro and craps. The next recommendation was a house with a high-class supply of day ladies or 'outside boarders', as they are sometimes known. *Friendly folk in Chicago,* I thought. *Helpful. Full of the joys of life.*

With dinner over, the lighting was discreet in the saloon bar, the cigar smoke thick and its patrons full of well-being and bourbon. A sense of privileged camaraderie prevailed, even among virtual strangers, that was excellent at breeding carelessness. I gave the pre-arranged signal to Oscar — a casual scratch above the left ear — while being subjected to the blusterations of a pig-eyed owner of a steel business in St Louis who, when he fell for the line that I was the Special (oh what glamour that word adds) Correspondent for *The Times*, began to snuffle with pride at the prospect of seeing his name in the pages of that illustrious journal. To his credit Oscar reacted at once from the corner where he lurked. There was an immense shattering of glass and crockery as he tripped over his chair and swept a flailing arm across the table in an attempt to keep his balance. A series of loud and colourful rustic oaths accompanied his collision with the floor. My stall, with this bravura performance, rose yet further in my esteem. The distraction was complete. Twenty braying bigwigs nearly swallowed their cigars at the commotion, and with what ease did I proceed to appropriate the steel man's fattened purse.

Back in our suite, I congratulated Oscar and rewarded him with a generous cut from the takings. He chose to go directly to a *bagnio* located in King Mike's domain but when my luck is in, I don't like to stop. I decided to mix celebration with a few more pilferies. I sallied forth to McVicker's Theater and watched an abominable play called *The Hero of Fort Dearborn*, set way back in the Middle Ages when

Chicago was still a snoozy one-horse town. A tale was told of how the founder Mr Kinzie failed to save some blockheaded soldiers from obliteration at the hands of bloodthirsty redskins. There was a moral in there as subtle as a herd of buffaloes so I ignored it, determined to enjoy myself regardless and applauded heartily. In the first intermission, I whisked (for almost $50) a man who must have been a politician, given the crowd that was pressed around him, before lifting a lady's purse in the second intermission while we climbed the stairs in tandem to go to our respective boxes. This pretty silk pouch contained a brooch worth $15, a diamond ring that would bring $35 and some loose bills that I donated to the Theater's collection in aid of supplying needy citizens with winter clothing.

The next day, I checked us out of the Palmer House and took some commodious rooms on Wabash Avenue. Within a week, King Mike and J. Patrick O'Cloke (touting exclusively, of course, his Irish accent) were business partners, and within a month the Brody Elevator Co. opened for business. King Mike and I were equal partners in the enterprise but we both shy away from unnecessary publicity. Oscar was only too pleased to step into the breach.

King Mike may have been interested in a quotidian business confined to the receiving, grading and shipping of grain, but I was not. This is not to imply that an elevator is anything other than an admirably profitable entity, especially under the management of Oscar and the Irish associate he recruited (called Dermot Something-or-other). Should any farmer be rash enough to object to the unorthodox grading of, say, top quality Spring Wheat No. 1 as the considerably less valuable Spring Wheat No. 2, the way Oscar cursed and glowered would soon persuade even the most hardened of them to accept his terms, or pay the requisite backhander. Yes, it was a profitable business.

Curiosity: where is the thrill? where are the odds? How, with an elevator, can one experience the dizzy pleasure of bringing one's opponent — or indeed oneself — to the brink of ruin? What point is there in life if we do not, from time to time, stake everything we own on the cards in our hand? For James P. Cloke, alias J. Patrick O'Cloke, the elevator was but a stepping-stone into the futures market and its 'corners'. I decided to take Oscar under my wing in this enterprise too. His healthy appetite for wrongdoing, combined with naked greed, deserved nurturing. Besides, one needs a pliant stall should things go wrong. Did I not hold information on the young man's past that would serve as excellent insurance, if needs be? We gamblers are, in the end, lone wolves.

1877

Editorial: *Chicago Daily Tribune*

FROM THE DESK OF THE EDITOR, MR JOSEPH MEDILL:

A case heard at the Board of Trade this morning brought into public view a deplorable practice that has been tolerated for far too long in Exchange Hall. I speak of that iniquitous construct — the 'corner'. For those readers unfamiliar with the workings of the futures market, let me begin by furnishing an introduction to this arcane institution. Not so long ago, a wheat farmer had to drive his loaded wagon along dangerous dugways to reach Chicago. He would then search for a buyer and negotiate a price. This was a risky, arduous procedure that — just fifteen or twenty years on — already sounds antiquated. In the modern world, a farmer simply loads his sacks of grain into a railroad wagon and, on arrival in Chicago, delivers them to one of the elevator companies. There, the grain is graded, shunted to the top of the hopper, weighed and sorted, and dispatched down an iron chute into the appropriate bin. That bin is emptied directly into the hold of a ship waiting at the quay. An efficient system that, managed honestly, would seem to be in everyone's best interests.

Mr Oscar Brody, the proprietor of the Brody Elevator Co.,

was summoned before the Board, accused of running the notorious corner that readers will remember brought the Exchange to a standstill at the end of June. I ask for patience from those readers who may find the following details dull, but they are essential if one is to understand the inherent corruption in the system. To put the puzzle into context, we must note two developments now taken for granted: the 'ticker' reports up-to-the-minute grain prices from across the world, and a standardized grading system means that No. 2 Spring Wheat is always No. 2 Spring Wheat, whether it comes from Illinois, Kansas, Iowa or Indiana. The only *lacuna* in this process is the time and cost of delivering the grain from, say, the Brody Elevator Co. in Chicago to a buyer in, say, New York. Hence, the appearance of the futures market and 'to arrive' contracts. These contracts fix a price today for the delivery of grain at a specified date in the future.

When the price of grain shifts, the speculator has his chance. Hence the division at the Exchange between the so-called Bulls who

bet on the price going up, and the Bears who bet on it going down. Whichever way it does go, one of them will make a profit, the other one a loss. What benefit their wager brings to anyone else in society, I have yet to discover.

In mid-May, it was alleged, Mr Brody — with as-yet-unidentified 'accomplices' — hatched a plan to buy, as gradually and discreetly as possible, futures contracts on No. 2 Spring Wheat for delivery on June 30. At the same time, the Brody Elevator Co. kept off the market the substantial stockpiles of No. 2 Spring Wheat held in its own warehouses. The inevitable duly happened. The price of wheat when Brody began to buy those contracts was $1.75 a bushel. By mid-June, when the market first suspected there might be a shortage, the price was up to $1.95. On June 30, when the contracts came due, the scarcity of the grain had pushed the price to $2.15. Brody and his associates made a profit, the Board was told, of over $100,000. Meanwhile, many unsophisticated small-scale traders went bankrupt and an even greater number of gullible farmers, persuaded by sharp-talking dealers to play the market, were ruined.

If this were the first time such a corner had been created, one might be more forgiving of the Board of Trade's lackluster response. But this has been going on for years. In the case of Mr Brody, the Board has once again decided that the reputation of the Exchange would be harmed more by the publicity attending a full-blown court case than by a quiet reprimand. The deciding factor in their pusillanimous behavior was the silver-tongued eloquence of an English barrister-at-law hired by Mr Brody — a man who styles himself 'The Honorable James Percival Cloke' — who argued that his client had simply enjoyed a run of good luck. On this occasion, although fluctuating prices happened to go in his client's favor, they might just as well have gone the other way. In short, the Board had no right to cast aspersions on the conduct of Mr Brody unless they could produce compelling evidence that a corner had indeed been created. This is a fiendishly difficult thing to do in hindsight,

when the market has moved on.

In a blatant ploy to divert the attention of the Board, Cloke focused his argument not on the corner but on some 'alleged misdemeanors' that had also been presented to the Board concerning one of Mr Brody's grain inspectors, a Mr Dermot O'Leary. Mr O'Leary himself was not present to defend himself. But under friendly questioning from his barrister, Mr Brody conceded that his grain inspector 'very occasionally, Honorable Cloke, if at all,' might have categorized No. 1 Spring Wheat as the less valuable No. 2 Spring Wheat. 'I don't doubt it would have been an honest mistake,' claimed Mr Brody.

'As the elevator owner,' proceeded the sly English advocate, 'you might therefore agree to accept responsibility for an occasional lack of oversight, and promise the Board this will never happen again?'

'I do,' said Mr Brody, with not a hint of apology or remorse. The Honorable Cloke paused, and regarded his client with a steely eye. 'But I would also like to point out to the Board,' added Mr Brody hastily, 'that I cannot be everywhere at once.'

The Honorable Cloke smiled. He turned to the Board. 'Of course, we cannot expect him to be everywhere at once, gentlemen, can we? He is only human!'

The Board took the bait. They suspended O'Leary's license to operate as a grain inspector, and agreed to forward the evidence put before them about the 'alleged misdemeanors' to Chicago's Court of Justice. The upshot, then, is that Mr Brody continues to own and operate one of the largest elevators in Chicago and remains free to trade on the futures market. If someone ever does have to spend a few nights in Joliet, it will not be Mr Brody but his henchman Mr O'Leary.

The disgraceful manner in which The Honorable Cloke traduced his profession and hoodwinked a docile Board of Trade was as clever as it was shameless. By yet again looking the other way, the Board jeopardizes not only the success of the Exchange, but also threatens the livelihood of all those farmers who depend on the honesty and efficiency of the grain market. This newspaper demands the Board come to its senses and re-opens the investigation. Rather than being diverted by small fry like Mr Dermot O'Leary, it should concentrate on bringing Mr Brody and his 'accomplices' to justice. Those unnamed accomplices, one suspects, were the true brains behind the corner.

1879–1886

Reception for the Settlers of Chicago

Address delivered by Professor Milton Winship, Faculty of History, University of Chicago at the 'Reception to the Settlers of Chicago prior to 1840', held at the Calumet Club of Chicago on Tuesday Evening, May 27, 1879.

(IT SHOULD BE NOTED THAT PROFESSOR WINSHIP WAS UNABLE TO DELIVER THE LATTER HALF OF HIS SPEECH DUE TO INTERRUPTIONS FROM GUESTS IN ATTENDANCE. IN THIS PAMPHLET WE HAVE CHOSEN TO PRINT THE PROFESSOR'S PROPOSED ADDRESS TO THE CLUB IN FULL.)

Ladies and Gentlemen,

Without any preamble, I proposition to read aloud extracts from the transcript I made of an interview conducted with Mrs Eulalie Van Voorhis, shortly before her death earlier this year at the age of eighty-three years. As some of you may know, I am a historian at the University of Chicago, and it was through my research into events that took place here at the beginning of this century that I would come to know Mrs Van Voorhis. I wanted to persuade her to talk to me about her recollections of the battle of Fort Dearborn in 1812 because she was, to the best of my knowledge, the last living witness of that tragic occurrence. Judging it best to lead her gently towards such a traumatic event, I asked her first about what I thought would be a happier memory — the arrival at Fort Dearborn of the man who would, briefly, become her husband.

Let me point out that I have made no alterations to the text I shall read out. The imperfections, the infelicities of expression, the contrarieties, are those of the elderly lady who uttered them. As you shall hear, she confused me at times with her late husband, addressing me as though I were he. I ask you to treat such slips with forbearance, and concentrate instead on the substance of her story. It has been said, by those infinitely better equipped than I to make such a judgment, that the memory of youth sharpens with age, and the mind begins to function like a telescope, no longer able to focus on what is near at hand, but marvelously proficient at looking into the distance. That would seem to have been the case with Mrs Van Voorhis's recollections of those far off days. I believe the story she tells has much to teach us about the origins of Chicago.

It was the coldest day of the year, Mr Winship. The same day one of the soldiers that went to fetch water from the river lost two fingers from frostbite. The same day the wind, how cruel it howled, cut through the timbers and unrooted a row of palisades better than an Indian attack ever could. The same day an ox froze to death. The day was so cold our breath, it came puffin' out like clouds, though we women was crammed together like slapjacks inside the barracks room of the Fort. It wasn't much, that room, neither in spacefulness nor comfort. How dark it was. Splintered stools for seats and a poor fire smoking damp wood, and prickly mats on the floor for sleeping,

that was the sum of it, but we had to borne up to it, as one had
to borne up to everything in those days.

I was a pretty one, though you won't believe it now. Hair on
my head like sheaves of corn with the color of a gold ring, not
that I ever had one on my finger like the ladies today, *heh heh*.
Wasn't the way, for a man to put a ring on your finger, not back
then. Wasn't the way to go to the church either, not when there
wasn't one to be found for a hundred miles or more. You did it
out in the open between the two of you. Yes, that was the way it
was and there was no shame in it. I kept my hair bobbed at one
ear, the same like in a picture they hung at the big house when
I was young. That picture came with us at the Banishment, all
the pictures did, excepting the one of the house itself — the
'first mansion' in Chicago, they called it. Everything else stayed.
Everything. The fine plates and candlesticks and kettles, the
mirrors and pewter basins, even the cabinet of French walnut
fitted with glass in each door.

No, I don't know about the picture of Lady Strafford — that
was her name, the one with the earlock curl — where it is now.
They were all sold, long time ago. I never saw a finer lady than
that one. She was a wealthy dame about to lose everything. I
reckon Gray Curls liked that picture the most, because he saw
his own future in it.

But to talk of fine ladies, I do remember one that was
special. A little lady she was, with a spirit to her like the breath
of God, for those that believe. Name like a church. *[Pauses]*
Chappell, that's what it was. Wed to a preacher man. Name
of Porter, I believe. Wrong man, if you ask me. Should have
taken the other one. I met him once, when he bought back the
picture of the 'first mansion' for me, though in the end I left it
in Chicago. Why? Because I didn't need it no more, not after I'd
told Miss Chappell about you, Isaac, and about what happened.

What do I mean, when I say Banishment? You ask a lot of questions, and some of them mayn't have no answers. But yes, to this one there is reason enough. Banishment was what we called it, when they drove us out of Chicago with nothing but a wagon full of pictures, a few loaves of bread and two broken legs. I was only a pup at the time, but I remember Gray Curls saying it like that. Yes, Gray Curls was my grandfather, that's how I called him. *We eat the bitter bread of banishment*, he'd say.

What's your meaning, that Shakespeare said it first? No, sir, I'm not so touched I never heard of that Englishman. And even if he did say it, I wasn't to know, was I? You've muddled me, with your talk of writers. Isaac was a fine writer. But not me. I don't write. And I never was one for talking much neither. I think though. I'm always thinking. Where was I? Yes, yes, I was the kind that primped myself good, soon as I was big enough to fasten my own buttons. I was gay in my colors as a hummingbird, the best I could make with homespun. My mother knew the loom better than most, and whenever a new cloth comes, she makes it into a bonnet or skirt or bloomers or something of the sort. No, bloomers came later, I reckon. Not that it matters, what came when anymore, whether it was before or after, not when you live this long, *heh heh*.

We were seated around a fire that day that was leaking heat into the barracks like the roof leaked water. There were only two thoughts in my mind. One was the cold, and how long it would last and if it would ever be over. The other was my belly, and the ache that growed there. For two weeks we'd lived on a diet of turnips and potatoes. The portions were getting smaller each day. There'd been no bread since the previous Sunday. Mrs Heald — she was the governor's wife — told us fresh supplies would come soon from St Joseph, but I didn't believe her. She'd said that before. It was in her character to be always hopeful, even when there wasn't no reason. Some people are like that, and they rise fast in the world, and Mrs Heald was one of them risers. You know what happened to her? When she was captured, the captain had to buy her back for a mule and a bottle of whiskey. After the fighting was done, they bought a farm in Stockton, Missouri. That's what I heard.

I'm ahead of myself, or maybe I'm behind, and it don't matter which. I'm touched, you see, that's what people say, though it ain't true. I keep to myself, that's all. You arrived, recall you this my husband, on the coldest day of the year and when the door scraped open and a hideous wind came rushing inside I turned on my stool, and through eyes watering with the cold I gazed upon you for the first time. Seeing through moistness makes a mirage, and there's shimmering in the air and hard things lose their edges and everything becomes more than it is. Remember those spring days on the prairies, when a carpet of primroses looks to be floating above the earth, when a tree far off looks like a tower leaning against the sky, and when the air vibrates like the strings of a violin with all the nature that's passing by? That was how I saw you, coming in from the cold like a mirage of nature, rubbing your hands together not fast like the rest of us but slowly, like you was only wanting to caress the cold, and I saw the snow shining like clusters of stars, bright on the tassels of your Hessian boots, sparkling on the folds of your blue velvet frock, twinkling on the brim of that round black hat — oh yes, I can see you as clearly now as I saw you then. You were as near to a god as can be made with flesh and blood. Your cheeks were pink, your eyes were bright as a blaze of sunlight, and when you spoke, your voice sounded like music inside my head, though I remember none of the fine words you spoke. I've never heard anyone speak or write the English tongue like you, Isaac, despite the Dutchness in your name.

Yes, it was the coldest day of the year when you arrived. An ox froze to death, a soldier lost two fingers from frostbite, our breath puffed out in clouds, but none of that mattered anymore because you had arrived. You had arrived, Isaac Van Voorhis, and the sweet madness of love was about to break my heart.

You say you want to hear how it happened, Mr Ship, *heh heh*? How we courted, and how we were wed? Those are secrets I can't tell, because it's a story that belongs only to Isaac and me. Don't think it's shame that prevents me from talking. The nearer I get to the end, the more shame I have and the less shame I feel. Every year we pile it up, don't we, all of us excepting the angels? But shame's easier to live with, the more time we spend with it. Maybe that's why we don't all go lunatic. And why some of us do. I feel more shame than you can imagine, about what I didn't do the day of the fighting. But I never felt shame about us, about you and me, Isaac, and how we loved.

What they're calling the Massacre Tree was our cottonwood. It was the biggest tree that side of the Lake with branches as high as the Towers of Babel they're building these days in New York. We aren't birds, are we Mr Ship? We don't walk on air, we only breathe it. Why do there be people who want to live with the birds? But times change, don't they? Yes, the times they change. We weren't to know what would happen there one day, when we took our vows beneath that tree. We went for love, that's all, because the tree was huge, and beautiful, and a long way from the wrong eyes. I wore a white calico skirt, and you wore a blue silk coatee, the same one in which you fell three months later. And that's how we pledged our troth beneath the cottonwood tree. You knew all the words, Isaac, in sickness and in health, to love and to cherish, until we are parted by death. Nobody could see us in that flowerful hollow. Nobody but the God I still believed in then. The leaves hung in a tangle of green triangles, thousands

of them, the fruit already splitting open in wisps of white. And
we lay there, didn't we, we lay in that hollow, day after day in
the long afternoons, and there we loved. And after the loving
was done and you were stretched on your back, staring up into
that green cloud of leaves, and as I slumbered fallen half across
you, one leg crooked over the both of yours, you would tell me
your visions of the future, and how things would come to pass
in America. I believed you, even though I didn't know how such
justice and kindness could ever be. I didn't think anyone could
see the future, except Gray Curls.

His birth name was Jean Baptiste Pointe de Sable. A
mulatto — French by the father, freed slave by the mother.
He was the first trader, and he built the mansion, he planted
the fields, he made a dairy and a stable and a barn, a poultry
house and bakehouse. He planted a row of Lombardy poplars.
Everyone liked him. That's how Chicago was birthed. One day
Mr Kinzie arrived and cheated him out of everything, and that's
when we came here, to St Charles.[7]

I use the memory of you, Isaac, to fight the nightmares.
It sounds silly, don't it, a woman as old as me, with only one
memory to keep me apart from madness? Or maybe not. Maybe
I'm a crazy old witch. You taught me everything about the herbs
and plants, Isaac, what was good and what cured what. Even
that last afternoon, before the journey, you brought me elk root
for the aches and bruises. And I remember how you said the
lunatic the lover and the poet, they're all the same. And we'd
laugh, and kiss again, and you'd say the taste of my lips was like
poetry and lunacy and love.

That was Shakespeare, again, Mr Ship? Shakespeare wrote it

---

7 At this point, the delivery of Professor Winship's lecture was delayed due to an uproar among
guests, outraged by the charge that Chicago was not founded by Mr Kinzie, but by an unknown
person of color.

too? I wouldn't be knowing about that. It's something Isaac used to say, that's all.

I thought those days would never end. I had no true fear, that's the oddness, that they could. We didn't have long, that last afternoon. Mrs Heald was calling for Cicely and me. Never mind. I told myself we would come back to our great tree one day, and lie again beneath its massy branches, the same as before. I was young, and in love, and that was my blindness.

You gave me your letters that last afternoon. It was safer for me to be taking them, you said. There were four or five addressed to Fishkill, New York. And there was one to me too, though I only found out later. You knew what would happen the next day, didn't you? How I wish I had told you, Isaac. But I thought there was no rush. That was the sum of it.

I slept well that night, like the innocent I was. When I woke up the next morning, I was more happy than afraid. The Fort was a dreary place thick with mosquitoes, the food was poor, life in the barracks room was hard, and the only two people who mattered to me, other than Gray Curls, were coming too. Yes, I mean Isaac and my friend Cicely. My mother was dead already, and so was Uncle Jean. He wasn't my real uncle, but I always called him that. No, he didn't die of sickness. Mr Kinzie killed him, stabbed him in the back eight times. Something to do with Mr Kinzie overcharging the governor, as I recall. No, Uncle Jean wouldn't hurt a fly. He was fat and lazy and full of laughter, and one of the gentlest men I ever met.[8]

There were two baggage wagons, and Cicely and me traveled in the second one with the children, screened by

---

8 Professor Winship was unable to continue his address beyond this point due to heated objections from the guests about the unflattering portrait of Mr Kinzie, and in particular the allegation that Mr Kinzie, the first settler and the man considered by many to have been the founder of Chicago, committed murder.

canvas. If there was to be any fighting, it wasn't for the eyes of the nippers. Cicely was a slave, and my best friend. We washed clothes in the river, and she kept watch for me when I was away with Isaac. She had the dearest, sweetest baby boy nursing at her breast. Name of Juba.

The day was warm and clear, the sky blue and empty. There was little wind, that I recall. The dust kicked up by the horses inside the stockade hung in the air. Everyone was running around like loons. Mrs Heald sent me into the wagon first, to get the children settled. They were the youngest ones, that was too small to walk on their own. I was so busy with them, I didn't even see the flag lowered, nor did I see you march past when the horn blew and the gate was thrown open, Isaac. You must have been looking for me, and I blame myself, that I wasn't there to look on you for the last time. You'd told me you were to ride at the front, with another captain — I've forgotten his name — a captain who'd arrived a day or two before with some braves from the Miami. That was the kind of man you were, to volunteer to go first.

The 'Dead March', Mr Ship? No, why would they play that?[9] They were trying to make our spirits high that morning, not despairful. And mine — young fool in love that I was — were high indeed. I remember exactly what the band played. I should have known, shouldn't I, that it could mean nothing good, for that it was Mr Kinzie I heard sing it first, before the Banishment. It was an old tune called 'Hail, Columbia, happy land!' You may be too young to be knowing it, Mr Ship. But that was a song we liked in those days. *[She sings]* 'Hail, Columbia, happy land! Hail ye heroes, heav'n borne band.'

---

9 Professor Winship notes that in Juliette Magill Kinzie's *Wau Bun: The 'Early Day' in the North West* (1856) the author claimed that the band played the 'Dead March'. As Mrs Van Voorhis says, it is inconceivable that Captain Heald would have ordered this to be played at a time when his primary concern would have been to raise morale.

That's how we left the Fort for the last time, with the band playing and the sun shining and thirteen nippers in the back of the wagon. Cicely and me, we'd taught them a game to play, in case of trouble. When I raised my hand and said 'Hide' they were to bury themselves like moles beneath the blankets, and not move nor make a sound, not until I told them they could. We were the last to leave the Fort.

Out into the open we pitched and rolled, like a boat on the Lake in a storm, the track was that rutted and rough. There was a gap in the canvas, a torn piece where it was tied at the seam, near where I was seated. Through the tear I could see where we were going. We followed the riverbank until it reached its mouth and then turned onto the path around the southern shore of the Lake. The track in the sand was even slower, and as bumpy. We were crossing between the water's edge and a line of sandhills on the other side.

[Long pause]

I'm sorry, Mr Ship, but I don't think I can say no more. I'm seeing it too clear, like it happened yesterday and nothing else has ever happened since. It's like the taste is in my mouth still, and the stench in the air too, and the blood sticky on my hands again. I've already said more than ...

[Long pause]

I'll try, then. Yes, I'll try.

As we were passing by the beach, I noticed the Indians with us begin to ride wide, away from the water's edge and near to the line of sandhills. One by one they disappeared. That was the first strangeness. But I kept mum. Cicely, she couldn't see out of the wagon but I knew she was watching me for news. She was also singing for the children, and playing with them and somehow she kept the babe Juba suckling at her breast. I never saw a woman more capable than she. I pretended to her I'd seen nothing, but she must've seen a sign in my eyes. Not fear there yet, I reckon, but suspectfulness. Suspectfulness that something wasn't right. I tried to smile, like I was easeful, but I don't think she was cheated by that.

We were nearly level with our cottonwood tree when I saw the Miamis come to a halt, and I knew you were there, Isaac, though I could not make you out. The leader removed his hat and waved it, round and round his head. We were surrounded: that was the story.

The enemy Indians rose mysterious above the sandhills, like a long line of turtle heads. There was a single, deceptful moment of quiet. Nobody seemed to be moving at all. It was like looking into a dream through that small tear in the canvas. Perhaps if I drew back, the dream would fade and the turtle heads vanish and the moment of danger would pass and be no more.

But it happened otherways. The silence ended as sudden as it started. I never knew what came first. A horn blew, there was a *rat-a-tat-tat* of musket fire, the turtle heads were grown big and become Indian braves on horseback, faces painted red and black, their heads shaven with a scalp-lock hanging at the back. They were beating one hand in front of their mouths as they rode, to make their ghost noises. And they were befeathered and waving guns and tomahawks. There was a *thud thud thud* of drumming or maybe it was the hooves of the horses or probably it was both. They galloped faster and faster, the closer they came. Where the air before had been still and empty, it was flashing with steel and blurry with smoke and kicking up fountains of sand. I raised my hand and, instead of shouting 'Hide' I shouted 'Snag.'

Those dear little souls understood well enough what I meant and they buried themselves beneath the blankets, and how I wish they'd been allowed to stay buried like that forever, out of sight, playing the game over and over amen, playing the game over and over without end.

But there was no God. They weren't allowed. No, they weren't allowed to go in peace.

[Pause, as Mrs Van Voorhis wipes tears from her eyes]

I didn't see you again, Isaac, not till the fighting was over and the bodies lay twisted like drunks beneath our tree, and I knew you only by your blue silk coatee, the one you wore when we pledged our troth, when it was as fresh and new as our love. It was the only proof I had that it was you. For they had crushed your face, and stolen your hat and taken a slice off your scalp, and over you, my darling, over your ruined head flew flies, a thousand flies in a hissing swarm.

[Long pause]

One of those devil-painted brutes came to our wagon. He leapt up and hacked the first child to death before he'd even finished pulling away the blanket, with one blow across the throat. The little children were paralyzed with terror. Some of them cried out, but most were whimpering or silent, huddled together. And all the time that savage whooped and yelled. After the first child fell, he swung his bloody tomahawk at another woman with us whose name was like to Mrs Corling or Corbin. She was using her fists to try to stop him but he slit her neck and must have struck an artery, for a fountain of blood splashed over those doomed children.

Yes, they were all doomed, all doomed but one. Or maybe I should say two, for the secret I was carrying in my own belly.

Cicely pleaded with the savage to spare baby Juba. But there was not a drop of mercy in his heart. And there should be no forgiveness for him neither, not even from God himself if He existed which, after this, He never could. The Indian tore Juba from Cicely's breast and smashed the little one's head on the timber planking. Cicely's lips were moving when he swung the blade high to drive into her throat. Her lips were moving with a prayer, and she was looking at me, her eyes not full of terror as mine were, but with a strange and wondrous light, and I thought I knew what it was. The love she'd preserved for herself and her babe, she was now passing on to me, because she had no further use for it. Yes, that was how she looked at me, all the kindness and love she'd saved up in her life, she was handing it to me. And what wretched use of it I've made. Cicely should have lived instead of me. Cicely and her child should have lived instead of me and mine.

Yes, you understood correct. I birthed a son, that I did.

Why did he spare us, while sparing no one else? You have still not understood, Mr Ship?

[Long pause. Mrs Van Voorhis, for the first time since this interview began, will not look at me. And when she does speak, she chokes on the first few words, though their meaning is unmistakable.]

Because he knew me, Mr Ship, the same as I knew him. That's why. He recognized me. Stained by the blood of the children he'd slain and the broken necks of Cicely and Mrs Corbin, Wabaunsee knew me for his kin.

I was more angry than afraid. I did not care what happened now. I threw myself at him, clawing at him, scratching him with my nails. I told him to kill me too. I ripped the cloth at my throat to bare my neck. Cut it, I demanded. But that was when his eyes lost something of their shine. He lowered his knife, pushed me back and smacked me down with his bare hands.

How I wish he had taken my life.

[Long pause]

He took me with him, didn't he Mr Ship? He took me with him to the camp. No, probably it wasn't like an Indian camp today, though I never seen one since. It was a big place, full of horses and children. There were four of us, I reckon, that they was keeping captive there. It's a blur, the memory of it. I was in a big tent, warm enough at night and cool during the day. I was fed better than I'd eaten in Fort Dearborn. There was a lot of corn and fresh meat. The Potawatomies were still wealthy then. Still proud and strong.

Yes, he protected me. I was sick with the babe and he brought the old squaws to nurse me. And he allowed no man near my bed. I can't say otherwise, that he did this, that he kept me safe. It was his guilt for the horror he'd done, I reckon, that saved me. Soon as I was strong enough for the journey, he took me to St Charles.

Yes, I saw him once again. The day the Indians left Chicago. No, we didn't speak. But I showed him he would never get no forgiveness from me.

There. It is said now. For the first time, it has been said.

[Long pause. Mrs Van Voorhis removes from her neck an antique necklace, strung with fine copper leaves, and hands it to me. She tells me she would like me to have it. She does not need it any more, because she no longer needs protection from anyone or anything. It once belonged, she said, to her grandfather. Only later would I discover, when Mrs Van Voorhis bequeathed Pointe de Sable's journals to me at her death, the necklace's remarkable provenance.]

I tell you this, Mr Ship. A long time ago, Miss Chappell wanted me to tell her all that happened. She said to speak about it would make me feel better. Sharing what hurts you with someone else is a remedy. That's how she talked, and she said she did the same herself too, with a cousin of hers. I didn't heed Miss Chappell because I knew she'd be reading from the Bible next, and I would have none of that. Probably something about mercy. She said without mercy we are lost. Utterly lost. Mercy and compassion, she'd say, that's what we need, *heh heh*. But just because Wabaunsee was kind to me once, that don't mean he earned my mercy. Nor compassion neither. Not to my mind. Not after the evil he'd done. I was saved by his guilt, that's all. He wanted to put me on the other side of the scales. But it don't work like that.

No, I never told Gray Curls what he did, for the hurt it would have done him. I never told no one. But I often wish I had told Miss Chappell, just for to see the answer she would be giving then, about her mercy and compassion.

I'm grateful that you made me tell you, Mr Ship. I feel the better for it. It is like a great weight has been lifted by the talking. Perhaps if I'd done this when Miss Chappell asked, it would have made all the difference. We shall never know, shall we Mr Ship? That's how life is. We never know what we'd best have done till it's too late.

1880

A Female Reporter

In the deserted lobby, you stand near enough to the window to keep an eye on the gaslit gloom of Madison Street, and silently curse Tom for being late. If you were to make a list of the ways in which you find him irritating, having no sense of time would be near the top, alongside his impracticality. Give him the simplest job, like painting a room or fixing a broken door hinge, and he will not only find a way to complicate it, he'll make a mess of it. Oh Tom, why tonight, of all nights?

You want to be there to applaud Mr George the moment he appears. You've been looking forward to this ever since the evening was first announced. And one thing is certain. Tom would have made damned sure he wasn't late if the speaker were one of his heroes: Henry James, for example, or William Dean Howells.

And then, suddenly, you spot him, loping tall and ungainly along the sidewalk through the wind and rain in that odd way of his when he's in a hurry, as though legs and arms are working simultaneously to paddle him along. He must have forgotten his umbrella, or lost it again. When he comes near, and sees you through the window, he frowns apologetically and mouths something, no doubt an excuse. His hat and tie are askew. He tries to push the door open instead of pulling it. In he comes, removing and shaking out his coat, throwing his arms around you in an embrace as he leans down to plant a kiss on your cheek. His beard is moist. He scatters you with raindrops. 'Terribly sorry, Antje,' he says. 'Getting the last few customers out was a nightmare.'

Probably because he was engaged in a fascinating literary conversation and quite forgot about his engagement at McVicker's. You want to be angry, but your irritation is already fading, as it always does. 'Come on,' you say, taking his arm and leading the way. The man at the door checks the tickets and you are soon making your way into the ornate, stuffy theatre hall. You glance around the auditorium and up at the grand circle. It looks sold out. And that makes you feel inordinately proud for Mr George, that he has filled all these seats on such a cold, wet Monday night.

You've hardly had time to get your notebook out before he's announced to a round of sustained applause. The stocky gentleman who crosses the stage towards the lectern looks at ease, acknowledging the warm reception with a modest smile and a raised hand. He bows three times, first to the sides of the hall, and then to the centre. You clap in what you realise, deep down, is a mood of wondrous astonishment. It shouldn't be a surprise, and yet it is, that he looks identical to the man in the photographs. You have to pinch yourself. Henry George is here in the flesh, on stage in Chicago, and you — Antje Hunter — are here to see him. You share a smirk with Tom before making some notes. You have always been a compulsive note-taker, whether or not it's for work. *Dark suit — smart but ordinary; white shirt and black tie, thick wavy brown hair combed over the ears, a distinctive mustache and goatee, prominent forehead with significant balding; bright, cheerful eyes with a steady gaze; confident, engaging smile.* If he could read what you've written, Tom would say it's too bland and doesn't capture anything of his inner essence. But you try to avoid speculation, and Tom's never learned shorthand.

It was an article he wrote in *Overland Monthly* about the expansion of the railroads that first alerted you to the work of Henry George. That must have been over ten years ago, shortly after 'Annie Borne' was given the opportunity to write an occasional column on food or fashion at the *Tribune*. In that article, Mr George argued that the railroads, for all the material benefits they promised, would profit only a privileged few while increasing the poverty of the many. He wrote about the concentration of wealth and resources in the hands of an elite, the problems created by a growing population and the need in the future — more than ever before — for 'public spirit, public virtue'.

His message was lucid and uncompromising. It felt as though he had shone a light on your own confusion about the mixed blessings of the railroads and the ways in which the rush for growth was being pursued in Chicago. And it was, you realised, exactly the kind of serious reporting to which you had always aspired. Now George has written a masterpiece, a book entitled *Progress and Poverty*, which can hardly be described as journalism at all. It reads more like a philosophical tract and, however much Tom may frown and call it 'indigestible', you've found it as gripping and imaginative as anything you have ever read.

Mr George really is here, in front of you. You glance across at Tom and it is disappointing to see that he is struggling to stay awake. How can he appreciate Mr George if he doesn't concentrate? You give him a gentle nudge and smile as he blinks, sits up straight, and pushes his spectacles up his forehead. You make more notes. *Speaks with naturalness and fluency. Only looks down when reading an extract from the book itself. His voice commands the hall, his sentences ebb and flow.*

When he begins to outline his proposals for the common ownership of property and the institution of a single tax on land, you feel again the primal surge of excitement you felt when you first read those words in the book — words that his political opponents have so unfairly maligned and misrepresented. You look across at Tom. With your eyes, you give him what you used to call, as a child, a 'speaking look': this one means, remember this part? He nods and stifles a yawn.

'All of us here tonight,' says Mr George, 'are immigrants, or we are the children of immigrants, or we are the grandchildren of immigrants. Our ancestors had no rights to the land on which they settled. So who owned it, before we immigrants took over? The answer, ladies and gentlemen, is that nobody owned it.' In shorthand, you write this down verbatim. 'But what of those indigenous Indian tribes,' he continues, 'that lived on the land. Did they not own it before we came?' He looks around the auditorium. 'No, ladies and gentlemen, the Indians never owned the land. They lived on the land, they used the land, but they never owned the land. And why did they never own the land? Because such a concept, the idea that a man could actually *own* land, that land could be bought and sold, that it could be traded like beads and whiskey, made no sense to them.' He pauses. *'And they were right.'*

The silence inside the auditorium is profound.

You lean across to Tom and whisper in his ear: 'The Old Magic Man, remember?'

Mr George's voice assumes a heightened cadence and rhythm as his argument builds. The thrill of hearing him lay down point after point with such clarity and passion fills you with joy. This, you think, is how you change the world, by confronting the real and the uncomfortable challenges faced by society. Land is a finite resource, he points out. As the population grows, and as material progress is made, the pressure on it inevitably increases. When land becomes a scarcer resource, its value goes up. And if we allow by law that such land is 'owned', the owner makes a profit for doing absolutely nothing.

Mr George raises both hands, as though appealing to common sense. 'Land,' he declares, 'was made by nature. It was not made by landlords.'

There is a round of applause.

'*The Great Spirit gave the land to all his children*,' you whisper to Tom.

As the applause dies down, someone shouts: 'Dirty socialist scum.' You look up. It seems to have come from the grand circle. And then, from the other side, as if taking a cue from the first disruption, another man yells: 'Anarchist.'

Mr George tries to continue. He raises his voice. He is neither a socialist nor an anarchist, he insists. But that is as far as he gets. Fights have broken out up there. This disturbance, it's clear to you, must have been organised beforehand. There are two small mobs, each about half-a-dozen strong. On each side, they have advanced down the aisles to the rails in the front row of the circle, from where they chant insults and swear, shaking their fists at the stage. 'Anarchist! Socialist! Scum!'

Pandemonium ensues, with everyone rising to their feet. Some policemen are coming through now. Tom is tugging your arm. But that is when you see, when you very clearly see, a man up there wearing a dark overcoat with his hat pulled down low, draw back his arm and hurl something towards the stage. There is a sound of smashing glass and, shortly afterwards, Mr George brings a handkerchief to his nose. With regret, you hear him say above the clamour, he will have to stop there.

People in the front few rows are coughing and holding their noses. Tom is leading you out, when the stench reaches you too. It is awful, like rotten eggs.

The next morning you wake up late, roused by the sound of Tom in the kitchen and the smell of coffee. The newspaper is propped up by your place, open at the front page. The front page? Your hand trembles as you pick it up and you can feel Tom turning to watch. Your eyes, for a moment, cannot focus. But there they are, your words in black and white. *Henry George's lecture at McVicker's Theater disrupted by a mob.* You begin to read, but stop and look back at the headline again. There is something not quite right. Then you realise it is not the headline that troubles you, it's the name of the correspondent. The article has not been written by 'Annie Borne'. The author, it says, is *Antje Hunter.* You gaze at the unfamiliar contours of its typescript form, remembering how you had toyed with using it, just to shock people, in that very first letter you ever wrote to the *Tribune.* At the last moment, you lost your nerve and merely signed it: *An Excluded Female of Voting Age.* So this, you marvel, this is how my name looks in print.

'Do you think it might have been a copy editor's mistake?'

Tom shrugs. 'I don't think the *Tribune* would allow a mistake like that in its leading article on the front page, would they?'

They have given you two full columns.

He places a cup of coffee next to you and stays by your side, one hand on your shoulder, while you read it through.

'They didn't change a word.'

He squeezes your shoulder. 'You've always deserved this.' The pride in his voice is unmistakable, and that touches you.

'If it wasn't for you ...'

'No, no. It was only a matter of time.'

You thank him, but you know in your heart that this is Tom Hunter talking, a dear kind loving man who has no idea how the world really works, let alone newspapers.

'The irony is that it would never have happened without those thugs.' The fact that you made the front page because of the premeditated disruption of a lecture by a great man, whose work has been an enormous influence on you, takes the edge off your excitement. 'Did you see how dignified he looked, even at the end?'

'Probably not the first time something like that's happened to him. At least nobody got seriously hurt.'

'Yes. At least there's that.'

He strokes your back. 'It was excellently composed. You were clear and succinct about the single tax.'

He finishes his coffee and urges you not to forget yours. 'I shall book a table tonight at The Lakeview, and would be grateful if the *Tribune* correspondent Antje Hunter might grace me with her company.'

'You mean, before on the stroke of midnight she has to turn into Annie Borne again, and write about ketchup and skirts?'

'I have no doubt that thousands of women are waiting anxiously for Annie to tell them what to wear, and how to make the best ketchup in Chicago.'

You reach up to run your fingers through his hair.

He hugs you, before throwing on his overcoat.

'Don't forget your umbrella. It looks as though it's going to rain again.'

He plucks it out of the basket by the front door. Pausing, he arches his neck and pushes up his spectacles. You recognise the gesture. He has had an idea. 'You know what Henry George should do,' he says, 'if he wants to convince people about his scheme? Write a story about how life improves for the ordinary person, when he begins living in a world of commonly owned property and a single tax. That way we could see how much better it might be. If the story's good enough, I'll try to have it considered for *The Dial*.' *The Dial* is a literary magazine for which he has started to work. 'I hear they're after stories with a political angle.'

'The next time I happen to bump into Mr George, I'll make sure I mention it.'

You exchange a smile before the door closes.

That's Tom all over, you think, but you love him for it. He wants to reduce everything to make-believe, turn it into a story, as if that's the only way the world can be understood.

In the empty apartment, you feel lost. You ought to go to the Public Library and look up some alternative recipes for ketchup with which to pad out the article. But the very dullness of the task makes you feel exhausted. It is hateful, writing just for the sake of writing. Maybe it's time to give up being the Annie Borne of food and fashion. Having the chance to spread the word to *Tribune* readers about Mr George's ideas, instead of writing about some silly recipe or new fashion, was exhilarating. But today, Mr Crewe is bound to be back at his desk.

It was Tom who pushed you to go home via the *Tribune* office, on the off chance that nobody had covered the meeting. When it turned out that Mr Crewe was supposed to have been there but had not yet been sighted, the night editor gave his grudging, conditional approval: 'We're a tad short of news tonight, so I guess you can have a shot at it. No promises, though.' Mr Crewe is one of those long-serving correspondents who has gotten lazy and behaves as though he owns the place. The joke in the office is that whenever he has to mention a lady in one of his articles, instead of bothering with a description, he uses the same stock expression: 'Mrs X was elegantly attired, as if on her way to tea at the Palmer House Hotel.' The count, they say, is currently nearing twenty.

You walk from room to room, pause over Tom's desk and touch his chair, imagining it filled by his long stooping back as he puzzles with his pencil over yet another manuscript. One day, he'll stop filling the bookshelves at McClurg's and write his own stories, or become an editor, or maybe both. You sit down in his chair, rest your elbows on the armrests and breathe in the scent of stale pipe smoke that rises from the cracked leather when you subside into it. You don't know what you would do without him. If you'd had children, maybe you wouldn't feel so protective of him. Maybe that's partly what this is about. But children or no children, that does not change the fact that his unworldliness can feel terribly fragile. That, you have no doubt, is exactly what attracted you to him in the first place.

You return to the kitchen and read the article again. It's good, you're sure it's good, as good as anything else on the front page. And why will they never again let you write about things that matter? Because you're a woman. It is that simple, and it infuriates you. Only Margaret Fuller ever managed to break the mould, but that was years ago with the *New York Tribune* and, sadly, she's long since gone. You seem to recall, strangely, that prior to the job at the *New York Tribune* she was the editor — in fact the first editor — of *The Dial*. That's an idea. Imagine Tom's face if you tell him you've decided to write a story on behalf of Mr George for *The Dial*. If fiction worked as a stepping-stone for Margaret Fuller, maybe it could work for you too.

There is a knock on the front door. A *Tribune* messenger boy is standing outside. You take the note and tear it open and your heart sinks. Mr Medill wants to see you.

Walking through the *Tribune* premises is always an ordeal. The women's small office is located on its own, away from the main newsroom. But that is not, today, where you go. You approach the stairs, looking straight ahead as you walk past the open door of the typesetting room, and take the steps carefully. You don't want to trip. Tripping is exactly the kind of thing Tom would do, if he were as nervous as you are. At the top of the stairs, you take a deep breath before pushing open the double doors.

You are struck by the usual mid-morning mayhem. The air is muggy with male sweat and tobacco smoke; the rows of desks look like listing wrecks, submerged beneath piles of papers, old files, books, notepads, ashtrays and coffee cups. Some reporters are seated at them, others are on the move, standing in earnest little groups, arguing and gesticulating, waving sheafs of paper, shouting to each other across the room. The airlessness makes you feel faint, as you begin to navigate your way forward. It always surprises you that newspaper men should need to make such a commotion simply to produce words on paper. Oddly, while you are traversing the newsroom, you experience a moment of epiphany as you reflect on the discrepancy between the chaos and noise of production, and the crafted perfection and silence of the final product.

As far as possible, you avoid meeting anyone's eyes. It's impossible not to overhear scraps of conversation. Sportswriter James Wendell is forecasting a win at the weekend for the White Stockings, columnist Frank Norten is boasting about an interview in which he 'put Mayor Harrison in his place on the Irish and anarchist problems. That should make the boss happy.' Hubert Moss, who writes about farming issues is pleading, as usual, to be given more space for his 'Life on the Prairies' section. Joey Sholder is being slapped down by tubby news editor Magnus French: 'You gotta have your facts straight, Joey. Otherwise there ain't no point in calling this a newspaper, now is there?' You glance across when he begins the Mr Gradgrind act which he does at least once a week. A short man with a yellowy smoke-stained beard, he rocks back on his heels and tugs at his waistcoat, as he adopts an exaggerated English accent. 'Now what I want, Mr Sholder, is Facts. Facts alone are wanted at *The Tribune*.' Mr French is a first-class bore and you have never liked Dickens. They go well together. There are some grins, some yawns and a call to 'Keep it down, Frenchie, can't you?'

They all look at you when you come in. They always do. You can feel their eyes follow you, as they always do. You are nearly there, at the far end of the room, and have had nothing more than a few nods of acknowledgement, and even a couple of compliments ('good piece, Mrs Hunter') when you hear the sandpaper drawl of Mr Grayson Crewe. He's leaning back in his chair, spinning a pencil with his fingertips. His eyes are red and sharp. 'Hey, look who's paying a visit, fellas. If that ain't our very own sweet apple dumpling Annie Borne ... no, no, no ... wait on ... Maybe I need a pair of spectacles. Because I'm not sure that's Annie, after all ...' He ruffles through a copy of the newspaper, pulling out pages, playing the fool until he's holding up the front page to show everyone. 'Blow me, if that ain't the oddest sounding name ... Ant. Jee. Hun. Ter.' He reads your name aloud again, mispronouncing it, making it sound unintelligible and silly. 'I prefer sweet ole Annie Borne. Wouldn't want her getting any ideas above her station and trying to migrate to other columns, now would we, fellas?'

You come to a halt and turn to face Mr Crewe. You let him finish before, with a smile, you say: 'Oh, don't worry, Mr Crewe, I wouldn't pass muster for your column.' You pause. He grins, flicking the pencil against his puffy cheeks. 'After all, I'm never *elegantly attired, as if on my way to the Palmer House Hotel for tea.*'

The newsroom breaks out into laughter. That gives you a much-needed boost of confidence as you reach the door, turn into the corridor and walk towards the office at the end where you have an appointment with the *Chicago Daily Tribune*'s owner and editor-in-chief.

Mr Medill is polite. He offers you a chair and calls for coffee to be brought. He asks for a minute, while he finishes what he is doing. 'I will then give you my full attention, Mrs Hunter.'

You settle on the edge of the chair, ankles crossed, hands in your lap, holding your pencil and notebook in what you hope is a relaxed but efficient-looking manner. You have dressed carefully, in what Tom calls your 'official outfit' — a long auburn skirt with a short velvet Eton jacket and a sensible felt hat with a bright blue bow at the side. It is smart without being ostentatious, serious but not dull. You try to act as if at ease, though you fear your nervousness will be written in the tightness of your expression, your tense posture. You glance across as he concentrates on the document in front of him. It seems that he can write as he thinks, quickly and efficiently. He crosses nothing out. Barely looking up, he dips his pen in the inkwell and continues. His grey hair, close cut, looks almost silver. His pen is gold-plated. His face is lean, well-proportioned, with a fine brow and firm mouth. He gives off an aura of decisiveness and intelligence. This is what power looks like, you think. And then you tell yourself to calm down and keep things in perspective.

You think back to the strangeness of how you have come to be seated here today in front of Mr Joseph Medill, the run of circumstances that began such a long time ago with that letter from *An Excluded Female of Voting Age*. You were twenty-seven years old. You can still remember the arguments you used in that missive, full of youthful fire and courage. That, doubtless, was why it caught Mr Medill's attention. Why should we halt the fight for universal women's suffrage, you wrote, until the battle for Negro male suffrage has been won? It wasn't that you did not agree wholeheartedly with both causes, but you failed to understand why one should be advanced at the expense of the other. You were fully behind those admirable campaigners Susan B. Anthony and Elizabeth Cady Stanton. *Women's suffrage is a right before God*, you wrote. *It should also be a right in the constitution of the United States.*

A few days later, there was a request on the Letters page from the editor that *An Excluded Female of Voting Age* should identify herself to the newspaper if she wanted to discover something to her advantage. Mr Medill, in those days, did not edit the paper. But he owned it, and when the editor of the day told you he would give you a chance with food and fashion, you were left in no doubt that this was done on the owner's instructions. Since Mr Medill's return to edit the paper, you have never seen him on his own.

He looks up, and apologises for having kept you waiting. He puts his elbows on the desk and frowns. He says he has asked you here to talk about your article. 'I think Mr George's ideas,' he says, 'are unworkable. I also think they lack rigour and vision. In the industrial age, land will become less important. Take the meatpacking industry in our city. How much land is used by Packingtown? One square mile? One square mile that produces an income ...'

At first, you are too much on edge to absorb what he is saying. You cannot challenge him or argue back. But the longer he speaks, the more you forget where you are and why you are here. There might be fragments of truth in what Mr Medill says, but the fallacies in his argument are glaring. When an opportunity occurs, you point out where you believe him to be misinformed. Packingtown, for instance, depends on a vast hinterland for the raising of the livestock, it depends on the railroads, it depends on the exploitation of an oversupply of labour. It is disingenuous, therefore, to claim that it uses only one square mile of land. And look at the way in which the stockyards pollute the Chicago River and take no responsibility for it, although the river is a common resource that should be the property of all. The Chicago River continues to contaminate the Lake, the dirty water has yet again caused an outbreak of cholera ...

You speak passionately, and at length, and — you come to realise — without interruption from Mr Medill. When you have finished, silence falls. He is leaning back in his chair, watching you. You cannot read his expression. But you know you have said too much, that you have likely roused his temper, that he is precisely one of those landowners who has made substantial profits from property speculation of the kind that Mr George's scheme would seek to abolish. You notice him rub his hands together. An expression of self-control or one of anger? When he throws one of his tantrums, he can be heard at the far end of the newsroom. You cringe at the thought of having to return through there, with the men sniggering behind your back. Oh how impulsive you can be, Antje Hunter. Was it not the hated Miss Trumbull who always snapped at you, for speaking before thinking? Maybe, for once, she was right. Because you have, haven't you, just argued against every position Mr Medill set out?

A wave of revolt runs through you. To hell with Miss Trumbull and her kind. Let Mr Medill fly off the handle if he wants. Let him speak sharply, let him lose his temper, let him insult you. There's no need to cower before him and agree to everything he says because — without even consulting Tom or thinking it through — you have made an irrevocable decision. You will do no more work for the *Tribune*. Annie Borne will speak no more. The citizens of Chicago can survive very well without Annie's advice about dressing for dinner or making ketchup. You will not write another line about food or fashion. Instead, you will find a way to write a book about something that really matters. You will find again the voice and courage of that young person who signed off as *An Excluded Woman of Voting Age*.

Mr Medill has begun to talk. He is not shouting. He does not even look angry. He seems to be saying he thought your article about Mr George was interesting, that the description of events was precise and the arguments regarding the content of his lecture were evenly balanced. 'I do not agree with Mr George,' he says. 'But I am always prepared to listen to an argument with which I do not agree, as long as it is cogently and fairly presented.'

You find it hard, again, to concentrate. This time, it's difficult because what he is saying is unexpected. You don't, at first, understand the gist of his speech for what it is.

'It has happened once before,' he says, 'though never on a Chicago newspaper. But I see no reason why the *Chicago Daily Tribune* should not have a female reporter,' he says. 'Do you?'

'No, sir.'

'Good.' He begins to make a list of topics that, he says, need examination — corrupt politicians, the anarchist movement, the city's sanitation problems, the failings in the construction industry.

The list goes on. You are taking notes. 'And I have no objection,' he says, 'if you would like to continue to explore the issues of Henry George's single tax and women's suffrage.'

You add those to the list.

'Yes sir.' You hear the tremble in your voice as the enormity of what Mr Medill is saying begins to sink in. You close your notebook. You thank him for the opportunity.

'The night editor says he used your real name as a temporary measure because he did not want to be responsible for making one up. And "Annie Borne" would hardly have been, in the circumstances ...' He smiles '... appropriate.'

'I would like to retain my own name,' you say. If a man can use his own name in a newspaper, why should a woman not do the same?

Mr Medill gives another thin, but not unkind, smile. 'I suspected you might. Very well, Mrs Hunter.'

You close the door behind you, and stand in the corridor. Your heart is beating so fast it makes you feel short of breath. After a silent prayer to the spirit of Margaret Fuller, to thank her for leading the way, you walk back towards the newsroom. This time, you do not care how they look at you or what they say. You're going straight to the bookstore to tell Tom.

Notes for a Photographic Exhibition

by S. Alfsson

AUTOBIOGRAPHICAL SKETCH

When the Hutchinson Art Gallery asked me to prepare an autobiographical sketch for this catalog, I replied that although I had no objection to speaking about myself, I believe it is the photograph, and only the photograph, that should occupy the viewer's attention. We therefore agreed that I would offer information about myself only where this might aid the interpretation of the exhibits. I hope this approach will cause no offense.

I was thirteen years old when the Great Fire swept through our city on October 8, 1871, old enough to remember some of the magnificent buildings that we lost. After the calamity, I felt like a child who had begun life with the gift of sight and then, suddenly and without warning, been struck blind. My recall of certain buildings was excellent. But they existed only in my mind and, unlike a blind person, I could no longer walk around them, touch them or sense their brooding physical presence. I made some drawings from memory. But how I wished I had the level of proof to back up those drawings, proof that only a photograph can provide. It therefore became my mission to seek out as many photographic records as I could of the city before the Fire. They were hard to find. This, I believe, is a tragedy. How dearly I would have liked to possess images of those buildings I badgered my father to keep taking me back to, like Mr Potter Palmer's marble-fronted hotel on State Street or Mr Chesbrough's North Side Waterworks with its huge fly-wheel and giant pumps.

This exhibition displays photographs of a single building, the Home Insurance Building, taken over a period of more than one year. My choice of this subject matter was mostly a matter of luck. I had long admired the Leiter Building, a seven-story warehouse on Wells and Monroe. The walls looked as though they were comprised more of glass than of stone, and its innumerable panes mirrored the sky into which they soared until they seemed almost indivisible from the air itself. How full of light was the interior, and with what delicate simplicity did the exterior please the eye. Which artist had conceived of such a building? It was the work, I discovered, of Major William Le Baron Jenney.

So when I heard that Mr Jenney had won a contract to build the Chicago headquarters for the New York Home Insurance Company, I was eager to see what he would do. I happened to make my first visit to the site in the spring of 1884, on a day when the bricklayers were on strike. I took advantage of the relative quiet to snoop around, and that was how I was discovered by Mr Jenney himself.

He engaged me in conversation before I had realized who he was, expressing surprise at seeing someone on site in such attire, and even more surprise when I told him I was a photographer. We discussed his frustration with the delays to the project caused by the strike. Nothing could be done until the bricklayers came back to work and finished the foundations. This was when the idea came to me that it might be fascinating to document the construction of Mr Jenney's new building, from this very early stage to its completion, whenever that might be. I seized my chance and asked his permission. My proposal was so speculative I was not even certain Mr Ayres would lend me his portable darkroom to set up on site, nor that I would find a patron like Mr Hutchinson, defender of photography as an art form, to fund my experiment. I am grateful to Mr Jenney for granting his permission at once. Neither he nor I had any idea that this particular building would be different from anything else that has ever been built.

PLATE I

THE FAT OF THE LAND

This print was taken shortly before the end of the bricklayers' strike to which I refer in my autobiographical sketch. I chose to position my lens at such a low angle to emphasize the immensity of the flattened site and of the sky itself (which the viewer will notice occupies approximately two thirds of the plate) while minimizing the two figures in the foreground. The scale renders the men insignificant, incidental to the scene in which they have been placed, more trespassers than participants. The title of the photograph is intended to be ironic. The land on which Chicago has been built is notorious for containing a subsoil of mud, sand and clay that is favorable for neither the cultivation of the land nor the erection of the multi-storied buildings that now dominate the downtown area. To establish foundations strong enough to hold firm on such an unstable base is the greatest of engineering challenges. The two men in the picture are the architect, Mr William Jenney, and his main contractor, Mr Gus Swanson. Mr Jenney is the shorter man on the left, seen here making an upward gesture with his arm, hence the blur on the plate, while Mr Swanson is the taller, leaner figure with his hat cocked backwards. He appears to be looking up at a specific point in the sky. Notice how, at this distance, his elongated form unconsciously imitates the iron columns he will one day install. Forgive my reading more into this than was known or intended at the time. But art often seems to work on a bigger canvas than we can visualize at the moment of its conception. In the poses my two subjects have struck in this plate, I like to imagine that the roles they are destined to play are being foreshadowed. Mr Jenney, a fount of innovative ideas, is making an extraordinary proposition about the height of the building, while Mr Swanson is pointing to the engineering details. Perhaps he can already see, in what to an untrained eye is merely an emptiness of sky, the topmost point of the building's ninth floor.

PLATE VIII
METAL SKELETON

This captures a moment in the late afternoon shortly before the end of the bricklayers' strike. I had taken a photograph earlier, in brighter conditions, but the glass negative cracked while I was processing it in the darkroom. As it happens, I believe this was fortunate. It is the silver-gray quality of the later afternoon light that provides such an evocative background for the ironwork of the wheelchair and the human figure seated in it. When I arrived on site that afternoon I expected to see work underway at last. Instead, I found Mr Jenney in animated discussion with the man in the wheelchair. Mr Jenney was as charming as always, though I cannot say the same for his elderly visitor, a Mr Atkins. He was offhand in his greeting and questioned why I was still using wet plates instead of dry. I told him I considered the quality of reproduction in a wet plate superior, and more consistent, than in a dry plate. It was clear he judged one such as I to have no place on a building site. I fear I may have brooded overmuch on his behavior, and this most likely prompted the moment of inattention in the darkroom when I dropped the first negative. I requested his permission to take a second portrait, but Mr Atkins criticized my 'ineptitude' at having ruined the first one and declined to sit for me again. If I wanted to take a photograph, that was a matter between Mr Jenney and myself, but he would waste no more time sitting for one. I suspect it was because he was trying to spoil the photograph that he is pictured leaning forwards, pointing. But, as the viewer will observe, that stretching movement integrates his figure into the complex network of interconnecting lines already created by the spokes and frame of the wheelchair, creating an effect that fortuitously imitates the construction style for which the Home Insurance Building would become famous. Afterwards, Mr Jenney told me that Mr Atkins had given him a good idea as to how he might make himself less reliant on bricklayers. Whether this was the idea that lay behind the structural innovations introduced by Mr Jenney over the next few months, I cannot say, but there must be good grounds for thinking it was. As far as I know, Mr Jenney never claimed those innovations for himself. He once told me there was absolutely nothing new about them, and that if anyone deserved the credit it should be the inventor of the balloon-frame house. He was using, he said, the very same principles of skeleton construction in the Home Insurance Building as are employed by a stack of two-by-fours and a bag of nails. Who will ever know the truth? In view, though, of the way in which this plate happens to imitate the construction techniques for which the Home Insurance Building has become renowned, I have taken the liberty of naming it 'Metal Skeleton'.

PLATE XVII

STAIRWAY RESTING ON THE EARTH

After construction work resumed, some months passed and there was nothing to distinguish the Home Insurance Building from any other big building. The solid pier foundations, embedded at their roots in a grillage of criss-crossed steel smothered in portland cement, rose as far as the second floor. The piers were encased in concrete (see plates X and XI). In the middle of September, though, something strange began to happen. I had recently observed the delivery of a large quantity of iron, in many different sizes and lengths (see plate XV), but I had no idea as to their purpose. I should mention that by this stage the contractor, Mr Swanson, had become my chief informant about the progress of the building (as well as my guardian in the face of a boisterous workforce). He had taken a special interest in my project and did everything possible to assist me, even ordering work to be halted on some occasions so that dust levels would subside, and movements that might spoil a picture were minimized. But I had not had an opportunity to consult with Mr Swanson on this occasion, and was therefore as surprised and puzzled as my subjects in this plate when I saw what was happening on site. It was impossible, given the field of vision to which my lens is subject, to include in the photograph what everyone was looking at. I hope this only serves to enhance the sense of mystery in the plate. Everything in the composition is posed as a question. Who are these people and what, out of camera, are they looking at? Why have such a disparate group of citizens paused to look up at the same thing? What drives their curiosity? Fascinating questions with no answers. A few years ago, when in Europe, I traveled to Brussels and was fortunate enough to see a work by Pieter Brueghel the Elder, titled 'Landscape with the Fall of Icarus'. In this painting are three human figures — a shepherd, a fisherman and a plowman — all of whom ignore the flailing legs of poor Icarus as he plunges into the sea. They lack curiosity. I see this plate as a mirror opposite to Brueghel's painting. Here, we see not three figures but an auspicious twelve. They are urban, not rural dwellers. They demonstrate the very opposite of indifference. The invisible (rather than the visible) object of their curiosity is not falling from the sky, but rising into it. Finally, the main subject has not been ejected from the heavens, as was the fate of Icarus, but is climbing towards them. Icarus was foolhardy, and features in a pagan myth. I hope it will not be considered taking the concept of the mirror-image too far to have named this plate after an event recorded in the Book of Genesis, in which Jacob dreams of a stairway resting on the earth, with its top reaching to Heaven.

PLATE XXIII
AN INSPECTOR VISITS

The metal skeleton was almost at the fourth floor, when work was halted without warning. Influential voices had spoken out against the structure. It was unsafe, it was destined to collapse, it would be unable to support the weight of a multi-storied building. This kind of reaction is normal with innovations. The inventor must endure the skepticism of his contemporaries. I am told that when the first balloon frame house was built the naysayers claimed it would take off from the earth like a balloon — hence the moniker. And much doubt and consternation greeted Daguerre, when he unveiled an image on a sheet of silver-plated copper. The unnamed subject in this plate, such an anomaly on site in his Sunday-go-to-meeting clothes, has been sent by the Home Insurance Company to evaluate whether or not the structure is safe. Notice that his eyes are not on the building works but on his own waistcoat, as though he is concerned some motes of dust or other foreign bodies have landed there and created a tiresome stain. This evaluator lasted a single day on site before Mr Jenney succeeded in having him replaced by a more competent man called Mr Burnham, a former draftsman of his. Mr Burnham (see plate XXV) would declare himself satisfied that the design was sound. The other aspect of this plate worth noting is the view afforded of a half-covered iron pier. By this stage of the exhibition the viewer will not need to be reminded that Mr Jenney's design innovation centered on the use of iron piers, iron columns and iron girders in place of traditional brickwork and masonry. The upper floors would be launched into the sky not on masonry-bearing walls but on an iron frame. Here, we see one such iron pier half-bricked up. Better than words could do, this photograph illustrates the enormity of the design change that has taken place. Brick walls are not being used to support the upper floors of the Home Insurance Building. They merely act as fire cladding for the iron frame.

PLATES XXX TO XLI
A PORTRAIT CYCLE

Since the subject of the next twelve plates is one and the same, I shall write a single introduction for them all. When taking a portrait I believe a photographer should aim to draw out particular, defining characteristics of the subject. No single photograph or painting can capture the full complexity of a human being. I say this because, without wanting to engage in a debate about the merits of photography versus painting, it is undeniable that while the painter remains at liberty to avoid a 'warts and all' approach, the camera's attachment to instantaneous truth dictates that the photographer cannot. Included in plates XXX to XLI are twelve portraitures of Mr Gus Swanson. I suggest that when taken together these plates present a composite artistic rendering of their subject. I have always encouraged my clients to be photographed in a place and/or with possessions that are important to them. I was therefore delighted when Mr Swanson agreed to pose on the remarkable metal skeleton he was building to support the higher floors of the Home Insurance Building. I have learned that the closer the relationship between photographer and subject, the more natural and revealing a portrait is likely to be. By this stage, I think it fair to say that I knew Mr Swanson reasonably well. It was helpful that we shared a Swedish background although, unlike Mr Swanson, I was born in America. The viewer will realize that for portraits to be taken at these elevations it was essential for the photographer and her equipment to go up there too. This was challenging, and I would like to put on record my gratitude to Mr Swanson for providing assistance in this regard.

These plates were taken on different days between September 1884 and December 1884. As portraits, they require no introduction. But I would like to talk about the intent behind one of them, plate XXXIX, as a way of introducing the compositional process common to them all. Mr Swanson led the work on site by example, taking personal responsibility for the construction of each new level. In plate XXXIX he is bolting down the first girder for the floor of the ninth and top floor. I am on the eighth floor, the tripod balanced in a way that angles the camera upwards. Just as it is hard to take a photograph at a height of eighty, ninety or a hundred feet (it was, necessarily, a windless day) so too is it a challenge for anyone to pose at that height in the way Mr Swanson does here. I held my breath as he climbed the ladder. One wrong move and who knows how many floors he would have fallen? Then came the agonizing process of raising the girder with ropes and pulleys. When that great length of iron was eventually balanced between two columns, it then had to be secured. There are two opposing forces at work in the plate. On the one hand, the way in which Gus kneels and looks down into the camera eye, while apparently turning the bolt (I asked him to pretend, for those long seconds needed to take the photograph) makes the whole process look effortless and safe. He might as well be at ground level, sharing a joke with the camera. It is a simple act, the turn of a screw, that has been done millions of times before. At the same time, though, the camera captures the terrifying truth. Mr Swanson is suspended on nothing more than a fragile triangle of iron while engaged on a task that requires great strength, agility and expertise. He is an acrobat, and there is no safety net. It would be the easiest thing in the world to err ever so slightly and lose his balance. Maybe the bolt gets stuck, but then unexpectedly spins free. Maybe he doesn't know that something slippery is gummed to the sole of his right boot so that when he leans forward, there is no friction at work and he cannot prevent himself from falling. Anything at all could happen. The viewer, on seeing this dangerous juxtaposition, feels a nervous tingling down the spine. Humans are neither fish of the sea, nor fowl of the air. This image puts everything we take for granted out of kilter. No wonder, then, that I feel a seizure in the stomach as with trembling fingers I set the wet glass in its light-box. If he were to fall, it would be my fault. And for what? For a photograph. He never even wanted to be photographed in the first place. I had observed that as a boss he was not a demonstrative man. His laborers respected him because he wasn't always shouting at them, the way some do in this trade. But they also recognized he was a perfectionist, and that if their work failed to meet the high standards he set, they would be out of a job. Demanding but fair, is how I would summarize his reputation. That, though, was only one side of him. Gus was a more driven man, more passionate about what he was doing, than anyone else I had ever met. A gleam came into his eyes whenever he climbed up his giant metal skeleton. I realized, in that moment, I was lost to him. His concentration was so absolute, his mental and physical energies so focused on pushing the Home Insurance Building higher and higher, that everything else was banished from his mind. It was like watching a boy play with his favorite toy. Maybe, I thought like that because I had learned there was a playful side to him too. I suggest we can see this in plate XXXIX in the self-conscious grin he is trying to hold back. He feels embarrassed to be enjoying himself so much on the job. When I first suggested I might take his portrait, he demurred for a long time. He did not like being the center of attention, nor did he want to be involved in anything that might distract him from the task at hand. I implored him. And so, I am grateful to record, did Mr Jenney. Finally, Mr Swanson relented. But whenever I asked him if I could take a photograph, I had the feeling he was doing it more for me than for himself. I confess I could not resist. The camera does not lie, though it might not always tell the whole truth. In these portraits of Mr Swanson (did I call him Gus earlier?) I knew I had found an artist who was an exemplar of his time and place. He was a man of air who had the balance of an angel. His feet gripped those girders like claws, he stood as still as a bird on a wire, he exhibited no sign of fear. While I was quivering like a leaf, even though I had wide solid timbers beneath my feet, he remained perfectly still. When he climbed, long arms reaching upwards, one leg bent and the other straight, head aligned with his back, he was like an iron column himself, melding into the frame around him. I asked him once whether he had ever suffered from a fear of heights. He said that as a child he had been terrified by heights. But then something happened. 'Falling down from high,' he said, 'is scareful to think about, but when I do this thing there is no afraid in my heart.' He said he would tell me more about it one day, if I wanted to hear. I said I would like that very much. I regret to say that I am still waiting. If I don't hear anything soon, I shall have to remind him. And, oh, what a handsome subject for the camera he is too. Not in a pampered way, but weathered, with a prominent brow and a firm but generous mouth that suggests to me warmth and finer feelings. A man with skin that is the perfect shade for my lens, dark enough to make key features stand out, not so dark that there is a danger of becoming lost in shadow. He is forty-five years old. I know because I asked him.

I must be going mad. What am i doing? it was going fine until i started with Gus. Must rewrite from plates XXX to XLI. also remember to check I kept any refs to myself 'neutral'. don't want to lie, but don't want to tell the whole truth either. make sure there is no stray 'she' or 'her' in there. Wouldn't do, would it, for people to know a weakly woman had taken these plates, something perverted and Against Nature in the proposition. Unless I called myself Blenda, but only the Swedes would understand. Check I don't sound too familiar with Gus. always MR SWANSON.

1886

An American

I am always waking early, but this morning there is much noise at the door. Open up, open up, they cry. Two police in blue caps are outside. They say come with us to the station. Now. I must be bringing papers. No possibility for to change into other clothes.

In the station they take me into one small room with a table and chair. I ask why am I here. They lock the door and go away. I wait. When I think why am I here, what for, I catch only straws in my hand.

I don't know how many hours before they come back. Another man is come with them. This is the police captain. He brings a newspaper. He sits on the chair by the desk. He asks questions.

My name is Gus Swanson, I reply. In age I am forty-six years. My parents are died long time before. My sister is living in New York. Yes, I am a citizen of America. Here are the papers.

No, sir, I not saying I am born in America. I am saying I am a citizen of America. Yes, it is true I am born in Sweden. But I came to America when I was very young.

One of the two police behind my back pokes me with his stick. You are not American, says the captain with a bad smile. You are born in Sweden, yes? Then you are a foreigner. Understand? It is foreigners that bring trouble to America.

I don't answer nothing to that. The captain asks me, have I a wife? No, I am not married up to this time, sir, I reply. But I am married today.

The police behind my back hits me on the shoulder. Answer the question, Squarehead, he says. I hear him spit to the floor. The police captain still is smiling in the bad way. I say this is true. I am not married now, but I am married today at twelve o'clock.

My wife her name is Miss Sofia Alfsson. She is American. Yes, her name is foreign. No, it is not German. Also it is a Swedish name. But she was born in America, sir. She was born in Chicago.

The captain asks me what am I doing one week before? One week before, I say, this is also Saturday like today. It was May 1. The day of the march. I tell him I went in the Richelieu Hotel to watch the march go past on South Michigan.

Do you know that march, what it was for? asks the captain. Yes, sir, I know. They want to make an eight-hour working day. No, I did not go in the march myself, sir.

Miss Alfsson is a photographer. I am helping her with the photographs on May 1. I make for her a dark room. I cleaned the glass plates and put on them collodion and then they must go into silver nitrate for three minutes.

The captain says I am telling lies. No woman can be taking

photographs. I answer nothing. Now I understand what is happening. It does not matter what I say, they will not believe me.

The police behind hits me in the back. I am hurting but I pretend it is nothing. Why he does that to me, I ask the captain. Because you don't tell the truth, his reply. You don't tell us you have your own company. And this your company built the Richelieu Hotel.

This is true, I reply, that Swanson & Co. is my company. It was started by my uncle but he is retired. Also it is true I was having the contract with the Richelieu Hotel. This is why I proposed to Miss Alfsson, that we go there to make photographs of the march.

There are in your company Germans, yes, asks the captain?

We have workers coming from different countries, I reply. This is normal. Some of them are living for a long time in Chicago, some not so long. When the captain asks this question, I fear I know what he is thinking.

You miss the question, he says.

No, sir. I don't miss the question. We have some workers coming from Germany, the same we have workers from ...

He asks do I like Germans.

Yes, I am liking Germans, I say. They are good workers. But I like all my workers, even they are not German.

The captain makes a big sigh to show he does not believe me. Now he is asking where I am Tuesday last at night.

I reply I am at the house of Miss Alfsson's parents. They live on 10th Street. We are doing preparations for the wedding. Yes, sir, of course I know what happened in Haymarket Square on Tuesday night. A bomb was thrown. We listened the explosion.

The captain again he says: You were there, wasn't it? No, I was not there, I say. Already I tell you I was at the house of Miss Alfsson's parents on 10th Street. So it is not possible for me also to be on Haymarket Square.

The captain smacks the desk with his hand. Only you answer the question, understand? Then the captain says do I know a Swedish man was making dynamite? I say yes, I heard this. But I never saw dynamite, I say, not even once in my life. I don't know how it is looking or how it is made. I am a builder, captain. That is all. I don't know someone who is making dynamite. No, I never met a Swedish called Mr Nobel.

The captain says if I know how many policemen were died on Haymarket Square? From the newspaper, I answer, I read seven policemen were died. No, I don't know the number for injured. Sixty, sir? That is very bad, I agree. I ask the captain how many other people died.

He smacks the desk again. Only you answer the question, understand?

Yes, captain, I say. But policemen shot people in the crowd with their guns. Not only policemen died at Haymarket. He is not listening me. He is showing me headlines on the front page of the newspaper. You know these men. They are friends to you, yes? The names he is meaning are Spies and Parsons. They are friends to you, yes, the anarchists?

No, I say. I never see these men in my life.

You also are an anarchist, yes?

No, I say. I am no anarchist.

You are friends to the anarchists, yes?

No, I am not.

You are lying.

I am not lying.

Even though I know the police are behind me, I am not ready when they attack. One knocks over my chair and pulls my arms behind my back. I fall on the floor. The man spits to my face. Liar, he shouts. You know Spies. You know Parsons. You know Engel. You know Fischer. You are friends with Germans. You are an anarchist.

No, I say. I never see these men. I never talk them. I am not an anarchist.

If it is true I not know them, why does Swanson & Co. have an eight-hour working day? Explain that, they shout. Explain that, Squarehead. Explain, you fucking Squarehead.

I try to stay calm but inside my heart is breaking with sadness. These police are like the loggers in St Clair, all those years before. They are a tribe. Either you are in the tribe, or you are out.

One police has his hand on my throat and it is hard to speak. I tell them we have an eight-hour working day at Swanson & Co. for two years already. Happy workers work good. I know nothing about the strikes or Germans or anarchists or the Haymarket bomb.

Lying Squarehead, shouts one police. He punches me at the eye. I feel the pain like a dizziness. The other is spitting to me and kicking my stomach. The captain is watching. I taste blood. I am panting for breath. The captain plays with his pen. He says: You are a foreigner and a Swedish and we are watching you. We know you and your friends make the dynamite for Spies and Parsons. We will catch you and you will hang.

When the captain speaks like this, I have the feeling that sometimes happens when I am on top of a metal skeleton. I am strong and filled by power. From the time in St Clair, the danger of falling makes me feel free. I have no afraid in my heart. At the top of the skeleton, I take in charge my destiny. This is how I feel when I decide to listen no more to the captain's lies.

I tell him he is wrong to speak like that to me. I am American the same as him, the same it says in my papers, the same like everyone else that come to America to live here their lives.

The captain goes silent when I begin to speak. Maybe he is surprised. Maybe he feels my new power. He is not smiling. The other police want to grab me, but the captain says 'no'.

I tell him it is wrong to use Haymarket for the excuse to attack foreigners. I tell him it is wrong to start calling Americans like me a foreigner, because I am born in another country. Captain, I say, I don't like anarchists. They are dangerous. And I don't like the police when they behave like this. They also are dangerous. Tribes divide a country. So if you believe in the future of America, captain, you must stop making tribes.

The captain stares at me, and I stare back. I do not care what he does, and he is feeling this. This is the power that comes when you take in charge your destiny. I am free to go, he says.

On the street, I feel bruised but I am happy too. There is blood on my clothes. My eye is swelling where they punched me. I walk fast as I can to 10th Street because I am married today.

I am not easy in a frock coat. The boiled shirt is stiff at the collar. Sofia bought me new pantaloons. The parlor is very full and hot. The air runs sweet with perfume of the ladies and pipe smoke and warm *brannvin*. There are small plates of pickled herrings and dumplings.

Sofia is wearing black. This is the Swedish custom. A black blouse with a white collar and a black skirt. But she has no veil or bridal crown, and that is not the custom. She holds a bouquet of flowers. She smiles the same smile when she takes a photograph on the metal skeleton. It is encouraging of me.

I cannot believe I am married today. All these years, I have only my work. And then Sofia arrive like a Småland girl from long time ago. Strong and beautiful, with straight blonde hair. A woman taking photographs that not even a man dares to try. I am the most lucky man I know.

We eat lunch at the Boston Oyster House. This is favorite for Americans. The table is beautiful. A long white tablecloth. Bronze candlestick holders. Vases full with purple sage flowers. A gleaming silver plate at each place, with six holders for the oyster shells. There is one seat at the table end. Sofia says this the place I must sit.

We eat Rockaways, Blue Points and Shrewsburys. We eat them fried and broiled. We eat them with different sides, dressings and sauces, with celery, mushroom, butter, cream and parsley. I like best the cotuit. This is poached in sherry and butter sauce, and sprinkling on bread crumbs.

Down here we are closed off from the city outside and its troubles. Those troubles will pass. I am certain of this. I look around my new family with happiness in my heart. And when they call Speech Speech, I am ready and on my feet.

I begin: Friends, Chicagoans, Countrymen.

1893–1900

1893

The Smiling Ghost

Stephen was in front of the mirror, combing his moustache, unaware that Billy was about to jump. Taken by surprise, his comb flew out of his hands and he stumbled backwards against the chest of drawers. Betty's bottles of perfumes and Magnolia Balm and Bloom of Youth and Chinese Skin Powder and God knew what else, arranged on top, rattled ominously, but he was lucky. Nothing fell and broke. He landed awkwardly on his back, with a view of the ceiling. Betty had been nagging him about its state. The plasterboard sagged; the paint was yellowed and peeling. Billy laughed and began to ride his belly like a horse. Soon they were galloping into the Wild West, and he was beginning to sweat uncomfortably.

That was how Betty found them. She swept Billy up in her arms and, with a withering look, slammed the bedroom door behind her. For a moment, he stayed where he was, panting. He remembered how, when he was that age, he used to do exactly what Billy had done whenever his father returned home from the store.

He heaved himself to his feet. He was dreading the day ahead. He returned to the mirror and resumed his grooming. His cheeks were an unpleasant blotchy red. Must be from Billy's horse ride, he told himself. He had always taken trouble over his appearance, even in the darkest of times. Feeling smart was a way of maintaining equilibrium. Perhaps that was something he had inherited from his mother. Everyone inherited something from their parents, didn't they?

He oiled what was left of his hair before trying to brush it over the bald crown. Even with moisture, it was hard to keep down the curls. He then applied a darkening lotion to his moustache. It was a trick he had learned from John Graves Shedd, the sales genius at Marshall Field. The deeper colour made the growth look more substantial. He adjusted the shirt collar, straightened the tie and brushed down his brown wool coat. Both sack suits and check designs were out of fashion, but it was the best he had. He had put on weight, which made it tight at the waist. His Oxfords were also showing signs of age. They were polished well enough, but it was hard to tell they had once been tan-coloured. He set his watch in his pocket.

After checking, with his ear to the door, that Betty was still in the kitchen (there was the scrape of a pan), he knelt down and felt behind the wardrobe. After withdrawing the bottle, he pulled out the cork and tipped it back, finishing what was left in one swallow. He contemplated hiding it behind the wardrobe again, but instead slipped the bottle in his coat's inside pocket. He rinsed his mouth with a mint and vinegar solution of Betty's meant to freshen the breath, grimacing when he had to swallow it, before popping in a piece of chewing gum.

Standing in front of the mirror, he smiled at himself. This was another trick he had learned from John Graves Shedd, who said it was not merely the act of smiling that boosted one's confidence. Just as important was *observing* oneself smile. 'Today's going to be my lucky day,' he told his reflection.

Taking a deep breath, he opened the door to the parlour where he found Jack and Billy on the floor, trying to tug open the lock on his grip. He charged across the room, telling them to stop that at once.

'There's no need to shout,' called Betty, from the kitchen.

'No dear,' he replied. 'My mistake.' He raised his eyebrows in a way that made Jack and Billy giggle, as he dragged them away from the grip. 'You should know better,' he told Jack, wagging his finger in a way that made them giggle again, 'leading your brother on like that.' Jack was eleven; Billy was six.

'But why can't we see?' Jack complained.

He was trying to herd them back to the breakfast table. 'Because there's a secret whim-wham inside,' he whispered. 'But *ssshhh*, don't tell anyone.'

'Are there whim-whams at the Fair?'

'Hundreds of them.'

'Are there whim-whams at Marble Fills?' asked Billy.

He laughed. 'Yes, there are also whim-whams at Marshall Field.'

'What's a whim-wham?' Jack wanted to know.

'A whim-wham's a new thing, that's all. A thing that's never been seen before.'

'It sounded like a bockle inside to me,' said Billy.

'Well, it's not,' he said, more defensively than he should have done. 'It's a whim-wham to show my customers.'

'Why won't you take us to the Fair? Everyone at school's gone already,' wailed Jack. 'I want to go with you to Buffalo Bill's show. I don't want to go with Grandpa.' Betty's father had promised to take them the next weekend.

'Now, now, Jack. Tell you what. When I get back, that's the first thing we'll do. You and Billy and your pa will go to the Fair, all three of us, and we'll have the day of our lives.'

'What about ma?' whined Billy. 'Can't she come too?'

'Why sure your ma can come too.'

Betty came in and put a mug of tea on the table for him, a plate with two slices of toast soaked in butter and a wedge of cheese to the side.

'You'll come to the White City with us when I get back, won't you honey?'

She told the children to come straight back to the table and finish their breakfasts. 'Jack, stop drawing.' Sitting down, she nibbled on her own piece of toast. 'Must you chew gum at breakfast?' she said, without looking at him.

He made an 'I've been caught' face which made the boys giggle again.

'I'm sorry, you're quite right dear.' He took out the gum and lodged it in a corner of his handkerchief.

Jack held out the drawing pad to show him his picture. Drawing was the boy's obsession. This picture showed two figures seated at a table. It took him some moments to work out who they were. The woman crying was Betty. The other person was him.

Jack was watching him closely. He smiled and patted the boy on the head. 'Very good. May I keep it?'

'Sure,' said Jack.

He tore the sheet off the pad, folded it and put it in his pocket. Jack had depicted him as a ghost. As a smiling ghost.

'We've run out of tea and coffee,' said Betty. 'And I shall need some money to buy kerosene.'

'Of course, dear.' He helped Billy onto his chair and rubbed his hands together with vigour. 'Well, my young soldiers, shall we tuck in?'

He and Betty had been married for over ten years. They met at work. He was a salesman, she was a cleaner. There had been no great romance. But she was sweet and pretty and he was doing all right in those days. She looked up to him. She thought it was fine to live in a German neighbourhood, with the church only a block away and a pretty choir hall to the side. The fact that a beer garden was also nearby did not seem to concern her and she turned a blind eye to the drunken Germans who staggered past on their way back home every Sunday afternoon. She said Jack and Billy should learn some German while they were still young. Now, Betty thought the house was too small, that Germans were rude and that they were all anarchists.

Couldn't he see this was no place to bring up children?

He raised his mug of tea. It was weak, more like hot water, but he pretended otherwise as he took a sip and licked his lips. 'Tea in the morning, boys. One day, you'll be tea drinkers too, I'm sure.'

A smiling ghost.

Betty had still not finished her toast. 'How long will you be gone?'

'Oh, the usual,' he said. 'Expect me back, if all goes well, in ten days' time.'

'Why do you have to go?' asked Jack.

'Now come on Jack. It's not for long. You know very well why. Your pa has to work, that's why. When you're older you'll realise it's a man's job to make sure there's food on the table for his family,' he said brightly, taking care to avoid Betty's eye.

'Where are you going?' she asked.

He began to reel off some names in northern Illinois and Michigan. And then — it was as bad as a nervous tic — he could not stop himself mentioning St Clair. 'That's an interesting one, boys. And I'll tell you why. In the old days, St Clair was so full of trees you had to fight your way through them to get to the river. Now it's big open country. And do you know what happened to those trees? They came here, to Chicago.'

He told them that their own house had probably been built with white pine from St Clair.

Betty stood up. Her arms were folded. 'I thought you went to St Clair on your last trip.'

Oh heck. He grinned at the boys. 'You're right, dear,' he said. 'I nearly did. It was on my schedule, but they cancelled the train.'

She went back into the kitchen without saying a word.

He cupped one hand and whispered to the boys. 'One day, my young lions, we'll leave the city and go live somewhere like St Clair. Get ourselves a farm, grow our own food, pick our own fruit. You'll walk across the fields to school every day, the same as your pa did when he was your age. Breathe fresh air. It'll be a wonderful life. You'd like that, wouldn't you?'

They looked at him, silent, mouths open.

'A wonderful life,' he repeated, biting his lip because he had a sudden, inexplicable urge to weep.

Around midday, Stephen gave up looking for work. He had scoured the advertisements in the *Daily News* and the *Tribune* but there was nothing new. It was not as though he was too proud, and circling only vacancies for a 'salesman' or a 'drummer'. He'd be happy if he never had to sell anything ever again. It wasn't something he had wanted to do in the first place. Selling was just what he had fallen into. It was five weeks since the debacle in St Clair and its humiliation still haunted him. There he was, scheduled to give a presentation at the town's main hotel, when he had become too drunk to do so. He had been highly intoxicated often enough before, but he had never been incapable. The telegram from Mr John Graves Shedd dismissing him from Marshall Field was delivered the next morning.

He should come clean with Betty. But more out of cowardice than in the genuine hope of finding work, he kept putting it off. He now knew that today would not be his lucky day after all, and that he would end up tonight at one of the cheap boarding houses somewhere in the 19th Ward where they'd serve cold tripe or half-cooked mutton broth on a plate rinsed in greasy water in a long leaden sink. After trying to eat, he'd sit in a stifling parlour with strangers for as long as he could, until he was so tired that he had a chance of falling asleep when he went up to the dormitory. He rarely joined in a conversation, not unless someone produced a bottle, which was hardly ever. He'd stare into space or pass the time by, say, watching a line of ants transport crumbs from here to there, or counting how many times his fellow transients missed the spittoon. Staggering upstairs he'd lie under an itchy blanket, coat and pantaloons folded beneath his head for a pillow. In the morning, it would start all over again.

He knew Betty suspected something. For one thing, his 'trips' had become shorter. He had run out of friends on whom he could lean for a loan and he could not go, yet again, on bended knee to his uncle. Every time he did, old Jearum fixed him with a look and wanted to know whether he had stopped drinking. Yes, he always lied, absolutely yes, he had stopped. Then there would be the lecture, on how alcohol rotted the brain and drained a man of ambition.

He now owed money to everyone he knew. That was why he was prepared to work anywhere at anything — as a store assistant, as a bricklayer and this morning he had applied at three different hotels for any post that was vacant, from porter to dishwasher. But it was the same everywhere. He could tell — from the way they looked at him — that he had no chance. He did not fit the mould. He was too old, he had the wrong face, he had no experience of bricklaying or washing up or whatever it was.

He pawned his grip for $4 and bought a bottle of bald face. Taking a swig, he relished the familiar burn of whiskey down his throat. He was so weary. He hated this city. He had never liked it, not even when he was young, and the feeling of entrapment, and of being an insignificant grain of sand, had grown stronger in him as the city grew. It was especially bad now, with all the visitors in Chicago come for the World's Fair. The streets of the city might be heaving with people and foreign money, but there was not so much as a dime that he seemed to be able to get his hands on.

It was a warm, pleasant summer afternoon. Time stretched out ahead of him, and that was the worst thing. He had no prospects, no ideas, no money to speak of and no energy, just time and time and more time. There was nothing to do and no end in sight. He should stop drinking. He knew that. He'd stopped in the past, for months on end. But deep down, he was no longer sure he could. He paused, leaning against a wall to take another swig. It was the hopelessness that hurt most. If only there was a point to this.

Wandering aimlessly, he found a cheap restaurant in a side alley off Randolph Street, advertising a plate of beans and batter for ten cents, with beef dodgers on top for another two. Pushing open the door, he was greeted by a fug of smoke and warmth and the crackle of fat frying on the stove. It was noisy. The tables were packed close, full of construction workers. As he went in, he looked down. He realised he had started doing that a lot these days, even though he had been trained not to. *Look your fellow man in the eye, show him your confidence and sense of purpose. Let him catch a glimpse of your soul and you will have gained his trust forever. He'll buy the world off you.* (John Graves Shedd)

He was aware that, behind the sales patter he could still summon up, his confidence had gone. He feared it would prove hard to recover. He could not have explained everything that had happened since it began to go wrong, whenever that was, nor how he might have saved himself. But he did know he was down at a level to which he never thought he'd sink.

He took out Jack's drawing and studied it. The likeness was frightening. Even the way in which the rigid smile on his ghostly face was unnaturally fixed. The boy was right, he thought. Nobody noticed him any more. He did not matter.

He ordered a plate of beans and batter with beef dodgers on top.

Maybe it was the food that revived his spirits and encouraged him to use the afternoon, and what little cash he had left, to see the World's Fair for himself. That way, he told himself, he would know his way around when he took Jack and Billy. Oh, and Betty too.

The floor of the Illinois Central cattle car, which he boarded at the Randolph Street Station, was covered in straw and it still stank of livestock. The jolting motion upset the beef dodgers in his belly. After twelve unpleasant minutes (he timed it, an old drumming habit: *Never forget that you're a man on time, to whom time is precious, John Graves Shedd*), the locomotive brakes began to squeal like a pig and he had to hold on tight while it came shuddering to a halt.

Blinded by the light, he stepped out of the car and followed everyone else down a flight of steps. Only when he reached the bottom, did he look up. The scales fell away from his eyes. In those twelve unpleasant minutes, he had travelled from one kind of city to another. His spirits lifted. Ahead of him, in all its splendour, stood the White City.

He made his way towards it. Everything here seemed to be for the best. The air was clean, the grass was mown, the inhabitants were healthy and well mannered and well dressed. The walkways were even and neatly signed and, as he moved in the direction of what was called the 'Court of Honor', along with the orderly crowd, he found himself gazing at a skyline dominated by magnificent white buildings, an identical and brilliant white stucco effect that shone like the marble it mimicked. High overhead, suspended on a series of arches, an electric train ran around the perimeter of the site like a planet orbiting its sun. Entranced by the beauty and perfection of what lay before him, Stephen forgot his problems.

He paused at one point to admire the scene. It was like one of those pastoral idylls over which he had fallen asleep at school, a scene from the classical world of gleaming temples set in verdant lawns and gardens awash with bright summer blooms, connected by wooden walkways and clear-watered canals and gracious bridges. Electric launches plied gently back and forth. There were even gondolas with ornately carved prows, reminiscent of ones he had seen in paintings of Venice in the Italian room at the Art Institute, in which elegantly attired couples sat on padded leather seats while gondoliers dressed as modern-day troubadours in baggy pants and bright felt hats propelled them sedately from building to building. Nobody looked unhappy or bored or poor. There were no vagrants, no dirt or trash, no dusty building sites, no horses, none of the noise or smells of that other city across the water.

But the truth was that by the time he arrived in the Court of Honor, he was already beginning to feel troubled. And when he caught his first sight of the turquoise blue waters of the Grand Lagoon and the giant golden dome on top of what (according to the map) was the Administration Building, a sense of fatigue was setting in. He loitered beneath a statue that resembled the Statue of Liberty, and gazed around the succession of vast buildings that flanked both sides of the lagoon, each flying a flag above its facade of colonnades, each with a flight of wide steps that led down to a velvety lawn dyed a deep shade of green. The White City was beginning to feel more like a mirage than reality. At the far end, as if to complete the illusion, stood the majestic centrepiece towards which all these frontages seemed to be paying homage, a massive fountain built in the form (they said) of Columbus's ship as he first caught sight of America four hundred years before.

The fountain was impressively big, but was it anything more than that? He knew the White City had been built to celebrate Columbus's arrival in America. But that did not explain what this was all for. He was in a city without houses or factories, a city without residents where nothing was made. To use Jack's analogy, it was the smiling ghost of a real city.

It was true there were some extraordinary inventions to see. But by the time he had seen wonders such as moving pictures and drawings sent over a telegraph line, and had listened to a long-distance telephone call from New York, he was beginning to find it hard to concentrate. He entered the Electricity Building, housed on another gigantic site behind a façade of Corinthian columns, and filled with glass-roofed pavilions. It was lit by thousands of electric lights, of different colours and sizes, blazing away like a multicoloured night sky. Just one of those lights at home and he could have read by it all night. He sat down on a bench. Squinting, he looked up at the Tower of Light, a pillar decorated by light bulbs that stretched from the floor to the roof, the light flitting up and down, back and forth as if a genie were being relayed from bulb to bulb. At times, it was like a delicate shower of light, at other times like a streak of lightning.

'You know what this Fair reminds me of?' he said to the man seated next to him. He had just finished off the bottle of whiskey. Maybe it was the alcohol that made him want to talk. 'Montgomery Ward's Big Book. Do you know what I mean, sir? It's like being trapped inside the Big Book, condemned to walk from page to page, back and forth like an automaton, your senses dulled because there's too much to look at. And, if you're like me, you get confused because everything under the sun looks to have been thrown together without rhyme or reason. At least in my line of work — I'm a drummer, sir, with Marshall Field — there are limits. We can only carry so much in a grip. And we still have old-fashioned contact with our customers. I would look you in the eye and if I had a couple of those bulbs in my grip I would tell you exactly how —' he pointed up at the Tower of Light '— the electricity jumps from one bulb to another. That's my job. But the Big Book doesn't explain a goddam thing. There are too many things and not enough space and nobody like me around to tell you. In fact, there's simply too much for the human mind to comprehend. Do you see what I'm saying, sir? Even if you were a professor, there'd still be too many new inventions for you to understand them all.

'In fact, when I look around, what I see is not exactly a Montgomery Ward Big Book but a Progress and Science Big Book.

But where are Progress and Science taking us?' He frowned. 'In a hundred different directions at once, I'd say. See that chair over there?' He pointed to a large armchair set on a plinth, equipped with a plethora of wires that ran along the arms and across the seat and around the back. 'As soon as I saw it, I thought to myself, now that's a wonder. The electricity must make the chair light up. Then I discovered what it's really been invented for. Shall I tell you, sir? Such a massive charge of electricity can be sent through those wires that anyone seated in the chair would be killed in a flash, so to speak. That's why they've got the straps on the armrests, to hold the victim down. Why would anyone invent a chair like that? What's the point? I have an uncle who's an inventor, but his inventions are *useful*. That chair might fit in a twisted German fairytale, but surely not in America at the end of the nineteenth century. If this is their vision of the future, a world in which I can buy in a mail order catalogue a chair that kills, then I — for one — want nothing to do with it. And you, sir? What about you?'

The man gave him an odd look, stood up and left.

Stephen spent the next few hours wandering along the Midway Plaisance. The anger he had felt earlier began to dissipate. The Midway was different from the main fairgrounds. Even though it felt as muddled, with one curiosity after another, and with no theme or order that he could see, it seemed more human. He walked through model villages from Egypt and Algeria, full of real Egyptians and Algerians. He circled a spiralling gold pagoda, he watched a boxing match where they wore padded gloves, he spent ten cents on a beer from a 'traditional' English inn that tasted flat and sour. He listened to a Negro playing the piano in a way he'd never heard anyone play, with a rhythm that seemed to hop and jump. That made him realise this pianist was the only Negro he had seen here all day. A 'white' city indeed.

At some point, he stood at the edge of a crowd gathered around an evangelist preacher who spoke with as much passion about God as Mr John Graves Shedd used to speak about the art of selling. Listening to the rise and fall of those sonorous words, he was filled with admiration for the confidence with which they were delivered, even as they reminded him of his own failings. Conviction was required to speak like that, and he was not a man to whom conviction had ever come easily. It occurred to him that a man who does not believe enough in anything else, cannot believe in himself either.

He paused at the base of the 'Ferris Wheel', whose top half he had seen over and over all day, making a graceful revolution through the sky. It was an absurd, outlandish creation. The iron axle at its base stood higher than a house. He raised his eyes and tried to count the number of timbered cabins that were making their slow way around. There must have been at least thirty, maybe even more. He was wondering whether to go up, when he felt a tap on the shoulder.

'Please, sir. Where does it go?'

He turned to find a group of four elderly Indians, wrapped in red blankets and with their hair in plaits, staring up at the wheel. Their long faces looked bewildered. He realised that despite being among crowds all day, this was the first time anyone had talked to him. He had not appreciated how lonely he was.

'The big wheel goes round and round,' he said. 'First it goes to the top, then back down to the bottom. The notice says it costs 50c, and for that price they take you round twice.'

The Indians conferred for a moment in their own tongue. The sound of their speech went up and down too, full of soft sounds and long vowels.

Their leader addressed him again. 'Who is pushing the wheel, sir?'

Steam, he thought. But he could not explain how. He wished he had listened better to old Jearum. One of his inventions had had something to do with steam. He began to explain what he knew about steam and pressure, but the Indians looked increasingly skeptical. When he had finished, they consulted together again.

Crossing his arms, the chief said: 'We will go with you.'

The other passengers kept their distance, and that suited him fine. They occupied a corner of the cabin, the Indians huddled around him as if he were their guide. They held on to him when the car first began to move, they asked questions about what they could see, they uttered excited shrieks as they neared the top. For the first time since he had left home that morning, he felt happy. He was not sure why the Indians had attached themselves to him, but he was pleased they had. He told them the names of the buildings he recognised, he assured them the Wheel was quite safe, that the best engineers in the world had built it. But they did not seem as worried about safety as he was. They were Potawatomies, he learned, and they had received a special invitation from white chiefs to attend the Fair. As they were descending, their leader pointed to the view below of an arena where some horses were parading. He had seen the signs earlier, to Buffalo Bill's Wild West show. He thought of little Billy riding his belly on the floor that morning, and it seemed an age ago. 'You go there with us, sir, when the Great Spirit has brought us back down to earth.'

But they did not go to the show. The last performance for the day had already taken place. He spent the evening with the four Indians. Their teepee was pitched outside the main fairground, not far from Buffalo Bill's arena. They gave him a blanket that smelled of smoke and horse sweat, and cooked a stew in a black pot that they suspended over an open fire. After they had eaten, a pipe was passed around filled with a bitter mix of kinnikinnick tobacco that made him choke until he had got used to it. The light began to fade. Other small fires lit the landscape beneath a starry sky. He felt as though he were floating above the worries of the world, so cheered were his spirits by this encounter. He smiled to himself. This had, after all, turned into a lucky day.

The Indians had travelled from a reservation in Michigan, they said, but their fathers used to live here for much of the year, around the shores of the Lake.

'It is important to come back,' said their leader, 'to honour the spirits of our ancestors.' He had a striking face. There was an elliptical perfection to his features, as though they had been sculpted out of a dark, luminous stone. His voice was soft, his eyes were wise. He sat in perfect stillness, cross-legged on the ground.

'You believe their spirits are still here?' asked Stephen.

The Indian smiled. 'Of course.' The others nodded. 'They pass their spirits on to us when they leave to join their fathers in the shades.'

'That is the way of the Great Spirit,' said another.

'You have children, sir?' asked their leader.

He said he had two boys.

'One day, they too will honour your spirit.'

That was unlikely, he said. He showed them the picture Jack had drawn that morning.

'He is afraid of losing you,' said their leader, after studying it. 'That is what he is saying.' He paused. 'And you sir, whose son are you?'

'My father passed on when I was young,' he said. 'I don't remember him well.'

The Indians nodded gravely. In the firelight, their leader's eyes seemed to grow opaque. 'That is why you look lost,' he said. 'You must find a way to connect with your ancestral spirits. That will help you put your life back on its path.'

'The spirits of our ancestors always make themselves known,' said another.

'If they did not, we would never know who we are.'

'Do you have anything with you, sir, that belongs to your father?'

As it happened, he always carried with him an antique watch

given to him by his mother. 'But,' he explained, 'it belonged originally to my father.'

The Indians nodded their approval. That would do well.

He removed it from his pocket, unhooked the chain and handed it to their leader. The silver sheen of its cover caught the light. The Indian turned it over, peered at the faded inscription on the back, and then closed his hands around it. There was great value, he said, to be found in precious objects that had been passed down from our ancestors. As these heirlooms aged, they acquired more power. And they were reminders to us of who we are.

'We are not the same as our ancestors, but a measure of their spirit always survives in us. That is what we must seek. You say you did not know your father well. But look into your heart. That is where your father's spirit moves within you. Look into your heart and you will find the dreams he never fulfilled. This is why we pass our spirit on to our children, that they should realise the dreams we have not realised ourselves. Look into your heart and you will find it. The dream is always there, even if you cannot recognise it for what it is.'

It was hard to imagine his father having harboured any grand unrealised dreams. He loved his wife and son, he enjoyed solving customers' problems in his hardware store, he liked making things with his hands. Stephen could imagine no more than that.

'We cannot forget our ancestors,' said the Indian. 'That is why we are here. That is why we are who we are.'

The Indians passed the old watch between them. Then they stood and raised their hands to the night sky. Stephen joined them. They chanted, their voices low and harmonious and although he could not understand what they were saying, he felt a peace come over him.

He burnt Jack's drawing in the fire.

———

The next morning he accompanied the Indians into the stands for a performance of what was described as: *Buffalo Bill's Wild West and the Congress of Rough Riders of the World*. They were going to witness what happened 'in every exactitude' on this land a long time ago.

The four elders watched impassively as a band of Indians, attacking a stagecoach, were driven off by Buffalo Bill in his big white hat. They watched the show that followed in silence too, right up to the last act that featured an attack by Potawatomies on a log cabin full of early settlers. Once more, Buffalo Bill came to the rescue.

It did not really happen like that, the Indians told him.

'Of course not,' he said. 'Nothing here is real.'

Before he said goodbye to his Indian friends, they asked for his help. One of them had found a copy of the *Chicago Daily Tribune*. To their delight, there was a sketch of the four of them printed on the front page. Would he please tell them what it said?

He skimmed the article. The ancestors of these Potawatomie Indians, it said, had been driven out of Chicago just sixty years ago. What a thoughtful gesture it was, on the part of the organisers of the World's Fair, to invite them back to their old hunting grounds to view the extraordinary achievements of their successors. How out of place these Indians looked in the new world created by Americans.

'It says,' he told them, to smiles, 'that we should never forget who was here first. It is like remembering our ancestors.'

They pointed to the title. *Indians Return as Freaks*. 'And this, sir?'

On Sunday afternoons, there was free entrance at the Art Institute. Some months after that encounter with the Indians at the White City, Stephen took Jack and Billy with him. By now, he knew his way around well. They held hands, one boy on each side of him, as they climbed the wide, low steps to the first floor. He wanted Jack to copy some of the portraits on display by Rembrandt and Van Dyck, but

Billy tugged at his arm. Couldn't they go over there instead?

He looked across to where he was pointing. A sign directed visitors into a newly opened display room.

'What does it say, pa?' asked Billy.

'It says that this exhibition contains works that once hung in the homes of the first settlers.'

'Was there a first first settler,' asked Jack. 'I mean, a founder?'

Stephen shrugged. 'I don't think anyone knows, not any more.'

'But there must have been,' he insisted.

'What's a founder?' asked Billy.

'The person who starts something,' said Jack.

'You mean somebody started Chicago?' Billy giggled. 'That's silly. How could someone start a city?'

They stepped inside.

'Now remember, Billy,' he said, 'no running around or we'll all be in trouble.'

It was a spacious room with a honey-coloured oak floor. Sunlight poured in through high oval windows. About two dozen paintings were on display. There were a few other people walking around, taking their turn and conversing quietly. In the centre of the room, cordoned off by rope, stood a copper kettle.

'That's the hugest keckle I ever seen,' said Billy.

Jack read out for them what it said on the sign. *This copper kettle (slightly damaged) is capable of holding 10 gallons. Date/place of manufacture unknown.*

Billy was on his knees. 'Pa, pa?' he cried. 'There's a hole.'

There wasn't a hole. It was a dent in the surface of the kettle, which was otherwise in immaculate condition.

'I'm copying that one, pa,' said Jack, opening up his drawing pad at a fresh sheet and sitting cross-legged on the floor. He had chosen a painting of a lady on a horse, posing in front of a large country house. It was an English scene. The notice explained that this painting had once belonged to Mr William Ogden, the first mayor of Chicago, but went missing after the Great Fire. Only recently had it been rediscovered. Jack, he thought, had chosen a melancholy but exquisitely executed painting. It seemed to him that the painter had captured the essence of both the lady and her horse. She had dignity and presence. Her posture and expression implied that she was a worried lady.

'You come with me, Billy,' he said, 'and help me draw this one, will you?'

The boy made a face. 'That one's boring.'

'You don't like it? It's a picture of an early settler's house.'

Stephen did not make copies of paintings any more when he came to the Art Institute, as he insisted Jack did. He used paintings like this one for inspiration. Before beginning to make a sketch, he inspected it in more detail. There had once been a title, but the letters were too faded to make out what it had been. Though not as accomplished a work as the one Jack had chosen, the portrayal of a large, lonesome cabin with a single figure on the porch was one that moved him. The owner sat in a rocking chair. He was smoking a pipe, and on the table beside him stood a glass. This was a man, decided Stephen, who had made his own destiny.

As he drew, the words of the Indians he'd met at the World's Fair sounded in his head. He wondered if, by painting, he might be achieving the unrealised dreams of his own father. Perhaps his father, instead of owning a hardware store, had always yearned to be an artist. A painter, perhaps, like him, or a musician or a poet. Perhaps his father had dreamed of venturing beyond the daily routines of his working life, as Stephen was doing now, but never dared to try.

The encounter with the Indians had been a turning point for him. He ceased trying to be the salesman he had never really wanted to be. He stopped drinking and, with a loan from old Jearum, he opened a small hardware store serving the local neighbourhood. Times were hard once the Fair closed, but he was surviving. He had already built up a core of loyal customers. Betty was helping him. She was beginning to look up to him again.

None of that would have been possible, he knew, without what he was doing now. It was painting that nourished him, that gave him confidence in himself, that made his heart thrum. Every Sunday he would bring Jack here and task him with copying Old Masters. Jack had talent. Maybe, one day, the boy would be able to make a living from his painting, just as Stephen had once yearned to do himself. Maybe Jack would fulfil his own unrealised dreams.

'Pa?'

He turned to find Billy hurtling towards him. Putting down his sketchbook, he rose to his feet. The paintings blazed like stained glass in a cathedral as the boy came skidding across the sheen of polished timbers. He stood firm and when Billy jumped, illuminated in a blinding arc of sunlight, he received him with open arms.

1894

An Interview

(The transcript of this interview, conducted by correspondent Mrs Antje Hunter, was used as the basis for an article exploring the work of Mr Milton Winship, Professor of American History at the University of Chicago, published in the *Chicago Daily Tribune* on February 15, 1894.)

Mrs Hunter: Let me begin by asking you, Professor, about your approach to the study of history. Other historians have claimed that you 'varnish' the facts, rather than let them speak for themselves.

Mr Winship: I confess there have been times when I've chosen to use my own experience of human nature to supposition how people might have behaved or what they might have said. I have done so knowing full well that this approach would not be to everyone's taste. But if what survives of our legacy is a patchwork of threads, I believe the historian has a duty to try to stitch them together. If the facts always did speak for themselves, history would be indisputable. But consider a situation where the facts are painful to digest, or where they weaken the thrust of a writer's argument. What could be easier for a historian than to make adjustments and deletions to suit his purpose? This is what happened in the case of your great-grandfather Jean Baptiste Pointe de Sable. *[Pauses]* I should explain, for the benefit of your readers, that I am in the process of writing an *Alternative History* of Chicago, a work that spans the nineteenth century, and I open with the story of our first settler. While conducting my research, it was my good fortune, of course, to be able to identify you as Pointe de Sable's great-granddaughter.

Mrs Hunter: A fact of which I was myself unaware, until you told me.

Mr Winship: Pointe de Sable's story is a perfect example of what happens when facts are not allowed to speak for themselves. He has either been ignored by my fellow historians or buried somewhere in a footnote. As I explain in my book, the fact that Pointe de Sable was born a mulatto made him a source of irritation and embarrassment to that stratum of Chicagoans who wanted to tell the story of a city not only built by white men, but also founded by them.

Mrs Hunter: But does it really matter, some may ask, whether Chicago was founded by Pointe de Sable or John Kinzie or, as many now like to say, William Ogden? Was it not the people who came later — men like John S. Wright, 'Long John' Wentworth, Potter Palmer, George Pullman, Marshall Field and Charles Hutchinson, to name a few, who have made the city what it is today?

Mr Winship: I grant their achievements may appear to dwarf those of Pointe de Sable, but don't forget they did not come — as he did — to a wilderness. Too often beginnings are lost in the mists of time and replacements fabricated to suit posterity. It is therefore a cause for celebration that ours can be reclaimed. I firmly believe that a beginning sets the tone for what follows.

<u>Mrs Hunter:</u> In that case, can we go back to an aspect of our beginning that puzzles me? I know you have investigated Mr Kinzie's visit to my great-grandfather in 1800. And I believe you have gathered information both from Pointe de Sable's journal and from interviews you were able to conduct with my grandmother Mrs Eulalie Van Voorhis before she died. You have told me that Pointe de Sable's journal breaks off at a critical moment, never to be resumed. Did my grandmother, in conversation with you, ever talk about what happened that evening?

<u>Mr Winship:</u> She did. And I would be happy to tell you what I believe took place. First, let me put things in context. It wasn't easy to track down your grandmother but I eventually found her living as a recluse in St Charles, Missouri. By that time, she was an elderly lady who got things confused in her day-to-day life. But she could remember those early days at Echicagou with remarkable clarity.

To recap. An extraordinary chess contest is in progress when Pointe de Sable's journal breaks off. Imagine the scene. It is a still, warm evening in early May. The two combatants are seated opposite each other at the dining table in the spacious, elegant keeping room of Pointe de Sable's timbered mansion, with its polished puncheon floor, the array of easy chairs set around the fireplace and the walls hung with fine, colorful paintings. A glowering Mr Kinzie sits on one side of the table, his breath soured by whiskey fumes as he chews on a wad of tobacco, while on the other side your great-grandfather is seated, a large, gentle brown-skinned gentleman in his mid-fifties with a shock of gray hair, his appearance disfigured by a black stocking with which he has been blindfolded. On the table between them lies his walrus ivory chessboard, a gift from Governor Sinclair at Michilimackinac, the pieces arranged in their starting positions. Jean Lalime, the game's referee, is positioned at the head of the table. Beside him stand a lantern and a sandglass. The sandglass lasts for ten minutes on each turn.

The rich furnishings and tasteful decorations inside the keeping room would normally project an atmosphere of conviviality and relaxation. Tonight, though, the tension is immense. Earlier, Mr Kinzie has whipped Pointe de Sable's grandson Wabaunsee, cruelly and inhumanely, scarring the boy for life, and despite being ordered to leave the house, Kinzie has refused to do so. Lalime, to present that shadowy figure in the best possible light, has advised Pointe de Sable that expelling Mr Kinzie from the house would, in any case, achieve nothing in the long term. Kinzie would only come back with reinforcements. Pointe de Sable himself, one must assume, has seen the futility of trying to fight a legal battle against opponents such as these.

That is why he has been driven to propose this contest on the chessboard. Mr Kinzie, regardless of whether he wins or loses the game, has undertaken to leave Echicagou and persuade the 'powerful men' in St Joseph, in whose behalf he is acting, that Pointe de Sable's property and possessions are worthless. If Kinzie loses the game, that will mark the end of the matter. But if Kinzie wins the game — and he is supremely confident, of course, that he will — Pointe de Sable has agreed to sell his estate, including all his livestock and household possessions, to his friend Jean Lalime for the advantageous price of six thousand livres. Pointe de Sable is certain this will never happen. But, unknown to him, Lalime has simultaneously pledged to Kinzie that, should this occur, he would be acting only as a caretaker owner. Kinzie could assume the legal title of the Pointe de Sable estate and property whenever he chose. Was Lalime also promised a reward by Kinzie for his trouble? Presumably, yes. Did Lalime have no other option, given Pointe de Sable's refusal to sell to Kinzie? We don't know. One matter, though, is clear. Mr Kinzie had no qualms about lying to his employers in St Joseph for his own gain.

Eulalie neither understands the rules of chess nor the significance of the game at hand. She can sense, though, with a child's intuition, that something very serious indeed is happening. The grown-ups are never able to hide their feelings when they're afraid. Her mother and grandmother try to make her stay with them in the bedroom where they are tending Wabaunsee, but she escapes and returns to the keeping room. She tugs on Pointe de Sable's coat and whispers a warning in his ear, before positioning herself in her favorite corner of the room, perched on a stool in the shadows by the kitchen door.

The game is tedious, if it truly is a game. Certainly, neither Mr Kinzie nor Gray Curls (her nickname for Pointe de Sable) seems to be enjoying himself. Why is it so slow? Why does so little happen? And why does Gray Curls have a black stocking over his eyes? It must be very uncomfortable. Sometimes she wonders if the game is already over, even though they are still seated at the table, because they take such a long time between turns. She does not doubt that Gray Curls will win, but she wishes he would hurry up because only when the game is over will the bad man Mr Kinzie leave them. Life can then go back to how it was before.

She can see Mr Kinzie is concentrating hard because he keeps his eyes on the board even while he's pulling on his pointy whiskers and chewing on his tobacco, spitting out a wad on the floor whenever he finally moves one of his white pieces. Sometimes he mutters under his breath; at other times he says a rude word aloud. Gray Curls, who stays upright and motionless, remains silent other than when he gives instructions to Uncle Jean (Lalime), speaking in what Eulalie will understand, later in life, are combinations of letters and numbers that respond to pieces and squares on the board.

She is sleepy. The room is smoky and it is late. Tiptoeing to the table, she slides along the bench until she is next to Gray Curls. There aren't as many black and white pieces on the board as before, and the ones still there have moved around, but that does not make the board look any prettier or more interesting. Lying down, she rests her head in Gray Curls' lap. His coat smells of kinnikinnick tobacco and grains of paradise. With his hand on her shoulder, she falls asleep.

How much time passes, she has no idea. But it is dark outside when she is woken by voices. Gray Curls soothes her as she sits up to see what is happening. There are fewer pieces on the board than before, and their arrangement looks even less pretty. Mr Kinzie moves one of the white pieces. Uncle Jean turns over the sandglass.

A long period of silence follows, broken only by the sound of creaking floorboards as Mr Kinzie paces around the room. She watches the sand fall through the narrow gap in the middle of the glass. The grains show a range of shiny colors in the lantern light. She could watch them all night, they are so beautiful, and much more interesting than the grown-ups' game. Uncle Jean speaks. He tells Gray Curls there are only two minutes remaining to make his move. Mr Kinzie returns to the table, but not to his seat. He stands over the board, rocking back and forth, arms folded, casting the pieces in shadow. She continues to watch the sand, wondering what the color will be, of the very last grain that falls through.

'Let My Euladie move the next piece,' she hears Gray Curls say. She stops watching the sand and looks up at him, but then remembers he cannot see her. Gray Curls gives instructions to Uncle Jean, who then shows her which piece she has to move where. There are more black pieces than white pieces, but while most of the white pieces are big, most of the black ones are small. It is one of those she has to move forward. She is about to do this when she catches a whiff of Mr Kinzie's perfume, the sharp mix of bitter oranges and the bite of salt and the flash of lightning that makes her eyes water. It reminds her of the last time she smelled it, and of how Mr Kinzie seized her by the throat and dragged her outside the bedroom door. For a moment, she fears he is going to do that again, but then she remembers that Gray Curls and Uncle Jean are here. He would never dare, would he? 'Hurry up, girl,' growls Mr Kinzie, waving the finger that had felt ice-cold against her lips. 'Make your move.'

He has distracted her. She is confused, no longer sure which piece she is supposed to move. Anyway, the small black figures — five or six of them — all look the same, so it will not make any difference. She chooses one in the middle and pushes it forward to the next square.

Suddenly, the grown-ups are all talking at once. She has made a mistake. Uncle Jean is telling her 'No, not that one.' He wants her to move it back. He's pointing to another one instead. But Mr Kinzie is speaking too, and when she tries to move the first one back, he grabs her by the hand and won't let go. He is saying it cannot be changed. That is the rule, and they know it. Then it's the silliest game she's ever seen. She wants to cry, but she does not because she is terrified by what is happening and what she has done. Uncle Jean is arguing with Mr Kinzie. He's saying it's unfair, that she's only a child, she doesn't understand what she's doing, that she's made a mistake and Mr Kinzie knows it.

She buries her head in her grandfather's coat and sobs. She knows she has ruined everything for everybody. All the bad things that happen to them from now on will be her fault. And she has no doubt that those bad things *will* happen. She wants to disappear and die. It is no consolation that Gray Curls is running his fingers through her hair, that he's telling her not to worry, that she has done nothing wrong, that it makes absolutely no difference.

The truth, though, is that her mistake does make a difference: a very significant difference. She is so busy feeling sorry for herself that it takes her a long time to realize the grown-ups have started to argue exactly the opposite to what they had been arguing before. Mr Kinzie wants her move to be changed back. Uncle Jean is saying it is too late to do that now. Did not Mr Kinzie himself insist, only a few minutes ago, that it had to stand, and had he not already played his next piece? Mr Pointe de Sable accepted that earlier decision, though it had seemed to go against his interests, and now it is Mr Kinzie's duty to do the same. She loses track of who says what or why, but she knows that Uncle Jean (to his credit, wouldn't you agree, Mrs Hunter?) refuses to alter his decision.

She does not remember how many more moves are made before Mr Kinzie says another rude word, very loudly, and storms out onto the porch. The door slams behind him. Uncle Jean removes the black stocking from around Gray Curls' eyes, and her mother and grandmother appear at the far end of the room. Mr Kinzie was a formidable opponent, Gray Curls tells them. 'And I was stuck, until My little Euladie, she comin' to the rescue. She must've seen six moves afore us, and gone done make the one move that would be winnin' the game.'

Is that really true? Has she really saved Gray Curls? She looks up at her grandfather. There are lines and stretch marks across his face from the black stocking, but otherwise he looks normal. He smiles, and nods. 'Until that point, we were drawn equal, and prob'ly nobody gonna win. You won't understan' this now, My Euladie. But people like Kinzie man, they thinkin' the game be won with the power of the few, with castles and knights, bish'ps and queens. That's why they don't take no notice of the pawns.' She looks at the board. 'Are those pawns?' she asks, pointing to the five or six small black pieces that surround the remaining duo of large white ones. Gray Curls nods. 'Remember this, My Euladie, that in the end it's the pawns that do the winnin' in chess, for they be the soul of the game, the same as we pawns be the soul of the world too, also.'

She does not know what that means, but she swears to remember it.

The next moment, the door from the porch is flung open. Mr Kinzie reappears. He sweeps the beautiful walrus ivory pieces off the table. They scatter across the floor. 'You cheated,' he says to Gray Curls. 'And you'll pay for it.'

'No, he didn't,' says Eulalie. 'You're a bad man and I hope you die.'

Mrs Hunter: She broke out into speech again. Real speech, this time?

Mr Winship: That's what your grandmother was always told. I guess she must have been so upset that the words came tumbling out.

Mrs Hunter: She was a courageous soul, wasn't she, from an early age?

Mr Winship: Indeed. How one shudders, when one thinks of the life that little girl was destined to lead. How unfairly the dice would fall. And the irony is that in an honest world, her mistake would have changed everything.

Mrs Hunter: The agreement signed by Mr Kinzie was worthless?

Mr Winship: I reckon honorable people of that era would have respected such an accord, lawyers or no lawyers. But, in retrospect, it does seem naïve of your great-grandfather to have trusted a man like Mr Kinzie to keep his word. Perhaps he had no choice.

In any case, Kinzie went to St Joseph and came back a week or so later with the reinforcements that had been threatened. Your grandmother did not, thankfully, witness the violence that took place on the afternoon of his return. This time, Eulalie was kept locked in one of the bedrooms with her mother and grandmother. She heard, though, a terrible disturbance. And in the middle of the night, when all was quiet again, she finally managed to sneak out. She found Gray Curls slumped in his rocker on the porch, smoking a pipe, with a horn of whiskey on the table beside him. He had a bandage over one eye, and his legs were limp. He once mentioned in his journal that Kinzie had threatened to break them. He and his henchmen had done exactly that. Your great-grandfather spent the rest of his life hobbling about on crutches.

Mr Hunter: I ... I had no idea.

Mr Winship: Eulalie fetched a blanket and slept out on the porch with him. She awoke sometime later, when it was growing light, and saw Gray Curls asleep in the rocker, a line of caked blood down one cheek. She found a moist cloth in the kitchen and dabbed at the blood. Although she was as careful as could be, he woke up. He thanked her. She said she thought he had won the game with the bad man Mr Kinzie. So why had they come back and done this to him? His reply surprised her. 'My little Euladie,' he said. 'I always thinkin' there be justice in the world. But now I ain't sure. This din't happen 'cause I lost. With these people, this is what happens when you win.'

She was only a little girl, she said. It took her a long time to understand how that could possibly be.

[Pause]

Mrs Hunter: If you take on somebody more powerful than yourself and play by the rules and beat them, they annul the result.

Mr Winship: Exactly. They behave as if they are above the law.

Mrs Hunter: Then nothing has changed.

Mr Winship: It appears that Mr Kinzie did, though, expect one aspect of the agreement to remain valid. When he returned to Echicagou, he did not travel on behalf of those 'powerful men' in St Joseph. He came back with his own men on his own account, having duly persuaded his employers that the Pointe de Sable property was worthless. He forced Pointe de Sable to sign a bill of sale that listed all his land, livestock and household possessions — the document is still held in Wayne County Building, Detroit. The buyer was a Monsieur

Jean Lalime, the sale price was 6000 livres. The only exclusions, we discover from Pointe de Sable's journal, were twenty-seven paintings. Four years later, in 1804, Jean Lalime transferred ownership of the Pointe de Sable house and property to a new resident, Mr John Kinzie.

Mrs Hunter: Who called himself the founder of Chicago. Not a beginning that sets an encouraging tone for what follows.

Mr Winship: No. That's why I start my *Alternative History* with the story of that chess game. The more I think about it, the more its significance has come to haunt me. Today, Chicago has the reputation, does it not, of being the most corrupt and violent city in America? We historians like to search for patterns and starting points. It's in our blood. So when I look at modern Chicago and see it controlled by a web of crooked politicians and millionaires, with their crooked police and crooked ward bosses, I ask myself how we got here, and how and when it all began, and how things might have been different. And I am always drawn back to May 6, 1800 when Kinzie ignored the result of the chess game and used violence to impose his will, with the collusion — willing or not — of Jean Lalime. That was when the rot set in, and when Chicago's destiny was decided.

Mrs Hunter: And if Kinzie had kept to that agreement?

Mr Winship: A very different city might have evolved, in which all races lived and worked together, in which Indians, Easterners, Negroes and immigrants held each other in mutual respect, in which wealth was more fairly and evenly distributed. *[Laughs]* I'm becoming sentimental in my old age.

Mrs Hunter: Could we turn to another subject, also of special interest to me because of my grandmother's ... I do apologize, Professor.

Please give me a moment. I did not realize I would find it so difficult to talk about her. I am referring to what is called 'The Massacre Tree'.

Mr Winship: You mean Mr Pullman's monument?

Mrs Hunter: Yes. As we know this was unveiled last year and is intended by Mr Pullman — and I quote — to be 'an enduring monument, which should serve not only to perpetuate and honor the memory of the brave men and women and innocent children — the pioneer settlers who suffered here — but should also stimulate a desire among us, and those who are to come after us, to know more of the struggles and sacrifices of those who laid the foundation of the greatness of this city'. I have not yet seen this monument for myself. But I understand it is a large bronze sculpture set on a marble base and is said to have cost over $30,000.

Mr Winship: I have not seen the monument either, and I should add for the record that I do not intend to see it. Let me explain. First, shall we assume, for the sake of argument, that this statue is a work of art? I have no idea whether it is or it isn't. But if it is, why, you might ask, would I choose not to see it? After all, what else but art can cast a light, and often an uplifting one, on man's inhumanity to man? The obstacle for me, Mrs Hunter, is the sculpture's location. I believe this bronze sculpture captures but a single moment in time?

Mrs Hunter: It records the occasion when Chief Black Partridge was said to have saved the life of a settler called Mrs Helm.

Mr Winship: As was described in Juliette Magill Kinzie's very fanciful *Wau Bun: The 'Early Day' in the North West*. She was Mr Kinzie's daughter-in-law, even though the two of them never actually met. That aside, my point is this. I believe the only work of art that should be installed as a commemoration on the very ground where such an event took place must illuminate the bigger story in which it plays a part. Should it fail to do so, it dishonors the memory of the other participants, and traduces history. Too often, history is told from only one point of view and, given your description of this sculpture, there is little doubt that it will have fallen into this trap. A monument that aspires to be a memorial can take many forms, but when it comprises a single incident that is atypical — rather than typical — of what happened we can be certain that it has been chosen to make a point. This particular event — which may or may not have taken place — was doubtless approved by Mr Pullman because it promotes a version of history he finds agreeable. The sculpture is close to where he lives?

Mrs Hunter: I believe it is sited in front of his house.

Mr Winship: How times change. And the tree itself? Does that still stand?

Mrs Hunter: I don't know.

Mr Winship: Do not let me discourage you from going to see Mr Pullman's monument, Mrs Hunter, though I understand you may have personal reasons for staying away that have nothing to do with the sculpture itself. If you do go, I would be fascinated to hear how you find it.

Mrs Hunter: I wondered whether, in preparation, I might read your account of what happened that day, when they abandoned Fort Dearborn?

Mr Winship: You may, but I must warn you that your grandmother's memory was vivid, and her experience traumatic.

1894

The Massacre Tree

Arm in arm, you walk along Van Buren's icy sidewalk in the direction of the station. There is a bitter wind and the sky has that swollen grey look that portends snow. But it feels too cold for that today. You curse Tom for suggesting it would be good exercise to walk instead of taking a trolley, like any normal person. Whether he likes it or not, you are going to have a cup of something hot at the station, even if it means missing the next train.

But perhaps you're being unfair. Is blaming Tom merely an excuse? Last night you read Professor Winship's account of your grandmother Eulalie's meetings with Isaac Van Voorhis beneath the cottonwood tree. There followed a harrowing description of what happened during the retreat from Fort Dearborn. It might have been better not to have read it. You cannot get her words out of your head.

You grip Tom's arm tight as you wait to cross the intersection at Pacific Avenue. Van Buren Station is already visible, its central tower — similar to the dome of a cathedral — rising solid against the sky. The limestone has a frosty glint this morning. The clock tower says it is half-past two which means the hands must have frozen. A railroad station is, some say, a temple to progress. What would Pointe de Sable have thought, if he could have seen it? He would not even have known what a railroad was, let alone imagine a building could be built as high as this. And six storeys is nothing, you'd tell him. Some buildings have over twenty.

'What would Pointe de Sable have thought,' you ask Tom, 'if he were with us now?'

His cheeks and ears are the most brilliant pink with cold. It makes him look so young and handsome, you have an urge to kiss him.

'He'd probably be as confused as we would be, if we suddenly had to stand on this same street corner a hundred years from now. Assuming, that is, it still exists.'

'Do you think he would have liked it?'

'I think he'd have been amazed. But like it? No, I don't think so. Would you really swap a picturesque log cabin in the wilderness for all this noise and stink and corruption and ...?'

'Okay, okay, enough!' The truth is that both of you love this city, for all its irritations. 'We'd never have been able to survive back then. Can you imagine it? Handyman Tom Hunter sawing down a few trees and knocking together a log cabin?'

He laughs. 'You chose the wrong man.'

Nobody will notice, will they, not on a day like this? On tiptoe, you reach up to kiss his pink cheek. 'What would I do without you?' You stamp your feet. 'I'm frozen.'

There are dark icy patches on the road and a stream of carriages rattling past both ways, drivers wrapped up like Eskimos, their horses labouring through clouds of their own breath. Even though the road must be slippery, nobody seems to care. They don't slow down. You watch one buggy take the corner and push straight into the traffic on Van Buren, which forces another carriage to skid sideways. Why should the poor pedestrian always have to stop and look both ways, and risk her life crossing a street, and never the other way around? Perhaps you should begin a campaign in the *Tribune* to introduce rights for pedestrians. Establish places where wheels have to stop and feet are given priority.

You are about to ask Tom what he thinks about the idea when he gives a little tug on your arm, and you are both on the move. He guides you across the street. You lean into him as a blast of wind chooses that moment to barrel down Van Buren. It pins your skirts to the back of your legs.

'Almost there,' says Tom.

It is indeed true that you are almost there, that a cup of hot broth could shortly be making you feel human again, except that Tom stops outside the entrance to hand some coins to a vagrant, who is slumped on the ground against the wall. Oh God, Tom, must you? But of course he must because he always does, especially now, when these unfortunate people are everywhere. It was in the paper only today, that since the Fair closed another fifty thousand jobs have been lost in Chicago. The number is too large to comprehend. What do fifty thousand people suddenly do? How do they eat? Where do they sleep at night? The article was not encouraging. Either they go to soup kitchens, often run by Irish boodlers, or they steal, or they starve. It can be frightening, just the way some of them look at you. It's not me, you want to say, it's the very rich who should be helping out but never do. While Tom searches his pockets for coins, you try not to think about broth and attempt to work some feeling back into your fingertips. Your gloves are next to useless and your toes are dead.

Tom frowns. 'Oh dear. I must have forgotten my purse at home,' he says. 'Antje? I'm sorry. Would you mind?'

A few minutes later, you are cradling a cup of soup in both hands at a small window table in the restaurant, waiting for Tom to return with the tickets. He said he didn't want any. Sometimes he eats like a bird, sometimes like a horse. You relish the sensation of the hot soup sliding down your throat. Feeling begins to come back to your fingers. You gaze out the window at the passersby and admire the station's lofty roof and spacious concourse. It is a safe haven, a place where travellers can rest and recuperate. In a way, you think, that's exactly what Pointe de Sable's house was too. The first station in Chicago. In those days, though, the world beyond its gates was a wilderness. Today, it's this beautiful, infuriating city.

You flip the mass of copper leaves on the necklace that Professor Winship gave you when the interview was over. This is the first time you have ever worn it. Lighter than it looks, the leaves make a whispering sound when you move. It is protection you remember, according to the Potawatomie myth, against the monster who lives beneath the Lake. You wonder if your grandmother actually believed that. It makes you shiver when you try to visualise this necklace being warmed against your grandmother's skin, worn exactly as you are wearing it now.

Tom comes into view, at the front of the line in the ticket office across the concourse. On a big board nearby a man on a ladder is chalking up the time for the next train along the South Shore. 10.25. The clock inside the station is working. Ten minutes. Tom catches your eye and gives you a speaking look. Just enough time to finish the soup and catch the train.

It must be seven miles to Pullman, and your journey takes well over half-an-hour, including stops on the way. It is a slow train and an old car, with worn wooden seats and drafty windows and a door that keeps swinging open and slamming shut. The iron roof rattles whenever the wheels cross a set of points. Once out of the centre, the train shunts through a bleak industrial district full of railroad tracks and warehouses. The Lake comes back into view, pearled with breakers. The air begins to clear and through the dirty, fogged up window, a number of elegant mansions flit by. On the other side runs the river, the same river where Eulalie and her friend Cicely must have taken clothes for washing. Today, the water looks brown and motionless.

The train slows. You wrap up tight again, fix your scarf inside your coat and button up.

'How long do you think it would have taken them to walk here from the Fort?'

'I'd say it's no more than a couple of miles, as the crow flies,' says Tom. 'But it wouldn't have been a straight path through the trees. And then there were the sandhills.'

'Yes, of course. I'd forgotten. The sandhills. They must have been flattened.'

You are the only people to step out onto Prairie Avenue at the 18th Street stop. A frozen-looking porter in the Pullman uniform of hard grey cap and coat with lapels pulls up and asks if he can help. Tom explains where you want to go.

'No more than five minutes, sir,' says the porter, after he's given directions.

You step down onto Prairie Avenue. It is a wide paved road lined on each side by pine trees and poplars, with flowerbeds every few yards in which clusters of snowdrops are breaking out. You hear little bursts of birdsong. A livoried victoria clips past, along the paved surface, its two top-hatted passengers wrapped in blankets. They do not look your way. In summer, you think, this must be glorious. Neither you nor Tom has been here before. This is one of those enclaves whose reputation goes before it. Millionaires Row is what some people call it. It is said that Marshall Field was one of the first to build here because the air was clean, it was within a reasonable distance of his store, and there was no need to cross the river. Others, like Mr Pullman, then joined him.

You walk fast and in silence, take a left turn as directed, and follow a long stone wall behind which you catch glimpses of a garden decorated with statues and curious figurines. There is a large house beyond with absurd turrets on each corner.

'A Moorish castle?' you suggest.

Tom chuckles. 'Maybe it was left over at the end of the Fair.'

'I was just thinking about that porter at the station,' you say. 'You know why Mr Pullman likes to employ former slaves?'

'Certainly not out of the generosity of his heart. They're cheap?'

'Yes, but also because they're "properly humble". That's the expression he used.'

'One day,' Tom says, 'Mr Pullman will get his comeuppance.'

'I hope you're right.'

A few yards further on, at the next corner, you come to a standstill.

There it is.

The statue looks massive, even from fifty yards away. It stands in a compound protected by barbed wire, directly opposite a forbidding grey mansion that you guess must be Mr Pullman's residence. Beyond the statue lie empty grasslands that lead down to the Lake. A few other visitors are already there, walking around it.

Tom squeezes your arm. 'Are you all right?'

'Fine,' you say. But you stop and look up at him. 'How important do you think a place is? In a story, I mean?'

'Sweetheart,' he says, putting his arm around your shoulder. 'We don't have to go any further.'

'No, tell me, Tom. I want to know what you think. Does a story always have to be tied to a place?'

He frowns, and with one gloved hand he pushes his spectacles up onto his forehead. 'Well, I don't think you can remove place altogether and say, effectively, that anything could have happened anywhere. Place, though, obviously affects the mood and the action in some stories more than in others. Sometimes place is only a backdrop, but at other times it can be everything.'

You think about what Professor Winship said, and wonder how you should be feeling.

A few minutes later, you are at the gate. A white man in the Pullman uniform — presumably white because there's an exchange of money involved — comes out of a small wooden hut with two tickets, for which you have to pay fifty cents apiece.

'Professor Winship wouldn't approve,' says Tom. 'That Mr Pullman is recovering the money he spent on the statue by making us pay to look at it.'

'Also,' you add, 'making us pay anything at all to visit the site.' You stop, and hold Tom back too. 'I'm not feeling anything. Maybe because it's so wintry and frozen when we know it happened in the middle of summer.'

It has dawned on you how much you have been wanting this place to affect you. And yet the truth is that you are standing underneath a huge bronze statue on a bitterly cold day, with the Lake on one side and Millionaires Row on the other. It does not fit with the place you have imagined.

'I suspect it's not unusual, Antje,' says Tom. 'We all like the *idea* of investing place with significance. *To think it happened right here.* But when we actually visit the spot, especially when it's been changed out of all recognition, we can't make the connection. It's not the same place any more.'

'You mean it could be anywhere?'

He shakes his head. 'I'm not saying that. It's just that we need a prompt, something that directly links now with then.'

'Well, it's not this,' you say sadly, looking up.

The bronze figures are larger than life-size, set on a great marble pediment, which is what you had been led to expect. An almost-naked Indian brave stands, with tomahawk raised, over a defenceless, fully clothed American lady. At her feet, a child is trying to escape. The brave is about to kill her. But the intended murder is being thwarted by another Indian who stands over the woman in stylised heroic pose, his right hand raised. This is Chief Black Partridge. He has been made significantly taller and broader than the other Indian. And you're supposed to understand he has been civilised by the white man because he is partly clothed, in a pair of buckskin trousers, and he is carrying a rifle over his shoulder.

'Notice that there's not an American soldier in sight,' says Tom.

'Indian braves went around murdering innocent white women,' you say in a flat voice, 'but it's possible for even savages to be inculcated with civilised, noble traits by the white man. The reformed Indian proves the efficacy of this treatment by saving the white woman and her child from a brutal savage.'

Tom nods. 'A notion that a man like Mr Pullman would be happy to promote.'

You remember with fondness the Old Magic Man you met in the Indian Camp when you were a child and how dignified he had been, even as he saw his own death approaching. He had needed no civilising instruction by white men. Rather the opposite.

'Remember what Professor Winship said?' you say. 'That a memorial should illuminate the bigger story in which it plays a part? If it doesn't, it dishonours the memory of the other participants. And it traduces history.'

You step back to allow a couple with a Kodak 'snapshot' camera to take photographs of themselves in front of the statue. That image will end up in their house, you think, proof that they visited a place where a terrible battle of some kind was fought a long time ago when this was still a wilderness.

'You know me,' says Tom. 'I don't believe facts need to be precise, as long as the gist is true. But this statue is a deliberate distraction from everything — from the gist, from the facts, from the truth. It's like using perfume to cover up a bad smell.'

You look at him. This has clearly touched a nerve.

'Let's go,' you say. 'I'm frozen and I've seen quite enough.' You need another cup of something hot after this excursion. 'When we get back to Van Buren,' you say, 'I'm going to make you drink something hot too. And we're not walking home.'

You move around the statue, out of the way of the people taking photographs, and head back towards the gate.

But you do not go far. 'Wait!'

A dead tree stands near the wall between Mr Pullman's garden and the park. The trunk, to which a few crooked branches still cling, is gnarled and shrunken. In what looks like an exhausted last fling, it forks into two stumps at the top.

You pause, arm in arm, but neither of you says a word. Tom, probably, is wondering the same as you, whether the dead tree might once have been the cottonwood. It would be better, you decide, not to know. There is something indecent about imagining it might have been. And who, after all this time, would know?

In silence, you walk back towards the station.

Preposterous Tales

A review of *Chicago: An Alternative History 1800–1900*
by Professor Milton Winship (A.C. McClurg
& Co., Chicago, 1902), published in 'North American
Review', June 1902.

The very title of Mr Winship's rambling, labyrinthine tome about
Chicago in the nineteenth century hints at the confusion that lies
in store for the unsuspecting reader. His *opus*, claims the author, is
both 'Alternative' and a 'History'. An 'Alternative', one wonders, to
what? Any attempt to compare Mr Winship's book with the work
of serious historians who have addressed key periods of the century
gone by would soon founder. For a text to be categorized as 'History'
implies, does it not, that attention has been paid to historical truth
and accuracy? Anyone, then, who ignores facts or, even worse,
blithely distorts facts for his own 'Alternative' purposes, has no right
to attach the label of 'History' to his offering.

   To read Mr Winship's motley, meandering collection of half-
truths, digressions and dilettante musings from beginning to end,
is an endeavor I would not wish on anyone. I have worked through
the long, dark nights on his typescript, only to prove the lie to that

otherwise admirable proverb 'in all labor there is profit'. On this occasion, I regret to report that none is to be gained. Mr Winship abjures the triumphs of our nobler forebears in favor of some whimsical tales about a cast of decidedly second-rate fellows.

Let me give an example that is fresh in your reviewer's mind. I shall address the final chapter of the book. Proof, readers, that I persevered until the bitter end! And because I doubt few will cross that finishing line, perhaps I can offer you the following courtesy. I shall illustrate the duplicity of the author's approach while relating in more detail than you might want, how this maladroit volume staggers, huffing and puffing, towards its shabby, improbable end.

I should mention, in fairness to Mr Winship, that he occasionally seems to remember that a book, like a building, needs a solid foundation. Whenever this notion re-occurs to him, he reverts to reflections about the land on which Chicago has been built. Hence, he starts at the beginning of the nineteenth century with the first of many a preposterous — to use his own word — tale. This one is about a mulatto trader involved in what Mr Winship claims was the first recorded land sale in Chicago. Not only does this lead him to the startling conclusion that this itinerant deserves to be called the founder of Chicago (the venerable Mr Ogden must be turning in his grave), he also strays into banal reflections about a board game. He claims (I do not jest) that the destiny of Chicago would 'hinge' on a game of chess.

We are treated to a stream of side stories that touch on real estate speculation, balloon houses, canal digging, railroads, sewage systems, agricultural machines, the timber trade, the Great Fire, the futures market, skyscrapers and the World's Fair. And while attempting, in this haphazard way, to document how the empty swamps and prairies were peopled and exploited over our first century, he also pokes his nose into the city's political, business and social affairs. He regularly chooses the wrong protagonists, thereby insulting our city's true visionaries and heroes, and credits his bumbling cast with achievements they do not deserve. Apparently, it was mad John Wright who not only brought the railroads to Chicago, but also revolutionized American agriculture. And how Mr Winship lavishes attention on the weaker sex, appropriating for them competencies and strengths far beyond their capabilities. In his fanciful picture of the city there are, can you believe, female photographers and female journalists. Worst of all, he insinuates that many of our leading businessmen and political leaders have been engaged in corrupt practices. Every city has the odd rotten apple. But why does Mr Winship imply that Chicago has a barrel full?

Enough of the charges. Let me now provide the evidence. To do so, I shall refer simply to that final 'Alternative' chapter, in which Mr Winship excels in all the aforesaid techniques.

Students of Chicago history will know that the provision of clean water has bedeviled the city for decades. For most of the century, Lake Michigan was both the source of our drinking water and the repository for our waste, with predictably dire consequences. An engineer named Ellis S. Chesbrough tried to solve the problem, first by tunneling beneath the Lake and then by enlarging the first 'canal' in a flawed attempt to reverse the flow of the Chicago River. I am sure the poor man tried his best but simply got his sums wrong (a fact from which Mr Winship chooses to distract us with one of his grubby asides about purported political corruption).

The magnificent new Chicago Sanitary and Ship Canal, built parallel to the original Chesbrough version, was officially opened on January 19, 1900, covering a distance of twenty-eight miles and connecting the Chicago and Des Plaines rivers. As promised, it has permanently reversed the flow of the Chicago River, thereby ensuring that the city's waste is no longer deposited in our Lake but, instead, flushed into the Mississippi and thence to the Gulf of Mexico. Readers will also recall with pride that the canal is the largest and most advanced sanitary engineering project that has ever been constructed, anywhere in the world. They would therefore assume that an honest, responsible and patriotic historian would praise the canal's technical feats and record the extraordinary exertions and achievements of the characterful men behind it. How upset they will be to discover that Mr Winship chooses to cover this triumphant moment in the annals of our city with a squalid little tale of intrigue about a buildings inspector, an alderman, a photographer and a journalist.

Mr Winship's version of events begins with an accident. In early December 1899, a buildings inspector slips and falls to his death off the top of a tenement block on West 60th Street in the 18th Ward while in the process of carrying out a safety inspection. The coroner records a verdict of accidental death and the case is closed. Some days later, though, the wife of the dead man makes contact with one of those female journalists on whom Mr Winship dotes. 'Mrs Swanson,' he writes, 'presented Mrs Hunter with a photograph taken on the day of the accident.'

It was a Kodak snapshot that might have been taken in any of the West Side slums. Pictured was a large tenement building with windows either boarded up or open to the elements. The building was not, though, abandoned. At some of the open windows, there were faces staring out, apparently unaware that a photograph was being taken.

The snapshot showed that the building was being raised from three stories to six. Two figures were visible on the incomplete top floor. In the foreground stood a slender man, his hat pulled down low, who seemed to be writing in a notebook. That was Mr Swanson, the buildings inspector. The other man was further away, his image more grainy and indistinct. What made the photograph striking, what added tension to it, was the fact that — as Mrs Swanson pointed out to Mrs Hunter — the second man was in the process of throwing something at her husband. Moments after taking the photograph, she witnessed her husband fall to his death.

Mrs Swanson alleged that it was no accident, but a case of murder. Her husband, she said, was experienced in working at heights. He had helped to build some of the most famous skyscrapers in Chicago, and it was only because the Depression forced him out of business that he was hired as an inspector. He would never have slipped of his own accord. The projectile must have struck her husband and knocked him over the edge.

Readers may be wondering, as was I, how on earth this incident could have any connection with the opening of the canal. A tenuous link is established a few lines later, with a digression about a column Mrs Hunter is preparing for the *Chicago Daily Tribune*. We are told this will not just be her final article of the year, but also of her career. With her sixtieth birthday in the offing, she has decided it is time to retire. The editor has requested that she use the column to make a series of predictions about the twentieth century. Mrs Hunter, Mr Winship is keen to point out, dislikes this task because she is a journalist for whom 'facts have always been paramount'. That does not, though, spare us from hearing what those predictions are, affording Mr Winship the opportunity to introduce Mrs Hunter's husband into the narrative. He is Mr Tom Hunter, editor and contributor to an arcane literary magazine called *The Dial*.

No doubt, then, Mr Hunter was behind some of the more fantastical ideas that would find their way into his wife's column. These include skyscrapers standing one hundred floors high, trains traveling at more than a hundred miles an hour, the establishment of universal women's suffrage, minimum wages of $5 an hour, equal health care for all citizens and, believe it or not, the use of fingerprints to solve crimes. Finally, citing the Sanitary and Ship Canal, Mrs Hunter predicts that the twentieth century will be an era of clean water for all. And so, in the nick of time, we are reminded that this is indeed supposed to be a chapter about the canal.

Do not, though, be fooled into thinking that our arrival at that engineering wonder is imminent. You will have gathered by now that Mr Winship does not write as the crow flies. First, we have to go back to the tenement building from which Mr Swanson, the buildings inspector, fell to his death. Sadly, another tragedy is about to take place there. Overnight, on December 15, the building collapses. There are eighteen dead, fourteen wounded, (details that have been corroborated by a variety of sources). According to Mr Winship, Mrs Hunter visits the site and is told that the building was being used as both accommodations and an illegal factory for about eighty recent immigrants, mostly Italian peasants and Russian Jews. When she hears that the building is said to belong to Alderman 'Burner' Brody, she requests an urgent audience with the alderman in his office at city hall.

Presumably because Mr Winship believes it will help bolster his research credentials, he includes a copy of Mrs Hunter's private journal entry about that meeting. This hardly furthers his cause. She comes across as a bitter, vindictive woman; the kind of cynical modern reporter — and a <u>female</u> one at that — who, beset by feelings of her own inferiority, casts anyone who has attained a position of power and influence in the worst possible light.

[THE FOLLOWING EXTRACT FROM *CHICAGO: AN ALTERNATIVE HISTORY, 1800–1900* WAS NOT INCLUDED IN THIS BOOK REVIEW BUT, IN THE INTERESTS OF BALANCE, WE HAVE CHOSEN TO QUOTE IT HERE IN FULL.]

Burner Brody: Controls the 18th Ward. Protege of 'King Mike' McDonald and J. Patrick O'Cloke. Associates with Boodler Johnny Powers (19th Ward), Hinky Dink Kenna, Bathhouse

John Coughlin (1st Ward). Runs a protection racket, owns saloons, *bagnios*, tenement buildings and an elevator. Often accused of running corners, but has always escaped charges. Drinks and gambles with the chief of police, plays golf with the mayor at the Lake Forest Club. Arranges jobs for men in his ward on the streetcars/building sites. Pays for 18th Ward funerals and buys the flowers. Provides turkeys at Christmas. Keeps poorest constituents in coal over the winter (hence, 'Burner').

Called into the lion's den, at last. The office is bright with electric lights. The carpet sinks beneath my heels. A stench of cigar smoke and whiskey. The walls are covered in photographs. Burner Brody is in every one of them. Also a massive larger-than-life portrait of him. Crude beyond belief. Reminds me of a giant hard-boiled egg propped up in an egg cup. Eyebrows are almost hairless, bald pate is oval-shaped, bloated florid cheeks, jowls swing smooth and low, and he has no neck.

The man himself is seated behind a desk the size of a billiards table, wedged into a dark green leather wing chair. He begins talking about the ghastly portrait. The reason he's depicted wearing a green jacket with an emerald stick-pin in his tie and a green sash over one shoulder is 'in memory of my dear father and out of respect for his love of the Old Country. Forgive me my maudlin mood this afternoon, Mrs Hunter,' he says, 'but you will understand my grief at such an unforeseeable tragedy.' Was it really unforeseeable, I try to ask, given the poor state of the tenement building …? But he does not let me finish.

He points to the portrait. 'That baseball bat I'm holding,' he says, 'was signed by Cap Anson. The greatest player the White Stockings ever had. Only twelve of those bats in the world, and

I own every one of them. You do remember Cap Anson, don't you? I'll send you the book I wrote about him.' He's written a book? I rather doubt it. I tell him not to bother sending it because I'm no baseball fan. 'No, no, it will be my pleasure. And if it's not to your taste, I'm sure your husband will like it. He's a bookish man, I believe. Please sit down.' Why should he know who Tom is, and what he does? Don't like that. Has he put Pinkertons on us?

As he drones on about the portrait, I notice that in real life he has a scar running like a worm from the edge of his left eye towards the top of the ear. An authentic touch for a thug. But the scar doesn't feature in the picture. Obviously not a wound for which the alderman wants to be remembered in these days of respectability.

Not difficult to understand the appeal of his deep, husky voice and what a soothing effect it must have on a poor immigrant who only half understands what he's saying. Everything will be all right, its tone seems to imply, as long as you do what I say. I will look after you, I will stand by your side through life's twists and turns, I will find you work, I will bring you food if you're desperate and coal in the winter when you're cold. Just make sure you vote for me at the next election.

The flattery and lies begin. What a pleasure it is to meet one of the finest journalists of our age, a true child of Chicago and champion of the same just causes for which he has battled throughout his political life. 'If only we could persuade our fellow citizens to believe as we do, that we must eliminate corruption and raise the daily pay of the working man to a fair level and clean up the levee and guarantee equality for all our

sisters, we would be the greatest city in America, the greatest city
in the world.' How excruciating.

'Let me tell you about my father.' *I'd rather you didn't,*
I think. 'His story, and what happened last night, are closely
connected.' Indeed? The logic escapes me, Alderman. 'Do
you know what my father had to do, when he first arrived in
America? Dig a canal. Fifteen hours a day with his bare hands, at
less than a dollar a day, fed on nothing but beans and grits, and
forced to sleep in a leaking, mosquito-ridden pine-board shack.'
He's shouting at me now, as though it is my fault. 'And why am
I telling you this? Because Mochta Bruaideadh, God Bless Him,
never lived to see the opening of the canal he'd dug. And why?
Because of an accident, an accident as unexpected and cruel as
the one that brought down the building on West 60th Street and
robbed those poor people of their closest family and friends. The
building in which my father died did not collapse. It caught on
fire. That is why, in his honor, I have pledged that nobody in my
ward will ever be short of coal in winter. You see why I'm telling
you this, Mrs Hunter?' *Because you are trying to cover up what
really happened. In your Old Country, Alderman, they'd call it a
load of blarney.* 'I'm telling you because I want you to appreciate
that I understand their pain. I have known that very same pain
myself. When accidents happen, we must club together.'

He dabs his eyes with a pressed white handkerchief. 'There was
a poet from Great Blasket, whom my father revered, called Old
Conn. And one of Old Conn's sayings was this: Do unto others
as you would have them do unto you.' The man's insufferable.
Even trying to pass off a common proverb as the wisdom of an
old Irish poet. Now he's smiling, as if all the bad news is out of
the way. 'I started out with nothing too, the same as my poor

father. But I think you'll agree I've made something of myself, Mrs Hunter.'

I point out that for one man to die in a fire, tragic accident though it must have been, is hardly the same as eighteen innocents being crushed to death because an unsafe tenement building collapsed on top of them. His smile vanishes. 'The building collapsed because it was illegally occupied by squatters, Mrs Hunter.' Is he denying, I say, that those 'squatters' were employed by him? He laughs. 'What a ridiculous idea.'

I have another go. Mr Swanson was a highly experienced builder who fell off the top of the very same unsafe tenement block he was investigating. Didn't that make his so-called accident look suspicious?

No laughter this time. Brody bristles. Tells me to remember my place (i.e. as a woman) and to mind my tone of voice, or he will make sure I never have access to city hall again. 'Accidents are always happening in a big city,' he says. 'It's a fact of life.'

I try one last throw of the dice. Show him Mrs Swanson's snapshot and tell two white lies. First — the man in the background has been identified as Mr Dermot O'Leary, his building contractor. Second — Mr O'Leary has a brick in his hand that he is in the process of throwing at Mr Swanson.

Brody claims it's impossible to see anything clearly in the photograph, and I am wasting his time. 'I am disappointed in you, Mrs Hunter. Do come back if you have something serious to say.' I'm already at the door when he tosses out a warning, dressed up as another homily from Old Conn the Poet. 'Neither luck nor good fortune ever came to anything that runs in people's talk,' he says. 'Do bear that in mind. Good day.'

I have the last word. Tell him I've checked the records.

I know he's the owner of that building.

By now, dear readers, you must feel mightily disoriented. I know I do. Why is Mr Winship taking us on such an extensive detour? When will he remember we have journeyed to this remote and distant chapter because we want to celebrate the opening of the Sanitary and Ship Canal?

The story about the tenement building staggers on. In her *Chicago Daily Tribune* column the next day Mrs Hunter writes in a provocative fashion: 'According to survivors interviewed by this reporter, the tenement building was used not only for accommodation, but also as a factory for manufacturing items of clothing. Conditions were abysmal. There were no drains or fireplaces.' She alleges that just as Chicago has the right to be proud of its magnificent downtown skyscrapers, so too it should be deeply ashamed of buildings such as this one. Finally, she calls for the City Building Inspector's Office to close off the site and to re-open its investigation. She demands an inquest into the tragedy. Those individuals found responsible, whether willfully or through negligence, should be tried before the chief justice.

The next day, we hear that a package is delivered at home to Mrs Hunter. It contains a ceremonial baseball bat signed by the legendary Cap Anson, along with a copy of a book on baseball written by Alderman Brody. The book was not actually written by him, Mr Winship hastens to point out, but was penned on his behalf. He includes a message that he says Mrs Hunter found on the flyleaf, allegedly written by the alderman himself. *Mrs Hunter, have you forgoten what Old Conn the Poet says, about what runs in people's talk?*

In baseball, if you don't play by the rules, you can't stay on the field. Take this as a worning.

Mr Winship's plot, I realize, is thickening, but to what end? And how much of what he reports as being 'factual' can be verified? Shortly, we will consider this in more detail. Suffice to say that, regarding this particular incident, Mrs Hunter was indeed found to be in possession of a Cap Anson baseball bat. But because no case would ever reach court, it has never been proven under oath how that baseball bat came into her possession, nor whether the misspelt flyleaf message is authentic or a fabrication by Mr Winship.

The next thing we know, Mrs Hunter has contrived to meet with Mr Brody's building contractor, his employee and boyhood friend, Dermot O'Leary. I suppose one must concede that the lady is persistent. Mr O'Leary is reluctant to speak out against his boss, which is what she desperately needs him to do so that she can build a story. Frustrated, she decides to fall back on an age-old reporter's technique. Burner Brody, she says, has alleged that Mr O'Leary has a professional history of cutting corners to save time and costs. 'He has also identified you as the man in the photograph with a brick in your hand.' The article containing these allegations, she tells him, will be published in the next day's *Tribune*.

Mr O'Leary, though visibly agitated, denies everything. Mrs Hunter tells him she will postpone publication of the article for one day.

That evening, we are told, Mrs Hunter discusses the story with her husband. He wants to know how far the 'projectile' — brick or otherwise — was thrown. He points out that if it knocked Mr Swanson over the edge, it must have been thrown hard and on target.

She shows him Mrs Swanson's snapshot.

'Maybe Burner Brody himself is the second man,' he suggests.

Mrs Hunter says that is highly unlikely. She explains that when a buildings inspector carries out a visit, there is never any prior notification. Not even the inspector knows where he is going until the last moment. So it would have been an extraordinary coincidence if Burner Brody had happened to be there.

'Unless he got a tip-off,' insists her husband.

'Even if he did, he's hardly going to murder the inspector. He's an alderman. If the report is negative, there are people he can talk to in the right places. He's got time on his side.'

'Perhaps what happened had nothing to do with the inspection. Or, let me rephrase that, perhaps it had very little to do with it. Have you thought of that?' Mr Hunter pushes his spectacles up his forehead. 'Maybe they knew each other. Maybe there was an old grudge. And if it's really not an accident and the alderman pushes the inspector over the edge, that means they must have a history.'

Do you see, dear readers, what has happened? Mr Winship writes not only as if he is present in the house that evening with Mr and Mrs Hunter (he is not), he also pretends that he knows (he cannot possibly know) what they say. And the more we read, the more we find ourselves being drawn into this 'Alternative' world where our author suddenly has the ability to read people's minds and transcribe their conversations. It is not unlike participation in a séance, with Mr Winship as our medium.

We must resist the lure of such narrative trickery and remember that this is no parlor game, but our living, breathing history. And what on earth has happened to the canal?

―――――

Mr O'Leary visits Mrs Hunter the next day in her office. He looks haggard and, she decides, scared. Nothing like this has ever happened before, he tells her, even if it's true that — always on the orders of the boss — he's saved a few cents here and there. Nobody was ever killed, even if there had been the odd accident. This time he told the boss — no, he begged him — not to build that high without putting in more foundations. Nobody should have been allowed inside while they were working on it. An accident was inevitable. She had to believe him, that he tried to persuade the boss to let him make it safer, to put in the proper supports. 'But Burner's a miser and a bully,' complains O'Leary. 'And he always makes me take the blame. Same with the elevator. You know I had to do a spell in Joliet once, so O'Cloke could get him off for fixing a corner?' And then he says, in a phrase that puzzles Mrs Hunter, 'He's got the memory of an elephant, ain't he, the boss? And Mr Swanson, it's true he was a feckin' Scandi, ain't it? Excuse the language.'

Before Mrs Hunter can either question or caution him, Mr O'Leary reaches into the bag at his shoulder and takes out a package, wrapped in brown paper and tied with string. He drops it on Mrs Hunter's desk. 'He told me to burn it. But I didn't.'

The next moment, he is gone.

Mrs Hunter considers opening the package there and then. But she decides, on balance, it would be safer to take it home, away from prying eyes in the office. She goes by streetcar and, after alighting at her stop, begins to walk home. That is when she realizes she is being followed by two men in dark greatcoats and slouch hats. She stops and confronts them.

'We know everything about you, Mrs Hunter,' says one of them. 'That wasn't a good idea, to meet with Mr O'Leary behind the back of the boss. Don't do it again.'

'Take a message to Mr Brody,' says our doughty heroine (for we can all agree that this is what Mr Winship has turned her into). 'Tell him he won't get away with this.'

'Is that all, Mrs Hunter?'

'No, that is not all. Tell him that I don't care what Old Conn said. I shall make d...d certain that what runs in people's talk is the truth. Is that understood?'

The bravado, readers! Mrs Hunter watches as her two would-be assailants stroll off along the macadam into the darkness, in boots that 'clip the road like crackers'. Her legs, she then realizes, are trembling. She turns to go home, breaking into a run, to seek comfort from her husband.

She is so distraught, in fact, that she does not even remember to open the package given to her by Mr O'Leary until the following morning. When she does, she finds a ceremonial baseball bat inside, smashed in two, signed by Cap Anson. The bat is stained with what she decides, in her wisdom, resembles dried blood.

In that afternoon's *Tribune,* she sees a notice.

Man dies in streetcar incident

A man was run over by a streetcar at 5.13pm yesterday afternoon in an incident at the junction of Clark and Kinzie Streets. The 56-year-old gentleman was pronounced dead on arrival at St Isidore's Hospital. He has been named as Mr Dermot O'Leary, resident in the 18th Ward. Alderman Brody has expressed his condolences to the surviving members of Mr O'Leary's family, and has undertaken to provide flowers at the funeral.

That same evening, Mrs Hunter is working at home, finalizing the column for the *Tribune* on her predictions for the twentieth century, when a brick is thrown through her window. Tied around the brick is a message.

YOU'LL END UP LIKE HIM. NO MORE WORNINGS

A reviewer, however strongly he holds a point of view, must also have the manners to stand back on occasion and act as an impartial referee. By this stage in the narrative, when the reader is beginning to feel doubtful that the author can ever find his way back to those twenty-eight miles of canal, there is a welcome shift towards the light. The first sign that it may be forthcoming is to be found in the quantity of verifiable facts that have begun to impregnate the text. Even though these facts will only be confirmed to the ordinary reader at the very end, there would seem to be no harm done, for illustrative purposes, in mentioning them now.

Fact — Mrs Hunter was indeed in possession of a 'Cap Anson' baseball bat, broken in two.

Fact — Mr O'Leary died in a streetcar accident, as indicated in the *Chicago Daily Tribune* notice.

Fact — Mrs Hunter produced a receipt from a glazier, dated December 31, 1899, for the emergency replacement of a window at her home.

Fact — Burner Brody's spelling can sometimes be erratic.

Fact — Sanitary and Ship Canal Trustees will be tipped off that the state of Missouri is preparing a court injunction to prevent the opening of the canal, scheduled for January 19, 1900, claiming that the reversal of the Chicago River will pollute their own water supply.

Fact — To beat the injunction, a top secret private opening of the Sanitary and Ship Canal will be arranged for dawn on January 2, 1900 on the basis that the canal, once it is open, will be impossible to close.

Fact — Mrs Hunter will be one of only two reporters invited to the secret opening.

Before we attend that opening, there is one final stop to make. Mr Winship insists that we return to the séance room and listen to more flights of fancy from Mr Hunter.

'My guess,' he says, 'is that Burner Brody gets a tip-off there's going to be an inspection. He takes along one of his precious baseball bats as a gift to bribe the inspector. For Gus Swanson, this is just another day, another dangerous, illegal construction site he will have evacuated and sealed off before a tragedy occurs. He's up there on the roof making notes for his report. Brody appears. Maybe they exchange a few words. Brody probably hails him: "Top of the morning to you, Inspector! How is your report coming along? Everything in order?" Perhaps Swanson looks up and greets him, before returning to his notes. Maybe he doesn't look up at all. The point is that Brody recognizes him, but Swanson doesn't recognize Brody. And that merely exacerbates the problem.

Whatever happened between them in the past was so unimportant to Swanson that he's forgotten about it. Being on the receiving end of something is always more memorable, though, isn't it? Brody doesn't just remember, the memory makes him absolutely furious, so furious that he picks up a brick or a hammer or ...'

Mrs Hunter shakes her head. 'Nobody holds a grudge that deeply,' she says. 'And nobody in his position would act so impulsively.'

'Not unless he's a psychopath.'

End of séance. Curtain falls.

Good news, patient reader. We have negotiated the maze of Mr Winship's concluding chapter and arrived at 'a little-known, little-visited, section of the Sanitary and Ship Canal in South Chicago on the bitterly cold winter morning of January 2, 1900. It is beginning to get light. About a dozen men, doing their best to keep warm, are gathered around an upturned handcart whereon stands Mr Wenter, President of the Board of Trustees of the Sanitary and Ship Canal.' From this cart, claims Mr Winship, Mr Wenter is delivering exactly the same speech that he would make two weeks later at the official opening to thousands of grateful, cheering citizens.

'"This is the most important day in the history of Chicago," declares Mr Wenter, "the most important day since the land was first settled in what is now the *last* century." *[Laughter]* "We have built the finest city in America, gentlemen. Over one and a half million citizens now live where, one hundred years ago, there were none. We are second in size only to New York. We are more than twice as big as St Louis." *[Cheers and applause]* "The Sanitary and Ship Canal is an engineering marvel. It is the largest excavation project ever undertaken by mankind. It will reverse the Chicago River. Welcome, gentlemen, to a new age of fresh air, of clean water, of good health."'

The speech continues for some time in this vein. 'When Mr Wenter's stock of rousing adjectives and adverbs has been exhausted,' reports Mr Winship, 'he approaches the flimsy dam that holds apart the waters of the Chicago River and the new canal.

'He raises his hat, a signal for the two men at the base of the dam to light their fuses and scramble back up their ladders to safety. Mr Wenter hurls a bottle at the dam wall that, ominously, fails to break on impact. The fuses below fizzle about like skittish cigarette butts until the powder catches. Blast follows blast, clouds of smoke billow forth and the odor of gunpowder fills the air, temporarily overwhelming the putrid stink of the river. They wait expectantly for the sound of sighing timber and the rush of breaking waters.

'To no avail. When the smoke clears, the dam becomes all too visible again, scalded here and there, but otherwise very much as it stood before.

'There is no more gunpowder. Everyone is bitterly cold and wants to go home. Nobody knows what to do next. The injunction from Missouri to prevent the opening could be delivered at any moment. This is the situation that prevails when, to Mrs Hunter's surprise and unease, Alderman Burner Brody appears. She neither knew he was there, nor that he had any involvement with the canal. The alderman mounts the upturned handcart. He raises his hands for quiet. "Gentlemen, gentlemen," he calls out. "Fellow trustees. Your attention, please.'"

Mr Winship's unwieldy epic is drawing to a close. I said I would go to the bitter end in this review but, on reflection, I fail to see the purpose it would serve. What happens after Alderman Brody mounts the handcart, as related by Mr Winship, has never been proven in a court of law. Dear readers, you have been warned. You venture into the final pages at your own risk.

Instead, I ask you to step back from the brink and consider the slant of Mr Winship's presentation. Mr Wenter is making the magnificent speech that would be heard by thousands and reported across the world at the official opening a couple of weeks later. But what is Mr Winship's setting for its delivery? An upturned handcart, a frozen audience of a dozen (albeit a distinguished dozen), a dull and ordinary section of the canal, an unsociable time of day, a screen of secrecy, a failed attempt to blow up the dam. In a word, ignominy.

Having plowed my way through the thousand-odd pages of this *Alternative History* I am wise by now to the authorial techniques at work, so this damp squib of an ending to the century comes as no surprise. Mr Winship has a tendency to shy away from celebrating great civic achievements and, as soon as a situation arises that is soured by unanticipated setbacks, however minor and inconsequential, he stands ready to exploit them.

Everything in this account, therefore, must be treated with a large dose of salt. His only source for what happened at the secret opening is his favorite female journalist — Mrs Hunter. Mr Winship is doubtless an intelligent man who is fond of Chicago. Why, then, does he not unreservedly applaud the remarkable triumph of engineering and mastery over Nature that the Sanitary and Ship

Canal represents? Why not bring our extraordinary first century to a close with the gay crowds, the flags and brass bands and ticker tape parades of those joyous celebrations staged on January 19, 1900? Would that not have been the proper thing to do? Is it asking too much, to tell the truth? Is it beyond him to furnish future generations of Americans with the historical record they deserve?

Instead, Mr Winship chooses to direct our attention away from that large, colorful canvas and take us into yet another of his little *culs-de-sac* of intrigue, populated by the minor characters he prefers, spiced up with the kind of séance talk that has no place in a serious work of history. I rest my case.

Let me just say this. If we entrust our past to the likes of Mr Winship, we shall never know the truth about anything. And that is not only intolerable, it is also, like so many of the tales in his *Alternative History*, quite preposterous.

Readers, I urge you to avoid this book.

My Lifelong Obsession

(Extract from *Chicago: An Alternative History 1800–1900* by Professor Milton Winship, University of Chicago, A.C. McClurg & Co., 1902)

'What's wrong with fire?' roars Burner Brody from atop the upturned handcart. 'We can burn down that d...d wall!'

There is a round of 'Here, here' and 'Bravo Burner!'.

He gives orders. Firewood is to be brought from the nearby pine cabin settlement and spread along the base of the wall. It will then be doused in kerosene.

'Mrs Hunter!' he calls out.

Despite the fact that she has been stalked by Burner Brody's henchmen, and recently threatened with the same fate as Mr O'Leary, she steps forward. Plucky, seasoned reporter though she is, even Mrs Hunter can have no notion of what lies in store.

Burner Brody announces that this is 'my good friend from the *Tribune*, Mrs Hunter'. Perhaps his fellow trustees do not know that yesterday, in the *Tribune*, Mrs Hunter predicted that we are embarking on a 'century of clean water', thanks to the Sanitary and Ship Canal. His words prompt an outbreak of applause. Mr Brody suggests it might therefore be fitting, given Mrs Hunter's public support for the project, that she be invited to light the fire that will bring down the dam and open the canal.

His fellow trustees find him charmingly, engagingly persuasive. Of course, they agree. It is a capital idea, Burner! An all-fired notion! Darned appropriate!

Mrs Hunter, on the other hand, is rendered unusually mute. She would like to declare that the man beside her is responsible for murder. She suspects that Burner Brody ordered the assassination of Mr Swanson, that he was responsible for the deaths of eighteen immigrants who were also his employees, and that he was behind the 'streetcar accident' that killed his old associate Dermot O'Leary. She wants to say these things, but as yet she lacks hard evidence.

Burner Brody takes her by the arm. He leads her across the frosty earth towards the dam wall. She feels nervous and vulnerable as she stands beside this huge, bearish man in his long black coat and high boots and wide-brimmed hat. It is exposed up there. The wind goes through her coat. The early fog is lifting to reveal a featureless prairie landscape beyond the far bank of the canal. The sky is spanned by a dull, gray light. The dam itself surprises her. It is nothing more than a wall of planks nailed together, about thirty feet across and twelve feet high, supported by a dozen or so lengths of timber, pitched at an angle in the bank of earth that separates the two bodies of water. The men sent down there look as though they have almost finished placing stacks of timber along its base. She turns the other way, towards the river. The surface is still, covered in a yellowish scum. The stench, even at this frigid hour, is revolting.

Burner Brody says he hopes there are no hard feelings, that as far as he is concerned the misunderstandings between them are now in the past, and as long as she doesn't make any more 'mistakes' he is happy to consider everything else to be water under the bridge.

'I admire your work, Mrs Hunter. That is why I made special representations to the Board, that you should be one of only two reporters allowed to come here today.' He only did that, she knows, to show he can fix anything, that he's untouchable. 'Remember I told you, Mrs Hunter, how my father dug the first canal with his bare hands? How proud he would be, don't you think, if he knew his son was a *trustee*.'

He takes off his hat and waves it to the men below as a signal to pour on the kerosene.

Mrs Hunter turns towards him. His bare head seems to be glowing. 'What happened to Mr O'Leary?' she asks.

'It was most unfortunate and out of character,' he replies, 'that he should step in front of a streetcar like that. Between you and me, I have wondered whether it might not have been deliberate, in the light of what has since become known about his affairs.'

She gives him a 'speaking look'.

'You didn't know?' he says. 'Dermot was not only a crooked building contractor, he was also the owner of the tenement building that collapsed on West 60th Street.'

With her fingertips, she touches the copper necklace she is wearing. 'Mr O'Leary did not own that building, Mr Brody. You do. You can't deny it.'

He grins. 'Oh, but I can, Mrs Hunter. If you care to look at those records again, you'll discover that the facts have changed. Poor Dermot bought the building off me shortly before he began — recklessly, in my view — to add those new stories.' He gestures towards the dam wall. 'And now, shall we ...?'

She holds his look. 'I'll get you in the end, Mr Brody,' she vows.

'Oh, please, Mrs Hunter. Surely you must know by now that life isn't a game, like baseball, where you can win by keeping to the rules. It's more complicated. There are events, not rules. We could be struck dead by a lightning bolt at any moment. A gust of wind could knock us off balance into the river. In life, anyone who sticks by the rules will lose.'

'That's where you're wrong, Mr Brody. When we play by the rules we may drop the odd game, but I can assure you we will win the series. In the end, people like you will be disqualified. And penalized.'

He shakes his head. 'What a dark humor you have, Mrs Hunter. I am afraid, though, that this is a conversation we must continue another time. Are you ready?'

'I know why you did it,' she says.

He frowns, in his lidless way. 'I said I was prepared to put this behind us. Now. Are you ready, Mrs Hunter?'

'I know everything, Mr Brody.' To her surprise, she hears herself repeating her husband's ideas. 'You were going to give the inspector the Cap Anson bat as a bribe, weren't you? Until, that is, you saw who he was.'

'Be quiet.'

'You recognized Gus Swanson, and that made you angry. And what made you even more angry was that when you greeted him, he didn't know who you were.'

He is staring straight ahead, pretending all is well, that they are having a pleasant chat. But she can sense his hackles are rising.

'And when he told you to close down the site, you picked up a brick or a hammer, and you hurled it at him. Pity you missed, and that Mr Swanson didn't even notice you'd done it. He just kept on making those stupid notes. And that made you mad. You lost control of yourself, didn't you, Mr Brody? You hated Swanson that much, because of what he'd done to you.'

He has gone deadly quiet and still. She glances sideways at him. His eyes are wide and bloodshot. And he is rubbing the scar above his eye, the same scar that was not included, it occurs to her, in the portrait on his office wall.

That inspires Mrs Hunter. She goes even further than her

husband. 'Yes, that's what he did to you, isn't it? You've had to wear that scar for life, but he was not even scratched. He didn't have to suffer, the way you've had to. In fact, he'd forgotten he ever did it to you. It was that insignificant to him. And now the "feckin' Scandi", as Mr O'Leary called him, is going to close down your building. It's too much, isn't it? You don't know what you're doing anymore, except that the bat is in your hand and you're beating his head and there's blood everywhere and when the bat is smashed in two but he's still alive, you push him over the edge. Then you tell your friend Dermot, who's watched everything from the start, to burn the bat.'

She pauses. He has turned a puce color.

'But he didn't burn it,' she says. 'He gave it to me.'

Burner Brody hands her a flaming brand: 'Throw it.'

She remembers, now, something else. When she first looked at the broken bat, she noticed strange, rather pretty, circular indentations in the dried brown stain. She wondered how sticky it must have been for those to form, how much blood must have flowed.

'Do you remember one of the other predictions I made in my column about the twentieth century?' she says. 'I have your fingerprints on the baseball bat. Your fingerprints, Mr Brody, are imprinted in Mr Swanson's blood. Those fingerprints are proof.'

'I said throw it.'

She feels his hand at her back. *Unless he's a psychopath.* He is going to push her over the edge, the same as he did with Gus Swanson.

Everyone will think it was an unfortunate accident. The coroner will record a verdict of accidental death, and there will be no shortage of respectable people to testify. *Sadly, it was clear that the act of throwing the firebrand must have caused her to lose her balance. There was nothing anyone could have done to save her.* She can even imagine how her death will be reported. Chicago Daily Tribune *journalist in fatal accident at top secret opening of Sanitary and Ship Canal. Alderman Brody is shocked and saddened by the tragic loss of a true champion of Chicago. He personally undertakes to fund the funeral procession and provide the flowers.*

'Get away from me,' she hisses, heaving her elbow into his stomach with as much force as she can muster before hurling the firebrand towards the dam wall. She feels him shove her in the back and the next moment, struck by an attack of vertigo at the sight of the drop, she trips forwards, scrabbling for purchase in the hard earth. As she slips towards the edge, she screams.

I began this *Alternative History* with an investigation into the shady dealings that led to the first recorded land sale in Chicago in 1800, and I am closing it here, precisely one century later, with the botched opening of an immense sanitary engineering project. I have chosen these two bookends for a reason, as I shall shortly explain. First, though, let me assure readers that I make no apology for the approach I have taken. I do not doubt that the topics on which I have chosen to dwell, and my interpretation of events, will often put me at odds with my fellow historians. However, I hope that on closer examination, they too will see the value in what I have done.

To be the chronicler of the fastest growing city in American history in its tumultuous first century is, obviously, beyond the capability of any one pen. There are too many stories to tell, too many threads to follow, too much material to condense. All that anyone can do is plot a course and do his best to follow it. I do not deny that I have occasionally digressed, that I have spent more time on some people than on others, but I hope that in large measure I have managed to present what might be described in contemporary terms as a 'moving picture' of our history over the last century that is truthful and informative, revelatory about the lives of some remarkable souls involved in its creation, and peppered here and there with moments of personal enlightenment.

To those who charge me with the omission of important people, I say this: consider the characters that I have chosen to follow, great and small, as representative of those I have left out. To those who complain that I have cast too cynical an eye on the behavior of our politicians and business leaders, I say look about you. To those who object to chapters that touch on the mistreatment of laborers, on civil unrest, on disparities of wealth, on poor health and sanitation, on governmental and judicial corruption, and go on to claim that our institutions have since matured and that our democracy has since strengthened, I say beware. As we know only too well, history finds ways to repeat itself. And to those of my fellow historians who persist in perpetuating myths, such as the one about a white man settling Chicago, or the one that pretends the opening of the Sanitary and Ship Canal was an unqualified triumph, I say I disagree with you, and here in my *Alternative History* — over and over again — are the reasons why.

To return, then, to my two bookends. I have said elsewhere that I believe a beginning sets the tone for what follows. Let us reflect, then, on that long-gone game of chess between Pointe de Sable and John Kinzie. Two intelligent people face each other across a checkered board to play one of the most deceptively complicated games man has ever devised. At stake is ownership of the substantial estate and trading post that has put Echicagou on the map. One of the contestants is a mulatto, one is white. One is honest, one is not. One is blindfolded, one is not. They play the game according to the rules. But when the honest man wins, the dishonest man breaks the agreement he has signed. He imposes his will by force.

In that chess game and its aftermath, I see seeds of a conduct and attitude that have been repeated *ad nauseam* throughout the century. On the one hand, what a fine thing it is, that we can claim an honest, self-made man of culture as our founder. On the other hand, how shameful that he should have been driven out and replaced in the way that he was. If I were to choose one theme that underlies everything else in this *Alternative History*, it would be the continuing struggle between the Pointe de Sables and the Kinzies of the world.

As readers will have noticed, my eye has been drawn above all to the land on which Chicago stands, and how it has been used and exploited. I still find it hard to credit, in my perambulations around the modern city, that these few square miles of former swamp land could have been so dramatically transformed in but a handful of decades. And yet they were. That is a complicated marvel I have done my best to illustrate, as I hope these pages testify, with a series of carefully chosen excerpts.

Among those excerpts, I have often dwelt on the problems of water and sanitation created by the city's rapid growth. The ability to provide its citizens with fresh drinking water is a basic requirement, in my view, of a city's competence and its leaders' sense of civic responsibility. The fact that it took so long, and so many needless deaths, before the city allocated the necessary resources to the problem is an indictment of our politicians and the clique of businessmen and ward bosses who keep them in power. That fact should be noted, and remembered, and remembered again.

While I am happy to applaud the Sanitary and Ship Canal as an engineering triumph, any such praise must be tempered by the knowledge that it was a long overdue investment. The historical record demands, too, that the true story of what happened when it was finally opened be told. I refer, of course, to the events of January 2, 1900, not to the grandiose civic party that was staged at a mock opening some two weeks later.

I have chosen, therefore, to bring my *Alternative History* to a close at the moment when Mrs Hunter throws the firebrand at the kerosene-soaked timber lying along the base of the dam wall, seconds before an enraged Alderman Brody attempts to push her over the edge to her death. He does not, I am glad to report, succeed. Some of his fellow aldermen, alarmed by what they are witnessing, apprehend him. Sadly, Mrs Hunter is too shaken to fully register what must have been the extraordinary sight of the dam going up in flames and giving way, as a torrent of canal water plunged into the river and began to reverse its flow. That should have been a moment to savor, the true realization of the deceased Mr Ellis Chesbrough's dream. How unfortunate, then, that the characters on the spot were diverted by Burner Brody, whose attempt at yet another murder, we should remember, was originally prompted by nothing more than an old grudge whose origin I witnessed in person, by chance, roughly forty years before. In such curious little aberrations and coincidences is history forged.

I would like to end by reporting that Burner Brody was arrested, tried, found guilty of all charges and imprisoned. Alas, it should be clear by now that this is not how Chicago functions. Although Mr Brody was indeed arrested and charged with the attempted murder of Mrs Hunter, by the time the case was ready to go to court, so many witness statements had been withdrawn or changed it was decided by a friendly judge that no case could be brought against him. And, regarding the death of Mr Swanson, the broken baseball bat on which Mr Brody's fingerprints were impressed in dried blood was handed to the police, only to be subsequently misplaced. Mr Brody was duly acquitted on all counts and discharged. At the time of writing, he is still the alderman for the 18th Ward, he still drinks and gambles with the chief of police, and plays golf with the mayor at the Lake Forest Club. He still keeps his poorest constituents in coal over the winter in return for votes.

It took Mrs Hunter a long time to recover from her ordeal. I am pleased to report, though, that the experience inspired her to delay her retirement from the *Chicago Daily Tribune*. She continues to use her column to fight for the causes she has always espoused. We live in dangerous times. As our political and business leaders become ever bolder in the corruption they practice, I believe it is in reporters like

Mrs Hunter in whom we must place our hope. I trust she may yet find a way to bring Mr Brody to justice and, in doing so, finally liberate the ghost of her great-grandfather, Jean Baptiste Pointe de Sable.

I am conscious that at the end of such a long book, readers may expect me to bring matters to a grand finale with a shining vision of the future, or offer a sagacious denouement on what we have learned from the century gone by. Far be it from me to attempt anything like that. But if I could mention one small thing I have noticed, it is this. Historical events are never as simple as they may look. Nobody acts alone and nothing happens in isolation. And not much occurs as a consequence of reason and good sense. And I believe it is in the cluster of smaller events, and in the lives of those who, in more traditional studies of the past, have been consigned to footnotes, that we can retrieve our history.

With that passing thought, I shall bid you farewell, offering my gratitude to all those voices from the past who have spoken through these pages. This book is dedicated to them, and is written in their memory. These are their stories, as best I could tell them. And whenever I have taken the liberty of using informed supposition, I have tried to remain true to the spirit of the truth, and to the unique, particular history of Chicago that has been my lifelong obsession.

Acknowledgements

I am immensely grateful to the writers and historians whose work about nineteenth century America/Chicago has been a source of inspiration to me, and to the many people — particularly my family, close friends and colleagues in Bath — who have encouraged me in my writing endeavours. Special thanks are due to: my agents Rebecca Carter and Emma Parry; my editors Molly Slight and Caroline Zancan; my first US editor Michael Signorelli; and key early readers Tom Melk, Beverly Stark and Tricia Wastvedt. Behind the scenes, I would not have survived without Eleonora's love, support and optimism.